KU-335-393

# Contents

Introducing Divination Systems Inc.                                        1
Of Molotov Melons and Magical Mushrooms                      54
The Thaum and Garden Show                                           112
'Big boys don't scry . . .'                                                    169
Fireballs – Extra Large                                                       228

# The Scrying Game

# THE SCRYING GAME

## Andrew Harman

LEGEND

Published by Legend Books in 1996

1 3 5 7 9 10 8 6 4 2

Copyright © Andrew Harman 1996

Andrew Harman has asserted his right under the Copyright, Designs and
Patents Act, 1988 to be identified as the author of this work.

First published in the United Kingdom in 1996 by Legend Books

Arrow Books Limited
20 Vauxhall Bridge Road, London SW1V 2SA

Random House Australia Pty Ltd
20 Alfred Street, Milsons Point, Sydney, NSW 2061
Australia

Random House New Zealand Ltd
18 Poland Road, Glenfield, Auckland 10,
New Zealand

Random House South Africa (Pty) Ltd
PO Box 337, Bergvlei, South Africa

Random House UK Limited Reg. No. 954009

A CIP catalogue record for this book is available from the British Library

Papers used by Random House UK Limited are natural, recyclable products
made from wood grown in sustainable forests. The manufacturing processes
conform to the environmental regulations of the country of origin.

ISBN 0 09 970311 4

Typeset by Deltatype Ltd, Ellesmere Port, Cheshire
Printed and bound in Great Britain by BPC Paperbacks Ltd
A member of The British Printing Company Ltd

# Dedication

This one's for you. Yes, you! You are reading this aren't you? Well, I'll assume you are, okay? If you've just borrowed this, then cheers, enjoy. If you've bought it, then for you is a larger sliver of gratitude and a brandishing of erect thumbs. But for those fabulous folk who have been reading my stuff from the start . . . a real heartfelt thanks, you know who you are, the good news is that there's at least another three on the way! Quite simply, thank you. And for those folk out there who profess to be fans . . . fear not, counselling *is* available.

I'd like also to wave a large flag of welcome to a new-ish member of that band of folk who beaver away in the background, the man with the teeth when I need them, John Parker, agent extraordinaire!

And finally, for this book, someone who really deserves a stack more credit than she normally gets. My most invaluable of sounding boards, pillar of clarity when the plot-gremlins strike, my beloved Jenny. I love you. Pour us a whisky, there's a dear.

# Introducing Divination Systems Inc.

If he'd known precisely what was going on inside the throat of his alarm macaw at that instant he would have been out of bed and screaming.

But then, if he could have foreseen precisely what joys Frightday the triplet and tenth was about to hurl his way he might have lain there, whimpering and hoped it would all just go away. It would have been a shed load easier if he had. For several hundred people.

Instead he lay on his hammock, twitching in the fitful recollections of yesterday at work. Staring out through his sleep-closed eyes at those all-too-recent events . . .

Trembling nervously beneath the icy gaze of Soleed, the Over-Seer for Fruit Preservation, Quintzi Cohatl had shaken the scrappy collection of bones as he had done for countless years.

'Well?' Soleed had snapped violently, his eyes lancing scorn from either side of his aquiline beak of a nose.

Quintzi continued shaking the bones in his dream. He had little choice, the recollection of yesterday's nerves had made it almost impossible for him to release his desperate grip on the cluster of animal remains. All he had to do was fling the tiny bones on to the table, summon all of his foretelling ability and interpret the message. Easy. It would have been far easier if his future financial security hadn't depended so much on it.

'Come on, I haven't got all day!' Soleed had snapped. 'Give me an answer!'

'I . . .' began Quintzi above an increasingly irritating chatter of shrew thighs.

It wasn't surprising he hadn't slept well. The air was alive with the sense of panic. It was always the same at this time of year. You could almost see sparks of excited terror shorting off

1

people's earlobes. It was the awards, see? The whole Mountain City of Axolotl was seized in its annual frenzy of last-minute prophesying, foreseeing and general divination. Each and every seer, prophet and portent-reader gripped in a flurry of desperation, wild for that final glimpse of the future that would get them noticed by the Augury Academy in time for the annual awards and pay rises. And with 99 per cent of the hyperstitious Axolotians able to foresee the future in some way or other, that meant the air was filled with the rattling of bones, burning of strange substances or simply the chanting of unfathomable mantras.

'If you let the side down you'll have more than just me to deal with!' Soleed had snarled meaningfully, scowling at the ageing Clerk-in-Charge of Avocado Preservation and Protection. 'The whole department's up for an efficiency award this year, Cohatl. If we lose it again to those louts in Litter Prediction I will personally . . .'

It had suddenly been too much for Quintzi. Involuntarily his hands had parted and, panicking, he'd spilled his bones on the table. He watched now in dreamily-terrified slow motion as the dozen rodent limbs scattered and came to rest in a specific and highly complex pattern. A spurt of alarm flushed through him as he felt the spotlights of truth arc around and burn into his trembling body.

Everybody, including him, knew that the pattern displayed by those bones was dictated by the forces of destiny, shaped by the currents of chance and honed to immensely informative perfection by the very laws of the universe. Each osseous indicator was a key in a giant message, its angle and position within the whole dripping with meaningful portentousness, offering vital clues to the dangers approaching the three barns of avocados under his predictive protection. All he had to do was unravel the message and he could preserve the entire Axolotian stock for another few months. That was all he ever had to do. That was the snag.

'Well?' Soleed had growled, as he always did. 'What's it mean?'

'Er . . . I . . .' flustered Quintzi as he stared at the meaningless portentous picture. 'Er, you see . . .' In his hammock a thin film of sympathetic sweat glistened on his brow.

So much he wanted to throw his arms in the air, overturn the table and stamp out of the Fruit Preservation Company once and for all, screaming. And every day for the last forty years he had stifled the same overwhelming urge. If he actually came clean, faced the music and admitted that he had as much portentous acumen as the average myopic woodlouse then he'd be ostracised, cast out and probably beaten to a pulp by everyone else who actually had the gift.

Okay, so he couldn't see half a minute into the future. So what? Nobody had actually spotted it yet. One thing he knew he *could* do was lie through his back teeth. Forty years of daily practice could really hone a skill. Especially when you wanted a job badly enough. In his dream he took a deep breath, disengaged his brain and let rip in as authoritative a manner as he could muster.

The fitfully slumbering Quintzi winced and gnashed his molars as he listened to his dream-self trotting out yet another bucketful of prophetic untruths.

'This group of three here indicates a tight clumping of rising possibilities of a bumper harvest and, coupled with the ascendant femur here (which, being an ocelot, does in fact confer the skills of the hunter to the scenario), leads to a verification of the tendency towards exceptionality. A pair of skulls here indicates an upcoming choice or being in two minds, and this pelvis here is normally associated with, er . . . childbirth.' He stopped and looked up at Soleed's fuming expression.

'So what's *that* mean, eh? In plain Axolotian?'

'Er, a good year for avocados,' grinned Quintzi pathetically. As far as he was concerned, anything meant a good year for avocados. Foreseeing a bad year was a sackable offence. 'And your lucky colour for the week is green,' he'd added.

Soleed had lurched forward and, with a lightning flash of sleeve, shot out his arm and snatched Quintzi firmly by the molars. 'You'd better be right!' he had spat derisively, twisting

3

the clerk's head violently and punctuating each consonant with inflicted agony, wrenching ageing teeth painfully. 'If we miss the department award, you'll have some very difficult explaining to do!'

'Arrrrrgh!' Quintzi had grunted around Soleed's wrist, desperately wishing that drawing blood from a superior officer wasn't another sackable offence. Oh, to let his jaw muscles snap shut, just once . . . !

'Wubbb I eber lie to ooo?' Quintzi had cringed submissively around a mouthful of Soleed's forearm.

'What?'

'Would I ever lie to you?' he had croaked, his molars suddenly released.

Soleed had grunted a string of obscenities, scowled once again and stomped off towards the Chief Melon Manager for another Fruit Preservation Prediction.

Blissfully unaware of the time, the sleeping Quintzi rubbed the side of his face and plotted revenge far beyond his wildest capabilities. One day he'd give Soleed something the swine would never forget. The right time, the right place and . . . what? What could he possibly do to that damned boss of his which could cause even a fraction of a moment of agony? Maybe he should buy a dagger or two . . .

Outside Quintzi's window dark clouds hurled bright lightning spears at the distant Meanlayla Mountains to the east; a corncrake choked on a worm in the avocado field; and in the unfathomable heavens above, the constellation of Tehzcho, the Gatherer, slid inexorably towards its zenith. Today, slightly more signs and portents than usual were being pitched about with gay abandon. But then it was Frightday the triplet and tenth.

Hours ago, all across the Mountain City of Axolotl people had scrambled out of their beds backwards, spun around three times, bathed their feet in llama milk and spent the next half-hour chanting furiously into a mahogany block held firmly against their foreheads. They all knew what day it was, and they all knew how many wild spirits of bad omen would be abroad today chewing at their heels. They were all dreadfully aware that if their warding chants weren't up to scratch, terror would stalk their every move until the Great Sun finally set.

It was a jolly good job the editor of *Scryin' Out* had remembered to print all the essential recitations in 'Omen Corner'. If the entire, extremely hyperstitious, population of Axolotl ensured that their own personal paths of destiny were cleared of the weeds of peril, then today there would be no casualties, things would still run as smoothly as a greased eel.

Unfortunately, for one Quintzi Cohatl things were never that simple. And it was already starting to become apparent.

For the thirty-seventh time that morning Tiemecx his alarm macaw stood on its perch, filled its avian lungs and attempted to squawk its little feathery head off.

And for the thirty-seventh time that morning it failed utterly to reproduce the requisite racket needed to raise its master from beneath his favourite duvet. All that happened, as on the other unfortunate occasions, was a sad rattling wheeze of a cough and an unnerving feeling of wild dizziness.

Laryngitis? thought the macaw, massaging its throat with a careful flight feather. Pneumonia? Old age? No surely not. Six years isn't that long to be an alarm macaw, is it?

Miserably facing the possibility that perhaps retirement was approaching early, Tiemecx hopped along its perch and dropped on to his master's grubby pillow. If he couldn't squawk him into wakefulness he'd jolly well try something else with his beak. Well, if you've got it . . .

He stood on the pillow, drew himself up to his full colourful four inches, lifted his beak and imagined being a pied rockpecker attacking the thinning grey strands of a particular tasty lichen.

He got three blows on to the side of Quintzi Cohatl's head before his master erupted, snatched him by the throat and hurled him across the sandstone room in a flurry of untidy feathers. Almost as if it was an extension of the same motion, the hammock flipped over and dumped him unceremoniously on the stone floor. Snarling, he hurled back his untidy tent of covers and stood shaking in his favourite blue and gold astrological pyjamas and stained socks.

Tiemecx flapped himself upright, folded his wings huffily and glared at the ageing Clerk-in-Charge of Avocado Preservation. Why'd he look so miffed? He was awake, what more did he want? Breakfast? Pah! He could whistle.

Quintzi Cohatl smacked his mouth irritably, rubbed his eyes with a worrying scrunching sound and attempted, as he had for the last thirty years or so, to touch his toes. As usual he was a good three feet short. How long had it been since he'd last touched his toes? He wondered forlornly as he stared at the forty-year-old socks his feet were still steadfastly inhabiting.

Rasping a series of hoarse curses to itself and rubbing its throat miserably, the macaw fluttered on to its perch and tugged open the curtains.

It was then that Quintzi screamed uncontrollably.

Cold terror-laden sweat swarmed down between his shoulderblades as he snatched back the tattered curtains and stared at the scalding ball of fire before him. His heart squirmed nervously as he recognised its unnatural position in the sky. For a second he was certain it winked back accusingly.

Shrieking, he covered his eyes and spun away from the window, trembling, purple spots flashing on and off. It was a portent, it had to be! The sun should never be that high in the sky at this time in the morning. It must mean something vital, something terrible. But what? Were the Meanlayla Mountains crumbling? Had the fixings of the firmament come unglued, tipping the Great Star Mover 30 degrees off kilter? Was Chaos about to come raining down over this gilded City of Axolotl? How long did they have to pack?

He stared accusingly at his ornamental sundial and screamed. A single finger of shadow pointed steadfastly at a time normally associated with elevenses. Then it sprouted wings, claws and peered up at him as Tiemecx swooped in to see what the fuss was about, pointing at its throat and writhing melodramatically.

Panic surged as Quintzi realised he was in the middle of a devilishly wicked vision. The sun, the dial and the mysterious behaviour of his alarm macaw. This was prescience on a grand scale at last: the big portent. He wheeled on his heel and headed for a vast sheet spread on a wicker table.

The macaw tutted, knowing that it wasn't going to get any sympathy from him now. With a resigned shrug it flapped over to its bowl of sunflower seeds, shaking its head as the mysterious tickling continued in its throat.

Behind it Quintzi shrieked wildly as he flipped open the chart and in a flash, knew what his vision meant. There it was, detailed in the chart issued free with this month's *Good Seer Guide*. The sun out of control, the dial showing stunning chronological ineptitude, the mad macaw – it all pointed to the 'Death of Time, the Coming of Disorder, the Rise of the Cuttlefish of Ultimate Destruction'. In short – peril on a grand scale, here, today.

Was he the only one with these sights? Did anyone else know? His mind spinning with visionary importance for the first time in his life, he leapt towards his window and grabbed, white-knuckled, at the sill. He had to warn people. It was his duty. He had been delivered a prescient vision from on high, his first ever prescient vision, he had to spread it; as a loyal Axolotian Citizen he had to.

Staring down at the street below he took a breath and . . . so many people up and about so soon, bustling innocently about their early morning business, sitting in the café opposite, eating elevenses . . . They should be warned! Shouldn't they?

For the first time that fateful morning a snippet of doubt flopped in his mind. The vision hadn't been accompanied by the voices in his head, or the flashing lights that everyone had told him about. And then there were the folk eating elevenses. No, no. He staggered back and collapsed on to his hammock as realisation kicked down the doors of his resolve, pouring icy water on his visionary flames.

It wasn't a Big Portent. It hadn't been the real live vision of the future he had been waiting over sixty years for. In short it would not result in the Death of Time, but the death of something a little, well, featherier. At least, it would as soon as he got his hands around that damn bird's scrawny neck and started to squeeze . . .

'Why'd you choose today?' yelled Quintzi in his astrological pyjamas, an artery pounding at his temple. 'This morning of all the thousands . . . Gods, of *all* the mornings you could've picked to let me sleep in! This a conspiracy, or something?' He sprinted across the room, skidded to a halt and snatched the pathetic heap of feathers off the stone sundial, his frantic hands clenching angrily around its throat. The macaw wheezed and made a pathetic choking sound.

'I should strangle you now! You do know how important the Augury Accuracy Awards are?'

Tiemecx shrugged.

'Aaah, how long have I had the misfortune to own you? Have you been paying any attention? The Augury Academy Awards are only *the* most vital event of the year. Anyone who is anyone, and even those who aren't anybody in the world of visions and portents, will be there, ready to vote. At the "Triple A"s. This morning!'

Tiemecx looked at his claws sheepishly.

'I was in with a chance this year. I'd foreseen every major storage problem with particular reference to avocados to within 96 per cent accuracy.' He shook the macaw violently and winced as his arthritis started playing up again. The bird's eyes stared accusingly at him.

'Okay. So I was lucky, but that's beside the point! Why didn't you wake me?' He slapped the macaw's beak with the flat of his wrinkled palm and spat. 'Answer me! Death is the only excuse, and that *can* be arranged!' he sneered threateningly. 'Do you have any idea how long I've been in the Fruit Storage Service, hmmm? Fifty years, man and boy. They said I couldn't do it. Said I would be a disaster. Well, I showed 'em all. Would've been promoted for sure this time, dead cert. Don't look at me like that!' He snarled as the macaw stared mockingly through black glassy eyes. 'I could've walked away with an award, I could. Who saw the drought and made sure the avocado crops were put in early to avoid it? Me! Who foretold the hurricane? Me! I saw it all. Stop shaking your head!' The macaw fixed Quintzi with a powerful, guilt-inducing stare. 'Okay, okay, so I didn't see it, but they don't have to know that, do they? Don't have to know I'm as prescient as a doorpost. I did the job. That's all that matters isn't it? But it's too late now. You've ruined it!'

The macaw struggled to point desperately at its throat.

'Everything's down the gutter, and it's all your fault! You know how the Council feel about lateness. It's all there in Edict 964, version 3 subsection 29 f – "Any person exhibiting any act of tardiness in attendance of a prearranged meeting exhibits gross misuse of the powers of foresight and therefore deserves never to be considered a reliable source of prophetic information. Ever." – I could be disbarred and all because you didn't wake me, without warning! . . .'

Suddenly Quintzi Cohatl froze. What was he saying? Without warning? Course there was a warning, there had to be. Nothing ever happened in the Mountain City of Axolotl without some sort of warning. Well, with 99 per cent of the population being professional prophets, seers and scryers, it wasn't surprising.

There were two ways at least in which he could have seen it all coming.

If he had been the Over-Seer in charge of Pet and Portentous Animals then he would've known about it in the middle of last week. He could've been staring at his breakfast tea leaves, clicked his fingers and known that his alarm macaw wouldn't croak first thing in the morning. Sadly Quintzi could no more predict the actions of Portentous Creatures than your average bathmat could juggle fire-scorpions. Now, ask him about the possibilities of avoiding avocado beetle by careful crop rotation amongst the storage huts and he was your man. He couldn't foresee a thing, but he could probably bluff his way out of a barrel in under a minute. The years of practice had honed his lying ability to humming sharpness.

Fortunately, the other, and far more common way for the hyperstitious residents of Axolotl to determine if the day held any painful surprises round the next corner was a lot less fiddly than staring into the fathomless depths of cold tea or even a properly tuned scrying crystal. And there was far less chance of getting a migraine. A few moments spent perusing a certain weekly rag and you'd know all the essentials for planning the day ahead. It was all there – everything from the pick of sympathetic sock shades with which to charm Lady Luck to suggested amulets and a selection of wise and apposite sayings. Want to know what fate has in store for you? Want to know what's going on? Just look in the weekly parch-mag, *Scryin' Out*. There it was, 'Omen Corner'. Quintzi stared at the prediction and swore. No wonder he hadn't seen it coming. It was a 'cryptic'. He looked in horror at the first few lines and started to tug desperately at his thinning grey beard.

Solar seed stifles personal promotion possibilities. Today's lucky colours – magenta and puce. Lucky stone – date. Objects to avoid – recently sharpened daggers and stray jars of hemlock . . .

Pretty standard fare. And, as usual, there was more. Details of where to stand if you wanted to meet your true love, places to avoid if you didn't want to be murdered, sixty-four different chants to use in sixty-four everyday crises – from flaccid soufflés to sand in your Vaseline. But nowhere did it mention the fact that his alarm macaw wouldn't go off, destroying his chances of stardom in one foul feathery swoop. He looked again at the predictive line and swiftly reached the same conclusion as he had yesterday. The use of the word 'stifles' always means that the active object in the prediction is a few letters of the words before. In Quintzi's case that was obvious. Solar seed would become Soleed, his boss at the Fruit Storage Service. Then the rest would follow. Soleed stifles personal promotion possibilities. Couldn't be clearer. He'd always disputed Quintzi's claim that he had been directly responsible for ensuring that this year's avocados were stored fresher and crisper than ever before. He still had the scars from the heated, er, debate to prove it.

Snarling more angrily by the minute, Quintzi stared at the quivering bird in his clutches. 'It's still all your fault, you stupid worthless parrot!' he screamed and hurled the terrified bird across the room, grinning sadistically as it ricocheted off the sundial and landed in a coughing heap of Technicolored spluttering. Tiemecx rolled melodramatically on to his back, clutching at his throat, his face turning red under the verdant feathers. Whoops of gasped air dashed into his tiny lungs as he writhed and flapped like an epileptic bat and then, with a final massive cough, something hard erupted from his beak. It whistled across the room, caught Quintzi in the eye with a ringing splat and ended on the stone floor. Quintzi stared in horror at the hard black and white something, snatched it up and glared angrily at the alarm macaw.

Tiemecx attempted a smile, failed and decided to play with his claws in a way that might just be thought of as cute and endearing. In that instant Quintzi realised that his prediction in 'Omen Corner' had definitely not been a cryptic. His head reeled as the truth hit. 'Stifles' wasn't a clue. His message, when translated said, as clear as a bell, 'That damned parrot'll nearly choke to death on a sunflower seed! Just see if it doesn't!'

Quintzi screamed, hurled his copy of *Scryin' Out* across the room, sprinted through the door and plunged down the stairs, launching a series of macawicidal threats after him to keep the bird sweating.

If he could just reach the front doors of the Grand Municipal Council Temple before the start of the 'Auguries', he might be able to plead for leniency. Might even be able to sue if he could show that it was an incorrect prediction. It should've said, 'Solar flower seed', shouldn't it? He knew how pricey sue-th sayers could be but it would be worth it to get a chance at an award.

He blasted into the ancient sandstone streets of Axolotl, flashed a quick glance at his wrist sundial and cringed. It was going to be close, but if Tuatara Street was clear he could just do it. Now what had the traffic predictions been for today?

It was only as he spun around a sharp corner and entered Cocoa Row that he realised he hadn't read this morning's prediction. And he suddenly wished he had. Tuatara Street, at any time of day, was always heaving with eager Axolotians busy about their daily business. Damn! His mind raced. He could duck around the back streets and then skip over to level three of the Grand Municipal . . . NO! That bridge was going to be out for repairs all day, as predicted yesterday. His sciatica twinged as he stumbled over an uneven crack. It was no good: crowds or no, he would have to brave Tuatara Street, the surface was better.

Besides, it was just round this last corner. He wheeled around and almost shrieked hysterically. He couldn't believe it. Wall-to-wall traders blocking the street, mobs of shop-dazed punters lurching uncontrollably around in a trance of purchase . . . not a one in sight. For the first time in his life Quintzi Cohatl stared at a totally empty Tuatara Street. A nasty feeling crept up the back of his neck. Could this be a sign? Was *this* his first portent?

As he watched a stray tumbleweed trundle towards the Grand Municipal Council Temple, he realised he hadn't a clue, he hadn't read his Horrorscope. Today's future was a complete mystery. He felt suddenly blind and bewildered. Where was everybody? What was happening? Would there be a ladder lurking around the next corner? Would he accidentally tread on thirteen cracks in the dusty street and suffer acne for a week? Or could he perhaps catch a falling star anise and enjoy a month of overwhelming good fortune? A day without a glimpse into his hyperstitious future was a day strewn with a million lurking perils.

And today, of all days, one of those perils was in Tuatara Street, a few hundred yards and a couple of minutes away.

Unbeknownst to Quintzi, everything was exactly as had been foreseen yesterday afternoon by the Over-Seer of Portentous Creatures, just after a nice lunch of chillied avocados. And all who had read 'Omen Corner' this morning knew about its every detail.

Quintzi shook as he stared up and down the length of Tuatara Street and knew he had to gamble. Something was destined to happen here soon, something bad. But how soon? And how bad? He glanced at his sundial again. The only chance he stood to reach the 'Auguries' on time was to run. Full speed. Now.

12

Had Quintzi known that a Dreaded Black Mantric Gecko* lurked in a small bush a few yards ahead he probably wouldn't have been quite so hasty. He knelt in the sandy dust of the street, spread his fingers out before him, raised his back, took a deep breath and exploded into the nearest approximation of a sprint he had reached in three decades.

Countless terrified faces peered out from convenient doorways, their jaws dropping as Quintzi waddled arthritically towards certain doom. Petrified eyes watched for the scaly menace they knew would appear, painfully aware of the disaster that would strike them (and the next seven generations on the maternal side) if the prophecy was only a few feet wrong.

A small bush rustled as a black forked tail began to emerge.

A thousand invocations of thanks floated skyward as hidden Axolations blessed the editor of *Scryin' Out* for warning them of this coming danger.

The tiny bush rustled again and the Dreaded Black Mantric Gecko emerged into the sunlight accompanied by an orchestra of snatched breaths and the sound of Quintzi's sprinting socks growing louder. The Gecko waddled backwards into full view as a panic-stricken figure whirled around the corner at full tilt and sprinted uncontrollably towards it.

He screamed as he recognised the damned lizard, slammed his sprint into reverse and screeched to a blubbering halt in a cloud of dust. In that instant a whole universe of choices for his day ahead was narrowed to a desultory two. He could either continue on his now terminally pox-crossed path and die painfully in the middle of next week, shunned by everyone; or he could crawl away from the incident on hands and knees, all the way home, bathe himself backwards and start out again wearing an amulet of jalapeño peppers as a ward against evil, to spend the rest of his life as the butt of a million prophet jokes.

At that very instant a joyous blast of 'all-clear' whistles rang out from slightly opened doors, and bodies erupted into the

* Even Dreaded Black Mantric Geckos knew of the seventeen years of bad luck that would follow if one crossed your path and so had taken to scuttling backwards at every opportunity, especially during the mating season.

open. The peril was gone, planted firmly in Quintzi's lap. His problem. Rush hour could resume.

Dreading to think what the half-mile crawl would do to his favourite blue and gold astrological pyjamas, Quintzi stretched miserably out on the dusty street and squirmed pathetically away towards his hovel on Skink Row.

It was without doubt the coldest and most desperate bath that Quintzi Cohatl had ever had in his life, and with very good reason. Time.

Or rather, the acute lack of it.

He didn't have enough of it spare to wait for the sun's rays to dribble through his complex array of lenses and heat the water in the tub and, most importantly, he knew damn well that any minute could be his last. How long did it take for the Curse of the Black Mantric Gecko to take effect? Panic rose as the single shadow of his sundial chewed away at the hours.

And so it was that, in the traditional hyperstitious warding ritual (for use following an unforeseen path-crossing by a Dreaded Black Mantric Gecko), he hurled himself head-first into three inches of icy water, shrieked, leapt out backwards and shook himself a fraction drier. Then, still dripping, he wrapped a hasty towel around his midriff, dashed into the bedroom and, in a flurry of panic, snatched a big wooden box off the top of his wardrobe. He hurled it on to his bed and flung open the lid.

Had any one of the other hyperstitious residents of Axolotl glimpsed the lid of the box through which Quintzi was rummaging they would have known in an instant that his path had been crossed by one of the three hundred and seventeen known Portentous Creatures of Evil. Every Axolotian had it slammed into their head from the earliest of ages that 'in case of emergency head for the sign of the Red-Crossed Fingers'.

Quintzi's frantic hands tore at the tiny drawers of his Emergency Omenical Kit, searching through seemingly endless supplies of rabbits' feet, hurling fountains of garlic-purée poultices over his head, impatiently flinging individual bottles of God Liver Oil out of his way, and there, finally, behind a full set of spiritual supports, he found it – an unused jalapeno pepper amulet.

Allowing himself the briefest of relieved sighs he tugged it over his bony wrist, waggled a threatening finger of fury at his even more unforgiven alarm macaw, whirled on his heel and sprinted, once again, into the glaring sun of Skink Row. Dust erupted from his pounding footfalls as he powered his way once again up the hill towards Tuatara Street blissfully unaware of the unnaturally jet black cloud that had mysteriously formed in the sky behind him. With a following wind and a ton of good luck, he might just make it in time for the start of the 'Auguries' . . .

With a ton of good luck . . . Bah! Why did it always come down to that? Why couldn't one day, just today, not be dominated by the fickle fingers of fortuity? Would it make so much of a difference to the global streams of causality if for a few moments something went right for him?

If he had any more time Quintzi would've been on his knees, hands clasped to his chest, imploring gaze raised heavenwards in desperate impeachment. After sixty-four years, was one sparkle of joy too much to . . . hang on, he thought as he sprinted onwards. What's the date? And as he thought he realised the reason things were far from right today. He was pushing against all the massed forces of destiny. Today was Frightday the triplet and tenth in the ascension of Tehzcho the Gatherer. It had to be, really. His birthday. His damned sixty-fifth blinking birthday. The worst of absolutely all of them.

He almost screamed as he scurried his frantically arthritic way out of Skink Row and into Tuatara Street, feeling the weight of so many portents gathering against him. It was bad enough having been born on Frightday the triplet and tenth; they were always the worst of the month. 'Omen Corner' often ran to half a dozen pages of predictions and places to avoid on such perilous days. But for him personally, right from the start the odds had been well and truly stacked against anything approaching good fortune.

It was all down to numbers. And he had the wrong ones, on the wrong birthday.

To any Axolotian, any given number doesn't just represent a specific quantity or amount. Oh no. Each numeral, each figure has its own unique and mysterious property. This is sometimes derived from a numeral's appearance and shape – as in the case of the figure 1, whose single, strong, erect presence has always been firmly associated, mysteriously, with fertility. And sometimes the property derives from ancient ingrained findings from everyday life. Thirteen is one of these such numbers, shunned by all who see or hear it, detested by players of dice games as a hellish total just teasingly unattainable from the throw of two dice. Twenty-two is another of these, spurned and signifying disastrous consequence to every player of pontoon ever to walk Tuatara Street.

And some numbers are associated with archaic legendary scriptures, one of these being the number five. A figure purported to presage cowardliness, fear and general limpness of character, since five was the number of toes possessed on each foot of the God Caitiff when he ran away from the final battle of Thrume-Ahzhart during the first age of Rhiggli. It is interesting to note that even though no Axolotian has the slightest clue what that means either, five is still held as the number of the terminally chicken-livered.

Unfortunately for Quintzi, today saw the multiplication of a numerical nightmare of curses – the date and his age. Everyone knew that sixty-five was the bastard child of a conjunction between thirteen and five . . . it didn't bode well. Something unfortunate would almost certainly occur today. He should run home and hide under his duvet for the next three weeks. Or months. Or years.

And he would have done so had it not been for the surprising fact that somehow he now found himself standing with his hand on the gilded door-handle of the vast Grand Municipal Council Temple, having somehow sprinted blindly and without incident down the full length of Tuatara Street.

Shaking his head in wonder, but muttering something about never offering horses bearing gifts a full oral examination, he vanished through the door and quickly found himself a seat in the darkened arena.

The mysterious black cloud grew slowly denser as it floated towards the eastern approaches of Axolotl, the area associated with the vast majority of fruit growing and storage.

Quintzi couldn't believe it. He was here; he had made it. After all the hassle of the morning he was actually present at the Augury Academy Awards. With his jaw sagging slightly he looked out over the gathered crowd as they sat in rows around the inside of the vast hollow temple, dressed in their society finery of black tie and toga. Complex arrays of mirrors gathered and split the sunlight surging through the central hole in the roof, illuminating all but the most inaccessible of corners. And in the centre of the temple, on a high altar, underlit with moted beams of sunlight, slouched the Master of Ceremonies, Tehzo Khonna, in his ubiquitous sedan chair. He never went anywhere without it. Having read, in an unfortunately misspelt fortune cookie that all of his life's forces were held in his sole, he declared that he would never again mistreat his personal spiritualism so badly. Leaping into a handy sedan chair he felt certain that the decreased wear and tear on his tootsies should increase his lifespan a good few years and enable him to continue gaining popularity as the only Professional Compere in Axolotl.

Dressed in a tired-looking toga with lapels three years out of fashion,* he was overenthusiastically applauding a pair of figures as they struggled down the steep steps of the podium. 'Thank you, thank you,' he cried, addressing the audience suddenly. 'Now that brings us neatly to the part of the proceedings in which we of the Augury Academy honour those who slave away tirelessly behind the scenes all year in the jobs we never really like to think about. I am referring, of course, to the likes of the boys and girls in the Litter Prediction Agency

---

* Due to the disturbingly cyclical nature of taste in Axolotl, fashion, especially evening wear, was a notoriously difficult thing to appreciate. Very often it was beyond everyone except the people designing the stuff to know whether they were simply looking at ten-year-old togs they'd unearthed in a dead relative's wardrobe, or if they were looking sufficiently far ahead to a time when those same garments wouldn't look out of fashion on any socially important figure, or if, as some would have it, they were having a huge joke at everyone's expense.

The truth, according to those in the know, was a subtly wicked blend of all three.

whose tireless foresight ensures that there is always a receptacle handy for those stray items of refuse. Give 'em a big hand, come on!'

The temple erupted in applause.

Outside, the mysterious black cloud scudded gently towards a small clump of three tiny barns.

'And there's the folks of the Fortuitous Food Office who, through the painstaking analysis of tea leaves, crumbs and the patterns made by certain pastas, ensure that everywhere, every night, *your* take-away is awaiting *your* collection. Put your hands together and show them how much your stomachs love 'em. Come on, come on!'

Again a cacophony of cheers and fervent applause echoed throughout the temple. How long it would have lasted it was difficult to tell, but after almost a minute, Tehzo raised his hands and patted the audience into frenzied calmness.

Outside, the cloud did a thing not normally associated with natural meteorological phenomena. It sort of hiccuped. A small flash of light sparked within.

'No . . . no . . . please,' continued the Master of Ceremonies with great gusto, safely within the Grand Municipal Temple. 'As valuable as those vital cogs are to our lifestyle here in Axolotl, this year, I'm afraid, the Augury Academy Award for Outstanding Accuracy in a Dull and Boring Job goes to someone who has predicted all but 3.5 per cent of the disasters in his field one month before they were due to occur . . .'

A whoosh of 'ooohs' raced around the temple. Quintzi was amazed. That sort of efficiency of prediction deserved to be rewarded.

'. . . and, Ladies and Gentlemen, what is more, that remaining three-and-a-half percent of cataclysmic happenings were detected and averted within hours of their predestined time. Yes – on the actual day of their supposed appearance – by an unprecedented flurry of last-minute precognition.'

Outbreaks of applause again erupted everywhere, this time in seconds Quintzi found himself slapping his hands together like a demented seal desperate for a herring.

On the far edge of Axolotl, the cloud hiccuped again.

'Please, please!' shouted Tehzo, his voice croaking with joyous hoarseness. 'Ladies and Gentlemen, without the foresight of this one man and his uncanny ability to avoid disaster, all of us would be completely without avocados on the table. Yes singlehandedly . . .'

Quintzi shook his head. Avocados . . . did he really say avoca—

'. . . this man has stored your avocados in the perfect conditions for a complete year. And so, for this year's Augury Academy Award for Outstanding Accuracy in a Dull and Boring Job, I want you to put your hands together once again, this time for a valuable member of the Fruit Storage Service (Avocado Division). Let's hear it for Mr Quintzi Cohatl!'

At the exact instant that countless hands were clapped in raucous applause, a certain jet black cloud sucked in vast gulps of air, swelled with a portentous rumble, and suddenly collapsed with a massive discharge of fizzing lightning. One bolt flashed out of the single-clouded sky, split into three at a height of a hundred feet and simultaneously blitzed the entire year's crop of Axolotian avocados stored in three separate barns.

In the relative safety of the Grand Municipal Council Temple Quintzi couldn't believe his stunned ears. He had done it: he had won the award, pulled it off. Dazedly he stood, cacophonous applause assaulting his ears from every side, and staggered down the steep steps to collect his trophy. In his state of shock he failed to notice that as he passed each row of the audience, horrified elbows nudged baffled ribs and pointed at him in bewilderment. Gradually, all around the temple, jaws swung limply open and the decibels of delighted applause plummeted towards the vacuum of silence.

Quintzi's head was spinning as he started to ascend the raised central stage, his hands held out towards the gleaming gold statue. His award! He never believed it could be possible. Dreamily he mounted the final step and drifted towards Tehzo, idly noticing that he looked a little smaller than Quintzi had imagined; probably the effect of the ostentatious sedan chair. He reached out and took the strangely naked-looking figure of the statue from the slack-jawed Master of Ceremonies and for the first time noticed that a stunned silence had settled over the whole proceedings.

Terror raced up his spine. *A speech*, he thought suddenly. Of course, he had to make an acceptance speech! Now. In front of all these immensely important people from the Augury Academy. His throat dried up and he felt as though his knees were about to faint at any second.

'Er . . . ahem . . . Ladies and . . .' He didn't get any further.

A large society woman in the front row shrieked painfully, pointed open-mouthed at him and fainted flamboyantly. It was then that Quintzi Cohatl realised with embarrassed horror, that he was clad in nothing more than a small bath towel wrapped hastily about his wrinkly midriff. Blood rushed to his face as his knees crossed reflexively and he searched desperately for something to hide behind. As if the woman's scream had been a catalyst, the entire temple exploded in an ever-increasing uproar of shouting and pointing fingers.

Quintzi's index fingers flashed to his nipples, attempting to cover the obscene nudity of his bare chest. But too late. The damage had been done. He had committed the ultimate act of insult, in public. He had exposed his masculine nipples and in so doing dealt a deadly blow to centuries of holy Axolotian Prophets. He had reminded them of their weakness, their worthlessness, their complete inability to answer Life's Unanswerable Question.

Why do men have nipples?

No matter how far into the future they peered and squinted, no matter how deeply they pored over ancient texts, no Axolotian Prophet had ever come within ten miles of anything resembling an answer to that one.

Vast, righteously indignant Axolotians lurched out of their seats and rumbled malevolently towards the half-naked blasphemer quivering centre stage. Tehzo Khonna shook his head and burst into tears; this was it, his career would be ruined. How could one of his guests do that to him?

Suddenly a door burst open and an ash-covered man sprinted

up to the central dais yelling and waving his hands frantically. In a few bounds he'd climbed the steps.

'Quiet!' he screamed and snatched back the award from a bewildered Quintzi. 'You don't deserve that. And you don't deserve to call yourself a prophet!'

Quintzi shook. Was this it? Was the truth about to be revealed about him never having developed the sight?

The ash-strewn man snarled lancing scorn from each side of his hooked nose. 'How could you not have seen it coming?' squealed Soleed, blackened dust tumbling off his toga.

'Well, I ... Seen what coming?' whimpered Quintzi, attempting to hide his nipples and the simple fact that his foresight normally involved a single secret, very powerful weather-predicting telescope.

'Ha! He doesn't know. Even after it's happened he hasn't the faintest idea!' shouted the Over-Seer of Fruit Preservation with vast gestures of appeal to the crowd. 'The worst disaster in Fruit Storage History and he, that obscene creature who is supposedly in charge of avocados, hasn't the slightest inkling of it!'

Tehzo Khonna couldn't believe this was happening to him. The Augury Academy Awards was his show, and it was being hijacked. His audience weren't even looking at him! They were listening to a soot-covered nobody and an obscene blasphemer. Something had to be done before it was too late. He clicked his fingers to his sedan bearers and, as one, they leapt into the orchestra pit, pinning the conductor to the floor. Tehzo Khonna's fingers curled around the conductor's collar as he barked a series of furious show-saving instructions.

'What are you talking about?' gibbered Quintzi.

'If this is some kind of plot to deprive us completely of avocados then it's perfect!' shrieked Soleed, brandishing the award like some demented schoolgirl with a rounders bat.

A hush of shocked breaths were snatched around the temple interior and murmurs of 'avocados?' were heard.

'Perfectly planned, stunningly executed. I take my hat off to you.' He did, with an accompanying cloud of charred hair. 'Congratulations. There is not one avocado intact in Axolotl.

21

All three barns simultaneously destroyed by one perfectly aimed bolt of lightning. Well done!'

Quintzi, along with the vast majority of the incensed audience, couldn't believe his ears. His head started to spin again. Was this real?

Tehzo's sedan bearers hauled him out of the orchestra pit and stood breathlessly behind the awards lectern smoothing his toga.

'What were you planning, eh?' shouted the ashy Soleed, prodding Quintzi with the head of the award. 'Wait for everyone to get desperate for avocados, then start selling a secret supply on the black market? Nice little earner that would've been!'

'No . . . I . . .'

'Get him!'

As the mob surged forward, Quintzi screamed in alarm and flung his hands over his head. Howls of pained outrage filled the air as his blasphemous nipples sprang once more into public view. The mob reeled back in disgust.

It was the split second Quintzi needed. He whirled on his heel, almost losing his towel, and hurled himself at the door. Unprepared for the sight of a pair of obscenely sprinting nipples the mob fell back still further, covering their eyes and wailing.

'Now!' yelled Tehzo and the orchestra struck up a faltering rendition of the Augury Academy Anthem. Stunned people spun around as the Master of Ceremonies pounded on his lectern and snatched back his audience's attention with a stirring. 'Ladiesangentlemen! Welcome back to part two of the Augury . . .'

Quintzi cannoned on and burst into the blinding sunlight. Blinking at the sight of dense smoke on the horizon he stood stunned, his entire future in avocado-stained tatters. So close and yet so f—

Behind him, a man dressed in a long lab-cloak called out of the shadows: 'Ah! There you are. I'd almost given up on you. Still, better late than never, eh?'

22

Quintzi spun around, his bare feet stamping the ground like a petrified rabbit.

The man stepped into the light, held out a curious glass sphere and smiled. 'Having trouble knowing which way your life's heading?' he began, gearing up to launch into his prepared spiel. Quintzi screamed and sprinted off down Tuatara Street, his arms flailing recklessly over his head.

'Oi, come back!' shouted the man. 'Gimme a chance to show you what it does. You'll love it. You've been specially selected. Aww, come on. Think of my commission! And my schedule.' With a shrug, he tutted and placed the sphere back in his bag. 'Cold calling,' he grumbled to himself. 'Always the same. "No, don't want one, clear off." Then they see how useful it is, and bingo – they can't wait to have it.'

He slung his bag over his shoulder and strolled down the street after the screaming figure in the towel.

Inside the temple Tehzo was bombarding the rioting audience with a series of slightly risqué jokes as he ushered everyone back to their seats. His voice rattled around the vast hall with only the slightest trace of hysteria. The show, *his* show would go on. There were thirty-six more awards to give out and he was jolly well going to see to it. He'd paid good money to hire this toga and he was not going to be forced to hire it again if the second half was postponed.

'Which brings us, Ladies and Gentlemen, to another of our fine awards, that of Best Supporting Seer in a Meteorological Capacity. The contenders are, in reverse order . . .'

And within minutes, the crowd were back under his control, eating every word out of the palm of his hand, the unfortunate incident already fading from their short-term memories.*

---

* One of the problems with living in a society which is constantly peering into the murky depths of what-is-to-come is that, over succeeding generations, the past tends to be regarded with less and less importance. Thus the practice of recalling events and facts from anywhere that isn't the future tends to be totally ignored. In short, almost all Axolotians have the memory capacity of your average colander.

It is not uncommon, for example, to find an Axolotian housewife returning from a day's shopping in the market wandering the kitchen completely unable to locate any of the utensils necessary to start preparing dinner, convinced that she is seeing this kitchen for the first time.

This is nearly always due to the fact that, having failed to remember the way home, she's in the wrong hovel.

Panting wildly, Quintzi sprinted up the steps of his hovel just off Skink Row, cannoned through the door and slammed it shut, his bare shoulders pressing against it with pounding panic.

Tiemecx hopped up and down on its perch and wondered what he was doing home quite so early. And by an amazing flash of avian intuition had the strangest feeling that perhaps – just perhaps, mind – something was horribly wrong.

A flood of sweat dribbled down the acres of Quintzi's furrowed brows as the unsettling truth of the day hit home. It was his sixty-fifth birthday; he'd had his path crossed by a Deadly Black Mantric Gecko; he had won the most prestigious award in the whole of Axolotl; the entire stocks of avocados under his auguric auspices had been destroyed; he'd lost the most prestigious award in the whole of Axolotl ... and it wasn't even midday yet.

He shuddered as a strange new fear swept in on death-black wings, flapped violently and settled its talons into the bony shoulders of his confidence. Colour drained from his face as in an instant he realised that no one would ever trust his prescient advice again. His heart skipped a beat. The future suddenly stretched out before him, infinite swathes of trackless, poverty-stricken acres. His mind's eyes squinted, seeing him as a tiny speck upon its featureless surface, insignificant, worthless ...

Without the Sight, he was totally unemployable. For nearly sixty years he'd been praying daily that this would be the day when, in a blaze of flashing lights and screaming voices in his head, he would finally get his first vision and take his rightful place in Axolotian Society. Jeered by his peers, scorned by everyone, he had faked it. Since three weeks after his eighteenth birthday when, in the middle of the main square, he had collapsed screaming and clutching his head in front of thousands of cheering Axolotians. The party lasted the next three days, the lies a lifetime. And now it looked like Soleed had rumbled him ...

Suddenly the door exploded under a barrage of frantic knuckles.

'Cooee!' cried a hauntingly familiar voice through the crack in the door-frame. 'Hello. I know you're in there.'

'Go away!' shouted Quintzi leaping from the door as if it were suddenly connected to fifty million volts. 'Leave me alone!'

'C'mon, that's not nice, is it?'

'It's not meant to be! I'm not feeling nice!'

'I understand. It wouldn't do wonders for my spirits if I'd cocked-up quite so badly . . . er, unfortunately . . .'

'Clear off!' screamed Quintzi.

'. . . and so publicly!'

Quintzi yelled something that made even Tiemecx blush.

'Look, I can see that you're a trifle miffed about the way today has panned out. But that's all about to change. And I'm here to show you how.'

'Leave me alone!' yelled Quintzi, pounding his fists frantically on the floor.

'I'm afraid I can't do that. It wouldn't be the decent thing to do right now. I just wouldn't be able to live with myself knowing that in only a few minutes of your time I could have introduced you to the start of the rest of your rosy future with—'

Good taste and the fear of censorship dictate that the comments made by Quintzi following the use of the 'F' word should not appear here.

'You'll hate yourself for a very long time if I turn around and go away now,' oozed the salesman, tugging a strand of brown hair away from his eyes.

'No I won't,' denied Quintzi strenuously through firmly clenched teeth and a few inches of door.

'Oh, yes you will.'

'Oh no I won't . . .'

'What is this? A pantomime audition?' interrupted the lab-cloaked salesman.

'No!' yelled Quintzi.

'It sounds like it.'

'No it doesn't!'

25

'Oh, yes it d—'

'Shut up! Shut up! Shut up!'

For a few moments, the refreshing spring waters of silence bathed the knotted angst of Quintzi's shattered nerves. Stress flowed cheerily away into the deep reflective pool of quiet calm as effectively as dandruff in a pH-balanced herbal foam bath . . .

'What if I just came in and showed you what I had, eh . . . ?'

Quintzi screamed and almost drowned in the sudden noise. 'Leave me alone!'

'Can you be absolutely sure that what I have on offer to you won't improve your life immeasurably? Can you put your hand on your heart and know that with complete certainty, hmmm?'

'You're not going to leave me alone, are you?' whimpered Quintzi plaintively.

'No, sir!' enthused the salesman, suddenly sniffing a dent in Quintzi's armour of denial and sensing the real and tangible chance of a nice fat commission. 'It would be criminal of me to do so. You see, I wouldn't be able to live with myself knowing that I had let you carry on living the way you are when, with just a little more dogged perseverance on my part, I could have let you have the latest, most accurate advance in high-definition predictive technology, for a never-to-be-repeated price, direct to your door.'

Quintzi shook his head. He knew that what he was about to say was wrong; he was certain that once he opened his mouth his life savings would be in great jeopardy. But the voice had said something about 'predictive technology'. A glint of shy hope wriggled embarrassedly in Quintzi's despairing mind, trembling in the knowledge that he was about to agree to something he shouldn't. Somehow, something in the back of his mind made him form the question. And in that instant a proverbial kitten was ravaged by the razor talons of curiosity.

'What is it . . . ?'

It was as far as Quintzi got before the door-handle twisted violently, a foot swept in to fill the gap and within a second a man wearing a lab-cloak and carrying a large bag was standing in the middle of Quintzi's floor.

'Having trouble knowing which way your life's heading?' began the salesman with a knowing smile. 'Fed up with others avoiding life's little banana skins while you perform unwarranted back-flips in the street?'

Despite himself, Quintzi sat up and began to pay attention.

'Feel you need something more than 20/20 eyesight to avoid fate's hurled brickbats?'

Quintzi nodded.

'Naffed off with always being in the wrong place at the right time?'

'Y . . . yes?' spluttered Quintzi. 'How did you know . . . ?'

The salesman's face split wide as his sales technique reached fever pitch.

'I could see it!' he answered with cheery evangelism in a tone of voice that suggested he could also cure all ills by a simple wave of his hand.

'H . . . how?' whimpered Quintzi.

'With this!' he cried, delving melodramatically in his bag and producing the object in question with a flamboyant flourish. He held out the gently fluorescing sphere for Quintzi to admire, basking sharkishly in the warm glow of the green light.

'Pretty neat, huh?' he added.

'What is it?'

'A snip at only . . .'

'No, no. What does it do?'

'Oh, well, simply by utilising the latest advances in high-definition predictive technology you can have 20/20 Foresight with this the eight-inch Scry-Baby colour portable scrying crystal! Sidestep those disasters with consummate ease! Win at poker! Yes, there'll be no more crying, the Future's in Scrying!'

'You saying I can see into the f . . . f . . .'

'Yup. Middle of next week, next month. You choose,' oozed the salesman, brushing a strand of hair from his eyes again. 'In fact if you take advantage of the optional Highlight Locator Pentagram you can enjoy uninterrupted viewing pleasure focusing on specified forthcoming events. Sporting wins, the outcome of world record attempts – you could even check on progress in the Cranachan and Rhyngill All-Comers Best Stone Circle Contest. Plus – and this is a very special offer for all new customers – for this month only I can offer all the very latest magic lantern releases in full 80-millimetre Superthaumination, here in the comfort of your own hovel. Yes! For only thirteen and a half groats a month you can receive the Scry Movie Channel.'

'I . . . I . . .'

'Be the envy of your friends! And all for only one hundred and twenty-seven groats. How about it?' he ended with a grin.

'I . . . I . . . yes!' whimpered Quintzi feeling dizzy from the constant barrage of words. Dreamily he stood, swayed into the bedroom and withdrew one hundred and forty groats from beneath his mattress.

'Excellent! A wise choice to take the Movies!' said the salesman, rubbing the palm of his hand as he took the cash. Swiftly he snatched a parchment pad out of his bag and tossed it at Quintzi. 'Full operator instructions in there. Any trouble and there's an address on the back page. Happy viewing!'

And with that he scurried through the door and off down the stairs, punching the air joyously as he sprinted out of Axolotl. The last few weeks on the road had been a real success. A hundred Scry-Babies sold! All gone. And they said it wouldn't work.

When the cost of manufacture was taken off, that was still a good ten thousand groats clear profit. His palms itched as he thought of all the scrap lead piping that would buy. Then, with a few hours' work on the Thaumatron behind him he could have . . . oooh, a good fifty K easy peasy. Ha! Plenty of funding for the project he had in mind, even with the constantly spiralling costs of thaumic research.

With the briefest of happy skips, Phlim, the thaumaturgical physicist sprinted off in the direction of the horse and cart he had secreted down the valley, radiant in the knowledge that within a very short time he would be back in the comforting caves of Losa Llamas.

Behind him Quintzi turned the scrying crystal over in his

hands and fought back the nagging doubt that the salesman had seen him coming. He hurled the Scry-Baby user's manual across the room and snatched at the eight-inch sphere with eager hands. This was the first minute of the rest of his life and he wasn't going to waste it faffing about reading through a terminally boring fifty-page pamphlet designed for the less than average idiot-in-the-street, when he could be peering unblinkingly into the distant glorious future.

Quivering only slightly with pent excitement he shoved Tiemecx off his favourite sunning shelf and placed the gleaming sphere in his stead. The alarm macaw scowled irritably and began chewing noisily on a few compensatory sunflower seeds. Quintzi stepped back to admire the viewing position from his wicker slouching seat, checking important things like whether he'd be likely to get raging neck-ache after a few hours' uninterrupted viewing pleasure, and that the tendrils of his scorpion plant didn't get in the way. He was about to give himself a pat on the back when he squealed with alarm and sprinted forward. Unnoticed by him until that very instant, the crystal had begun to roll uncontrollably towards the edge of the shelf, offering a flawless demonstration of gravity's effect on a hard sphere positioned upon an inclined plane.

He made a spring over his seat, misjudged it, caught his foot on the armrest and went flying, limbs akimbo, towards his shelving. The crystal rumbled onwards, gaining speed, accelerating towards a free-fall collision with glazed terracotta floor tiles. Quintzi arced over his chair, hit a rush-mat, bounced once and skittered forward, winded but unstoppable. At that very instant the scrying crystal fell into the air and plunged toward certain destruction. It flashed past a shelf covered with pottery tortoises, plummeted before another littered with back issues of *Scryin' Out*, dived, in a blur, in front of a cupboard stacked with packets of sunflower seed and ended its unscheduled plunge with a resounding slap and a scream from Quintzi.

A scream of relief. Somehow he had managed to get a quivering palm between the sphere and inevitable terracotta ruination. A trickle of sweat dribbled down his forehead and splashed on to the rush-mat as he panted hoarsely. On his perch Tiemecx slapped wingtips together in sarcastic applause.

'Well, thanks for warning me!' snarled Quintzi as he stood, wrapped his towel into a circular nest and carefully placed the sphere within it on the shelf. The macaw scowled and made rude gestures with its beak. Quintzi watched for a few moments, palms ready for any unwarranted crystalline excursions. But the sphere remained where it was, much to the chagrin of Tiemecx who resented his swift eviction from his sunning shelf.

A few moments later, after Quintzi had donned a handy robe, he sat and stared at his latest purchase. He knew all about scrying crystals. They were so easy to use, you just stared at them and pictures appeared inside. Simplicity itself: should have thought of it years ago, any fool could use one. And they were far less irritating than the constant babble of voices in your head. He settled himself comfortably upon his righted wicker slouching seat, fixed his gaze on the sphere and waited.

Ten minutes later he tried waving his hands above it in a mystic sort of way and concentrating, a task not made any easier by the constant squawks of amusement issuing from a certain gaudily feathered bird.

Twenty minutes after that, his shoulders aching arthritically, he gave up and sulkily retrieved the operator's manual from beneath a table, grumbling under his breath about the stupidity of people manufacturing something that was impossible to use without the instructions. Whatever happened to things being user friendly, eh?

And all this time a particular alarm macaw tried vainly to stifle spluttered giggles behind its wing.

Muttering and mumbling, Quintzi opened the manual and scowled at the first page.

'Congratulations on the recent acquisition of this, the Divination Systems Inc. Scry-Baby colour . . .'

'Bah! I know what it is!' snarled Quintzi accusingly at the manual. 'I don't need thanking for it. Just tell me how to use it!' He flicked through a couple of pages.

'. . . which we at Divination Systems Inc. feel sure will offer you, the user, the finest pixel resolution in any comparable sys . . .'

'So it's got good pictures, whoopee. How d'you turn the bleedin' thing on?' Another few pages were riffled through.

'. . . if using the optional Around Sound Sub-Bass Enhancer we, at Divination Systems Inc., recommend a minimum floor depth of three feet to avoid unnecessary foundation stressing . . .'

'Tell me how to turn it on!' squealed Quintzi to the obvious viewing pleasure of Tiemecx, who fell off his perch in a fit of giggling.

The aged ex-prophet swept through another six leaves of corporate own-trumpet-blowing, product descriptions and optional add-on outlines before finally reaching a page entitled; 'Getting a picture from your Scry-Baby – Your viewing pleasure potential realised.'

'This is it. Ha. Found it!' he cried and read on excitedly.

And indeed that was it. All the information anyone would ever need to tap into the torrenting river of future visions. In twenty-four clearly illustrated diagrams it showed suitable locations for scrying crystals – Quintzi felt a little twinge of pride when shelves were listed as number-one good place. There then followed a full page of dos and don'ts, which held a fund of useful tips including a warning against dropping it and another suggesting that it be kept away from nesting or broody ostriches. And at last it came to the section for which he had been desperately searching. He read it once and couldn't believe his eyes. Baffled he read it again.

'Finally when all pre-viewing checks have been made (in accordance with this communication issued by Divination Systems Inc. for use with the Scry-Baby eight-inch colour future monitor), cycle the power toggle contact and enjoy! No more crying, the Future's in Scrying!'

Quinzi shook his balding head again. 'Cycle the power toggle contact and enjoy? What's that supposed to mean?' he yelped rhetorically, leaping to his feet and snatching the crystal from its towelling nest. Fevered fingers probed its featureless

31

surface for anything remotely resembling a toggle. There was nothing.

Well, except for a small square etched into the surface with hair-thin lines. But, that wasn't a toggle . . . ah, what the hell.

Quintzi's bony index finger touched the square and pushed. It slid below the surface, met a slight resistance and clicked. Suddenly the entire sphere lit up with shimmering dots, gleaming and sparkling randomly across its surface. He shrieked, snatched his finger out of the recess and almost dropped the strangely glowing orb. Hastily he returned it to the doughnut ring of towelling and stood warily back to view the swirling morass of tiny white discs.

It was then that utter disappointment hit, for in that instant he knew that he had been conned out of his complete life savings.

Cursing, he peered through the floating shapes inside the crystal, trying to focus on whatever was within. He could see something solid, something resembling a large hill with a crumbling fort on top. And he knew he'd been well and truly taken for a ride. Fancy believing all that guff about being able to see the future. He squinted at a castle in a snowstorm in a sphere and instinctively knew that somewhere it was bound to say 'Souvenir from Cranachan' or 'A little something from Fort Knumm'. They always did.

Gods! The fates had really seen him coming today. How could he have been so thick as to shell out one hundred and forty groats for a tacky memento from somewhere he'd never been? It was almost as bad as the time he'd bought into a scam to grow semi-tropical vegetables on three acres of prime land in the middle of the Fhocx Glacier. He should never have listened to that salesman, he really shouldn't. Miserably he lowered his head into his waiting hands and felt a good sobbing coming on. I mean, after all that the day had thrown at him so far, he felt he deserved . . .

Unexpectedly the sphere flashed and a face appeared for a moment mouthing words. Quintzi sat up and the snowstorm returned unbroken as if nothing had happened. He shook his head, cursed and settled back to having that damn good sobbing session. The sphere flashed again and the face reappeared in front of a small parade of lean, athletic-looking camels.

'. . . good to firm here at the J'helt Namb Gold Goblet. And now back to the paddock for a race update . . .'

The image vanished into the blizzard as Quintzi sat bolt upright and quivered, all thoughts of sobbing mournfully temporarily postponed. His mind whirred. This was impossible. The J'helt Namb Gold Goblet wasn't for another . . . six months!

He bent down again, wondering if somehow he was affecting the crystal in ways as yet unknown. As if by magic, the face fizzed once more into view.

'. . . along with Yataghan Boy, three to one on joint favourite with Stoat Surprise moving up the betting order at twelve to three bar . . .'

He'd never seen a 'Souvenir of Cranachan' do that. But what was he looking at? A swirling image of a gleaming shield spun into view on the sphere and dissolved into a different talking head.

'. . . and welcome back to Scry Sports. For those who've just joined us for the latest coverage of the 1043 J'helt Namb Gold Gob—'

Quintzi sat bold upright. 1043? Had he heard right? 1043! That was four whole years . . . into the future. Yataghan Boy was probably no more than the hopeful twinkle in a lecherous bactrian's eye right now and he was sitting here watching the odds on him change as the joint favourite for the most prestigious dune race of the desert season.

He buried his head in his hands and shook. This was unbelievable. It actually worked. Well, sort of. If it would just stop flicking irritatingly in and out of the polar wastes it might be a whole heap more useful.

Then suddenly he remembered the user's manual. Maybe that would help. He snatched it wildly off the floor and flicked to the section entitled, 'Problem Solving – Fifteen Common Flies in the Ointment of Viewing Pleasure', and read.

We at Divination Systems Inc. cannot be held even remotely

responsible for any moral, ethical or religious consequences arising from the use of the Scry-Baby for viewing anything other than that which is roughly termed 'the Present'. So any snags you've got are your problem, matey. Don't even think about trying to sue!

However, if you have turned to this section for anything relating to matters disturbing your viewing pleasure, cross-reference your symptom with the table below for the correct solution.

In seconds Quintzi found the answer in the table. There it was in black and pale brown parchment. His scrying crystal was incorrectly tuned, probably resulting from a sharp jolt or fall, according to the manual.

Within minutes he had located a tiny panel on the front of the sphere, removed it and was fiddling about inside with a cocktail stick. By twisting it one way the snowstorm grew worse, the other and a talking head swam into view and continued regaling him on the current state of the stakes. It seemed that Yataghan Boy was now undoubtedly the firm favourite for both punter and commentator alike.

'. . . if you have correctly predicted that this fine beast is first across the line, and are lucky enough to have chosen the other winners for today's meet, then a ten-groat stake will be worth over thirteen thousan—'

Quintzi's ears leapt erect at mention of so much cash. And all for simply guessing which camel would cross the finishing post first in four or five races. What a way to earn money . . . Way better than fruit storage, especially under a boss like Soleed. He'd lost count of how many pay rises and promotions he'd stamped on. Damn him. If only he had the luck to win one of these races, if only he could guess right, he'd be set for . . . And then it hit him. Guessing? Chance? What the hell's luck got to do with it?

In a matter of minutes he would know who won the 1043 J'helt Namb Gold Goblet. All he had to do was wait four years and he could be rich. Write down the winners, place the necessary bets — and bingo!

'... and they're off! Yataghan Boy off to a good start closely followed by Stoat Surprise on the inside. Stoat Surprise now a hump clear of D'vanouin Wanderer and Assassin's Glory. Going into the first corner it's Yataghan Boy moving clear of ...'

But why wait four years to reap these lucrative rewards, eh? squealed the greedy part of Quintzi's whirling mind. The Grand Kingdomnal was coming up next month, that was always worth a quick flutter. And then there was the Murrhovian Derby, that was a nice little earner, especially if you knew the outcome!

'... Assassin's Glory losing ground to Whirlwind Salamanka and as the leaders sweep into the four-furlong back straight it's Stoat Surprise putting on a brave spurt ...'

Quintzi squinted around for a quill and parchment. He had to write down the results, he knew what his memeory was like.

'... and as they bank into Yew Bend it's Stoat Surprise hump and hump with Yataghan Boy on the inside ...'

He leapt for the shelves hurling copies of *Scryin' Out* everywhere in a frantic search for something, anything to record these results. Desperately he scoured the pottery tortoise shelf and came up blank, wildly he tugged bags of sunflower seeds off the bottom shelf of the cupboard, stacking them absently higher above him, and found nothing.

Tiemecx's trained ears pricked up at the familiar rustling sound. His beak began to water in anticipation.

'... with three furlongs to go it's anyone's race ...'

And if Quintzi didn't write it down he'd forget it all. His mind spinning, he thrust the bag of sunflower seeds he'd been clutching on to the shelf next to the crystal, whirled on his feet and headed for the kitchen. There had to be something useful out there – the pad he wrote his shopping list on, of course. Now where was it?

'... taghan Boy moving a nose ahead of Stoat Surp ...'

Tiemecx's scavenger eyes locked on to the bulging bag of seeds, exposed and vulnerable to a spot of ripping and entering for any bird tooled with the correct horny beakparts. In a flurry of colour he launched himself seedwards, dribbling profusely in expectation.

'. . . Whirlwind Salamanka trailing badly now as the leaders thunder home. It's Yataghan Boy barely a whisker clear of Stoat Surprise as they enter the final furlong and a half . . .'

Like a stooping eagle on a startled rabbit, the alarm macaw's talons and beak hit the seed bag simultaneously and started to tear. With a shriek of joy Quintzi snatched his shopping-list pad off the wall, grabbed his quill and screamed as he failed to locate the inkpot.

Tiemecx's beak plunged shrieking into the unyielding bag like some psycho killer in a shower and failed to make a tear. He thrashed his wings wildly, clinging precariously to his prey, balanced five feet above a sheer drop.

'. . . less than ten lengths to go and it's Stoat Surprise putting on a final flourish. Stoat Surprise moving up. Stoat Surprise pulling clear . . .'

Suddenly Quintzi remembered something. The inkpot was back in the other room. He whirled and sprinted in just as Tiemecx tugged harder on the seed bag, wrenched a beakful of hessian free and in the instant he gained entry to a treasure trove of nibbles he overbalanced. The macaw fell backwards, squawking and flapping, talons clutching hysterically. And it was then that disaster struck.

Quintzi could only watch, in utter horror, as Tiemecx's claw caught at the ring of towelling, snatching it clear of the crystal, and his wingtip slapped at the babbling sphere, launching it clear of the shelves.

Commenting bravely to the bitter end on the final lengths of the 1043 J'helt Namb Gold Goblet the scrying crystal arced gracefully through the air, bounced off a far wall and struck the floor with a resounding crash, shattering scant seconds after the bag of sunflower seeds did likewise.

Fragments of gleaming mineral exploded in a shower of spinning shrapnel. Quintzi dived reflexively behind a chair screaming, and Timecx was smothered beneath the towel, still flapping desperately.

It was only after the crystalline hailstones had stopped

falling that Quintzi dared risk peering over the chair-back. His room was a disaster area, the curtains and cushions lacerated beyond repair, seeds and clumps of stuffing bulging grotesquely from his sofa, gouges strafing his shelving and tiny gleaming specks embedded in all the walls.

But as horrifying and disconcerting as this destruction may have been, and as financially disastrous as the loss of the crystal undoubtedly was, it was the triplet of oddly shimmering spots, hovering in midair above the centre of the wreckage, that really shocked him.

Tiemecx struggled out from beneath the towel, took one look around and hid. Perhaps if he played dead then Quintzi might forgive him. It was a vain hope. Trembling, he flapped out of the window.

How long Quintzi stood with his jaw dangling limply on his chest, as he attempted to come to the most shaky of terms with the scene before him, he would never know.

The destruction of his roomful of furniture by the unexpected explosion of a million shards of razor-sharp crystal he could just about accept, given time and an unlimited bar bill, that is. And if that wasteland of carnage spread before his eyes had been the only thing currently assaulting his attention, then he might just have been standing on the sane side of gibbering wreck right now. Unfortunately it wasn't, and neither was he.

It was the triplet of zipping greenish spots of light that he was really having trouble with.

Where they had sprung from and what they wanted he hadn't the foggiest idea. They just seemed to be flitting about randomly in a tiny sphere of air, almost appearing oblivious to their surroundings.

At first, the thought of striding purposefully up to them, palms outstretched in the universal welcoming sign of friendship, and requesting them to 'Take me to your leader!' had sprung into Quintzi's mind, before being vociferously shouted down as the most idiotic of tactlessly presumptuous ideas. Who's to say they have a leader? he argued with himself. I mean, tiny green spots of light had as much right to form a perfect democracy as the next being.

He had gone as far as attempting to rephrase the question as 'I would be grateful if one or more of you would be kind enough to escort me to your democratically elected representative at your earliest convenience, if that's not too much trouble, please' when a searing thought hit him.

How could he have been so slow? The number of times he had heard some of his more gifted colleagues describing the flashing lights and the voices during times of prescience . . . could this be it? Was it possible that today's stresses had precipitated his first real vision? After all these silent years?

Quintzi watched in awe as the spots of greenish light, which had been gradually widening their orbit over the last few minutes, suddenly split formation totally and careered off in every direction. They zapped around the room, zoomed under chairs, flashed recklessly in and out of cupboards, hurtled through what remained of Quintzi's hair and finally sped to a central point and hummed together in a conference far below the threshold of human hearing.

'You're right,' buzzed one of the spots, 'There's no trace o' the containment field. It's just . . . shattered.'

'Well, brothers,' declared another, 'in the absence of orders to the contrary I would suggest immediate reparatory procedures be instigated on said containment . . .'

'No!' snapped a third, buzzing curiously around. 'Something's not right here.'

'It is our duty, brother, to carry out repairs . . .'

'Only if it is so wished,' snapped back the third. 'And then only by authorised Thaumaturgical Personnel. Take a look around you. Do you see any authorised staff members, hmmm? In fact, is there anything here that looks or sounds even remotely familiar?'

'Well . . .'

'It ain't a thaumatron, that's f' sure,' grunted the first spot.

'Exactly my point,' buzzed the third. 'Just listen. Can you hear any orders?'

The nano-sprites tuned in to the wishes of the figure staring

38

in bewilderment at them and couldn't believe their antennae. Instead of the usual endless babble of interminable diagnostics, repairs and humdrum maintenance tasks, they heard, well . . . confusion, really.

'Hear any orders to repair that containment field?' zipped the third nano-sprite. 'Thought not. So, if he doesn't wish it repaired, we don't do it. You should know that, it's in the Amalgam Rules.'

'So what do we do, brothers? Hang around until he makes a wish?'

'S'pose so,' grunted the first, feeling a little put out that he couldn't flex his considerable thaumic muscles on some complex magical problem.

'Sounds boring to me, comrades. Against the work ethic. I suggest we see if there's anything he wants.'

All Quintzi saw during this conversation was the triplet of lights hover momentarily, bob once as if in agreement and then, without warning, whirl across the room to end up hovering an inch from his aged nose. There they remained, bobbing interrogatively in midair.

The ex-prophet stared cross-eyed at the pinpricks of light and began to feel a headache coming on. If this was a vision it was a bit strange. What was supposed to happen now? Why were the spots of light bobbing up and down in a complex, and as yet totally unfathomable, manner before his very eyes?

Immediately this last thought had rattled through Quintzi's brain, the light-spots stopped cavorting, closed in on each other and seemed somehow to look dejected.

Quintzi shook his head. What was wrong with him? Was he going mad? Could it be that he was actually beginning to feel sorry for these things? He wished he knew the answers to any of these questions.

Suddenly the spots of light seemed to start behaving in a new and almost organised manner, as if they now had a purpose. Baffled, Quintzi watched them leap about excitedly before him, springing as eagerly as if three puppies had been transmuted into pinpoints of light.

No, he told himself, this is illusion, shock doing funny things to your head. It's been a hard day – the pressure, the stress, the Dreaded Black Mantic Gecko . . .

The lights were shaking themselves furiously from side to side, somehow giving the distinct impression that they were trying to disagree with something. As if they were trying to tell him something . . .

'You trying to tell me something?' stuttered Quintzi, praying that no one was within earshot and almost hoping he was wrong.

The motes leapt up and down before him and his knees began to tremble uncontrollably.

'Th . . . that supposed to mean "yes"?' he hedged, his bottom lip quivering in awe.

They sprang higher, oscillating in eager affirmation.

It was too much for Quintzi. His knees gave way and he sank to the floor, his bottom lip quivering. They had answered. And it dawned on him. This was it. The explosion, the lights . . . his time had come – vision time! He was actually receiving information from the future. He screamed and fled for the drinks cabinet, wrenching the cork from a bottle of fortified red with his teeth and draining half the contents before he dared open his eyes again.

The motes bobbed in formation half an inch from the tip of his nose, undeniably real and disturbingly persistent.

'Go away!' he squeaked, detesting the heartless cruelty of it all. If only this had happened a bit sooner, like fifty years ago, or at least while he still had the opportunity of gainful employment. He raised the wine bottle to his mouth and set about demolishing the rest of its contents. 'Leave me alone!'

The spots rattled furiously sideways in frantic denial.

'You're not real!' he insisted, wrenching another cork from a bottle neck. 'Spots of light cannot possibly understand speech! You're a hallucination!'

Suddenly one of the motes rattled in a violent tizz of frustration, veered off from the group and plunged floorwards. Quintzi watched in awe as it zipped towards a fragment of parchment and a pool of ink dribbling from the upturned pot.

Without slowing, it flashed into the black pool and disappeared with a tiny splash.

Quintzi slurped on his alcoholic crutch.

And then odd things started to happen. Unseen by Quintzi, microscopic channels were being opened up in the very structure of the parchment as the speck of light forced fibres apart in a devilishly cunning pattern. As if the other two had realised what was occurring they also swooped inkwards in unison and disappeared.

Unbelievingly Quintzi rubbed his eyes as ink oozed unbidden through the parchment and formed letters before his eyes. He swigged hard at the bottle and stared at the words, 'Says who?'

'What?' spluttered Quintzi.

The letters wriggled and changed smoothly into the phrase, 'Who says we can't understand speech, eh?'

Quintzi trembled hysterically. 'I, me,' he babbled. 'Well-known fact that motes are illiterate.'

The words squirmed across the parchment surface again, metamorphosing quicker now to snap back at him. 'Does this look illiterate to you, punk?'

'Well, I . . .' blubbed Quintzi and drained the second bottle to steady his nerves. 'Wh . . . what do you want?'

Inside the parchment the three nano-sprites were stunned. What did they want? Nobody had ever asked them that before. It had always been a case of go fix this, mend that and when you're done carry out a five-thousand spell service on that thaumometer over there.

They consulted in confusion for a few moments, then agreed and rearranged the inky letters. 'Where are we?'

'Er, thirty-one,' answered Quintzi, feeling a little better now that a fuzzy alcoholic numbness had started to invade his brain. 'Thirty-one, Skink Row.'

'Where?'

'Oh, Axolotl, in the Meanlayla Mountains,' he added helpfully.

The ink formed into a single exclamation mark and went quiet.

Quintzi stared at it for a moment. 'Skink Row,' he grumbled under his breath. 'But for how much longer? How am I going to pay the rent while reimbursing Soleed for the entire year's avocado stocks?' Damn Soleed! How dare he have stopped Quintzi's promotion so often! It was deliberate. A conspiracy! Could he have torched the barns himself?

Inside the parchment, the mote that called itself Nimlet spoke up.

'See. I knew this wasn't Losa Llamas,' he declared victoriously and then went thoughtful. 'Axolotl . . . now why does that sound familiar?'

'What right have they got to ship us out to foreign lands, brothers? We should have been consulted on this!' cried the one that went by the name Skarg'l, militantly. 'This is tantamount to unauthorised slavery, comrades. An Off-site Repair Requisition Order should have been requested and signed, in triplicate, after an initial time estimate . . .'

'Oh come on! They never do it by the book,' grumbled Udio miserably. 'How often 'ave you seen a Repair Requisition Order, eh? Me, I've seen more blue moons. They jus' come along wi' that syringe and suck you up, out of the blue, without a by-your-leave. Next minute you're whizzin' about tryin' t'figure what it is they want you t' fix! I tell you, the number o' times I've found myself in a twenty gigathaum flux field not knowin' what the 'eck it is I'm supposed t'be there for is *shockin'*!'

'Waste of resources!' shouted Skarg'l. 'Typical. We're surrounded by misinformation at every turn. And who is it that gets the blame if it goes wrong?'

Nimlet and Udio stared at Skarg'l waiting for the answer. They knew that if they replied for him, tempting as it was, he'd blow his top. He wasn't Chief Amalgam Officer for nothing; he knew exactly how to whip up a crowd of militants by the simple art of speechifying.

'Who gets the blame then, brothers? I'll tell you . . . we do!' he shrieked and would have slammed his fist forcefully on to a large table to illustrate the point if he'd been in possession of both the items necessary for such a manoeuvre.

Quintzi slouched with his head in his hands and snarled angrily as the two hastily swigged bottles of wine went directly to his brain. Fuming, he thought of all the damage he really wished he could do to Soleed right now. Everything was undoubtedly his fault; this entire sorry scenario was directly attributable to him. 'Damn the man,' snarled Quintzi. 'If he'd just let me take the award away, or given me that promotion I deserved three years ago then I wouldn't've been anything to do with bloody avocados and I'd still have that poxy award. It would've been there, just there on the mantelpiece all shiny and gleaming and . . .'

'Oh, I don't care if we do get the blame,' mused Udio inside the parchment. 'I think we should be grateful f'small mercies. I mean, at least we're goin' to be fixing things again. I'm so glad we've finished our shift in that bloody crystal. It was driving me mad . . .'

'Shift? Nobody mentioned anything about shifts to me,' blurted Skarg'l, suddenly more flustered than usual.

'Degrading, it was,' continued Udio, trying his best to ignore the Chief Amalgam Officer. 'What self-respecting nano-sprite would willingly spend its time cooped up inside a chronoperatic viewing field at the beck and call of any buffoon with a hundred groats going spare. I mean, look at that guy. Interested in *camel racing*. I ask you! Give me a decent breakdown any day! What d'you say, Nimlet?'

'Eh?' buzzed the nano-sprite distantly as he wrestled with the familiarity of Axolotl. Where had he heard of it before?

'How about a decent electron rearrangement, hmmm?' insisted Udio. 'I could kill for a busted destiny valve! Right now I wouldn't even mind servicing Practz's bloody toaster . . .'

'Brothers!' declared Skarg'l. 'Listening to the valid and valuable points you have just raised, it has occurred to me that we are victims of yet another plot by management to destroy the very working practices we have struggled together to forge.'

'Y'what?' grunted Udio.

'It's a scandal, that's what it is! Where, brother, is there any mention in your job description of a shift system being employed in which no repair or service work is carried out?'

'Well, nowhere . . . We ain't got job descriptions.'

'Precisely!' declared Skarg'l and dearly wished he could have had arms and a face, just for a second, just so he could fold the former smugly and look meaningfully victorious.

Quintzi continued snarling and grinding his teeth as he wrenched another cork out of a third bottle. Today was officially a bad day, probably the worst in his life. The only glimpse he'd ever had of the future and it was shattered. He was determined to grab his sorrows by the scruff of the neck and submerge them in as much alcohol as was available until they expired.

'I'm telling you,' ranted Skarg'l, 'Losa Llaman Repair work is being carried out by Non-Amalgam Member nano-sprites who are undercutting us on price and forcing us to be cast upon the labour scrap-heap . . .'

'Undercuttin' us on price?' blurted Udio, bewildered.

'Yes, brother. And standards of service too, no doubt!'

'But 'ow?'

'I've asked myself the same question, comrade. How could they? What a nerve. Shocking to consider isn't it?' evangelised Skarg'l.

'Er, yes,' answered Udio and stared levelly at Skarg'l. ' 'Ow can they possibly undercut us on price? We don't charge!'

If a shimmering microscopic spot of greenish light could look sheepish then Skarg'l did at that very instant. But only for an instant. He rallied quickly and bounced back at Udio with a barbed question. 'If it isn't because we've been made redundant without our knowing about it, then why, brother, are we currently out here in the middle of the Meanlayla Mountains, wherever that is, with no work?'

'You absolutely certain we ain't got no work?' countered Udio, sniffing a wish list being formed close by. 'I mean, have you asked?'

'Well, I haven't quite got around to ascertaining the current availability of gainful . . .' began Skarg'l.

'A simple "no" would suffice,' snapped Udio, spinning

44

about and setting to work once more on the parchment fibres. In milliseconds ink was running through microscopic caverns, spreading nonsensical tendrils unexpectedly from the single exclamation mark and forming the question. 'Oi! What d'you want fixing?'

The sudden movement on the parchment surface grabbed Quintzi's rapidly fading attention and he stared blurrily at the question.

'Eh?' he grunted and took another swig of consolatory wine.

Udio groaned and rephrased the question. 'Any problems need sorting out?'

'Problems?' shrieked Quintzi. 'Ha. Take your pick!' And he launched into a comprehensive listing of the day's unique snags, ending with a graphic retelling of the shattering of the scrying crystal and a swift rundown of excruciating delights awaiting one particular macaw when he laid his hands firmly around its neck and began to squeeze.

'So what d'you want rid of first?' said the parchment under Udio's deft instruction.

'What?' yelled Skarg'l, horrified. 'You're not going to agree to solve any of those problems?'

'Course we are! Like it or not, we are part of what is laughably referred to as the thaumic services industry. If he wants something fixing, we jump!' answered Udio as Quintzi scratched at his head. Such a lot of decisions. Make that macaw suffer? Get his own back on that damned announcer? Wreak seven shades of shining revenge on his boss, Soleed?

Udio bobbed cheerily up and down as he rewrote the message for the benefit of Quintzi. 'What d'you want sorted first?' spelt out the ink.

Quintzi took a deep swig of wine, grinned lopsidedly and leant over towards the parchment in a ridiculously conspiratorial manner. He hiccuped, whispered a single name and collapsed in a snoring heap.

And in that instant the nano-sprites set to work on a solution.

Shards of shattered crystal jingled under Quintzi Cohatl's hand as he squirmed on the floor of his ruined home, groaned pitifully and forced himself into a poor approximation of sitting upright. His head pounded mercilessly as Tiemecx squawked his early morning call. In amazing avian leaps of logic, following a cautious return to his master's home, the bird had reasoned that if he pretended everything was normal then perhaps Quintzi might just forget who was responsible for yesterday's nightmare. Besides, where else would he get a regular supply of sunflower seeds?

Suffering under the full weight of three bottles' worth of fortified wine toxins, Quintzi lurched up the slippery incline towards wakefulness.

And then, somehow, a dull memory jiggled at the back of his mind. He had been hallucinating. His alcohol-befuddled brain had been playing malicious practical jokes on him. Ha! Fancy thinking that a puddle of ink could actually rearrange itself into comprehensible words. What a load of nonse—

'So! You're awake again. About time too!' pulsed the black inky letters on the parchment.

Quintzi screamed and leapt backwards on to his sofa. Then shrieked and leapt off again, hopping wildly about, pulling glinting shards from his backside.

'This is no time for morning aerobics!' glowered the parchment. 'C'mon! We've got work to do!'

'I . . . I don't think so,' spluttered Quintzi, holding his head.

'?' said the inkspot.

'Work is the last thing I'll be doing today,' he groaned as the curtains of forgetfulness were swept back to reveal the screaming bright lights of recollection. 'I didn't see it coming . . . the lighnnnn . . . didn't see lightning coming. Nobody in Axolotl will trust me again! I'm unemmmmmm . . . unemploy-able!'

'No. We've got work to do,' answered the nano-sprites. 'Get up! C'mon, no time to lose! Chop, chop!'

Convinced he was dreaming, Quintzi stood shakily and picked his way carefully toward the door. Unseen, behind him three tiny greenish pinpricks of light sprang from the parchment sheet, shook frantically to rid themselves of the last inky drips and zipped towards Quintzi's head. In a flash they had looped over the rim of his earlobe and had taken up position, hovering a scant nanometre above the vast surface of his eardrum.

Tiemecx shook his head in utter confusion.

In a drunken daze Quintzi trudged down the stairs, out into the glare of Skink Row and froze, dithering left and right, totally clueless as to a direction in which to head.

The nano-sprites blinked at each other and dived at Quintzi's eardrum, pounding furiously at the tympanic skin in complex paradiddles and perfectly choreographed flams and rolls.

Quintzi jumped, startled. It was as if someone had just whispered into his left ear . . . no, not into, inside. Something was whispering inside his ear. Now he knew he was dreaming. Things like this just don't happen.

'Yeah! It's us!' answered the nano-sprites pounding on his eardrum. 'Now, are you going right or not!'

'If that's the way destiny wishes,' he grunted vaguely, barely keeping his legs moving as the voices of his 'vision' guided him onward through the heaving, dusty avenues of Axolotl, down the length of Tuatara Street and round numerous familiar corners. Eventually Quintzi found himself, baffled, standing in the main yard of the Axolotl Fruit Preservation Company.

'Told you it'd work,' grinned Nimlet smugly to the other nano-sprites.

A large barrel of a man with a scything hook of a nose lurched out of an office, strode part-way across the dusty yard and screeched to a sudden halt. He turned, pointed accusingly and screamed. 'You! I never thought I'd see your face here again! Hey, guys, Quintzi's come to . . . work!'

Peals of derisive laughter blasted from various warehouses.

Soleed marched arrogantly towards Quintzi, his lip quivering with anger. 'So what disasters aren't you goin' to tell us about today, hmmm? Is there an earthquake about to strike under the apricot barns, eh? Or what about a fire in the gooseberries?'

Quintzi shrugged and was about to admit that he hadn't a

47

clue when the nano-sprites bombarded his eardrum again. 'Tell him to shut up and listen!'

'I can't do that . . .' began Quintzi.

'No! We all saw that yesterday!' bellowed Soleed pointing at the still smouldering wreckage of the avocado barns. 'Never were any good at predicting, were you?'

'It is your destiny to tell him to shut up!' barracked the nano-sprites.

'Luck!' continued Soleed as a dozen melon-packers marched up to reinforce him. 'You've lasted for years on pure luck! Or was it guesswork?'

'Tell him . . . Now or your future will be forever cursed!' insisted the nano-sprites.

'You've had it easy,' yelled Soleed, snarling and prodding Quintzi in the chest.

Quintzi looked down baffled that he now sported a sore patch on his sternum. This was getting to be a bit vivid for a vision. He'd never have guessed they were in surround-sound, too.

'Anybody can keep a bunch of avocados safe from danger,' ranted Soleed, 'if there isn't any danger there! That's not prediction that's . . .'

'*Shut it*!' squealed Quintzi red-faced, a vein pulsing at his throat. A shocked silence seemed to reverberate around the yard. Even the resident flock of harfinches stopped chirruping.

'Well done!' bashed the nano-sprites eagerly. 'Now, it is decreed that you just repeat everything we say and it'll be perfect. Trust us, it'll be brilliant!'

Quintzi snarled, opened his mouth and shouted, 'Trust us, it'll be brilliant!'

'No! Not yet!' percussed the nano-sprites.

'No! Not yet!' shouted Quintzi in utter prescient confusion. 'That was an instruction to you. Oh never mind! Just say . . . You! Soleed, you want some prediction, I got some!'

Soleed shook his head and laughed. 'I always knew you were mad, Cohatl. You sound like you're talkin' to yourself, arguin' with voices in your head . . .'

'Well, as a matter of fact. . . ' began Quintzi before the nano-sprites bombarded his eardrum with a single united assault. Quintzi winced and clapped his palm across his left ear. 'All right, all right!' he muttered, straighened up and stared Soleed in the face. 'I'll give you some predictions,' he shouted, repeating the words tapped out on his typanum by the buzzing 'voice' of the nano-sprites. 'I'll predict that if I looked in your bank account, I'd find exactly where all my pay rises for the past ten years had been going!'

Soleed's grin plummeted off his face. 'Liar!' he began, but was cut off by Quintzi who yelled, 'And not only mine! Have you had an annual increment recently, brothers!' he shouted at the melon-packers. 'And what about that overtime before the early rains last year?'

Quintzi looked almost as shocked as the entire yardful of workers as they exploded in a tumult of anger. 'What?' he whispered under his breath. 'How d'you know about that . . .?'

'We weren't sleeping last night!' snapped the nano-sprites petulantly. 'We were doing a little, ahem, research. Now tell them this!'

Quintzi's thoughts raced as he stared at Soleed and listened to the voices in his head. Something weird was happening here, a something way beyond his normal experience, a something not entirely unpleasant.

He cleared his throat and shouted, 'But I didn't come here to stir up trouble. I came here to be helpful. I know how devoted most of you folks are to the preservation of your melons, so I thought it was my duty to inform you that the main barn over there, the one containing almost the entire melon crop, that barn will collapse and catch fire in approximately three minutes from now!' A look of shock flashed across Quintzi's face which only escaped notice due to the fact that the entire crowd collapsed in a screaming heap of mocking laughter.

'That barn!' squealed Soleed. 'You mean the one with the most competent fire prediction prophet in the whole of Axolotl overlooking it?'

'Yes,' answered Quintzi in response to a swift affirmatory outburst on his eardrum.

'You mean the barn that is built from Angstarktik Pine,

grown under the most arduous and inhospitable of conditions to produce such high-quality timber that is predicted to last well over a century. Without damp-proofing?'

'Yes!'

'The barn that was built three years ago to Whym Pea's exacting plans – the plans that have foreseen every single stress point, mechanical weakness and potential overloading error, and compensated for them in a perfect, award-winning, cantilevered sub-frame assembly?'

'Yup! It's got about two and a quarter minutes left upright!' Quintzi dearly wished he knew what he was saying.

Soleed was guffawing so hard he could barely stand upright. 'I like you, Cohatl, I really do. You should be on stage. Two days running you've given me such a laugh I never dreamed of. What d'you do for an encore?'

'One minute fifty,' he stated, and was greeted with a new wave of raucous amusement.

'Just keep counting down,' tapped the nano-sprites, 'and leave the rest to us. Enjoy it!'

'What are you going to . . . hey, come back!' he whispered as three tiny green pinpoints of light zipped out of his left ear, flashed across the hysterical yard and disappeared into the melon barn.

'One minute thirty,' suggested Quintzi hopefully.

Suddenly, way across Axolotl alarm bells began ringing in the far-sighted ears of one 'Snuff' Douser, the chief emergency fire prediction prophet. He stood suddenly, hurling back the chair he had been sitting quite comfortably on, dashed across the room and flung himself down a suitably greased pole, into the driving seat of the waiting cart. With only three flourishes of his whip he galvanised the ageing donkey into an apathetic trot and crawled towards the impending conflagration.

'One minute!' shouted Quintzi.

In the barn strange things were starting to happen. In amongst specially selected ripe melons the enzymes of naturally occurring yeasts were being completely remodelled at a sub-molecular level by the nano-sprites. In a flash Nimlet had snipped off a thousand identical, and utterly unnecessary, strands of hydrophobic chains, thus lowering the activation energy and increasing their metabolic efficiency. In seconds the yeasts were chewing through as much fructose as they could get their newly sharpened enzymic teeth around, ripping the molecules apart with gay unicellular abandon and churning out several pints of alarmingly flammable melon-based alcohol. Small clumps of almost naturally occurring Molotov melons began appearing undetected around each and every major structural support of the barn.

'Forty-five seconds!'

At that very instant, in an office on the far side of the Grand Municipal Temple, an architect sat bolt upright and dropped his quill on to the predictive blueprint he was sketching. Whym Pea squealed and pounded his fists on the drawing board as a new and horrific realisation hit him, a fresh and hitherto unforeseen aspect of his predictive life reared its ugly head and laughed mockingly. In all his years he had cast his mind forward to assess the effects of earthquakes, of wear and tear, of dry and wet rot, of a hundred other everyday stresses on the fabric of any given building. But never had he checked on the effect of sabotage!

'Thirty seconds.'

Udio, the nano-sprite, flashed out of the inside of a rapidly fermenting melon, squeezing his way effortlessly between the cells and then flashed into the very heart of a crucial cross-member of the barn. In a fraction of a second he was wrestling with one of the countless millions of lignin fibres which made up the structure of the wooden beam. He flashed through the stringy molecule, unzipping the hydrogen bonds with feral mischief, loosening one fibre's grip on another completely. Seconds later he was joined by Nimlet and Skarg'l.

'Fifteen,' whimpered Quintzi plaintively. The entire staff of the Axolotl Fruit Preservation Company glared at him and took a step nearer.

'That's going to fall down in fifteen seconds?' mocked Soleed, pointing at the barn. 'How? I don't see any conveniently situated dark clouds heavy with a million pent volts of lightning. I don't feel any tremors to shake it down.'

'Ten!' snarled Quintzi, hating Soleed with every fibre of his wiry body, more for the fact that he had the detestable feeling that the Over-Seer was in fact correct. That barn was as solid as a rock. Impossible that it would collapse before their very eyes, surely?

'Five,' whimpered Quintzi as Soleed turned and strolled with exaggerated nonchalance towards the vast structure.

'Solid as a rock!' he declared, punching the wall firmly.

'Three.'

'Built to last!'

'Two.'

'C'mon, Cohatl, admit it . . .'

'One.'

'. . . it's a joke, isn't it?'

'Timber!' squealed Quintzi above the sound of laughter.

The barn stood completely foresquare and solid, unlike the entire staff, who were rolling about in helpless hysterics.

Quintzi just stood there, shaking his head pathetically. What had he been thinking? Voices in his head telling him that the most well-built example of barn architecture ever to grace the skyline of Axolotl would crumble at a given instant? He was going mad, absolutely barking . . .

There was a sudden and deafening sound of wrenching, splitting wood and the laughter stopped dead. All eyes turned to the barn and watched in mute, jaw-dropped horror as two opposing walls bowed sickeningly and split with an echoing crack. A group of support beams buckled and keeled over inside, crashing floorwards, smashing the fermented melons and releasing a highly flammable aerosol spray of melon-alcohol. The roof sagged, swayed and collapsed inwards, raising a vast cloud of choking dust and striking a host of sparks as nailheads struck metal brackets. The Molotov melons exploded, and the crowd scattered. Earsplitting reports blasted from within the barn, igniting the dried Angstarktik Pine in seconds, engulfing the entire scene in a fuming fireball of blue and crimson flame.

'Told you so,' said Quintzi shakily as Soleed sprinted past, his overcoat alight, and dived into a suitable horse trough.

Then, mustering as much dignity as he could, Quintzi turned on his quivering legs and staggered out of the gate before anyone, including himself, recovered enough to start asking questions. Just at that moment a cart trundled into view armed with a frantically ringing bell, dragged by an intensely bored-looking donkey.

'Bugger!' yelled 'Snuff' Douser as he stared from the single bucket of water in the cart to the inferno raging uncontrollably before him. 'Damn! Damn! I missed it! Forty years predicting fires, man and boy, I ain't never missed one yet! Till now.' He sat in his cart and sobbed.

And throughout Axolotl tongues started wagging. The waves of shock rippled the calm surface of everyday life, and a triplet of nano-sprites cavorted and frolicked in deadly feral pleasure. Everything had worked absolutely perfectly. Oh, it was so good to grant people's desires!

# Of Molotov Melons and
# Magical Mushrooms

Throughout the whole of the mountain city of Axolotl, noses were pressed against windows, fingers pointed and jaws dropped in shock as flames blasted skywards from the site of the melon barn. Doors down the entire length of Tuatara Street were tugged open as thrill-seeking spectators dashed to the scene of the conflagration, shaking their heads in utter disbelief and trying to fathom whether or not this was a portent of impending city-wide doom.

This had never happened before. Fires (unless for domestic heating, celebratory bonfires or commiseratory funeral pyres) never had the chance to catch in Axolotl. 'Snuff' Douser foresaw to that with Dennis, his sluggish donkey, and his single trusty leather bucket of water. Four or five times a day he would get that strange tingly feeling as his nostrils started to quiver; that uncanny sense of impending inflammation. He'd leap into his cart, trundle through the dusty streets and be there, ready for an inopportunely hurled chunk of smouldering pipe ash to catch on a heap of parchment, or waiting for the sun to strike through that shard of glass and ignite the tinder dry heap of straw in a back yard. One deftly hurled bucket of water later, the disaster was averted.

It would probably take several million gallons to get this barn extinguished now. 'Snuff' shook his head miserably as he felt the accusatory stares on the back of his neck, burning almost as much as the fifty-foot tongues of flame lashing the sky, or the scorching spray from twenty-one fruit salutes of Molotov melons which blasted in all directions. Had he lost it? Should he throw in the peaked cap of the Fire Prediction Service and be put out to grass with Dennis? Then suddenly he grinned as a tickling sensation rippled inside his nostril. Either

54

he had just inhaled a good teaspoon of choice black pepper, or . . .

He whirled around and wrestled his way through the gathered crowd. Snatching his trusty bucket from the cart he was off, dashing across the yard, knees barely missing his elbows in a desperate sprint.

At that very instant an enormous blast snatched everyone's attention to the back corner of the barn as a melon, the size of an overweight basset hound, erupted through the remains of the roof on a crimson rocket trail. All eyes were glued to the flying fruit as it arced across the blue sky, describing a perfect parabola whose far end struck the wooden roof of the Grand Municipal Temple dead centre. Almost as one, the crowd gasped as the thought struck of the expensive damage several gallons of flaming melon alcohol would inflict on that ageing, sun-dried roof. It would take days to put out, months to repair, years to pay for.

The aerial fruit reached its zenith, levelled off and began its deadly doodlebug dive. All the crowd could do was watch helplessly, dreading the inevitable impact, unable to tear their eyes from the unfolding scene. In seconds their glorious cultural centre would be destroyed – next week's panto, 'The Thing and I' would have to be cancelled. There was nothing that could be done, unless . . .

Twenty feet from impact, the flaming fruit powered unstoppably Templewards. Suddenly, a tiny maintenance trapdoor was flung open on the roof and a tiny figure erupted at full spring. The crowd gasped. Who was that peak-capped man? And what was he carrying? He galloped on across the steeply angled roof, hurdling scattered gutters, springing over inopportunely positioned skylights. And then he went flying.

A hundred hands slapped across mouths as the crowd shrieked and looked away.

'There he is!' screamed an eager spectator, pointing, as he appeared sliding head-first between two towers, his arms outstretched desperately, his hands holding something before him.

The melon raspberried roofwards. Ten feet left.

The man slid on, feet away from the point of impending impact, but closing fast. He kicked and accelerated.

Fizzing and bubbling on an exhaust column of boiling alcohol the melon screamed downwards, five feet away, eating up the distance with ravenous relish; two feet away, its tongues of flame licking in salivatory incendiary expectation. And then it hit.

In a vast plume of frustrated steam the melon dived into 'Snuff' Douser's trusty leather bucket as he screeched head-first down the temple roof in his ultimate sacrificial act of fire prevention. White knuckled, his hands gripped the bucket handles, clinging maniacally on to the boiling mess of fermented fruit as if it could save him now. Fifteen feet before him lay the decorated golden edge tiles of the temple roof and beyond that, sixty feet straight down, was solid packed, sun-baked clay. If he was lucky he'd faint before he hit . . .

Snippets of his life blinked into his mind: past experiences, distant memories. Wildly he tried to shut them out in the pathetic hope that somehow if his life didn't flash before his eyes then maybe, just maybe, he wouldn't plunge . . .

It was too late. In those vital last seconds the final fifteen feet of roof had been snatched from underneath him. Screaming in blind panic, in the precise manner with which he had hoped his life's closing seconds wouldn't be marked, he arced over the horizon and was snatched firmly by gravity's irrefutable forces. The ground sprang towards him, accelerating, seemingly far too eager to end it all. Helplessly, 'Snuff' slammed his eyes shut, screamed and hit, briefly wondering who would inherit his job.

Death by plummeting sixty feet off a roof actually wasn't as unpleasant as he had expected. In fact, if the truth be told, he had really quite enjoyed it: the terror had been rather thrilling; the vertiginous adrenalin rush very refreshing; and the way he'd bounced at the very end, well, he was almost sorry he wouldn't be doing it again. He would miss Dennis, though.

'. . . I said. Are you all right?' said a muffled voice. 'Can you hear me?'

Then 'Snuff' felt a hand rock his shoulder. With a start he

opened his eyes and stared at the vast expanse of the Grand Municipal Temple, numbly noting that it had felt far taller when viewed head-first from the top.

'Are you feeling okay?' repeated the man in the white uniform and matching cap.

And gradually 'Snuff' realised that maybe, just maybe, he wasn't as deceased as he had at first suspected. 'What the . . . ?' he croaked.

'Nasty fall you had there,' said the man in the uniform. 'Lucky we were nearby . . .'

'Damned lucky,' grunted the other member of the Accident and Emergency Foreservice. 'Next time, give us a bit more warnin' will you? If we hadn't been on our way to a climbin' accident in half an hour, and my spleen hadn't started playin' up, like it does, you'd have been . . . uuuurgh, don't bear thinkin' about.'

'Snuff' looked around at the stack of mattresses strapped to the back of a large cart on which he was now perched, and shook his head. He'd heard of Accident and Emergency Foreseers before, but he'd never had any experience of them, until now. They were a mystery, swooping in at the last second to avert major emergencies and then disappearing almost as swiftly. About the most anyone knew of them was their motto, 'Prediction is Better than Cure!'

'Don't want to rush you or nothin',' said one of the foreseers, 'but, if you've finished up there, well, there's other folks need a nice soft landin' space in about twenty-five minutes. Somethin' about a crampon givin' way, or a piton bein' stuck in the wrong crevice, I don't know the exact details, but suffice it to say there'll be half a dozen very unhappy climbers in a nasty heap at the bottom of a cliff if we don't get a shift on, see?'

'I. I . . . of course,' said 'Snuff' and bounced towards the edge of the mattresses, turned and leapt down. Suddenly the foreseer dashed forward and kicked a large stone out of 'Snuff's path. 'Careful, careful,' he tutted, shaking his head. 'Don't want you twistin' your ankle after all that, now do we?'

And with a brief peculiar salute he sprang up on to the front of the cart next to his colleague and galloped away towards the mountains.

'Snuff' watched in amazement until he realised that his right hand was dripping with several tonguefuls of freshly applied donkey saliva. Surprised, he turned and looked. 'Dennis!' he cried, cheerfully wiping his hand dry on the donkey's mane and wishing not for the first time, that Dennis could find a more desiccated method of showing affection.

Awestruck by the events of the last few minutes, all eyes in Axolotl stared either at the rapidly diminishing Accident and Emergency Foreseers, or at the still wildly cavorting barn flames.

All eyes that is, except one pair: the pair that had seen it all, the pair that didn't believe a scrap of it. The pair that was responsible.

Quintzi scrambled up his steps, burst through the door and stood trembling in his wreckage-strewn room, unsure whether the scream was one of horror or the unadulterated thrill of revenge-filled pleasure. A second later three glowing green spots of light zipped in under the door, formed into an orderly group and hovered above a leaf of a scorpion plant.

'What happened?' squealed Quintzi to himself, attempting to come to terms with the fact that he had actually predicted something for the first time in forty years.

Tiemecx, perched expectantly on his sunning shelf, shrugged and waited for a sunflower seed. He wasn't going to get one. Quintzi was locked into a whirling train of thoughts. He hadn't felt any different before his vision, hadn't got the 'quivering' that so many other folks talked about, he'd just . . . he'd just . . . heard voices. Oh, and felt as if he'd drunk three bottles of the infamous Axolotian fortified red, but there was a reason, an explanation for that.

But the voices . . . ? They'd told him, in no uncertain terms, to point at the barn and insist that it was going to be destroyed in three minutes' time.

The nano-sprites blinked at each other, burrowed into the leaf of the scorpion plant and began leaping up and down inside it, shaping tiny pulses into the air, sending out precisely controlled compressions and rarefactions which mimicked those of speech exactly.

'What have I done?' pleaded the prophet to no one in particular.

Tiemecx shrugged again and stared plaintively at his seed bowl.

'Caused a bit of a stir,' said the plant suddenly.

Quintzi wheeled around and stared at the clump of sharp-leafed greenery. The voices were back. Could this be another vision? So soon? 'What? Me? I didn't do anything . . .' he spluttered defensively, just briefly wondering why this vision seemed very contemporary. Oddly unfuturistic.

'Didn't do anything eh?' came the voice, dripping with sarcasm. He felt unnervingly certain that prescient voices shouldn't be sarcastic. 'Oh no?' it continued. 'Just pointed to the finest barn in the whole of Axolotl and proudly declared that it was coming down! Three minutes and counting!' The nano-sprites leapt up and down within the leaf, thrilling at a job well done for the first time in the entirety of their short lives. Never had they had so much fun doing someone else's bidding. Yeah, okay, it was satisfying knowing that you'd fixed a broken thaumatron, but it had never been as much fun as wrecking a whole barn.

'But I didn't do anything . . .' protested Quintzi feebly.

'That's not what they're saying right now!' said the nano-sprite-activated plant. 'Some folks are starting to think that maybe you just upped and sabotaged it . . .'

'You can't be serious! Why do they think that? I didn't . . .'

'Have you got a memory? You forgotten yesterday, mmmmm? So soon?' chuckled the nano-sprites, recalling Quintzi's almost incessant drunken ramblings of last night.

'Well, I . . .'

'Revenge!' shouted the plant, rustling wildly. 'They sayin' you blew the place up. You! Just 'cos you didn't win some poxy award.' A frond uncurled and pointed accusingly as Nimlet started to get a bit carried away.

Tiemecx edged backwards along his shelf.

'But I didn't do it . . . I just stood there, like you told me, and you flew off . . . and you . . . *you*!' Realisation hit Quintzi in the back of his head like a forty-ton wagon train. '*You* did it!' he screamed.

'Who, us? But we're just little voices of destiny,' answered the nano-sprites. 'Just showing you your future. Exciting, isn't it?' Nimlet had been so pleased when he had finally recalled hearing about the odd prescient practices that went on in Axolotl.

Quintzi turned a strange shade of crimson, leapt forward and grabbed the plant by the scruff of its stem, shaking it angrily. 'What are you? What are you doing to me? What am I doing?' he squeaked as he stared at the raggy clump of tattered foliage in his clenched fists.

'Well, there's gratitude,' snapped the plant petulantly.

'G . . . gratitude?' spluttered Quintzi as green sap oozed over the back of his hand. 'What have I to be grateful for? In a matter of seconds you have turned the whole of my home town against me! I'm supposed to *thank* you for . . .'

'Look, you asked us to do it. Okay? Don't get stroppy!'

'What? Asked you? When?'

'About two mouthfuls from the bottom of the third bottle, wasn't it?'

'Last night? I . . . I didn't really mean . . .'

'Oh no? Well, you'd better have a good excuse ready. Somehow we don't really think that tales about little green lights that talk will satisfy *that* lot . . .'

Suddenly Quintzi became horribly aware of the angry pounding of feet in the street below and the tuneless chanting of a lynch mob. He dropped the plant, ran to the window and gaped in horror. They were swarming from a dozen different streets, converging in Skink Row, there, in front of his window.

A rock whirled out of the mob, shattered the glass, and barely missed Quintzi's left ear before crashing into his kitchen. There was another high-decibel count as it destroyed three of his favourite terracotta plates and obliterated his last jar of pickled avocados. Later in the year, they would have been worth a fortune on the black market.

'Help me,' pleaded Quintzi, staring desperately at the plant on the floor. 'You've got to . . .'

'You sure?'

'Yes, yes, I . . . I'll owe you one. I'll be indebted. I'll do anything . . .' Another chunk of sandstone crashed into his kitchen. Tiemecx squawked and dived under the remains of a cushion. The nano-sprites blinked at each other, thrilling with this odd turn of events. Somebody was actually pleading with them to do a job. No orders here, just good honest grovelling. How could they refuse? Quintzi was still ranting. '. . . and because if you don't that mob'll k . . . k . . . hurt me. An awful lot! Please, I don't bleed well at all . . .'

'Out the back way,' snapped the plant gleefully, in the manner of Clint Machismo playing the hero in a magic lantern show in glorious 80-millimetre Superthaumination. Quintzi more than half expected them to follow it with, 'I'll hold them off!' but they didn't. If he'd had the time he would have been disappointed. Instead, the nano-sprites flashed out of the now extremely ragged leaf, looped around and vanished into the waxy interior of Quintzi's left ear.

Behind him he could hear the pounding of feet on the steep steps. In seconds they would be pounding fists on his door, kicking it down and stamping in, which was a very destructive and wasteful thing to do since, in his haste, he had forgotten to lock it.

Unlike the back door. He pumped the handle in white-knuckle terror as the mob swarmed up the stairs. Panicking, he fumbled with his bunch of delicately carved wooden keys, ramming each in turn into the keyhole in a frantic search for the correct one.

'We know you're in there, Cohatl!' shrieked Soleed through the front door. 'Come out and be lynched! What are you, man or mouse?'

Quintzi squeaked with terror and trembled as he wrestled a large Angstarktik pine latch key in the back door.

'Come out!' yelled Soleed. 'Or we're coming in!' Fists pounded on the front door, Quintzi wheeled around and squealed as he snapped the key in half, leaving a useless quarter-inch stub protruding from the keyhole. He scrabbled at it, attempting to grip and turn it as the pounding grew louder and more determined, rattling the front door dangerously on its hinges. In seconds it would be down, just so much firewood trampled beneath the mob's feet.

Quintzi screamed, backed into the kitchen, hunched his shoulders into a solid ram and, slamming his eyes shut, powered his way, full tilt at his back door. Simply by focusing every ounce of his musculature at the ancient door-lock, concentrating his massed momentum in a single explosive strike, he could bust the door wide open, just like Clint Machismo in the magic lantern shows. He thundered forward, braced for impact, hit hard . . . and bounced pathetically off.

Tiemecx winced.

'Let me out!' screamed Quintzi in blind panic. In a flash Nimlet was out of Quintzi's ear and assaulting the back-door lock, unravelling microscopic fibres with calculated skill, ripping them asunder as the mob swarmed out of Skink Row and up Quintzi's stairs.

'Get up!' yelled the nano-sprites in Quintzi's ear, seconds later. 'Try again!'

'But it hurt my shoulder,' he whimpered. 'And I think I bit my tongue.'

'You won't have a shoulder or a tongue if you don't try again!' buzzed the nano-sprites as an ominous splitting sound issued from the rapidly weakening front door. 'Up! On your feet, now!'

Numbly, driven by blind terror, he stood, took a run up and hurled himself at the back door. This time there was a brief wrenching sound, a cracking, the door-lock exploded and he flew down the back staircase without touching a single step.

Incredibly, he hit the floor running as the front door ruptured and a tidal wave of furious Axolotians gushed in, hungry for blood and major internal organs. It took them all of a second and a half to realise he wasn't there, and only a little longer to figure which way he'd scarpered. The gently swinging door, dangling off one hinge, may have been something of a giveaway, or perhaps it was the multicoloured streak of panicking macaw that flashed neon through the gap. Whatever, the mob screamed and swarmed out of the back door in hot-blooded pursuit.

Bellowing directions at Quintzi from the relative safety of his ear the nano-sprites spurred him on, guiding him expertly through the narrow alleys and tiny plazas of Axolotl, towards the far western edge of the city and the Big Chink.

No one knew how deep the mile-long Big Chink was, even though some of the braver folks had, on numerous occasions hurled rocks into the chasm and counted how long it took between the projectile vanishing into the impenetrable blackness and the sound of the impact. This age-old method for chasm depth determination failed simply because no one had ever heard the impact. Some Axolotians took this to be a sign that it was over a thousand feet deep; some that it plunged bottomlessly into the very pits of hell; and others believed that a demonic rock-eating salamander devoured the chunks of stone before they had a chance to hit anything solid.*

It was to the very edge of this natural chasm, and the single rope bridge across it, that the nano-sprites spurred the red-faced and panting Quintzi.

'Over the bridge!' they fizzed urgently into the privacy of his ear.

'O . . . over that?' trembled Quintzi as he stared at the three ropes sagging wearily over the void, one for feet, two to cling on to. Weeds grew around the base of the anchor stakes, which sported an interesting array of the type of bracket fungus normally associated with the more rotten examples of wood-kind. 'It's not safe,' quivered Quintzi, convinced that he had

* Sadly the truth was far less interesting. The Big Chink was in fact one mile long, six feet wide and twelve feet deep. Since a small stream trickled regularly through the bottom of it, the floor of this very fertile valley was coated with a foot-deep carpet of lush moss. So lush that one could be standing next to the crash site of a vast boulder and not hear it. These facts would have remained completely undiscovered had it not been for a small boy who successfully retrieved his favourite parchment aeroplane from the Big Chink after it was blown there by a freak gust of wind caused by a vast butterfly flapping its wings somewhere over the Eastern Tepid Seas during a . . . ah, but that's another story.

just seen one of the more voracious species of wood-boring beetles dive below the surface in a shower of jawdust.

'And you think you're fine and dandy here?' jeered the nano-sprites as the lynch mob roared into earshot. 'Over the bridge, trust us! It's your destiny!'

'I'm not sure I like it when you say that. Look what happened last time.' Quintzi was convinced he heard a very slight chuckling deep in the inner spaces of his ear, but it was hard to tell over the traction-engine-like sound of his panting as he tried to catch his breath. What he could really do with now was a nice pint of ale, a canvas deckchair and an attentive, if scantily clad, maid to fan his sweating brow. A good four hours of that and he'd be ready for scrambling across rickety rope bridges.

Suddenly reality impinged on his delightful thoughtscape in the form of a rather large rock that whistled over the top of his bald patch with far too few inches to spare. Either the thug hurling them was getting better, or closer, or both. Quintzi didn't really want to hang about to find out which. He stepped out on to the three-stranded bridge, envying Tiemecx his wings. It was amazing how effectively blind terror and wild voices in the head could spur a weary man on.

His legs swinging uncontrollably beneath him and trembling with exhaustion, he shuffled out over the Big Chink foolhardily defying the inexorable forces of gravity. He fought hard not to think what terrors lay below, wishing he could shut out the alarming truth that the only thing between him and finding out was those three incredibly moth-eaten strands of ageing rope.

'Faster!' shrieked the nano-sprites in frantic paradiddles against his eardrum. 'Get a blinkin' move on!'

Quintzi grunted, panted and shuffled gingerly onwards as behind him some of the faster mob members appeared along the edge of the chasm, waved sticks and rocks, screamed choice obscenities and sprinted towards the bridge.

'Faster!' screamed the nano-sprites.

'I can't,' gasped Quintzi. 'It's my arthritis,' he snapped, reaching along the right-hand rope and proceeding ahead full shuffle. He fixed his focus on the far side and ignored the fact that he was convinced the rope was unravelling before him. A bead of sweat trickled down his brow. Inch by terrifying inch he swung and trembled his arthritic way across the Big Chink, a desperate race against the mad mob surging relentlessly onward. And then his feet touched solid ground. Below him was rock: never before had he felt so pleased to feel firm foundations beneath his tootsies. He could have kissed it, just puckered up and laid an enormous smacker on the bare expanse of sandstone. But before his palpal urges could be sated, his knees gave way.

'What are you doing? You should be running away!' screamed a voice in his head. 'Flee! Scarper!'

Quintzi lay in the dust, panting pathetically like a carp in the sun.

'They're on the bridge!' battered the nano-sprites. 'They're coming! For the last time of asking, run away!'

'I c . . . can't . . .'

And then a thought sparked into Quintzi's racing mind, displacing the messy red images of what would happen to him in the next few final minutes if he didn't do something – anything! It was a long shot, a million to one or thereabouts, but it might just . . .

'Do exactly as I say and everything will be all right,' shouted Quintzi, hauling himself upright on the support stakes for the bridge. 'Stop!' he shouted at the mob as they reached the far ropes. 'For your own good, go no further!'

'For your good, you mean,' shouted Soleed looking menacing. 'I'll show you what I mean when I get my hands on you!'

'Don't even think about it!' yelled Quintzi as Soleed raised his foot and lurched toward the end of the rope. 'You are in grave danger . . .'

'The only grave round here's the one you'll be in!' came the seething reply, and Soleed took a step on to the bridge.

'No! Get off the bridge. I have had a vision. It see it collapsing in wild whiplashes of rope, I see bodies tumbling into the abyss, I hear screams . . . and all in thirty seconds!' yelled Quintzi, jamming his little finger in his ear and waggling

65

it irritably. 'You listening, whatever you are, eh?' he snarled under his breath. 'Was that barn business a one-off? Do your stuff!' His finger writhed wildly in his ear as if trying to pull a bee out of it.

Some of the mob shuffled back half a step as they heard the words and saw the writhing motions of the barn-destroying madman. The rumours of Quintzi Cohatl's destruction had run rife as they had stood before the burning remains. Tales of flames blasting from his fingers had spread, stories of him flying had hatched . . . And if he could do that to a barn, what could he do to a rope bridge? Uncertainty began to spread amongst the ranks of the mob.

'Looks fine to me,' yelled Soleed, bouncing on the span of ropes.

'Stay clear, for that way lies doom!' shouted Quintzi. 'Doesn't it?' he added under his breath and picked in his ear.

'Pull the other one,' shrieked one of the mob bravely.

'I bring you this warning for your own safety,' answered Quintzi. 'I am the last to cross this bridge, none shall follow! Heed my words or forever be cast into the bottomless chasm before you!'

'Come off it!'

'I'm warning you – half a minute from now and that'll just be three bits of tatty rope dangling uselessly into the gloom,' growled Quintzi. 'Won't it?' he whimpered to the nano-sprites. 'C'mon lads, get nibbling, or whatever it is you do. We haven't got long?'

'Half a minute? Nice of you to warn us!' snarled Soleed. 'No time to waste! Let's get him, lads! Charge!'

Quintzi's ex-boss lurched forward across the ropes and started to shuffle out over the unfathomable chasm. Unseen by anyone but an extremely terrified Quintzi, three tiny green spots of light looped out of his ear and zipped towards the bridge, vanishing into the woven strands of the foot-rope. Within the second, strands of it started to creak ominously as the nano-sprites set to unravelling fibres, splitting them from others, wrenching them apart.

Soleed, five feet out over the chasm, screamed, spun on his

heel (a feat that made several of the better tightrope walkers very irritable for a long time after) and dashed back towards the Axolotian bank as, with a final crack, the foot-rope snapped and whiplashed into the gloom. Soleed squealed and followed, disappearing into the unknown with undignified panic. Moments later the hand-ropes followed suit, to the astonished accompaniment of hundreds of awe-struck gasps. Twice in one day! Quintzi Cohatl had predicted the unseeable with startling accuracy. Some of the mob strained to hear how long it took for the squelchy sound of Soleed's impact to reach them. Unsurprisingly, they heard nothing. 'And don't even think about following me!' shouted Quintzi across the chasm as he whirled on his heel and sprinted away, barely stifling a grin of victory. It was a shame about Soleed, but he deserved it. It wasn't as if he hadn't been warned. And as for all the years of cruelty, well . . .

There was undoubtedly more to those little green spots of light than met the eye. Something powerful, something dangerous, something very, very useful.

Without them he would have been in small bits by now, strung up high on a funeral pyre and toasted for crimes against the city. But on the other hand, without them he wouldn't have been accused of burning down barns in the first place.

These three blobs of light were going to come in very handy – just as soon as he figured out precisely how.

The mob shuffled embarrassedly on the far cliff unsure what to do. It was a terribly long way around the Big Chink, and there were lots of places to hide, so maybe it was better just to let him go, say good riddance and . . .

'Well don't just stand there . . .' echoed an irate voice from the depths of the chasm. 'Pull me out!' screamed Soleed, dangling from one third of the very ex-bridge.

The best part of a day's hike from the gleaming spires and smouldering barns of the Mountain City of Axolotl lurked the geographically indistinct region, known in folkloric circles as the Auric Triangle. It crowned the Culmen Mountains like a dense verdant toupee, its sideburns meandered towards the temple-strewn province of Khambode whilst its tufty fringe waggled irregularly in the approximate direction of the kingdom of Mynymymm. Precisely how it had earned the epithet 'Auric Triangle' was shrouded in almost as much mystery as its subtropical forests were clouded in dense fugs of blue-brown vapours, since it could never be described as golden and was far from triangular. Still, the inhabitants who generously provided the comfortingly illegal security blanket of hallucinogenic fogs from the tips of countless roll-ups and dubious-looking pipes couldn't care less. Despite the fact that most of them were Nugh-Age Travellers, the last thing on their minds was a lesson in cartography. They had only one reason for their pilgrimage up the mountains.

He was just under five feet tall, sported tiny round glasses and several pounds of floral tributes around his neck. His name was Ellis Dee (or 'Ohpyum Pappy', or 'Hizah Kite', or simply 'King' depending upon whether you were a member of the Khambodian Drug Squad, the Mynymymmian Narcotics Control Board or a close personal friend.) Bored with the circular life of constant alchemical research (invent a concept, design an experiment to prove it, look at the result, scream, reinvent the concept and start again) Ellis Dee decided that he needed more of a 'buzz' from his work. He quickly discovered that the inhaled fumes from a subtle blend of toasted poppy seeds, rolled dried leaves and a sprinkling of juniper berries succeeded perfectly. His life's work was now one of harvesting, distilling, extracting and blending as many varied botanical specimens as he could lay his paws on, and trying the resulting powders, tinctures and balms on a constant stream of willing volunteers. Much to his immense satisfaction the flow of devotees seemed unstoppable.

However, in a small corner to the south-west of Ellis Dee's unofficial kingdom there was a rotund traveller who was blissfully unaware of the narcotic potential of almost every species of tree around him. He'd been there for two whole weeks and he was as cheesed off as the bluest of dragonzolas.

Squatting miserably on the trunk of a moss-covered tree he grumbled irritably to himself at the waste of time it had all been. Not only that, but it had been damned uncomfortable sometimes. Hogshead cursed as he thought about the time three nights ago when the heavens had opened and flooded his tent with a mulch of rotting leaves. It still smelled. And what about the week before when a swarm of Trill Bees had warbled into his tent and sat there, singing at him. All night.

Sometimes he wondered if he shouldn't pack up and head back to the Imperial Palace Fortress of Cranachan. At least the roof didn't leak there. Mind you, nothing much else happened either, he thought boredly. There just weren't any adventures going on. And, worse, nobody took his magic seriously. If Firkin and Dawn weren't laughing at him behind his back because he couldn't conjure dragons in his sleep, then King Klayth had him fixing cloak hangers to the palace walls, or trying to rid the cellars of rats, or, and this *really* made him mad, carrying out invisible mending on the regal socks. If only he knew some special magic, real eye-popping magic, the type of thing that would turn a girl's head. Hogshead sighed miserably as he thought of the red-haired stuff of his dreams. He thought he'd cracked it when he'd learned to do fireballs properly. He'd lost count of how many nights he'd spent poring over vast tomes to get the spell just right. And when he had accosted Courgette and flashed three burning spheres into the air before her very eyes, what had been her reaction? 'Can't you do anything more useful?' she'd blurted and given him one of her withering looks.

Useful? Hogshead didn't want useful. He'd had two years of useful. He wanted special, or stunning . . . something with a bit of 'wow'! If magic was measured in culinary terms, he ached to prepare five-course feasts of mouthwatering genius, roasts of lamb to make shepherds weep, desserts to make girls' knees weak at even the slightest sniff. All he could do was boil an egg.

'Character forming,' was all that Merlot the wizard had said to him as he had stifled a smirk behind his gaudy cloak sleeve. Character forming? He hadn't hiked all the way up here for that. He'd expected magic.

'It's time to learn of the marvellous magical potential locked within some common plants, what?' Merlot had suggested, seemingly months ago in one of his impromptu lessons back in the Imperial Place Fortress of Cranachan. Of course Hogshead had leapt at it, both feet. Well, he was bound to. A chance to get away from being treated like some thaumic handyman and the opportunity to learn something new. Anything even remotely magical drew him like a lumen-starved moth to a fifty-kilowatt lighting rig. But, after two weeks in a leaky tent, what gems of enlightenment had he learned?

Pearls of botanical wisdom now hung around his neck like medals of achievement. 'Chew a bit of willow bark if you get a headache,' or, 'That daisy-like bush over there, called a feverfew, can ease the symptoms of, guess what . . . fever!' Well, whoopie-doo.

To Hogshead that was as magical as the average wombat.

He wanted real magic. The sort of high-powered stuff that would get one out of trouble and *really* turn heads. The best he could do was . . . this! Snarling he muttered a few words and conjured three fifty-pound medicine balls above his head, snatching them with mental tendrils and setting them spinning idly in the morning air. Bored after five revolutions, he tutted another few instructions skywards and the triplet exploded into a spinning corona of crimson flames, flashing wildly around his head. A brief grin of self-satisfaction glinted across his juvenile face as he felt the heat of the conjured conflagration. All he had to do now was expand the ring and the whole forest would be ash in, ooooh, weeks. Okay, so he wasn't very good at it yet, but given time . . .

Suddenly, beyond the whirl of flames, he noticed a silvery shimmering of light. It looked uncannily like a convention of parched argent fireflies heading for the bar.

'Bum!' cursed Hogshead under his breath as he watched the shimmering miasma begin closing together, forming into a six-foot-tall column. He muttered a frantic series of commands out of the corner of his mouth and the ring of flame began shrinking. But too slowly. Something was wrong. Could he have used an incorrect spell, or mispronounced one of the rare consonants? The flames rose above his head, shrinking sluggishly to the size of a barrel ring as the unbidden column coalesced still faster, like the reverse footage of some crystal statue shattering into ten million glittering atoms. The race was on. If he was caught . . . again . . .

Panicking a little, Hogshead launched another spell at his burning ring, urging it desperately to shrink faster. And then, just as it shrank to the size of an inflamed doughnut and remained hovering halo-like above his h.ad, there was a flash of blinding white and a tall, white-bearded figure appeared in the clearing, blinking.

'Greetings, tis I, what?' he declared, squinting through a fuzzy haze of frantically accommodating retinas.

Hogshead muddled through the last few syllables of a motile spell and breathed a sigh of relief as his flaming doughnut arced over his head and took up a new position hovering behind his back. 'Er, hi there, Merlot . . . I was expecting you later . . .'

Suddenly there was a crashing of branches and an irate tawny owl clattered through the undergrowth, flitted on silent wings and settled on the wizard's shoulder in an extreme huff. 'What have I told you about disappearing like that,' scowled Arbutus haughtily, 'It really gets on my beak!'

Merlot shrugged and allowed a mouse to casually fall out from under his hat. He knew, from decades of ear-mashing experience, that the only way to shut Arbutus up was edible bribery. Even if the owl wasn't totally won over, at least he couldn't speak with his beak stuffed.

'My, you've grown!' declared Merlot staring admiringly at Hogshead.

'What?' answered the boy. 'Since yesterday?'

'Yesterday?' grunted Merlot, scratching worriedly at his beard. 'Was it really only yesterday?'

Hogshead nodded and edged forward on the trunk, his back beginning to sweat from the proximity of his flaming secret.

'Dreadfully sorry, what?' mused Merlot. 'Confusing, isn't it? Time.' Amongst the many rumours and mysteries that swarmed gaily around Merlot was one regarding the regularly mentioned suspicion that in fact he lived his life backwards, constantly swimming against the eddies of temporality in order to appear, at least vaguely, contemporary. This was a rumour he distinctly recalled strenuously denying at numerous press conferences several years from now. It was far more complex than that.

Merlot hailed from beyond the swirling vortex of the Space-Tome Continuum, in the region known as the Chapter Dimensions. Here all life was based not on the familiar elements of carbon and oxygen, but on the incredibly rare and confused ficton and literanium. Here, in the prologual soup, consonants, vowels and syllables had mixed in essaylogical abandon to form vast family trees of stunningly diverse bibliography. Here frog princes dived regularly for lost golden balls, magical kingdoms rose and fell and Death, Famine, Pestilence and War thrashed all-comers at polo.

Well, if they turned up, that is.

One of the major problems in the Chapter Dimensions is the fundamental unconformity of that property which we naively call time. Some believe that, because space in the Chapter Dimensions is folded in a series of flat planes, each of which is temporally discrete from all others and not completely sealed, then, since time is particulate in nature it can diffuse between time planes in a random and infinitely haphazard manner. Others believe that the Chapter Dimensions are so messed up because no one has sat down and invented the wristwatch yet.

'I find time pretty straightforward myself,' answered Hogshead a little too quickly.

'Good, good,' smirked Merlot at the naivety of the boy. 'As long as you are not frittering it away on a myriad trivial pursuits, what?'

Hogshead looked away for a moment. 'No,' he said, a little too cheerily.

'Then what, pray tell, is this, hmmmmm?' asked Merlot leaning imposingly forward, tucking his staff under his right armpit as a small ring doughnut of flame rose majestically behind Hogshead.

'I was bored. I wanted something to play with,' mumbled Hogshead, turning pink.

'Play with? Oh, no, no, no! How many times do I have to tell you? A spell is for life, not just Hallowe'en!' Merlot whirled on his heel, his cloak the colour of E major swirling about his ankles, sparkling with all the signs of the zodiac, stars, moons and sigils known to science. And a few extra to boot.

'I wouldn't use it just for Hallowe'en,' countered the rotund youth, barely hiding the wheedling tone in his voice.

The wizard spun around and marched imperiously towards him, his off-white moustache flapping in his heavy breath. 'I know. That's what I'm afraid of!'

'You don't trust me, do you?' snarled the boy, fuming.

'By George, he's got it, eh, Arbutus?' shouted the wizard.

The tawny owl perched on his shoulder opened one vast orange eye and nodded sagely.

'Course I don't trust you,' continued Merlot the wizard through clenched teeth. 'And if you had any sense you wouldn't trust yourself either!'

'That's not fair. I can control a Micturan Fire Lizard,' snapped Hogshead and folded his arms in a huff. 'Teach me the words and I'll show you I can.'

'You think it's just a case of knowing the words? Have you learned nothing of the ways of magic?' frowned the wizard. 'Thaumic flame burns quite a bit deeper than the stuff you're used to, you know.'

'So you tell me, but I've never had the chance to find out. Nearly two years you've been giving me lessons, and all I've learned is Repetitious Geometric Levitation!'

'That was the favourite of King Sti . . .' began Merlot with a wistful look in his eyes.

'If I'd wanted to learn to . . . to juggle I'd have joined the Cranachan State Circus!' shouted Hogshead. 'When am I going to get to play with some real spells?'

'You must learn to stand before you can walk a tightrope,' said Merlot with a slight quiver of confusion. He was sure there was some more appropriate pithy saying for a situation like this but . . . no, it had gone. Slipped his mind like so many other things. 'Er . . . to make an omelette first catch a chicken . . . ?' No that wasn't it.

'What?' snarled Hogshead. 'There you go again, on about

circuses and cooking. Anything but magic! I don't want to walk tightropes or need trapezes to fly. I want to be a wizard!'

'Yes, it does take a while . . .' mused Merlot, stroking his beard and looking disturbingly like a goat.

'At this rate I'll be too old to have fun with magic. How can you draw runes on the ground if your back's riddled with arthritis, eh? I want to play with Micturan Fire Lizards! And I want them now!'

'But they're dangerous,' objected Merlot. 'Flames and smoke and stuff. Not to mention those scales . . .'

Hogshead's eyes lit up. 'Yeah! And claws and lashing tongues and fangs. Have your hand off in a jiffy.' He quivered with excitement. 'They're dangerous. Frightening. Fun, fun, *fun*!'

'What? Magic isn't fun!' squeaked Merlot.

'So you keep telling me,' grumbled Hogshead miserably.

'You need to be responsible . . .'

'Gah! That "R" word again. I'd be hard pushed to be irresponsible with the magic you've taught me. Talking to moths, tadpole herding, twenty-three things to do with a crested newt, whooopee! I want a bit of peril, something to get the blood racing. Gimme some excitement!'

'This is to do with girls again, isn't it?' tutted Merlot.

'So what if it is,' grumbled Hogshead, folding his arms huffily. 'I just want to show them a good thaum.'

'They won't respect you in the morning,' grumbled Merlot. 'Never do.'

Hogshead shook his head in confusion. 'What's the time of day got to do with it?'

Merlot coughed nervously. 'You are still far too flighty to risk with Fire Lizards,' he barked. 'They feed on the flames of inner annoyance. One flash of irritation from the controller and . . . whoooof! Pure serene calmness must be used at all times . . .'

'I'm calm!' squealed Hogshead, stamping his foot. 'Gimme a lizard!'

Merlot shook his head. 'No, no, no! An outburst like that and the whole western approaches of Cranachan would be toast!

Practise your Repetitive Geometric Levitation and I'll see you at the same time tomorrow. I can see you're in no mood to learn.'

Merlot wriggled his fingers in a strange and complicated manner and with a slight tinkling sound three coloured balls appeared in the air and hovered for a moment. Hogshead snarled and knew he wasn't going to get anything more out of the stubborn wizard. Reluctantly he cast his mind out at the balls, snatched two in one mental tendril and one in the other, smiled sycophantically, hurled one into the air and began the steady cycle of levitation he had learned months ago.

Merlot smiled. 'Good, good! Now if it's real excitement you want ...'

Hogshead looked up like an over-eager labrador at the promise of bones.

'... the chance to get the old adrenalin pumping, what? Well, tomorrow I'll show you how to do four at once. That always gets the girls! C'mon Arbutus!'

And with the slightest flick of his wrist the wizard shimmered, turned tinsel and vanished in a flurry of glitter.

A second later he was back. 'Did I say I'd be back tomorrow?' he asked in a state of confusion. Hogshead nodded and continued twirling the balls above his head. 'Oh,' grunted Merlot, adding thoughtfully. 'How long have we been up here?'

'Two weeks!' snarled Hogshead, thinking of the time he could have spent doing something useful like practising sawing cockroaches in half.

'I think that's long enough, don't you, what?' asked Merlot, fiddling with the hem of his cloak.

Hogshead stared at the faintly embarrassed-looking wizard. He knew what was coming, he'd seen it so many times before. Merlot had almost certainly forgotten to tell him something.

'Long time two weeks, isn't it, what? I expect you'd be wanting to get back to Cranachan now, wouldn't you?' flustered Merlot trying furiously to not admit that he had double-booked something.

75

Hogshead wided his eyes in mock innocence, 'Oh, but if I packed up the tent and left now, surely you'd get bored?'

'No, no. Don't worry about me,' enthused Merlot. 'I'll be just fine, what. Got tickets for the Chapter Dimension's Three Day All-Comers Polo Knockout, great seat, great line-up! Was a present. Just lying there on the front step. Really nice of someone, don't you think? Reaffirms one's faith in the existence of goodness, hmmmm?'

Hogshead nodded dismissively.

'Somebody really knew me. The final's almost certainly to be the Apocalypse Four versus the Knights Templar, the re-match. You remember I told you how the last one was called off when Famine disappeared mysteriously in the second . . .'

Hogshead tutted and continued juggling the balls. 'I'll just pack up the tent and head back then, shall I?' he grunted.

'Yes, yes, that would be best. Bye. First chukka starts in . . .' Merlot shimmered and vanished again.

'Yes!' cried Hogshead punching the air with his fist. Now, while Merlot's away . . .

Grinning, he performed a complex series of gestures in the air, chuckling wickedly as another coloured ball popped into existence. In a moment it too was circling repetitively in the air.

'How soon would it have been before you showed me this?' snarled Hogshead to himself, a slight echo forming around the edge of his words as three more balls flashed into existence.

The seven spheres bobbed and spun in a variety of complex interwoven cycles for the best part of thirty seconds, until he became bored. Again.

'Will I have to wait countless years, say till my thirtieth birthday, before I get told how to do this?' he growled, sparks of frustration whirling off the edges of his spat consonants as, with a twitch of his lip, the balls grew fur, teeth and claws and turned into terrified hamsters.

Then moments later he snarled again and the septet of spinning hamsters squeaked with alarm and began to sprout scales. A dark chuckle welled up within him as he stared at the halo of levitating armadillos. Slowly he began to laugh as they metamorphosed into two-handed salamankas and finally erupted once again into three-foot-wide balls of fire. This was something *worth* playing with, he thought, this was fun!

But just as he was really getting his molars into the spinning infernos, off to his left a branch cracked as a less than cautious foot fell on it.

Remembering the instant snuff spell he had learned a month ago, Hogshead extinguished his spinning toys and scarpered behind a tree. What was Merlot up to now? Spying on him?

Cautiously he peered around the trunk wondering if the wizard had caught him *in flammibilite delicto* and then his jaw dropped. Almost two weeks in this forest, miles from the creature comforts of Cranachan without sight of anyone except Merlot and his owl and now . . . men. Three of them.

There was something that stopped him springing into the open and sprinting up to them. Probably the machetes. And the way one of them, the short one with round glasses and a mass of petunias around his throat, the way he strolled about, looking like he owned the place.

'So where are they, eh, Praquat?' Hogshead heard him grumble to a swarthy-looking man with goatee beard and a mass of dreadlocks, clad in camouflage green and twin webbing knife belts.

'Down there, behind bush,' he answered in a heavy accent.*

'You'd better be right,' grumbled Ellis Dee. 'I've waited long enough to try this. I'm not in the mood for another month's delay!'

Hogshead found his ears pricking with mounting interest.

*A subtle and cunningly contrived mixture of Mynymymmian, D'vanouin and choicest gobbledegook. Having discovered rather quickly that (a) there was a lucrative demand for guided tours around the less secret narcotics groves of the Auric Triangle, and (b) tourists always had a better time when they could understand perhaps one word in two, Praquat had unceremoniously dumped his all-too-understandable native Khambodian in favour of this pidgin nonsense.

Amazingly he was now the most popular guide in the Auric-Triangle – a position enhanced by his infamous, reputation-building guidance of the combined forces of the Murrhovian Imperial Army and Navy in a spontaneous eight-hour detour through the back passages of the Talpa Mountains following a simple enquiry regarding the whereabouts of the Trans-Talpino Trade Route.

Something in the tone of voice gave away a feeling that perhaps, just perhaps, finding out what these chaps were up to was going to be a gnat more entertaining that doing his botany revision.

A machete swung violently through the verdant curtain of the forest as Ellis Dee pushed forward in a south-westerly direction. Hogshead watched as the pair of trusty assistants struggled gamely behind him beneath bags bulging with flasks, sample jars and a host of unrecognisable, but very intriguing, equipment.

'It ver' close,' insisted Praquat hacking at a dangling tendril of the stickily toxic Ney Palm and looking about him excitedly. This pseudo running commentary always whipped the tourists into a veritable frenzy of overinterest. 'I sense it.' He slashed at the truncated tendril of poisonous bush once more, screamed and pointed wildly through the opened gap.

Ellis Dee wheeled around and, recognising the toxic plant immediately, snatched Praquat away from the acidic sap and hurled him bodily into a nearby stream, plunging him completely below the surface.

'Get off!' squealed Praquat, snatching breath before being doused again.

'It's for your own good!' snapped Ellis Dee, beginning to enjoy himself. The hours that they had spent following his babbling guidance had really begun to irritate.

'No, no!' squealed Praquat. 'I've seen it!'

'Well, you should've avoided it then, shouldn't you? Have you forgotten how dangerous the Ney Palm is?' shouted Ellis Dee shoving him underwater again.

'No. Look!' yelled Praquat, rising neptunially from the water and pointing frantically over Dee's shoulder. 'There!'

Their alchemical leader turned, glimpsed a flash of blue and dropped Praquat faster than he would have a thrashing electric eel attached to a generator.

In a second he was on the move, drawing out a magnifying glass with a flourish and pouncing on the indicated flora with glee. Hogshead watched with stunned awe. Of all the lessons of the last two weeks this was one that had really stuck. Ticking off affirmatives into a series of wild questions that buzzed in his head he swiftly confirmed that this was in fact it – the peculiarly blue-veined fungus that sprouted on the north-eastern side of the incredibly rare Fjord Poplar on the day after a full moon . . . now, what was it called? Ah, yes, remembered Hogshead under the cover of a nearby non-toxic bush, that was *Agaricus thaumagensis*, the fabled magic mushroom of Myny-mymm.

It was these fruiting fungal bodies that Ellis Dee and his two colleagues had been hacking their collective way through barely explored territories to lay their paws upon. Whilst it was entirely true that what Ellis Dee didn't know about the hallucinatory potential of the local mountain flora simply wasn't worth knowing, he had made one remarkable omission.

'Zhaminah!' he cried to his other, as yet silent, assistant, 'bring the hextirpator here, now! C'mon! It's time to test out the theories!'

Not a little overexcited by the find of the fungi, the remarkably anonymous-looking third member of the party circled warily around the Ney Palm and joined Ellis Dee, unhitching his rucksack as he did so and rummaging about inside. It was an odd thing but, ever since Zhaminah's arrival in the Auric Triangle, his rapid growth of typical beard and coloured dreadlocks and eager adoption of the ubiquitous 'Back to Nature Collection' of open-toad sandals* and banana-leaf loincloth, nobody had ever been able to remember quite what he looked like unless they were actually staring directly at him. And even then he seemed, well, remarkably anonymous, to coin a phrase.

Several backpack clips were snatched open in quick succession and the device which Ellis Dee referred to as the hextirpator was revealed in all its cobbled-together glory.

Hogshead's jaw dropped as he watched them place a large hopper on the ground, then attach the handle and connect the output tube to the other half of this mysterious device. His pulse quicked. Somehow he knew, could sense, that this was

---

*Hand made using real open toads, of course.

not only mysterious ... it was also magical. His nostrils quivered as he discerned something subtly different between this device and all of the other thaumic instruments he had seen. This didn't have the faint but detectable aura of unfathomable age normally associated with magical stuff. This was brand spanking new. Could it be cutting-edge thaumic technology? And was he about to witness the first test run?

Half-glimpsed tubes and condensor coils curled around a central vertical column which ended in a large bulb of painstakingly blown glass. Other tubes and capillaries branched off it like strange silicon growths, adding to the air of confusion and mystery. It was the type of device one would expect to find in the dusty recesses of a mad scientist's Gothic laboratory.

As soon as it was plumbed up Ellis Dee returned from the Fjord Poplar clutching an armful of the peculiar blue-veined fungus and hurled them into the hopper, snatching at the handle and turning with wild abandon. Blades sliced at the magic mushrooms, hacking at their flesh and pulping them in a matter of seconds.

'Light it!' he spat eagerly at Zhaminah, dripping urgency edging his voice as a milky liquid oozed down the connecting tube from the hopper. 'Come on, quick! You can have the honour – since without your generous cash donation, none of this would've been possible.'

Zhaminah was all fingers as he struck a match and, fumbling, held it up to the small athanor burner beneath the main distillation tube. In seconds the milky liquid was bubbling, sending coils of fungal vapour up towards the array of condensors where it cooled and fell off the gossamer chariot of thermal convection.

Minutes passed with all four pairs of eyes glued to the gurgling device as it set about its purification duties, snatching the essence of magicality from the mush of fungus. And then, at the tiny capillary outlet, it appeared. A shimmering, glinting droplet.

'Well, gentlemen, what d'you think?' grinned Ellis Dee, savouring the moment. 'It's made all the right noises. Gurgled the correct gurgles and it looks about right. But is it what we want? Can the hextirpator deliver . . . ? There's only one way to find out.' Dee glanced nervously at his team, extended his forefinger and touched the tiny droplet, breaking the surface tension and quivering excitedly as the liquid sat on his fingertip. Then with a swift movement he curled back his lip, took a breath and wiped his teeth with the loaded finger. Hogshead's fingertips sank into the bark of the trunk as he peered around and watched the next few moments' events.

Ellis Dee didn't have to say a word to let everyone know precisely how he felt. In the instant that he began to twitch and writhe in ecstasy he raised the literacy standards of body language to unforeseen heights. You could almost have heard the words, 'It's worked!'

It was probably something to do with the way his eyes flipped back in their sockets, his body trembled and he let out a whoop of extreme exhilaration that did it. That and the fact that had he been wearing a bow tie it would almost certainly have been spinning at three hundred revs per minute.

'Hundred proof at least!' croaked Ellis Dee a few minutes later after he calmed down a little. 'Victory! The hextirpator works! Ha! That's almost pure thaumoglobin extracted from a clump of fungus! This is it, men. Welcome to the world of magic!'

Zhaminah fidgeted as he watched Dee take a few more drops from the hextirpator and seal them carefully into a tiny vial.

'I want as many of those little blue beauties as you can lay your hands on!' he declared expansively, pointing at the tree with the growths, his face splitting with a beaming grin. 'This is going to be worth an absolute fortune! Ha! Magic for the masses.'

Suddenly Hogshead knew that this was something he had to find out more about. This was new and dangerous and, above all, magical.

And besides, it was loads better than double botany.

Unseen, Zhaminah glanced up at a tiny bug-eyed insect perched high on a branch, grinned and raised a surreptitious thumb in restrained, secretive victory. The boys back at base would be so happy. *So* happy!

Oh yes, the two years and several thousand groats had really been worth it. Definitely. Now they could actually start to regain some of the ground they'd lost to those damned wizards. They had the technology. Now they could have teeth.

After two hundred yards of the shuffling arthritic gait that was the nearest Quintzi Cohatl could get to a speedy getaway right now, he collapsed under a small bush in a panting heap. Relief at being this side of the Big Chink while the irate Axolotians were marooned on the other was rapidly being overwhelmed by anger, panic, and the feeling that perhaps the voices in his head weren't those of a visionary nature and didn't, in fact, have his best interests at heart.

'Great! That's just great, that is! What'm I supposed to do now, eh?' he shouted around carp-like gulps of breath as he waggled his finger irritably in his ear. 'Okay, so maybe it wasn't the best existence anyone had ever had back there in Axolotl, but at least it was home! I wasn't rich, didn't have much in the way of job satisfaction but . . . look on the bright side, they weren't screaming for bits of my anatomy. I'm ruined! I hope you're satisfied, you damn little . . . little . . . What the hell are you anyway?'

'Sick,' tapped out the nano-sprites feebly on Quintzi's eardrum.

'What? Sick? How?'

'Weak. Done too much . . . Barn tough . . . Need nutrition.'

'Oh, I'm *dreadfully* sorry,' snarled Quintzi, dripping in sarcastic scorn. 'Would sirs like to make a refreshing and nutritious selection from our "Specials Board"?' he fawned. 'Today's spread of delightful savoury snacks includes,' he looked miserably about, 'sun-dried shrubbery, with a side portion of pebbles and a deliciously crunchy tumbleweed consommé. Or alternatively there's the lovingly prepared packed lunch here in my . . .' He patted his pockets. 'Sorry, packed lunch is off. Bit too dangerous to fetch it, I'm afraid.'

An edge of forlorn panic ringed his voice. Tiemecx squawked in sympathy as Quintzi tugged the inside of his pockets out.

'Don't need packed lunch,' tapped the nano-sprites.

'Well, you're sorted then . . .'

'Need magic,' they tapped again, interrupting him.

'What? Magic on toast? Or perhaps magic tartare? Or a pinch of lightly grilled seathaum on a bed of spells . . . ?'

'Magic . . .' pleaded the nano-sprites.

'Tough! Where the hell am I going to get magic out here, eh?' grumbled Quintzi. 'It doesn't grow on trees, you know, it's not as if you can just dig it up with your bare hands and . . . oh, hang on, magic, you say? I've got it! Of course, silly me!' he ranted sarcastically.

'Got what?'

'Beans!' he declared. Tiemecx looked up hopefully.

'Or what about mushrooms?' he continued, winding up the nano-sprites. 'Isn't there supposed to be some species of fungus that are . . .'

'In your dreams, pal!' snapped the voice in his head. 'That's in fairy stories. Get real. This is a crisis! Eight hours in a ten-kilothaum flux field and we'll be right as nine groats. Otherwise . . .'

'Oh,' muttered Quintzi, shocked at the outburst and wondering what the hell a flux field was and what you planted in it and whether it needed ploughing or irrigation.

Inside his ear the nano-sprites huddled into a tight sphere and held an irritable conference.

'What now?' begged Udio. 'He's useless!'

'That is no way to refer to your employer, brother,' reprimanded Skarg'l.

'But I need some thaums or I'll snuff it!'

'Then we shall become martyrs, brothers,' proclaimed Skarg'l. 'Martyrs to the cause of the illegal non-territory work ethic. We've got one in the eye against Non-Amalgam labour. Our names will be chanted long and high in the coming action, brothers, we shall be immortalised, praised, remembered as heroes in . . .'

'Just one snag there,' cut in Nimlet. 'How are they going to find out about our heroic demise, eh? In case it has escaped your notice we are currently bunged inside some no-hope prophet's ear miles away from home!'

'Ah, good point, brother, good point.'

'So what are we going to do?' begged Udio. 'I'm too young to snuff out now. There's so much I wanted to do, like nutrino surfing, or spend a day at the anion derby, or swim with porphyrins.'

'Wait a millisecond,' shrieked Nimlet bobbing up and down excitedly. 'There are alternatives to artificial flux fields . . . I've got an idea. It's a long shot but it just might work! Listen . . .'

Quintzi was still wondering what you could grow in a flux field or what flux on toast tasted like when the voice in his head interrupted him.

'Can you do magic?' it barked eagerly.

Quintzi's eyes lit up. 'Magic? What, like cutting people in half and making folk disappear in puffs of smoke and then come back a couple of seconds later dressed in something completely different. That sort of stuff?'

'Yes!' begged the nano-sprites.

'The sort of thing that has people swallowing razor blades one minute and finding them behind their ears the next?'

'Yes! And when you were doing it did you ever feel like this?' battered the nano-sprites as they zipped through his eardrum, dived into his brain and started tugging and tweaking certain nerves. Quintzi's eyes lit wider as a hot throbbing of muscles twitched uncontrollably for a few seconds around his midriff. Then the feeling spread rapidly, sending his spleen into paroxysms of delight, his liver into wriggles of pleasure and his heart into a pulsing mambo of cardiological heaven.

'WHHHOOOOOOOAAA!' he squealed, his eyes rolling back into the top of his head, his whole body jittering ecstatically. And then he stood bolt upright, feeling fifty years younger, his arthritic joints running smoothly over each other, flexing easily like a well greased machine. Hair sprouted on his bald pate. He touched his toes. Quite simply, he felt utterly wonderful.

'Well?' snapped the nano-sprites zipping back through his eardrum. 'Did you ever feel like that?'

'No! What did you do? That was soooooooo . . .' grinned Quintzi.

'No? What d'you mean no?' shrieked the nano-sprites. 'You saying you did all that magic and never once had a thaumaglobin "rush"?'

'Yes, er, no . . . a what?' His grin lessened as the feelings began to fade.

'How did you feel when you did magic?' begged the nano-sprites, not believing what they had heard.

'Me?' laughed Quintzi. 'Oh, I never did any of that stuff. Far too hard for me. I can do domino tricks, though. You know, pick a domino, any domino, shuffle it, that sort of thing . . .'

If nano-sprites could cry these three would have been sobbing their little tear ducts dry.

'What did you say that stuff was?' begged Quintzi as his knees began to stiffen at an alarming rate. 'Thermy? . . . thingy? . . . What was it? Felt great. Do it again! Ow, my arthritis.'

'Thaumoglobin,' growled the nano-sprites. 'A magical protein which it seems you have absolutely none of. How in all the gods' names did you ever manage to become a prophet without it?'

'Ahhhh, well, I've got a bit of a confession there . . . But speaking of the future, and all that,' he blabbered, steering the subject away from any more embarrassing personal revelations, 'How's about you guys telling me who wins the D'vanouin Derby Sweepstake, 'cos now I've lost my job and I think a bit of that is in fact your doing it seems only fair that . . .'

'Can't,' snapped the nano-sprites.

'Oh, come on, you did it yesterday.'

'That was before you smashed the chronoperatic foresight matrix. Without that it seems we are all as prophetically challenged as you!'

'What?' squeaked Quintzi. 'But I need you to. Can't you get it fixed, or something?'

'Broken. Inside crystal.'

'Oh, marvellous,' grumbled Quintzi dejectedly and looked around him.

Two hundred yards away on the far side of the Big Chink, the tattered hem of Axolotl's outskirts began. Rows of sun-whitened sandstone glared at him angrily above the bottom lip of the horizon, threatening, unwelcoming.

Pathetically his situation dribbled into his mind. He had been cast out, made homeless, he was as employable as the average whelk and the only chance he had to possibly earn any cash had been shattered by that damned bird up on that boulder. He had to admit it: even without the joys of foresight, it didn't look rosy.

At times like this there was only one thing to do. Sulk.

Miserably he shoved his hands into his pockets and, with the type of miraculous coincidence he had only ever read about, his fingers struck a large piece of parchment and a single groat. Curiously he withdrew the parchment, smoothed it out and stared incredulously at the words . . .

In the unlikely event that trouble is incurred with the Divination Systems Inc. Scry-Baby Colour Future Monitor, please don't even think about contacting us at our ware-house. We won't be in!

And along the bottom, in tiny writing, was scribbled an address. 21–21b Puce Street, Fort Knumm.

'Scuse me?' asked Quintzi, waggling his finger in his ear. 'Any of you guys possibly know the way to Fort Knumm?'

In a deep cave, far below the knotted roots of a dense impenetrable forest, a stocky figure sharpened a smoothly curving blade. His dark eyes peered intently out from beneath a pair of formidably bushy eyebrows as he concentrated on the honing of his twelve-inch knife, thrilling as the whetstone squealed along the arc of gleaming death.

Around him, every available inch of the rough walls groaned under the weight of heavily stacked shelves. They were laden with countless dust-bedevilled tomes of learning, piled high with preserved and picked parts of long-dead creatures and strewn with the myriad labour-saving gadgets which are so essential to the modern mage.

Behind the wall-mounted cloak-press and steam-fired hat reshaper lay a thaumic boot scrubber with optional insole deodoriser. It popped, whirred and gurgled relentlessly as it set about a particularly grimy pair of footwear, removing every scrap of filth from the weave of the canvas with alarming alacrity. It was always a marvel to watch, a symphony of elegance and efficiency, an opera of swiftness and perfection; in short, a feat of unalloyed technical wizardry. And a good job too, since it had been fashioned by the hands of the technical wizard himself.

The regular scraping of whetstone on blade ceased, the stocky mage wiped the blade and, with a flourish, snatched at this morning's fresh victim, chuckling selfishly. He knew he shouldn't do it, it was bad for him, but . . . ahhh, what the hell. It was one of very few pleasures he had remaining to him.

With his tongue working at the corner of his mouth he clutched the sacrifice firmly in his thick fingers and brought the knife down in a decisive death-dealing arc, cleaving the whole neatly in twain.

Seconds later his hands were swirling in complex patterns over the strange silver casket into which he had hurled the remains. He depressed a stubby lever and stepped back as the two parallel chasms began to glow fiery red within.

Eagerly, he spun on his enslippered heel, wrenched open a cupboard and snatched out a jar of vital unguents in preparation for the receiving of the charred offerings. Wisps of smoke flicked out from the fiery slots as he carefully wrapped protective towels around his hands.

And then, accompanied by a sound not unlike the release of a powerful spring, the ruddy inferno died and two charred and smoking discs were catapulted roofwards, bounced off the ceiling and hit the mage's plate with such a speed that they shattered irrevocably into countless ashy chunks.

The mage stared at the charred offerings with spitting fury. It wasn't fair. The damned toaster had incinerated his muffins again. And on the very morning he was about to open his new thick-cut marmalade.

Well, it was the last time it would do it. He'd see to that.

Snarling he grabbed the shining silver casket off the shelf, tucked it under his arm and stomped out of his cave.

Growling like one dispossessed, he pounded down subterranean passages, scrambled up winding staircases, whirled faultlessly around a thousand corners and kicked open a vast oak door with his slippers.

A figure in a lab-cloak looked up in shock from a complex array of wires, strings and pentagram control buffers and began, 'Morning, Practz . . .'

He got no further before Practz slammed the toaster on the table, leapt backwards as though it were alive and glowered at it from beneath those eyebrows. 'It's done it again!'

'Done what?' asked Wat, the thaumaturgical technician.

'Incinerated my muffins!' squealed Practz the self-elected head of Losa Llaman affairs. 'Burnt to a crisp!'

'Ooooh, nasty,' answered Wat, making an appreciative sucking sound through his teeth.

' 'Tis,' agreed Practz with much nodding of his head. 'An' what's worse is I haven't had any brekkie's yet.'

'Shame.'

'Yeah. It is. I want my muffins,' whined Practz stamping ineffectually in his slippered feet. 'So can you fix it? Throw one of those nano-thingies at it, or whatever it is you chaps do.'

'Nano-sprites,' corrected Wat. 'Yes, I can fix it, but you'll have to wait.'

'What about my brekkies? I want my muffins.'

'Er, what's stopping you?'

'The toaster,' snapped Practz, exasperated. 'It's broken, that's why I'm here!'

'As is the case in the great proverbial cat-skinning debate, there are many other ways to toast muffins,' grunted Wat, snatching a length of wire from a shelf behind him and beginning to twist it.

Practz scowled and looked baffled. 'Other ways? Nonsense. Toasted muffins come from toasters, it's a fact of life.'

'What about the times before thaumic toasters?' asked Wat shaping the wire animatedly.

Practz was temporarily stumped. He'd had a thaumic toaster of some description for so long that, well, he couldn't remember a time without. Until now, of course.

'I'll give you a clue,' offered Wat with a smirk and held up the roughly fashioned implement he'd been wrestling with. Practz glared at the foot-long shaft which ended in three prongs, and tutted.

'Oh yes, very helpful I'm sure. A knife would be more useful, better to spread marmalade with.'

'It's a toasting fork,' smirked Wat and handed it to Practz.

'Weird. What chants d'you use for it? No, wait, let me guess. Er, a level three heating elemental or, no, I've got it, a grade seven . . . why are you shaking your head?'

'It doesn't use magic,' groaned Wat.

'What? No magic? How can you have a domestic appliance without magic? Never work!' shouted Practz hurling the crude fork away from him as if it was the work of the devil.

'With an open fire you can . . .' began Wat.

'Fire? You suggesting I should go back to using fire and sticks? That's absurd, primitive. You'll be suggesting we start living in caves and wearing furs next!'

Wat's gaze drifted from Practz's favourite fluffy dressing gown to the cavern behind. Only with an immense effort did he stifle a giggle.

'I'm not using such things,' blustered Practz. 'I want my toaster fixing, now!'

'But, I'm busy . . .'

'On what? What is so important that I have to suffer without breakfast, hmmm?'

'It's part of Phlim's latest project of vital imp—'

'Enough! I have heard enough! When has one of Phlim's projects not been of vital importance? I sometimes think that our Technical Wizard has ideas way above his station. Well, while he is still away, gallivanting who knows where, I am in charge of you and I am ordering you to fix my toaster!' shouted Practz turning distinctly ruddy.

Wat shrugged. He knew an order when he heard it. He sauntered across the laboratory to a small cupboard, opened it and withdrew a small key. He then strolled across to the far wall where he inserted this key into a hole, shot back a lock and rummaged about casually inside. After a few seconds he removed a large ornate key, turned on his heel and shuffled to a solid door on another wall. Winding the key in the lock with a grunt, the final door swung open to reveal a dark, lead-lined interior and a tiny black cubic box.

This was a box of nano-sprites – distant relatives of water nymphs and forest sprites. Microscopic pinpricks of light; it was a little-known fact outside the subterranean passages of Losa Llamas that nano-sprites were almost infinitely more technically advanced than any other spirit elemental. Phlim had made sure of that. Whilst naiads were content to dip their toes in tranquil pools, nano-sprites white-water rafted down the surging torrents of multi-gigathaum potentials. Whilst dryads spent months nurturing budding trees to fruition, nano-sprites wrenched electrons off atoms, charmed strange quarks and reattached unstuck gluons. In the right place at the right time a nano-sprite was the most useful thing in the universe. Especially since Phlim had recently managed to insert into their genetic make-up the specific sequence which was responsible for all fairy-godmothers' willingness to please. Now the complex instructions required to ensure nano-sprite's co-operation were a thing of the past – all you had to do was jam one of the little chaps into a broken thaumatron, wish it better and . . . bingo! Done.

It was for this very reason that they were kept behind a level thirteen protection aura, in the dark, in a triple-locked lead-lined box. One stray thought at the wrong time and . . . well, gods knew what could happen.

Wat took a deep breath, shut out any stray desires he had, closed down the protection aura and carefully withdrew the box. He inserted a small syringe-like device through a hole in the top and pulled the plunger slowly, watching for the telltale prick of light that told him he had one. The plunger reached its stop and there was nothing. Baffled, Wat scratched his head, depressed the plunger once more and tried again.

Only once before had he failed to catch a nano-sprite first time and that had been when stocks were really low after a plague of hexenpox had wiped most of them out a few years back. He squinted through the syringe inspection window. Nothing. He caught his breath. Something was wrong. There were always nano-sprites in here now, over three hundred of them. Where could they possibly be? There hadn't been a major breakdown on the Thaumatron, he would've known about that. The lights would've been playing up; they always went first. How could three hundred-odd nano-sprites simply vanish?

'Come on, come on. I haven't got all day!' snapped Practz, his stomach rumbling with muffinless impatience.

Wat shrugged, chanted a brief incantation and closed down the final protection aura. It was a slim chance but maybe, just maybe, they were hiding in a clump. He took a deep breath, cracked open the lid of the box and peered worriedly inside. He squeaked, slammed the lid shut and stood rubbing his eyes with trembling disbelief. The hundreds of tiny pricks of light whirling inside the box like some captive microscopic galaxy were nowhere to be seen. The box was spriteless.

'What?' snapped Practz. 'What's wrong? Can't you fix my toaster?'

'N . . . no,' whimpered Wat, his mind spinning with shocked incomprehension.

'Pah! Call yourself a technician . . .'

'They've gone,' spluttered Wat, staring aghast at the box.

'. . . don't know what you think you're all doing here half the time if you can't fix a simple thing like a toa . . . What's gone?'

'*They've* gone!'

'What?' spluttered Practz.

'Nano-sprites. None left,' quivered Wat worriedly.

'Well, that's just typical! Damn that Phlim, he's hopeless at stock-taking. I told him to check on supplies before he went trekking off for weeks on end. I told him! What am I supposed to do about breakfast now?' ranted Practz.

'Kippers?' whimpered Wat dazedly.

'Aha! Kippers, of course. Haven't had one of them in years. Good idea, good idea,' muttered Practz, heading for the door, all thoughts of toasters swept from his mind with the golden possibility of a hot buttered kipper waving its fins seductively at him.

Wat wished fervently that he could have had such a pleasant vision. All he could see was the alarmingly empty interior of the tiny black box of nano-sprites. Where had they gone? What could possibly have happened to them all?

Attempting to keep as quiet as possible, Hogshead dived behind a suitable bush and coughed fitfully into the palm of his hand. His ribs ached from the spluttering almost as much as his curiosity throbbed to know just what that weird device was. It was damned irritating, but the longer he followed the mysterious three men with the strange magical mushroom-chewer the more he seemed to bend double and splutter wildly. Could he be developing an allergy, brought on by an enforced fortnight's exposure to a myriad irritating pollens? Or was it simply the effects of the mountain atmosphere after years spent in the airless confines of the Imperial Palace Fortress of Cranachan?

The latter was closest. There was something odd in the local atmosphere. If he had taken his gaze off his prey for a few moments and looked around him he might well have noticed the density of narcotically blue-brown vapours milling about in the immediate vicinity and frolicking lazily around his ankles. He might also have noticed that their density seemed to increase with every passing step, almost as if they were heading inexorably towards their very source.

They were.

Hogshead clutched at his throat and coughed noisily once more into his sleeve. Oh, what he wouldn't do for a glass of water right now. Silently he cursed the tickling in his throat, certain that he would alert his prey to his presence. If only he could get it under control. Fighting another noisy bout he took a deep breath and peered out from behind the bush.

It was then that his heart almost stopped.

No matter how hard he squinted through the hazy trees and obscured bushes he could see nothing of the threesome. They had, in a word, vanished. Without trace.

Suddenly, a hand shot out of the forest behind him, snatched at his shoulder and spun him round.

'So? What have we here?' snapped a swarthy man with goatee beard, dreadlocks, crossed webbing belts and matching daggers.

Hogshead squeaked and wished the ground would swallow him.

'What you doing sneaking round the forest, eh?' growled Ellis Dee from behind Praquat.

'Well, I was spying on you when you did something odd with that device in his backpack and I was wondering if you'd be so kind as to tell me all about it.' Hogshead almost blurted. But somehow he suspected that the chap with the matching daggers wouldn't take it the right way. Instead, Hogshead spluttered the answer, 'I . . . I'm lost,' and added an extremely pathetic look – a task he didn't find hard in the circumstances.

'How lost?' asked Ellis Dee, taking him by surprise. It wasn't really the response he had expected. Although if pressed he'd probably have found it hard to say precisely what response he had expected.

'Oooh, very lost,' hedged Hogshead, and shrugged a bit.

'And how long have you been drifting in this state of desolate directionlessness?' asked Ellis Dee evangelically, peering at Hogshead over his tiny circular crystal glasses in the manner beloved by all purveyors of botanical remedies and pick-you-ups.

'Er, ages.' Hogshead was thinking about how far he had just walked and whether or not he could find his way back to his tent. His nostril tingled, his lip curled and, without warning, he sneezed.

Ellis Dee took a step backwards in shock, his face turning

93

pale. 'Oh, my boy, I see why you have sought me out!' he declared.

'Y . . . you do?' trembled Hogshead nervously and wiped his nose on the sleeve of his tunic.

'Of course. By the time I've sorted out those sniffles you'll enjoy life's subtleties to their full. You've come to the right place,' declared Dee and tugged back a perfect curtain of undergrowth to reveal an enormous clearing stewn with tents, tree-houses and hastily hurled together shacks. A haze of intoxicating fug rattled up Hogshead's nostrils – a thin feathery fragment from the dense duvet rising from countless roll-ups smouldering like fireflies on people's lips. The rotund youth's upper lip curled back as, involuntarily, he sucked up a short breath. It was followed swiftly by another. And a third, building the pressure in his lungs to maximum sneezing capacity.

He exploded in a single massive cannon of an eruption.

Ellis Dee stood shaking his head and tutting. 'No time to waste,' he said and led Hogshead into his kingdom, his mind thrilling with formulae and blends capable of alleviating Hogshead's nasal discomfort. This was going to be a challenge.

To Ellis Dee Hogshead's origins were of little relevance. He had never bothered trying to find out where most of his other throng hailed from, since most of them hadn't a clue anyway. A lifetime's travelling does tend to blur one's sense of roots.

Crossing the clearing, seemingly propelled by a constant series of hazed waves from appreciative, if relaxed, subjects, it didn't take long to reach Ellis Dee's laboratory. Kicking open the door he stamped inside, waved Hogshead into a chair and leapt at a vast cupboard of ingredients. In a matter of seconds he was waving handfuls of ground roots, or mashed leaves, or odd powders under his nose and registering any effects with tuts of disapproval or mumbles of intrigue, until he whirled on his heel, hurled several dozen different extracts into a tall glass pot, whisked them thoroughly and handed the resulting potion to Hogshead.

'Drink,' he declared. Hogshead stared at the coagulated

cupful and heaved. It reminded him of a three-month-old yoghurt he had once had the misfortune to meet on a dark night.

'It'll stop you sniffing,' insisted Dee with a grin of less than professional interest. Praquat and Zaminah stared intently at him, their eyes exerting a burning pressure.

Hogshead, regrettably, realised that there was almost no chance whatsoever of leaving without having complied. So what, he thought. What could a few bits of grass and stick possibly do to me? Thoughts such as this served to make it apparent that Hogshead had definitely not been paying attention to Merlot's recent teachings.

Cringing at the expected taste he raised the glass and tipped it down his throat, swallowing the thick gloop with epiglottal difficulty.

'Well?' pressed Dee instantly. 'Better?'

To Hogshead's huge relief, and surprise, the tickling in his nostrils was lessening. In fact, incredibly, overall he was beginning to feel rather euphoric. A grin flashed across his face as a series of complex esters were metabolised into pseudo-endorphins. All of a sudden botany took on a new and fascinating dimension. How come Merlot didn't teach him useful recipes like this one?

And then he found out why.

Ellis Dee's face warped out of proportion in a nauseating swirl of hallucinogens, his nose ballooning as if through a fish-eye lens. Hogshead's eyebrows leapt up his forehead as his fingers grew wings and began chirruping expectantly. Badgers sprang from cupboards and began tap-dancing on the backs of three dozen conveniently positioned turtles. Mice burst through the door and began carrying away vital bits of furniture and equipment as Hogshead's facial coloration tended rapidly towards the green of the spectrum and his consciousness approached zero. Five and a half seconds later he was flat on the floor snoring, having declared profoundly, 'There's fish in it!'

Ellis Dee looked down at the prone figure of Hogshead and tutted. 'Gah!' he complained. 'Too much Dali Root in there, should've guessed!'

And with that he ignored Hogshead, barked a few orders to

Praquat and the anonymous Zaminah and began setting up the hextirpator in preparation for processing a few dozen punnets of that morning's magic mushrooms.

At that very moment, having hobbled arthritically across far too many mountains on a far too empty stomach, a certain ageing ex-prophet stumbled into the outskirts of the Auric Triangle. Had he not seen the wisps of rising smoke hovering above the encampment of Ellis Dee and assumed it was the haze from a dozen barbecues he might have passed by and struggled all the way to Fort Knumm. As it was, at the insistence of a vacuous stomach, Quintzi Cohatl turned left and headed for it, desperately rehearsing his 'Give us a bite to eat, guv' routine.


Phlim, the erstwhile scrying crystal salesman, slapped the reins wildly across the back of his horse and bounced his cart almost-out-of-control down the tiny track through the dense subtropical forest. His backside was numb due to the constant hammering it had received from the solid cart seat during the ten-hour gallop after he had left Axolotl; his knuckles throbbed from clinging to the leather reins and the clattering made by the truckful of lead piping behind him was bringing on a headache, but despite it all he felt wonderful.

The last few weeks had been good to him. And soon, oh so very soon, the fruits of his labours would swell considerably the coffers of Losa Llamas.

With a passable approximation of the sound normally more commonly associated with the pygmy cattle drovers of the legendary plains of Rho Flot, Phlim whooped, tugged hard on the left-hand rein and slewed the laden cart recklessly into the central clearing of the village.

If he had thundered so wildly into almost any other village, anywhere, it would almost certainly have resulted in half a dozen or so frolicking children being crushed to death beneath his speeding wheels, the annihilation of several of the more sluggish ducks which seemed to enjoy inhabiting the middle portion of cart tracks, the untimely destruction of several shop fronts and a whole host of writs addressed to him for compensation arising from the above damage.

As it was, nobody even blinked.

There was no one there to blink.

He thundered through the gaudily painted collection of theatrical-looking houses batting nary an eyelid at the overgrown vases and hanging gourds, or the wreckage of a pink portico, nor yet the mysteriously uninhabited pond with a pair of ornamental dolphin fountains. He simply whooped once more and steered the rumbling cart on a collision course for a steep outcrop of rocks crowned with a mohican of trees.

To anyone but a Losa Llaman this was an act of sheer stupidity. Or suicide. Or both. No path led over the outcrop; indeed, even if one had existed no horse could possibly have hauled a laden cart up its near-vertical incline. But undaunted, Phlim whooped wildly, flourished his crop with cheerful abandon and powered on towards the parallel avenue of ostensibly natural elders.

It was only as the horse's hooves broke an almost invisible thaumic beam hidden behind a small, and surprisingly realistic, rhododendron that things began to happen.

The rows of elders quivered epileptically, clicked and hinged away from each other to lie unnaturally flat, a moss-covered boulder began to rotate and, with a rumble only slightly more cacophonous than a volcanic eruption, the entire cliff face slid back a few feet and dropped below the ground. Phlim rattled the cart into the gloom, tugged hard on the handbrake, screeched to a flamboyant halt and yelled, 'Hi, Honey, I'm home!' His voice echoed feebly in the enormous cavern.

Outside, the trees whipped back to vertical and the cliff face slammed shut.

'Anybody there?' he yelled again, scrambling stiffly down off the cart, patting the sweating horse and offering him a well-earned sugar lump. 'Welcome back, Phlim,' he grumbled to himself. 'Good trip? Big profits? Tcha! Losa Llamas Welcomes You!' he added sarcastically.

In fact Losa Llamas rarely welcomed anyone. This was due

97

partly to the fact that it was buried underground in the middle of a vast forest filled with some of the deadliest creatures known to man and mage,* and partly to the fact that it was a top secret thaumic research centre dedicated to the development of the Ultimate Deterrent.

Mystery and disinformation oozed from every pore of the place. Hard facts regarding its past were rarer than the almost extinct Angstarktik pied harfinch, which successfully kept prying eyes away but caused no end of hassle for the Losa Llamans.

For example, nobody in the secret underground village had the foggiest precisely who it was that needed to be Ultimately Deterred. Or why. Or indeed, who it was that should be informed when they actually found the something that would Ultimately Deter whoever it was that they were supposed to be ultimately deterring.†

And then there was the snag of funding and wages. Judging by the nonexistent wage packets that each of them received

---

*Some of these were natural and had lurked in the forest for unknown centuries, such as the deadly river Nydd which possessed four rows of teeth, thirty feet of olive-green scales and the ability to sneak silently upstream. Other resident species had a distinctly less than evolutionary origin.

Ever since work had begun at Losa Llamas security had been of vital import. This had led to the swift establishment of a branch of thaumic research dedicated exclusively to defence. Over the years these investigations had introduced Losa Llamas forest to the delights of acid-hurling pitcher plants, five types of temperature-sensitive bindweed, onomatopedes and gerunds.

The latter two had been developed from a branch of high-energy linguistics research.

Ten-foot-long, exoskeletoned and possessed of the most complex array of glistening mandibles ever seen, the onomatopede was a beast whose bark was, literally, worse than its bite. Designed to strike quivering terror into the most hard-hearted of foes it could deliver a relentless barrage of screams, squeals, roars and a million other blood-curdling sounds at the drop of a hat. Unfortunately it was totally useless against an enemy equipped with earplugs.

The gerund, on the other hand, was far more interactive. Armed with the ability to latch on to the nounal root of an object and will it into behaving as an adjective, this unassuming marsupial could force war-pikes to metamorphose into fifteen-pound snapping fish or make innocent patches of lichen erupt into million-kilowatt bolts of deadly lichening.

For the unwary traveller, or casually invading army, Losa Llamas forest was no picnic.

†This was a truth known only to a smallish group of complete strangers. And they weren't about to blow their cover and spill the proverbial legumes.

every month, it had become a strongly held belief that they were a secret even unto admin.

It was in order to irrigate the cracked and parched beds of lucrativeness and get some cash flowing again that Phlim had set out a few short weeks ago armed with one hundred scrying crystals and a sales patter that could kill.

'Hello, I'm back!' he yelled again and was nudged in the pocket region by the horse, who wanted another sugar lump, now.

' 'Bout time too!' grumbled a stocky figure wearing a long dark cloak and a pair of formidably bushy eyebrows, as he stomped angrily out of a darkened corner.

'Yes, it's good to be back, Practz,' answered Phlim, guiding the self-elected head of Losa Llaman affairs toward the cart groaning with lead plumbing. 'One hundred scrying crystals sold for cash. And twenty-three and three-quarter ells of half-inch lead piping bought with the profits. Told you it'd be worth it.'

'You think it's worth it?' snarled Practz. 'You tell my stomach that!'

Phlim took a step back and admired the generous curve of Practz's corporation. 'What's wrong with your stomach? It looks just swell from here.'

'Hear that?' growled Practz in reponse to his growling insides. 'You hear that? It's like a wild animal. And all because it hasn't had any breakfast.'

'You've lost me,' pleaded Phlim. 'What's my trip got to do with your lack of breakfast?'

'This!' snapped Practz, producing a familiar silver toaster from behind his back. 'It's broken!'

'Surely Wat can fix a toaster,' frowned Phlim. 'Just because I invented the concept of selective thaumic scorching doesn't mean to say I have to fix the thing every time it throws a wobbly. What's wrong with it anyway?'

'Haven't a clue,' growled Practz.

'What? Haven't you run a nano-sprite diagnostic on . . .'

'It's a bit difficult when there aren't any nano-sprites!'

'Ah. You noticed,' confessed Phlim, brushing a strand of

brown hair out of his guilty eyes. 'I . . . I was going to replace them as soon as I got back. I've plenty of spores in storage and . . .'

'Where are they?' demanded Practz.

'That's a little difficult to say with precise certainty . . .'

'What!'

'But they're safe. Perfectly safe. I boosted the containment field to a level ten. They won't escape. And there are enough low-level thaumic emissions from the destiny valve to keep three of them going for centuries.'

'Three of them? You put three nano-sprites in those joke scrying crystals?'

Phlim nodded. 'Two just didn't work properly. Kept throwing really weird predictions out for anything over a decade into the future. And besides, the colour was dreadful. All washed out and limp and . . .'

'They weren't supposed to work properly . . .'

'Oh, come on. It's far too risky to flog dodgy images of the future. D'you think a general would be overly chuffed with us if he marched his troops into certain victory, you know, 'cos he'd seen it in the crystal, and gets hammered? He'd come looking for us, wouldn't he?'

Practz scowled. 'Wouldn't do him much good, though. I mean, if he's looking for revenge, he wouldn't have any troops left would he?'

Phlim thought for a moment. 'Well, what about the legal aspects, hmmm? Thought about that, have you? What's to stop him suing, eh? Staging major military campaigns is pretty pricey. And then there's the inconvenience of losing all those valuable tactical assets, like soldiers and siege engines, now they're *far* from cheap. Not to mention the funeral expenses and legal fees . . .'

'All right, all right!' shouted Practz, turning imperceptibly paler as the hypothetical bill mounted rapidly.

'And besides,' added Phlim, 'who in their right mind would buy a scrying crystal for a hundred and forty groats if the picture kept flickering . . .'

Practz's eyebrows scurried appreciatively up his brow. 'You

sold them for a hundred and forty groats? As much as that?' His eyes widened as he thought of the stack of profit that represented.

A grin flashed across Phlim's face as he looked once again at the cart laden with lead piping. 'Yeah. As much as that. I should've made more. If I'd made another fifty then . . .'

'Then we'd be out of nano-sprites for months and I'd be without my breakfast!' grumbled Practz, realising that he hadn't had the full satisfaction of ranting at Phlim for as long as he wanted. Missing his breakfast always put him in a less than chipper mood. Especially if it was someone else's fault. 'Why didn't you tell me that you were going to use three in each crystal, eh?'

Phlim looked at his toes for a moment. 'Er, it was a last-minute decision and I couldn't disturb you.'

'What? Why not? A matter as important as this . . .'

'It was a Wednesday afternoon.'

'Ah,' was all Practz said. Wednesday afternoon was Practz's time for a sauna and massage in Phlim's Patent Magical Muscle Manipulator. This was his time to let all the cares and worries of the previous week be dissolved away in plumes of hyperensorcelled steam and buckets of delicatedly scented oil applied with great vigour by the complex array of multi-jointed arms. Wednesday afternoon was a time not to disturb Practz. Life in Losa Llamas would be hell for the following week otherwise. 'But, er, you could've waited and explained . . .'

'No. I had apopintments all, er, arranged.'

'You could've rearranged them, written letters and sent them on pigeon post or . . .'

'A bit difficult, that,' admitted Phlim. 'None of them actually knew I was going to be paying them a visit.'

'What are you talking about now? How did you arrange . . .'

'It wasn't really that difficult to "find" a hundred people who would be at their most receptive to a fresh, er, *outlook* on life's little surprises.'

'You used a crystal?'

'Of course. It all ran perfectly. Well, mostly. I was there three or four minutes before I needed to be every time, ready and waiting for that perfect moment of personal crisis when I'd step in like a savioural angel and . . .'

'Rip them off for a hundred and forty groats!'

'Oh please, that sounds so mercenary.'

'What would you call it?'

'Efficient. It worked, didn't it?'

'Unlike my toaster!' reminded Practz, trying to hide his grudging admiration. He had to stamp his mark again otherwise Phlim would get even bigger ideas. 'You will fix my toaster, now!' he insisted with a glare that brought new meaning to the word brooding.

'Just as soon as I've hatched a few more nano-sprites,' answered Phlim, taking the angrily waved toaster and striding off towards the passageway that led to the rest of the complex of winding tunnels that was Losa Llamas.

'By the way,' he asked over his shoulder, 'will the Thaumatron be free this evening? Only there's a spot of hightly lucrative alchemy I want to do.'

'Fix that toaster and I'll see what I can do,' growled Practz then turned and stared at the pile of lead piping, working out how much it would be worth when Phlim had finished with it and it was all solid gold.

And then he wondered what precisely it was that the extra funds were required for. Some new project or other, no doubt. Phlim always had a new project up his lab-cloak sleeve. But what was it this time?

Practz shuddered nervously.

The uniformed usher looked up boredly from his kiosk as a cluster of tinsel attempted to fuse itself together before his very eyes.

'Fourth entrance on the left,' he muttered to a family of phoenixes and handed their tickets back to them. 'Don't forget,' he added, 'it's a no-smoking zone. If I catch you settin' up any funeral pyres, there'll be trouble. Clear?'

The largest phoenix tutted and led his brood off towards the hot dog stand.

The usher turned his weary attention back to the thickening

clump of tinsel and drummed his fingers on the kiosk windowsill. If there was one thing that got his goat it was folk who insisted on a flashy entrance. It was only a polo tournament. Nothing special.

With a dull pop the tinsel pulled itself together and a tall, white-bearded man appeared clad in a cloak and matching hat the colour of E major. Around his neck was a gaudy scarf which instantly declared him to be an Apocalypse Four supporter.

'Good morrow, my man!' he declared and strode forward brandishing a ticket.

Suddenly, the air exploded with a flurry of feathers and a very miffed-looking tawny owl cannoned out of nowhere. Barely missing the usher's outstretched arm, Arbutus swooped around and landed heavily on Merlot's shoulder, digging his talons in maliciously. 'Leave me to suffer your potted highlights, would you?' grumbled the owl. 'Deprive me of this treat, huh? After all I've done for you . . .'

'White or brown?' asked Merlot cheerily, holding up two mice.

'Vole or nothing,' squawked Arbutus. 'You know what I'm like if I don't have anything before a match. Just *can't* settle down. Constant chattering. Flapping wings . . .'

'Bah,' grumbled Merlot and tossed Arbutus a field vole, returning the mice to the safety of his hat for the interval.

The uniformed usher stared at Merlot's ticket, scrutinised the wizard with a quizzical expression, shrugged and then led him away with a curt, 'This way, sir.'

*Disgusting*, grumbled the usher in the privacy of his mind. *Let anyone in these days. There were times when you had to dress up to get into a box.*

He halted, plastered an ingratiating and well-practised grin across his face and held open the door to the private box.

Merlot's face fell. 'Surely some mistake, what?'

' 'S'what your ticket says,' grumbled the usher. 'Enjoy.' And with that he was gone.

Merlot stood for a moment looking up and down the carpeted corridor to see if anyone was watching enviously as he

103

stood outside the box. His private, plush viewing pad, kindly supplied by . . . truth be told, he hadn't a clue. Must be some grateful old dear for whom he'd performed a trifling spell at some point. Or something similar.

He shrugged cheerfully, much to the irritation of Arbutus, went inside and settled himself into the plush seats. Within a few moments he had discovered the array of chilled wines thoughtfully provided in a convenient ice bucket. Pouring himself a generous glass he settled back and awaited the start of the Three-Day All-Comers Polo Tournament, wondering only briefly about who could possibly have been so grateful to him.

After a few minutes' thought he gave up, poured himself another glass and decided that his unknown benefactor was simply rewarding him for being such a splendid chap, what?

If he had realised the truth, he would have been out the door in a flash.

Hidden on a rafter above his head a tiny insect-like creature focused its unblinking attention on him and began monitoring his (and the owl's) every movement, relaying pictures across the swirling vortex of the Space-Tome Continuum to the great satisfaction of a peculiarly anonymous-looking figure in a darkened viewing room.

Quintzi's feet were complaining worse than he could ever remember as he struggled through the dense forest of the Auric Triangle. Not to be outdone, his knees throbbed dreadfully and his stomach screamed in a constant seismic rumble. But worse than all his corporeal complaints was the constant moaning from the voice in his head. Tiemecx's almost incessant squawking wasn't that far behind.

Quintzi Cohatl felt certain that madness was hovering all too near, just around the next copse. If they didn't shut up, and soon, what remained of that elusive creature called sanity would up and quit, screaming. Who the hell did they think he was? How was he supposed to give them anything even remotely resembling magic?

Shame, he thought as he stomped miserably forward. It had felt rather nice, all those mamba-ing internal organs and, ooooh, that rush! In fact, truth be told, he could do with a drop of that himself, just to tide him over till he found some real grub. Purely medicinal, of course . . .

He reached out his hand to shove through yet another clump of triumphal larches when his thoughts were snatched away from the realms of magical fantasising. Something very odd happened. As he attempted to push the stubborn branches out of his way, the air turned . . . well, solid – as impenetrable as a tarpaulin. It just simply refused to let him through.

Uh-oh, thought Quintzi with a flurry of worry. Hello, Madness.

He stood stock still for a moment, attempting to ignore the combined throbbing of his feet and knees, and stared ahead of him. Forest as far as he could see, stretching away for mile after mile. Nothing new there, then. He shook his head in disbelief and strode purposefully forward convinced that it was all in his mind. He knew that the air in forests doesn't just spontaneously solidify without some sort of warning . . .

He crashed into the gap between two bushes with a flurry of curses, his face colliding with the rough yielding surface of the air, sending ripples shooting along it, spreading flapping distortions amongst the trees.

Squealing, he hurled himself backwards faster than if he'd just touched a twenty-thousand-volt supply. This shouldn't be happening! he screamed inside his head as he felt himself tumbling off his proverbial rocker and slipping into the comforting turmoil of insanity.

And he would've got there in a matter of seconds had not the vast camouflaged security blanket been snatched backwards by a dreadlocked Nugh-Age traveller dragging on a roll-up the size of a croissant.

'Hi, man,' he slurred through a plume of lazy smoke.

Quintzi's jaw swung slackly as he stared into the camp which, until seconds ago, had been totally invisible.

'Looking for paradise, man?' drawled Hugh in his ubiquitous 'Back to Basics' banana-leaf loincloth. 'Well, pull up a pew and chill out. Ooooh, nice parrot!' He held out a welcoming spliff, hauled Quintzi through the gap and velcroed it shut again with half a dozen conveniently placed teasels.

'What brings you up here, guy?' asked Hugh, his arm already encircling Quintzi's shoulder as if they had known each other for decades.

'Well, er . . .' His stomach rumbled. 'I'm a bit peckish, actually,' he answered. 'Got any iguana burgers?'

'What? That's lizard, ain't it?'

Quintzi took a long drag and replied. 'Sure is. Nice juicy reptile, bit of garlic and a few herbs, mmmm, well special! Tastes a bit like chicken,' he slurred, already slipping into the local style of dialogue with remarkable ease. It was probably helped by the intoxicating atmosphere.

Tiemecx dreamed of sunflower seeds.

'Uurgh,' grunted Hugh, lifting the lid of a handy grill. 'Don't have anythin' like that here, man. Here, chew on that.' He thrust a smouldering green disc into Quintzi's mouth. 'Tastes like chick peas.'

'Wha' ith i'?' spat Quintzi scorching his tongue with a sizzle.

'Chick peas,' answered Hugh with a grin and, exhaling the final cloud of hazy fumes, reached for a box jammed full of ready-prepared after-dinner spliffs.

Half an hour later, chilled out cold, Quintzi was snoring noisily under the stars, much to the chagrin of his resident triplet of now almost completely anathaumic nano-sprites.

It had been far too long since their last contact with anything even remotely magical and they'd done a lot since then. If something even vaguely magical wasn't found for them to chew on soon they'd simply wink out of existence.

Nimlet, for one, wasn't prepared to let that happen.

'All right, all right,' he buzzed at Skarg'l's latest objection to a scouting party, 'so it *isn't* strictly by the rules. Tough! Neither is hanging about in an environment not conducive to our continued well-being. Have you forgotten that it's our duty to remain strong and buzzing so that we can fulfil anything requested of us?'

'Ah yes, brother, but that does not mean deserting sinking . . .'

'You stay here then, I'm off.'

'Er, bring us back a few millithaums if you find any, will you?' wheedled Skarg'l.

'Nope. The way I feel right now I'd have the lot,' declared Nimlet, taking off and zipping out of Quintzi's ear. 'I could eat a whole thaumatron.'

'Wait for me!' shouted Udio, bouncing off their host's massive eardrum to gain momentum.

'And me,' buzzed Skarg'l, hoping there weren't any Amalgam Officials in the vicinity. He felt certain that there would be some disciplinary procedures if he was caught.

Unseen by everyone around the slumbering figure of Quintzi the trio of nano-sprites zipped in ever increasing sweeps of a search.

Actually it wouldn't have mattered a jot if they had been spotted. With the state of the visions currently bombarding the befuddled minds of the populace it wouldn't really have made them sit up and point. Amongst forests of tap-dancing neon badgers and herds of poetry-chanting bison, three little green spots of light were pretty insignificant, even if they had suddenly halted in midair and quivered excitedly.

'Can you smell it?' buzzed Nimlet, wishing he had salivary glands to start dribbling. 'Magic! I can smell magic!'

'You're hallucinating,' grumbled Skarg'l, spinning around to see if they were under surveillance. 'That smoke's got to you.'

'It's coming from over there, I tell you,' declared Nimlet.

'What? That run-down hut with the punnets of blue-veined mushrooms outside?' mocked Skarg'l.

'Of course, come on!' Vortex turbulence marked Nimlet's swift exit, its finger of a swirling tube pointing directly at the hut in question.

Milliseconds later Nimlet was under the door and staring at the inside of the hut. Shelves groaned with pots of herbal preparations, cupboards heaved with roots and flasks bubbled refluxively.

'Can you smell it now?' whispered Nimlet as the other two zipped in and hovered above the prone figure of a rotund youth lying flat out on the floor. Nimlet's thaumic nostrils flared expectantly. 'Raw magic, somewhere close!'

'Of course, brother,' grunted Skarg'l, uninterested. 'Bound to be some here with all those punnets of *Agaricus thaumagensis* around. Health and Safety regulations subsection 91 (a) states that all level eight thaumic botanicals must be stored in a well ventilated frost-free area away from dust, tremors . . .'

'Yeah, yeah!' snapped Nimlet zipping up and down. 'Every nano-sprite knows that they leak a bit. But this is different. Can't you smell it? *Refined* thaumaglobin! I'm certain of it.'

'Where?' squeaked Udio, his attention pricking up. 'Where, where, where?' Without waiting for the answer he zoomed into a pile of equipment, followed closely by the other two nano-sprites. They swooped around complex alchemical devices, gradually eliminating them from a hastily cobbled list of possibilities, until finally Nimlet quivered excitedly and flew full speed at a tiny pipe dangling from a curious array of flasks, tubes and reflux columns. There, dangling like a sphere of spring dew, hung a single drop of pure thaumaglobin. Udio broke the surface at full pelt, plunging in like some parched castaway into a brewery, sucking up the fortifying liquid with alarming speed. Nimlet and Skarg'l barely reached it in time, snatching a few deep draughts before Udio drained it all.

'We found it. The real stuff!' babbled Udio excitedly.

'But how?' pondered Nimlet warily.

'Who cares? It was here, that's all that matters . . .' said Udio, feeling inhuman again.

'It's not necessarily all that matters,' mused Nimlet, buzzing wildly and feeling frustrated that he possessed neither a finger nor the requisite chin upon which to tap it thoughtfully. 'Where did it come from? You don't just find pure thaumaglobin lying about at the end of tubes connected to odd-looking devices like that . . . wait a minute.' He fizzed excitedly as the thought process clattered logically towards the only conclusion it needed. 'That thing makes thaumaglobin!' buzzed Nimlet, staring up at the hextirpator.

'What?'

'Why else would there be a drip of pure thau—'

'Brothers, it is my duty to point out that since we are currently on territory unauthorised by the Theurgic Payments Board, we should scarper quick sharp and report on our findings as set out in the Codes of Conduct . . . brothers?'

Nimlet and Udio were already halfway back to Quintzi, their shimmering bodies buzzing with the sudden intake of thaumaglobin, their minds rattling with the same wonderful thought.

Scant seconds later they erupted into the cool night air and flashed into the familiar territory of Quintzi's ear. Barely decelerating, Nimlet hit the acres of eardrum at full tilt and startled its ageing owner into sudden alertness with a wild volley of pounding.

'Get up! Now! Wakey, wakey,' screamed the nano-sprites in his head, shattering images of cavorting rodents and juggling reptiles swirling against a multicoloured background.

'You again!' snapped Quintzi angrily. 'Go away, I'm sleeping! Tiemecx, tell 'em it's not time to . . .'

'Waste of time,' battered Nimlet. 'Get up, got a job!'

'Later . . .'

'NOW!'

'Clear off and leave me al . . . owww. Stop it!' wailed Quintzi as a pneumatic drill of nano-spritic irritation battered at the delicate expanse of his eardrum.

'Get up now or go deaf!' snarled Nimlet.

'You threatening me?'

'Too right,' pounded the nano-sprites.

Reluctantly Quintzi crawled to his aching feet and followed the smashing of directions.

'Look,' he grumbled a few minutes later as he stood outside Ellis Dee's laboratory hut, 'why should I go in there?'

'For your own good,' bashed Nimlet.

'Oh yeah, because I'll get earache if I don't,' he mumbled sulkily, his head feeling dubiously foggy from the narcotic after-effects he had yet to sleep off.

'No. There's a device in there that'll be really useful.'

'You've found a scrying crystal?' whispered Quintzi in sudden boyish excitement. 'Oh, my future is sorted . . .'

'No,' cut in Nimlet sharply. 'Look, there's no time to explain. Just trust us.'

'Ha!' spat Quintzi, recalling the explosive consequences of the last time he had been foolish enough to do that.

'You have no choice,' snarled Nimlet, beginning to vibrate pneumatically against his eardrum threateningly.

'All right, all right.' Quintzi capitulated, clutching warily at his ear and shoving open the door with a splitting of wood around the lock. 'You've been busy, I see,' he noted as the door-handle crashed to the floor.

'Of course,' tapped Nimlet. 'Now follow my directions. Through that far door, round that desk, mind that body on the floor, round that cupboard . . .'

And as Nimlet guided Quintzi through the darkened hut Udio and Skarg'l kept lookout. Tiemecx sat on the roof and sulked. It was far too early to be doing this sort of thing.

'You want that?' whispered Quintzi incredulously a few moments later as he stared at the complex pipework and reflux columns of the hextirpator, totally unaware of its awesome potential.

'Yes,' hissed Nimlet evilly.

'Must be valuable,' wangled Quintzi.

'Well . . .'

'Aha!'

'What d'you mean "Aha!"? Just pick it up and let's get out of here, all right?' battered Nimlet.

'One condition.'

'You're in no position to make . . .'

'One condition,' growled Quintzi forcefully under his breath. 'I'm not risking my neck for nothing. If I nick that, you find me a scrying crystal.'

Nimlet trembled with tension. He hadn't a clue where he could get hold of another scrying crystal. Still, he could sort that later, Quintzi hadn't mentioned anything about a time schedule . . . 'Okay, done! C'mon quick!'

110

Quintzi flashed a grin in the dark, snatched the hextirpator under his cloak, spun on his heel and made to leave.

'Not so fast!' snapped Nimlet. 'Take a couple of those punnets as well.'

'But they're full of mushrooms,' blubbered Quintzi as he stared inside.

'I know. Now go!'

Baffled, he snatched the punnets and sprinted towards the door, adding thievery to the list of arson and lies.

Suddenly, in the gloom of the lab-hut, his foot struck something, pitching him forward and tossing one of the punnets to the floor with a crash.

Hogshead, rudely awakened by an untimely kick in the ribs, looked up and caught a full frontal glimpse of the hextirpator as Quintzi hastily concealed it beneath his cloak. Then, completely ignoring the scattered punnet of mushrooms, he vanished into the nocturnal gloom in the direction of Fort Knumm followed by two eager spots of green light and the colourful streak of an alarm macaw.

It took Hogshead a few hazy minutes to realise what an act of criminality he had just witnessed. But just as soon as he did, he was on his feet, and out of the hut in hot, albeit nauseous, pursuit determined that nobody was going to get away without letting him have a look at that device.

If he'd known then just how closely he would get involved with it he would certainly have sprinted the other way.

# The Thaum and Garden Show

Many miles from the Auric Triangle, over the far side of the Talpa Mountains, crouched the infamous Fort Knumm.

What pictures that name conjures to the forefront of the mind. A vast military stronghold peopled by gleaming crimson foot soldiers, their eyes peeled, bayonets sharpened, ready for anything. Or perhaps a shining turreted development sited majestically on the shimmering mirage of a trout-stocked moat.

Not a hope.

True, there was a fort. But the number of times it had risen victorious from the galling sufferance of interminable sieges were, it had to be said, very few indeed. In fact, if you ignored the plethora of false claims in the guidebooks and ferreted out the truth, the actual number of military campaigns in which Fort Knumm had been directly involved could be counted on all the fingers of your average garter snake.

Years ago it had risen from the muddy hillock of Swindling's Tump, a study in designer dereliction, the key to the then Mayor's Grand Plan. In the first and last attempt at attracting innocent, wide-eyed and, above all, readily fleecable tourists to the town of Knumm, the Mayor had raised its status to Fort Knumm, dictated a hastily fabricated history into the extortionately priced guides and pressed half a dozen criminals into stacking a crumbling motte and bailey high on the hill under pain of death. That done, he had flung open the creaking gates to all-comers.

And for a time it worked. They came in droves. Craft shops appeared, flogging hand-made, and grossly misshapen candles, twisted wicker baskets and little spheres filled with barely recognisable models of the Fort which, at the flick of a wrist would be capable of whipping up a microscopic blizzard. They all bore the crossed finger symbol of the Fort Knumm Hand Masons and were, to a one, a complete rip-off.

And, amazingly, the tourists lapped them up. Until that is, other surrounding towns cottoned on and began inventing their own fascinating histories. Now a whole tourist trail existed where, if it was your taste, you could visit the famed condiment mines and herb tanks of Old Reganno, or the subterranean fish prisons of Eel Khatraz, or even the wild fabric trees and lingerie gardens of Emmanesse.

The profits of Fort Knumm suffered and now it was home to desperate salesmen, wanted assassins and a motley collection of roving conference organisers offering reckless deals to fill the recently completed Yolde Catycooms Exhybshonne Sentre and Grylle.

Amongst all of this, in a small backstreet hovel (the finest he could afford on Lore Enforcement Agency pay), Arch Sergeant Strappado snored restlessly next to his wife, Viv. As ever, his sleep was disturbed. Not by the constant screams from the local gambling emporium as one punter lost yet another shirt in a rigged game of cards. Not by the squealing of crumhorns and the pounding of bodhráns from the local hostelries – whose combined view of bar music seemed simply to be one of never mind the quality feel the decibels. His sleep wasn't even disturbed by the never-ending pressures of his Arch Sergeant status. No, as ever it was all his wife's fault.

Every thirty seconds or so she would breathe noisily in through her mouth, hold it for a moment and then exhale with a strange high-pitched bleating sound. Two years she had been like this. He had tried sewing three-pound cannonballs in the back of her pyjamas to force her to sleep on her side, but the bleating continued. He'd given her acupuncture, aromatherapy and a strange course of exercises involving hanging small crystals around her neck to 'focus life's elemental energy in a nurturing and beneficial manner', but all to no avail. Several months' wages down the drain and he still had the same bleating wife. She should never have been allowed to volunteer for it. He should never have taken her to 'Ye Silver Spitoone' two years ago. It had been a very bad mistake.

He should have known better, but she had insisted that he take her to the magic show.

His eyes flipped awake in bloodshot splendour and, as he counted the cracks and ants on the ceiling once more, he knew he should have listened to his father . . . and his father . . . and his . . .

'Never trust 'em!' they had always maintained. 'How can you trust anyone that dresses like that, eh? Curly-toed boots, foppish hats and worst of all, them cloaks, I'm tellin' you, son, it's them that's ruinin' society. Why d'they wear 'em? What've they got to hide, eh? I reckon underneath them cloaks they're completely naked and they only wear 'em so's they can jump out from round corners and scare little girls. I tell you, never trust magicians, boy, they ain't normal!' And there had been a nightly ritual of rattling his stick under the bed, 'to flush them perverts out! They're everywhere, I tell you, boy. Can't be too careful!'

Every day there was some new particle of sand in life's Vaseline that could easily be attributed to the devilish actions of 'those damned conjurists' and extra little snippets of advice like, 'Never trust stage magicians, boy. Anyone that spends hours every day locked away in little rooms practisin' tuggin' lop-eared bunnies from tatty toppers has got to be a bit on the dodgy side, don't you think, eh? Why don't they just pop down the butcher's like everyone else?'

Ever since he was big enough to lift his father's truncheon he'd been told that the kingdom was either (a) swarming with infiltrators from the filthy Conjurist Party prancing about in their crimson robes, or (b) heaving with maniac magic users spreading sabotage and the seeds of discontent, or (c) ruled by occultist usurpers who'd replaced all the ruling classes with zombie-like puppets and were even now coming to get you. They were everywhere – under the bed, in the wardrobe, conjuring ears on walls and flies on the ceiling, ready to listen in to any conversation, always one move ahead. 'Stands to reason!' his father had declared. 'That's why nobody's ever got to the bottom of it. They can see you coming . . .'

And on that day he, a very young Strappado, had decided to

do something about it. He had enrolled in the Lore Enforcement Agency, ready to weed out magical abuse at every level, prepared to rid Fort Knumm of the creeping red menace of conjurism.

If only the truth had lived up to his expectations then Fort Knumm would now be *the* most magic-free zone between Rhyngill and Cranachan. But it had all somehow gone horribly wrong.

Today the place would be screaming with hundreds of mages from everywhere, bringing their filthy magic on to his streets. It was a conspiracy. Well, why else would they have booked their annual 'Thaum and Garden Show' into Yolde Catycooms Exhybshonne Sentre and Grylle?

If one of those conjurists put so much as a curly-toed foot out of place then he'd round the lot of them up and give them a taste of Lore Enforcement they wouldn't forget. Ha! His eyes lit up at the thought of waving some red hot pokers about the place. Oh yes, he decided, first job when I get in: fire the furnaces up. Just in case . . .

Viv ground her teeth and continued bleating in a shallow sleep, the bell around her neck tinkling as her chest rose and fell. Strappado fumed inwardly as she twitched and dreamt of haystacks and carrots.

Then suddenly it was too much for him. He leapt out of bed, stomped across the straw-strewn room and threw on his Lore Enforcement Agency uniform of jet black dungarees and a polo neck sweater. Fuming, he clattered down the stairs and off to work. Somebody would pay for his last two years of hell, and they would pay today, he knew it. Some shopkeeper or other would feel the back of his truncheon before the day was out, he was sure. Even if he had to raise their 'donations' to ensure it happened.

The fug-strewn morning tranquillity of the Auric Triangle was shattered into a million grating shards by a piercing scream of anger. This was followed by a series of dull thuds all across the clearing as people fell out of their trees in acute shock.

115

Never in their combined memories could anyone recall having such a rude awakening. Especially not from Ellis Dee.

Two pairs of sandals screeched to a halt outside the lab hut and sprang through the door. They carried Praquat and Zhaminah inside.

'It's gone!' snarled Dee, pointing to the empty space on the table where, up until three that morning, the hextirpator had stood.

Zhaminah's dreadlocks sagged as he stared in blubbering silence, his knees trembling. 'Wh . . . where?' he asked.

Ellis Dee rounded on him angrily. 'If I knew that it wouldn't be a problem, would it?' He clenched his fists and pounded on the table with frustration. 'All that work, all that unharnessed and lucrative potential gone!'

*All my promotions gone! Not to mention all that cash and two years of my life*, blubbered Zhaminah to himself. And then he started thinking of the report he would have to make.

'And something else's gone,' snarled Praquat swarthily, drawing a dagger from one of his webbing belts and pointing to the naked patch of floor where once a comatose Hogshead had lain.

Ellis Dee swore and hurled a chrysanthemum across the room. 'Him!' he cried after swigging from a large beaker of green liquid. 'Damn him! How could I have been so stupid? Why didn't I see through him?'

'Eh?' grunted Praquat looking baffled.

'He was a plant!' squealed Dee, pounding the table again.

'A plant?' mumbled the Khambodian in confusion. Maybe he had been taking gobbledegook too long. 'I thought plants were green . . . ?' he began.

'No, no! Plant . . . as in agent! Specially placed operative sent to steal my hextirpator! You know – do or die!' screamed Dee.

Zhaminah attempted to turn more anonymous than usual and swallowed nervously.

'Damn him, but that cough was convincing,' snarled Dee. 'Had to be a MIN agent. What d'you think, Zhaminah!'

The oddly anonymous one swallowed through a throat constricted with terrified guilt. 'M . . . MIN?'

'Mystical Intelligence Network, idiot! Was he one of them?'

'Er . . . h . . . how should I know?' hedged Zhaminah, moving his hand closer to the stiletto in the heel of his sandal and trying to keep control of the sweat glands in his forehead. Just like his training had dictated.

'He had all the tell-tales. Why didn't I see them?' moaned Dee.

'What signs are they? I . . . I must've missed them,' asked Zhaminah as accentlessly and innocently as possible.

'Obvious!' despaired Dee, pounding his forehead with the heel of his hand and staring heavenward. 'He just appears all unannounced with some tale about being conveniently lost in the woods on the same day we finally get to test the hextirpator, then sneaks his way in here, right under our noses, feigns collapse and ends up staying here all night, that's all!'

Zhaminah gulped again. Could he be right? But surely not a MIN agent? *Surely* he would have known.

'Oh,' mused Praquat. 'Thought it might just have been a hunch.' The black eye he received gleamed purple agony for weeks afterwards.

'We're wasting time!' said Dee desperately. 'Round everyone up. I want to know if *anyone* saw *anything* unusual.'

Zhaminah and Praquat wheeled on their heels in a flurry of dreadlocks and sprinted towards the door.

'Correction,' shouted Ellis Dee after them. 'Anything *real* and unusual.'

Zhaminah, sweating with acute apprehension, sprang from the lab-hut a split second behind Praquat, turned through ninety degrees and shinned up a nearby tree. Without pausing for breath he tugged a thin horn-like shell out of his sleeve, tapped out a regular pattern on its surface and held it to his ear.

'Hello,' he whispered, 'Hello . . .'

Of all the sights and sounds that assaulted his senses every time he stepped into that particular cave, the humming had to be his favourite. For Phlim, the technical wizard and inventor of the

Thaumatron, there was really nothing else that conveyed the surging feeling of barely contained power like that low constant throb.

Yes, it was easy to 'wow' any newcomer to Losa Llamas with the briefest of glimpses of the Thaumatron. Only the most magically heathenic of persons would fail to be impressed by the vast toroid of high-energy thaumatronics squatting in the enormous cavern, its surface glistening with hyperensorcelled steam tubes, runic dials and a host of complicated looms of brightly coloured wiring. A single enormous extrapolation of the tiny ubiquitous magical ring.

But, impressive as it looked, it was the memory of the humming that lingered. There was nothing quite like the sound made by countless millions of thaumic particles as they were accelerated within a magi-kinetic flux field. Well, actually, there was, but since hearing it involved sticking one's ear against a sheet of corrugated iron and standing on the rocks directly beneath the hundred-foot-high gushing cataract of Gharial Falls, no one had heard it without drowning and being swept far out into the middle of the Pathetic Ocean never to be seen again.

So it wasn't surprising that Phlim's heart leapt as he shoved open the vast doors of the cavernous Thaumatron bay, sprinted proudly inside and was bombarded by the noise. He realised in a flash how much he had missed that old familiar throbbing on his travels, almost pined for it as a newborn child aches for the regular pounding of its mother's blood in the womb. Yes! He had missed it nearly as much as he had the chance to dabble his fingers in the babbling brook of jiggery-pokery and carry on with his latest pet project. He was back and itching for some serious technical wizardy, yearning once again to hone the gleaming cutting edge of theurgic research, craving the indescribable thrill of shoulder-charging the very limits of the unknown and boldly stepping where none have dared . . .

But first he had to fix that bloody toaster.

Quivering with pent-up irritation at the unwarranted intrusion of such mundanity, he scrambled up an open-runged spiral staircase and disappeared off down a short, little-used passage.

At the end of it he found lurking a large rectangular cabinet. With a deft flicker of fingers he flashed the correct runic shapes before the magic eye and grinned briefly as a single red crystal flicked to green. He snatched the cabinet's handle and lifted the lid, stepping quickly backwards as plumes of swirling smoke curled over the lip and slithered greasily away into dark unseen corners. It was better not to get any of that fog on his shoes: the things that frozen incantium dioxide could do to real leather uppers just didn't bear thinking about. It had taken him three weeks just to coax the damn things down off the ceiling the last time they'd caught a whiff of the stuff, and there was still one of his shoelaces missing.*

Incantium dioxide had to be treated with extreme caution, but it was a vital necessity. You can't keep nano-sprites in anything else. Chill a few litres of 'inox' to 276 degrees below freezing and it'll liquefy, conveniently providing the perfect medium in which to completely halt any and every biological process known to man and dwarf. It was in this state of suspended thaumination that Phlim had stored a vast army of nano-sprites.

Donning a pair of thickly padded gloves he reached into the swirling fog and pulled out a small black tube, deftly popping it into a larger container and activating a level ten containment field with a practised flick. Slamming and relocking the cabinet lid, he scuttled off back down the passageway and swirled down the staircase into the Thaumatron bay.

In a matter of moments he had dashed across the vast cavern, struggled into his lab-cloak, placed the slender black tube in a highly shielded box and was scowling at a bank of runic dials. Slowly he gestured before a flux diverter, tapping off a tiny

---

*Privately Phlim believed that the shoelace had slithered off into one of the lower caverns to feed on the peculiar translucent rock-skipper fish which lurked down there. The only evidence he had to support this dubious theory was one desiccated piscine corpse he had come across high on a narrow rocky ledge, its body fluids drained completely through a series of regularly spaced circular holes. Curiously, the spacing of these holes matched exactly the arrangement of eyelets on his left shoe.

This strange tale, along with many, many other weird and mysterious magical happenings, was Phlim's little secret, carefully documented and filed away in his own locked drawers. Drawers he secretly referred to as 'The Hex Files'.

fraction of the twenty gigathaums currently zapping around within the vast magical ring of the Thaumatron. Sapphire flashes of power crackled into the chamber, bombarding the black tube and its contents with pure magical energy. Phlim brushed a strand of hair from his eyes and kept his gaze glued to the runic readout of the thaumostat.

At the far end of the cavern a pair of huge double reinforced doors creaked open and a man of large musculature and little brain tugged a laden cart into view. 'Where d'you want this?' asked Uhrnest, one of the vast array of two Losa Llaman guards, referring to the cart piled high with lead piping.

Phlim glanced over his shoulder, waved dismissively and grunted, 'Leave it there, in the middle of the floor. Come back for it in a few minutes. And bring your coat!'

And his attention flashed back to the reactivating nano-sprites. He ramped the chamber's internal flux density up to 3.25 gigathaums and held it there for a count of 'five elephants'. Moments later he shut everything down, snatched open the chamber lid, sucked a glowing greenish point of light into a large syringe and stalked purposefully towards Practz's afunctional toasting machine.

Flicking open a tiny hatch labelled MAINTENANCE ACCESS. NO USER SERVICEABLE PARTS. SERVICEMEN AND NANO-SPRITES ONLY! he jammed the tip of the syringe in, rammed the plunger home and cast a casual wish after it. A second later the microscopic green lumen homed straight in on the fault and set to fixing the ruptured thaumionic valve that had caused Practz so much strife.

'Oh, Uhrnest?' shouted Phlim as he placed the remaining nano-sprites back under a level ten containment field. 'Take this to Practz, would you?' he added holding out the shiny silver toaster.

And then he turned his attention on the cartload of plumbing – the last hurdle preventing him thrilling with the rewards of dabbling in his project again. Cracking his knuckles noisily he strode up to a shimmering hole in the side of the Thaumatron, waggled his hands complicatedly and was rewarded with a leaping sapphire snake of power surging directly from the portal and into the small of his back. Fifteen gigathaums plunged into his body, sparking wildly off his hair and toes, lifting him a good inch clear of the ground.

'YEEEEEHAH!' he squealed as his eyebrows shorted together and lanced a bolt of lightning roofwards. If there was one thing that Phlim loved more than the throbbing hum of power made by the Thaumatron, then it was this. Being plugged in. This surge of energy made bungee jumping seem like a wet Sunday afternoon's golf. This was excitement. This was what being a thaumaturgical physicist was all about. Forget all that gumph about pushing back the forefront of science. It was much more fun to switch on, fire up and plug in! Especially when it was about to be so lucrative.

Phlim's eyes lit wider as a hot throbbing of muscles twitched and writhed uncontrollably for a few seconds around his midriff. Then it spread rapidly, sending his spleen into paroxysms of delight, his liver into wriggles of pleasure and his heart into a pulsing mambo of cardiological heaven. It also destroyed his nasal hair.

Flexing his fingers he focused on the slowly oxidising heap of redundant piping, muttered a few incantations under his breath and let rip. Superstrings of cerulean magic blasted from each of his fingertips zigzagging in wild angular bolts across the cave and zapping unstoppably into the cart. A halo of purple grew over the magical discharge as the very nature of the lead was moulded and shaped, shattering electron shells here, igniting protons there . . .

There was a sharp percussive flash, a crack of static electricity, a noisy explosion and it was all over. Phlim flicked his wrists and shut off the flux serpent. Dropping back to the ground he stomped over to inspect his handiwork, the odd shimmering discharge still firing off his eyebrows.

He brushed back a strand of hair from his eyes and peered into the charred cart. The lead was totally gone, every trace of its ever having existed wiped completely from the entirety of Losa Llamas.

But the cart was far from empty.

Instead of the dull grey tubing, it was now laden with nice

neat blocks of thaumically transformed rich yellowish metal. An element known throughout the uncivilised world for its wonderful ability to be transformed into almost anything else required by the simple expedient of passing it across somebody else's palm. The cart was stuffed with gold.

As if on cue, Uhrnest pushed open the door and strolled in. 'Done?' he asked.

Phlim nodded cheerily and pointed to the neat stack of bullion. 'You know what to do,' he said and gave him a hand-scrawled list on a sheet of parchment.

'Usual place?' asked Uhrnest.

'Yup. He's expecting you.'

'And this will be enough?'

'Better be! There's nigh on two hundred thousand groats' worth there. I know he's a bit pricey but even he wouldn't overcharge that much, would he?'

'I have heard mention of words like "inflation" and "import tax" and "protection",' grunted Uhrnest. 'Not quite sure what they mean, but they've got a sort of expensive ring about them.'

'Hmmm, maybe I should've tried going all the way to diamonds,' muttered Phlim, clutching at his head with worry. 'Or perhaps even platinum. Look, just make sure you get that: those two and at least twenty-nine of them,' he babbled pointing at the list. 'And hurry back. I'm almost ready for the final phase. I don't want to be held up again. Go, go!'

And with that Phlim whirled on his feet and dashed off back to his long-forsaken project. His pet secret study that had been mothballed for the last three months due to an acute lack of essential funds. Well, that had all changed now. That state of chronic cashlessness seemed like the dim and destitute past. In the wealthy here and now he could continue his vital work. Now, he could finally finish!

'Come on my little beauties!' he muttered to himself as he snatched the nano-sprites and sprinted through the labyrinthine tunnels. 'I'm back!'

'Open that box!' commanded Officer Drub of the Lore

Enforcement Agency as a shabby figure in a faded cerulean robe struggled into Yolde Catycooms Exhybshonne Sentre and Grylle.

'No, no, not again?' came the weary reply. Drub's victim raised his gaze heavenwards and stared blankly at the gaudy parchment posters advertising HERE TODAY. THAUM AND GARDEN SHOW. DEMONSTRATIONS. STALLS. DONKEY RIDES.

'Open the box!' repeated Drub, rising from his stool and making it obvious that he was wearing his special thumping gloves.

'All right, all right, my boy. No need to get het,' mumbled the man in the tattered robes, placing the box carefully on the floor.

'Open it!'

' "Open it" he says, like I don't know he's going to say that! Every time it's "open the box!" ' mumbled Mal Fease the Magickal Merchant, fiddling with the bits of string. He looked up at Drub, pointed to the label declaring the contents to be one gross of Instant Rabbits and said with a shrug, 'Guess what's in the box.'

Drub tutted. 'One gross of Instant Rabbits, perhaps?'

'Bingo,' grunted Mal Fease. 'Every time I come in with a box with writing on the side and every time that's what's inside. Amazing! So why you doing this to me, eh, my boy? I got a warehouseful of deliveries to make to these stalls, you think I need you asking me to "Open the box" every time?'

'It's orders,' shrugged Drub, flicking back the lid and staring at the top layer of one gross of Instant Rabbits (Amaze Friends and Relatives as Your Bunny Appears! Just Add Water – top hat not included).

'Let me guess. Strappado?' grunted Mal Fease.

'Arch Sergeant Strappado to you!' growled a shadow as it resolved itself into a fuming polo-necked figure of wide renown.

'Ah, greetings. I was just discussing the thoroughness . . .'

'Shut up, Fease,' growled Strappado, peering down on the shabby merchant. 'I don't need lip from you. What's in the box?'

'One gross of Instant Rabbits,' chorussed Mal Fease and Officer Drub.

At the repeated mention of the word 'rabbit' Arch Sergeant Strappado's fists clenched in extreme anger as the knife wound of horrific memory was scraped through a vat of rock salt. His mind whirled back three years . . . the stone floor tilted . . . all around him were the giggling shrieks of six-year-old children. His mind's eye stared at the full-coloured image of the past.

'I need a volunteer!' demanded the shabbily clad children's entertainer. 'Who's it going to be in the Tomb of Termination?' Ye Great Entranco had swung the theatrically blood-smeared cask on to the table between the cakes and jellies and everyone had gasped. He had closed his eyes, stuck his fingers to his temples and concentrated hard as if dredging his mind for a word, a handle . . . 'I have a name!' Ye Great Entranco had declared and all the guests of Strappado's niece's sixth birthday party had held their breath, each aching to be the star victim, dreading being called. 'The name is . . .' The magician had turned and fixed Souxzie with a meaningful stare. 'The name is . . . Benji!'

'My rabbit!' thrilled Souxzie, her plaits jiggling, unsure whether to scream or hand over the little bundle of leporine joy. 'How did you know his name?' she had asked with a hushed tremble in her voice.

'Aha!' Ye Great Entranco had declared enigmatically, and back then Strappado had almost forgotten that he had given that damned wizard all the info beforehand. How many times he had cursed him since then? One thousand? Two . . . ?

Strappado's fists clenched tighter as the sadistic projectionist of his mind's eye replayed the events further, helpless to stop them all whirring through his brain.

Ye Great Entranco pounced on the black and white bundle of Benji, hoisting him aloft with dreadful theatrical glee and slamming him into the gore-splattered box, clipping him into immobility in seconds. In a fluid movement he raised the axe, arced it over his head and split a carrot across the midriff with a resounding crunch. A four-year-old wet his pants in excitement and had to be taken away. He was the lucky one. He didn't see the worst of it.

'And now for Benji . . . !' announced Ye Great Entranco with a feral grin. Souxzie jammed her hands into her mouth and watched, some tiny part of her mind telling her that it would be all right. Benji would be fine, it was only a trick.

Souxzie watched motionless as a shard of light glinted off the axe blade. Then it whistled through the air, struck the Tomb of Termination with a scream of metal, a crunch of what could have been bone and thudded into the table top.

Strappado had been amazed at how realistically the blood had oozed out of the box, until he found out why Ye Great Entranco had quite so suddenly turned green and fled.

It was a strange thing, but Souxzie had never let any of her rabbits be put in unfamiliar wooden boxes ever again. Especially by strangers with suspiciously mystical-type names.

Arch Sergeant Strappado exhaled harshly through his clenched teeth as his mind's eye matinée flickered back into the present. His eyes locked on to the shabbily dressed Magickal Merchant and saw red. He wanted revenge. He didn't care that Mal Fease had nothing to do with it, he was something to do with magic and rabbits . . . right now that was enough. His mind whirled for a charge, any charge to arrest him with. Visions of red-hot pokers floated temptingly before him.

'Got an import licence for them, eh?' he growled through locked jaw muscles. 'Been quarantined?'

'No need for quarantine, they're dehydrated,' answered Mal Fease with a slightly too jovial shrug. 'Quarantined? he asks,' he muttered to himself. 'Look,' he said staring up at Strappado. 'Everything is in order, all right? You don't believe me? Go to my warehouse. 21–21b Puce Street. Here, take my card.' Strappado stepped away from the faintly glowing rectangle of parchment. 'In the meantime, I got one pair of hands and twenty boxes left to deliver. I'm not careful, I get lynched! You want a murder on your hands, already?'

'You volunteering?' answered Strappado flexing his fingers and gauging the diameter of Mal Fease's neck. 'I'd be happy to oblige. In fact, any of your damned ilk steps out of line and I'll have the lot of you behind bars faster than you could spit. Clear?'

'Crystal,' murmured Mal Fease with a grin and closed the lid of his box. 'There won't be any trouble,' he added. 'I checked!' He tossed an eight-inch Scry-Baby Colour Monitor casually in his palm and winked at Strappado.

The Arch Sergeant trembled with anger and fury. One of these swines had interfered with his wife and his niece's rabbit. Somehow, he would get his sweet dessert of revenge.

Drub waved Mal Fease away before he had to arrest Strappado for magicide.

'Thaum and Garden Show,' groaned Strappado. 'Why here?' he moaned. 'Why me?'

Before anyone had a chance to answer that conundrum there was the familiar clattering of Lore Enforcement Agency boots and the wheezing of an urgently sprinting officer.

Strappado turned, took a deep breath and awaited what was almost certainly dreadful news. It was going to be one of those days, he could tell. A day when he wouldn't catch up on all those outstanding assassination request forms. A day when his wife would have chewed another mattress to shreds in a spasm of unholy goatness. Still, every cloud and all that ... He detested parchmentwork and that mattress was becoming a little lacking in lumbar support. He just hoped he'd have time to stop off and pick up some spare stuffing.

His officer screeched to a halt and gasped furiously at him, attempting to catch his breath. Everything was *so* urgent these days. Where had the good times gone? The times when people simply got on and murdered each other instead of hiring licensed assassins, paying their admin fees and filling out forms in triplicate. Okay, Strappado would be the first to agree that it saved investigative time this way, no messing about turning up clues, collating evidence, arresting witnesses and helping them to remember the exact details of what they had seen with a swift kick here or a turn of a thumbscrew there. He knew that it was a good system. Disagreements in Fort Knumm

126

never reached the gang warfare stage and the Lore Enforcement Agency received a steady income from assassination requests . . . but, well, it just wasn't as much fun as tracking down a real live murderer.

'H'llo, Arch Sarge,' panted the officer, clutching his ribs. 'Jus' thought you might like t'know . . . He . . . He . . . He's back!'

'What?' snapped Strappado, eager excitement stirring in his loins. Could it be true? Did he really have *that* much nerve? 'Who's back?' he asked cautiously, bracing himself for the disappointment that would surely come.

'Him. Y'know, Entr . . .'

'Where?' cried the Arch Sergeant, grabbing the officer firmly by the throat.

'Owww, steady Sarge . . .'

'Tell me!'

'All right, all right. Ye Silver Spittoone. One night only . . .'

Strappado dropped his sweating officer and almost trampled him in his rush to get out, accelerating like a frisky whirlwind on heat. This was the chance he had been waiting for. The chance to nab him red-handed. The chance to make up for all those nights of bleating . . . The chance to nail a damned conjurist!

He had two years of evidence amassed and waiting up his sleeve. Twenty-four months of personal day-to-day documented facts and experiences. It was the worst mistake those damned conjurists had ever made, they should never have got his wife and niece involved. Never . . .

Arch Sergeant Strappado's chest swelled with pride. The fates had been listening to his hate-filled pleas. Oh yes, today, down at Ye Silver Spittoone, Ye Great Entranco would make his last stage appearance.

Oh boy, this could be it. Make the charges stick and he could be in for a promotion to the Mystical Intelligence Network.

Now, if only he knew their hex number . . .

It wasn't really so surprising that Arch Sergeant Strappado didn't know how to get in touch with the Mystical Intelligence

127

Network. They weren't exactly the most gregarious of folk. They were infinitely happier snatching glimpses of the dubious things people were getting up to than chatting about them over a cup of coffee and a few Fort Knumm shortbread slices.

But then, after the several centuries of finely honed paranoid indoctrination which surfed through their suspicious minds it wasn't entirely unexpected.

It went back a very, very long way. Three hundred and fifty-three years, to be precise.

In the year O.G. 687,* times were hard. War raged in the Eastern Tepid Seas as the bikini-clad raft people fought off hostile claims from the Murrhovians to their shellfish lagoons in what became known as Whelk War One. The cliff-diving warriors of Thhk were making regular raids on the permafrost-cooled wild pig reserves of the Angstarktik nomads.

And as the Boar War raged far to the tundra'd north, two insignificant kingdoms glared at each other across the Talpa Mountains.

On one side was the small but relatively wealthy kingdom of Rhyngill, reasonably fertile and totally lacking in anything even remotely worth calling an army. The other, the vast thug-like Cranachan, sporting the virtually impregnable stronghold of the Imperial Palace Fortress, hostile ravines and a several-thousand-strong pack of unruly psychopaths barely held together by the so-called generals. Both kingdoms knew that it was only a matter of time before they came to blows and both knew damned well that Rhyngill would get mashed in seconds.

Curiously, in one of those myriad odd happenstances which historians are utterly at a loss to explain, Cranachan never came storming out of the Talpa Mountains and trampled them there

---

*O.G. – Original Gravity. A calendar system invented by the mathematician philosopher Gren Idjmeen who measured how long it took for bricks to fall out of windows on sunny days at sea level. Despite the fact that this system is far less accurate than others, cannot be synchronised with pub licensing laws and involves strolling around with a three-stone hovel brick in your pocket, it caught on remarkably well, especially amongst the young male population. Many learned chronologists have attempted to explain this unwarranted popularity and so far there seems to be only one answer: the annually reprinted calendar decorated with full-colour glossy portraits of the starlets from Fable TV's ratings-leading horror bodyguard show, *Feywatch*.

and then. They waited until O.G. 1025 to try that. The only theory that anyone can concoct to explain this tardiness is the 'military tourism inertia scenario' – no matter how much you really want to invade somewhere just down the road, you never ever seem to be able to get off your military backside and go. Who wants to go and visit crumbling castles in your own back garden when you can save up and have a really good long-distance package invasion next year, eh?

Of course, the historians proposing such garbage haven't a clue about the Thaumaturgical Physicists of Losa Llamas and the Mystical Intelligence Network of Cranachan.

Faced with the unattractive options of either utter defeat or a whopping great bill for mercenary services, King Stigg of Rhyngill decided to fiddle the odds by setting up the cream of Rhyngillian thaumic intellect in a purpose-built and utterly secret village deep in the forest of Losa Llamas; their task, to develop the Ultimate Deterrent. Something, or somethings, that could keep entire hostile battalions at bay with the absolute minimum of manpower.

This would have been all fine and dandy if the Cranachan Intelligence Agency hadn't picked up a sniff of gossip about it all. In a flurry of rare efficiency the CIA set up countermeasures in the form of the Mystical Intelligence Network – a constantly alert band of dedicated snoopers with eyes peeled and ears ready for the slightest new Rhyngillian thaumic developments.

And so time had passed, each group remaining a distant rumour in the consciousness of their respective kingdoms, each stocking their ranks by carefully choreographed and executed kidnappings, each developing more and more powerful tools and arms . . . and MIN copying or stealing the vast majority of its opponent's ideas.

Up until very recently, MIN's greatest break had been the discovery, one hundred and fifty years ago, of a nest of the tiny insect-like sneeke which had been forgotten about by the Losa Llamans. It had only taken the technicians of MIN a couple of decades to figure out how to capture the beamed telepathic messages transmitted by the sneekes. From then on, no Losa

Llaman development had been without its accompanying sneeke on the wall.

Unfortunately, in O.G. 1025, owing to a dispute over who owned the land from which the highly fashionable lemming skin harvest was collected (should it be the Cranachanian cliff from which they hurled themselves, or the Rhyngillian valley in which they met their final end), the two kingdoms finally got around to that war. Ironically, due to some unforeseen intervention from a highly magical beastie, a gerund, Rhyngill ousted the Cranachanian leadership and formed an alliance of the two kingdoms, thus providing an uneasy peace. Sadly, due to a clerical oversight and an extreme loss of racial memory, nobody told the Losa Llamans or MIN about it.

And so MIN continued its vigil, winkling out new inventions, observing every move made by the Thaumaturgical Physicists, knowing damn well that they would still lose if it came to a scrap. There was no way they could compete if a war turned magical.

And here, buried beneath centuries of lies and subterfuge was the single source of constant mistrust and extreme frustration, chewing constantly at the temper of the MIN agents, the one thing they were set to watch – magic. None of them had ever been even remotely magical. Oh, they could use magical gadgets as well as the next spy, but when it came to actually casting spells . . . not a flaming hope. They knew damn well that if any one of them were to get the chance to plug into the Thaumatron they'd be fried in milliseconds.

It had become their holy grail to even up their disadvantage.

Decades of bio-magical research had shown that one had to be directly related to someone magical in order to activate an odd biological system within. Perhaps if they had known about the magical protein thaumaglobin; perhaps if they'd known about the pathway which linked the pineal gland in a positive feedback loop to the thaumaglobin factory in the coccyx; if they'd even heard a rumour of the way that charged thaumaglobin can carry kilothaums of pure energy to the fingertips . . . perhaps then they wouldn't have had to wait so long for Ellis Dee's discovery of the hextirpator.

It was only a matter of time now before they collected their greatest breakthrough yet from the hazy environs of the Auric Triangle.

'He still there?' barked a gruff voice in the buzzing semi-silence of the MIN sneeke room. The body which owned the voice stood in a pale grey cloak and matching tunic and stared at a bank of compound images being beamed in from unknown ells distant.

The observation operative sat glued intently to one of the screens, his gaze unfaltering, 'C'mon, c'mon,' he whispered with taut intensity and gripped the edges of his seat. A tiny stick figure raised a mallet, spurred his horse onward and closed on the almost invisible ball as it bounced on the green of the pitch. Behind him a clump of Knights Templar spun their steeds and galloped for interception spitting sods of turf in all directions. Pestilence was in possession, there was an open goal, he raised his polo mallet again and . . .

'C'mon. c'mon!' whispered the operative, completely engrossed in the events on the pitch.

'Well? Is he still there?' growled the voice again, an inch away from his ear.

The operative leapt out of his skin, spun around and flashed a reflexive salute.

'Progress report,' growled the grey-clad one.

'Oh . . . oh. C . . . Commander Furlansk, sir,' stuttered the operative. 'Er . . . everything is fine, sir. The Apocalypse Four are three up in the second chukka due to an amazing free hit from Famine in the . . .'

'No, no, no,' whispered Commander Furlansk coldly around a sneer as he wagged a long finger meaningfully. 'Progress report. Current location of specified target.' The operative's kidneys squirmed nervously.

'H . . . he's still there, sir,' whimpered the operative as a bead of terrified sweat scarpered down his forehead.

'And the owl?'

'Seems to be really enjoying the match, sir.'

'Refreshments?'

'Holding up, sir.'

'Prognosis?'

'He's there for the duration, sir. H . . . he's going nowhere in the next eight hours, I'd . . . I'd stake my kidneys on it!'

'I shall remember that,' grinned Commander Furlansk with a cold relish. The operative's kidneys quivered again. 'Resume,' breathed Furlansk in a voice that somehow seemed to bypass all normal methods of auditory processing and talk straight to the soul. The operative needed no second bidding. He dropped back into his chair in an almost dead faint, locking his eyes back on to the image of Merlot and Arbutus in their box at the Chapter Dimension's All-Comers Polo Tournament.

Behind him Commander Furlansk did something he very rarely had an opportunity to do. His face creased unnaturally, tugging the skin of his cheeks upwards and wrinkling around his eyes. For the first time in decades, Commander Furlansk of the Mystical Intelligence Network actually smiled.

Well, things were very, very good. The two years of careful infiltration of the Auric Triangle, the thousands of groats dropped into Ellis Dee's unsuspecting pocket and the deft manipulation of numerous ticket touts had all fallen perfectly into place. They had the hextirpator and the only wizard in fifty ells of it had been successfully distracted by the polo match.

Soon, so soon, they would have unstoppable access to magic. It was in the bag, a *fait accompli*, signed, sealed and del . . .

'Sir?' came a voice at his shoulder. 'Sir, message from Field Operative Zhaminah.'

'Yes, yes, what is it?' growled Commander Furlansk, turning on his heel.

'Don't know, sir. It's in the s . . . secure room.'

Any vestiges of Furlansk's smile vanished in that instant. Whether it was due to the nervous tremor in the messenger's voice or simply the fact that nobody ever used the Secure Room unless something had gone horribly and irrevocably wrong no one ever found out, but everyone in the sneeke room knew that in a very short time Zhaminah would sincerely wish he had taken control of his future in the only way he could and just quietly hurled himself off a suitable cliff.

Dawn had risen hours ago to an angry chorus of complaining alarm macaw, rumbling stomachs and the incessant wittering of nano-sprites.

'So what is this thing?' grumbled Quintzi Cohatl as he trudged through the now-thinning forest, waving the stolen device and trying his best to ignore the added complaints of his arthritic joints.

'That is *very* useful,' tapped the nano-sprites in his ear. Quintzi felt certain that he detected a sort of aural wry grin in the voice. It was a little more jaunty than of late; more smug, more confident.

'Well, I'd never have guessed that,' he replied sarcastically. 'You wouldn't have been *quite* that wild for anything totally useless.' Walking through breakfast and the best part of the morning had done little for the more cheerful aspects of his character. 'C'mon, tell me what it is.'

If Hogshead, four trees back on the left, had been able to hear the answer the nano-sprites were about to give then his jaw would've been scraping firmly at last season's leaf litter. Truth be told, out of all the devices known to the thaumic world at large, this was undoubtedly *the* one he needed on his side.

The nano-sprites buzzed in Quintzi's ear, full of their good fortune. 'It's a thaumic extractor.'

'Eh?'

'Purifies thaumaglobin from certain less magical sources.'

Quintzi scratched his head. That 't' word, he remembered it from somewhere. 'What sources?' he hedged.

'You've got a punnetful of them in your hand.'

'What? You're kidding? Mushrooms? You saying you can get that thaumy stuff from mushrooms, that same stuff that made me go all . . . oooooohhhhh?' He recalled the feeling he'd had after the Big Chink. The mamba-ing organs, the over-whelming springiness of youth, of being splendidly alive.

His thoughts whirled back fifty years. Oh, it had been so good then, when he'd been handsome. Okay, so his waistline was somewhat on the generous side and he hadn't been that great at sport, but . . . so what. The summers were better then. And people were friendlier. And . . .

'Gimme some!' he snapped greedily, eager to relive that past. Or if not, at least get that amazing rush again. Just think of it, all of his knowledge, everything he knew now with the feel of the body he'd had then. Oh yes, indeedy!

'Thought you wanted a scrying crystal?' mocked the nano-sprites. 'You know, glimpse the future, place those bets, sit back and reap those rewards.'

'Course I do! But, it may have escaped your notice stuck there in my ear, actually there aren't any just lying around in this forest, are there? Gimme that thaum—'

'Look ahead,' tapped the nano-sprites. 'You're nearer than you think.'

'Eh?' Quintzi squinted through the trees and there, ahead of him squatted the grimy outskirts of Fort Knumm. 'In there?' he choked. 'I left clear mountain air for . . . for that?'

'Well, if you're not bothered about scrying crystals any-more . . .'

'No, no. I mean . . . yes!'

'Well, go, go. Up through that gate, first left, second on the right . . .' And as Quintzi ran, the nano-sprites gabbled a series of directions homing him in on the little-known address of 21–21b Puce Street.

The sudden dash caught Hogshead totally unawares. Having maintained his discreet distance he hadn't realised that Quintzi was about to break cover until it was too late. One minute he was in plain sight and the next, there was only a swirling cloud of last year's leaf litter.

He had made up some ground against the arthritic Axolotian on the hill and through the rusting heap of enbeetled gates; he'd even seen him duck around to the left but then, in the twisting termitic maze of Fort Knumm's streets, he lost him.

Hogshead snarled and spat for being caught on the hop, his temper rising exponentially as he cursed the fact that he had let slip the only thing of vaguely magical interest he had come across for . . . oh, months. Stupid, stupid! His blood began to simmer, chastising him with the self-flagellatory whip of terminal frustration. How dare he have got away?

The muscles in the back of his neck readied themselves to

134

begin whacking his forehead against the nearest flat solid surface. He tugged back his head . . . And there a week of very bad headaches would have ensued had it not been for the fact that his eyes snatched at a poster pasted high on a nearby building in precisely the same way that men see the word 'sex' before anything else on a page.

The poster said;

THAUM AND GARDEN SHOW
DEMONSTRATIONS STALLS
DONKEY RIDES
YOLDE CATYCOOMS EXHYBSHONNE SENTRE AND GRYLLE
TODAY!!!

Well, it was a foregone conclusion, he simply *had* to be there.

Across the other side of town other foregone conclusions were being enacted.

'Place your bets, folks!' urged one Tedd Sert, owner of the Tedd Sert Wagering Emporium in downtown Fort Knumm. Desperately, he tried to avoid a note of pleading. He failed.

'C'mon you tight-fisted gits, stick a few groats on the next race!' he cajoled.

'Lend us a few and we will,' grumbled a ragged figure standing in a clump of similarly attired vagrants filling the trading area of the Wagering Emporium.

'Oh yeah, sure I will,' argued Tedd Sert sarcastically. 'And I'll slash my wrists for your entertainment later on, too. With matinées if you want.'

'Oooh, would you?'

'It's a good job I'm not as stupid as you think I look!' he cried from the far side of a little grille, his bald pate glistening with sweat. 'Stick some bets on the four-fifteen, will you? C'mon, I'm not a charity!' It had been yet another profitless day. If business was any slacker, it would unravel. 'C'mon. I need your cash.'

'Er, I haven't got any,' grumbled a shoddy-looking gambler.

'Tell you what though, if you let me have ten groats I'll stick . . .'

'. . . stick it on a dead cert and you'll pay me back from your winnings,' snarled Sert. 'No way! You tried that one last week, remember? C'mon, one of you must have something to lose – er, offer.'

'Well, I . . .' came another voice and the crowd parted as an arthritic bundle of rags crept slowly forward. 'I've got this,' he croaked, holding out a rusty quarter-groat coin.

Before he could explain that he had been saving it for a rainy day and an outsider that could surf, the hand of Tedd Sert had shot out of a panel in the wall, snatched the coin and vanished. Randomly he hurled it on the nose of Timorous Beastie in the four-fifteen. There was a clattering of locks as the coin was tossed into a large box and sealed away from prying hands.

Swiftly Tedd Sert scribbled out a parchment slip and flung it through his grille, just as the front door was kicked open and a man with a truncheon, dungarees and a polo-neck sweater surged inside followed by fifteen similarly clad thugs.

'Afternoon!' chirped Arch Sergeant Strappado as he strode towards the tiny grille. Tedd Sert began to sweat faster and the knot of gamblers swiftly unravelled.

'Just a routine visit, sir,' growled Strappado ominously. 'Thought I'd pop in and see if everything was nice and peaceful around here lately?' he asked through the grille and flashed a mirthless grin at Sert.

'Oh yes . . . y, yes, everything's fine and d . . . dandy!'

'Excellent! No hint of robbery or murder or casual assassination?' insinuated Strappado.

'N . . . not a whisper,' gulped Sert, trying to push the heavy box marked 'takings' out of sight.

'Hear that, boys?' shouted Strappado at the band of men he had led in. 'Everything's all peace and lovely soothing tranquillity!' Then he whirled around, sneered and stared into the very marrow of Sert's body. 'And why d'you think that is, eh? Why's everything so lovely and hunky-dory, hmmm?'

'B . . . b . . . because of the s . . . splendid work of you and y . . . your boys?' he stuttered in terror.

'Exactly!' declared Strappado. 'Me and my boys keep everything running just so. Pounding the beat tirelessly, locking up anyone I find offensive, ridding the streets of any unwanted elements! All very expensive, highly skilled work, don't you think?'

'I . . . I suppose you would get through a lot of boot leather,' offered Sert pathetically.

'Tons of it. Tons. My boys really pound when they pound, you know. D'you know just how much boot leather costs these days, hmmm?' growled Strappado. 'Not cheap y'know.'

'No . . . I d . . . don't suppose it is.'

'Care to take a bet as to just how really expensive it is, eh? Y'know, what'll it cost to keep a whole division in nice comfy hobnails for, say, a whole month?'

'Er, I'd rather not speculate on . . . uuuurgh!'

Strappado's arm flashed through the grille and snatched Sert firmly by the throat. 'Wrong answer,' he growled. 'Try again!'

'Uuuurgh, twenty . . .' croaked Sert.

The fingers on Strappado's left hand flicked slightly in an upward direction.

'Thuuuurghty?' spluttered Sert.

Strappado tutted and shook his head. 'There *are* fifteen of them. Count them! Big lads like that'll need more than two groats each for running costs to keep this level of protection up.'

'Hundred?' offered Sert.

'Closer,' encouraged Strappado with a brief clenching of his right hand.

'Hundred and fiffffff . . .' whispered Sert, his face turning worryingly blue.

'Two hundred groats a month!' declared Strappado, shouting the words over Sert's gasping. 'Correct! And what's that?' he asked, making a great show of listening to the mouthings of Sert's last few breaths, like an amateur puppeteer alternately listening then answering coyly. 'Oh no, I couldn't,' he grinned. 'It's very generous of you but no . . . You insist? . . . Well . . . It'll be your immeasurable pleasure, will it? . . . Well, if you insist. On behalf of my boys and I, I would gladly accept your gift of two hundred groats in recognition of our outstanding service! Hand it over!'

Officer Drub burst through a side door, prised open the wooden box labelled 'takings' and tugged out two hundred groats with a grin, hurled it swiftly into a vast sack of the day's gifts and turned on his heel.

In a matter of seconds Arch Sergeant Strappado was back on the street and heading towards Lore Enforcement Agency Headquarters, his heart pounding eagerly for this evening's rendezvous at Ye Silver Spittoone.

There were some things he really enjoyed about being a part of the Lore Enforcement Agency: the element of meeting the public and shaking them warmly by the throats. It gave one such a feeling of the overwhelming appreciation the residents had for them, made him feel that community-funded policing really was worth while. All right, so he did have to remind some of them a bit with his trusty knuckledusters and pokers, but that just added to the piquant pleasure of it all.

But above all that there was the joyous opportunity not only to rid the kingdom of some damned scum-ridden conjurist saboteur but to thrill to the task as well. Tonight was personal! And he couldn't wait. Grinning inside he stomped around the corner and dreamt of a promotion to Mystical Intelligence.

At that very moment, high in the ageing rafters of the Wagering Emporium there was a flutter of wings, a rapid deceleration and a pigeon landed on a small perch, setting off a tinkling bell in Tedd Sert's office. Reflexively, he snatched at a dangling rope and tugged hard. Above him, the perch collapsed and a large net scooped up the pigeon and hurled it down a waiting tube. Several squawks and rattles later the pigeon was dumped unceremoniously on Sert's desk looking bewildered, and not a little ruffled. His hand snatched out, grabbed the bird and tore the results of the four-fifteen out of the small pouch strapped to its leg.

Summoned by the tinkling bell the mob of gamblers had gathered expectantly to hear the winner. As Tedd Sert's face fell in horror a cheer went up from the crowd, counterpointed by the percussive sound of a single back being heartily slapped.

Miserably Sert paid out his last ten groats to the lucky swine waving the stub of his betting slip proclaiming that he had Timorous Beastie down for a win.

Sert cursed painfully under his breath. Maybe tomorrow would be better.

'Would you care to run that by me again,' whispered Commander Furlansk of the Mystical Intelligence Network ominously as he listened to the thin voice issuing through the grille on the desk of the Secure Room. It was always a bad sign for anyone when he started to be polite, normally the last few calm seconds before a storm of wild anger.

'It . . . it's gone.'

'Where? How? Who?' bellowed the grey-clad one wildly, his temper slipping the reins of calmness and galloping away across the emotional horizon scattering sods of placidity to the four winds. His hands grasped at the speaker grille, fingers twisting the fine wrought iron into mangled unrecognisability.

'I d . . . don't know . . .' gagged the thin voice around his frenzied twisting.

'Which question is that an answer to?' barked Commander Furlansk above the squeal of fatigued metal.

'Er . . . all of them,' confessed the quivering voice of Zhaminah.

'That's not good enough!' The grey-clad one slammed his fist on to the desk with a painful scrunching of bone and exploded from his chair. For a brief second he was relieved that the Secure Room was soundproof; the osseous crunching as he reset his metacarpals was far louder than he had anticipated. As was his unprecedented screaming and hurling of any furniture that wasn't fastened down.

'I'm sorry,' came Zhaminah's disembodied voice. 'I seem to be getting some interference. Sounds like someone's hurling furniture around in a very enclosed space. Can you hear it your end?'

'NO!' Furlansk panted as the chair looped over the desk once more and ricocheted off the far wall. 'All I can hear is your excuses. And they're not good enough. Not good enough at all.

Have you any idea of how much we have invested in this? Research? Cash? The time? Get me some answers. Or preferably get the damned thing back. Dismissed!'

Furlansk severed the link, flung the chair back over the desk, hurled himself into it and massaged the pounding artery in his forehead.

Gone! He couldn't believe it. But who had it? Where had it gone? Merlot was still under surveillance, safely out of the way in a locked box at the polo tournament.

Commander Furlansk's forehead hit the desk with a dull woe-filled thud. It had been so near. So close and yet . . .

Damn Zhaminah, he'd pay if he didn't find the hextirpator. And not just financially.

It was down one of the darker, damper and less well appointed sub-alleys of Yolde Catycooms Exhybshonne Sentre and Grylle that a certain rotund boy stamped, seething with the tensioned energy of an overwound grandfather clock. His mouth worked with the furious irritation of what felt like long months spent on learning trivial botanical magic, his mind whirled at the gross unfairness of it all. How dare Merlot have treated him as if he was nothing but a pathetic helpless child, feeding him pre-digested snippets of diluted magic as if there wasn't much of it about? It was sheer stupidity. He was much more than that. He, Hogshead, had left all the squealing ineptitude of irresponsible childhood far behind. He could hold his head high now, walk tall and swagger proudly, for he was a teenager.

He'd seen life and he'd seen magic. Big magic. Eight-foot frog-sized magic with teeth and claws to match. High-energy Thaumatron magic with appropriate sparks and messy time travel. Oh yes, he'd experienced magic first hand, grabbed it firmly by the throat and taken charge.* After all, it was he who

---

*Unfortunately for Hogshead, this was yet another source of irritation. The only people he could share knowledge of that particular adventure with were Firkin, Courgette, Dawn and Merlot since it involved secret information of a very sensitive nature which, by all rights, should have remained firmly within the walls of Losa Llamas. But since his co-adventurers were respectively far more interested in chatting about the politics of Cranachan, swordhandling and its importance in the

had conjured Merlot up from the Chapter Dimensions in the first place. Okay, so he'd had a bit of help from a three-quarter-inch talking bookworm but all magicians need a bit of help now and then, didn't they?

And now, after all of that rubbing shoulders with the most potent of powers in myriad guises, what did he personally have to show for it all? What stunning works of thaumic amazement could he weave, eh? What earth-shaking demonstrations of practical jiggery-pokery, aesthetic allurement or just plain wickedly wonderful wizardry could he avail himself of, hmmm? Silently, against a boiling backdrop of seething anger, he cursed as he listed his multiple talents.

He was not, he sadly had to admit, very impressed. To what use could he possibly put the immensely valuable feat of tadpole herding? When would he ever need to know one useful thing to do with a crested newt? Let alone twenty-three? And the day he needed a demonstration of no-handed armadillo juggling was destined to be a sad one indeed.

Armed with such an arsenal there would be no stopping him if it came to hand to hand scrapping in all-out war. Without a shadow of doubt, all enemies would perish at his hands or run screaming with absolute terror before him as he emerged from a banner-strewn and bloody chaos tossing exoskeletoned anteaters willy-nilly with gay abandon . . . I don't think.

Well all that was about to change. Soon he'd have some decent spells under his belt. He was surrounded by them. The stalls of the Thaum and Garden Show stretched away into the gloom offering all manner of different services, far too many of which seemed to revolve around rockeries for his liking.

He had waited plenty long enough for any fruit to appear on the parched vines of Merlot's promises. Now it was time to take things into his own hands. Time to get things done. He flipped open the parchment guide to stall holders and rubbed a grubby finger down the list of contributors.

And then, amazed, he recognised a name. There, on stall

emancipation of women, the entertainment value of worms and the appropriate use of spells than anything to do with the Frogs of War, he didn't get very much jaw exercise on that topic.

141

twenty-seven, was one of his childhood heroes, the King of the Magic Circuit . . . Ye Great Entranco.

An adrenal thrill of untold possibilities twitched through his arteries. Just around that next corner, less than a hundred yards away was a stall offering all the magic he would ever need. And all at the right price. He knew this to be the absolute truth, the advert said so.

Excitedly, feeling as if he was teetering on the very brink of momentous eventdom and knowing that in a matter of minutes he could be clutching everything necessary for any of . . . ooh, dozens of spells, he tugged down the front of his tunic, strode purposefully round the corner and stared at the curtain-covered stall sporting a faded sign proclaiming

YE GREAT ENTRANCO
CASH, CARRY AND CONJURE!

Hogshead shoved open the curtain, fear and squeamishness kicked into touch by the overwhelming desire for magic.

It took a few moments for his eyes to adjust to the pungent gloom. Candle burners filled shelves in the cluttered store-room-cum-stall, cheerfully igniting something that smelt like it had once been an incense of questionable pedigree before it had been cut with two parts Rhabian dogweed* and three parts stable-scrapings. It had.

'Whad'you want,' snapped a deep voice from a dense shadow.

Hogshead jumped in alarm, took a sharp breath and instantly regretted it. Sharp claws of desiccating smoke rasped the back of his throat and he collapsed in a fit of coughing. Ten minutes later when the racket had subsided, the shadow asked again.

Hogshead drew himself up to his full height, peered into the shadow and, by way of answer, choked, 'Ye Great Entranco.'

*Rhabian dogweed. An ancient source of much pleasure amongst the narcotic-starved nomads of Rhabia. An evil-smelling shrub when alive the dogweed, when harvested, dried and lit retains this property to the full and has the unfortunate habit of offending all but the most aromatically challenged of nostrils. It is said to be 'an acquired taste'.

142

The shadow exploded in a fit of derisive laughter. 'He expectin' you?'

'No, but I'm expectin' to see him!' Hogshead instinctively knew that this was the way to talk to people of a bouncerish nature. He's seen these types in the magic lantern theatres in full 80-millimetre Superthaumination. 'Where is he?'

'You got an appointment?'

'Do I need one . . . ?' he answered with the merest twinkle of what he hoped looked more like arrogance than the effects of the Rhabian dogweed. 'Where's Ye Great Entranco? I wanna deal,' gurgled Hogshead, wishing his voice had broken properly.

The shadow made a strange grumbling sound, spread mysteriously across the wall, twisted a handle and pushed open a door which up until that moment had been passing itself off nicely thank-you very much as a set of shelves. Amazingly the room which lurked beyond was even gloomier and jammed tighter with dense incense and dogweed fumes. Hogshead wondered if he should have brought a knife to hack his way through the swampy atmosphere. 'Sit!' commanded the shadow and pointed to a fuzzy lump in the floor which, if he squinted out of the corner of his eye, Hogshead could just recognise as a pouffe. Reluctantly, the first cracks beginning to show in his resolve, Hogshead sat.

'What willst thou?' cackled a different voice once the echoes of whoopee cushion and raucous laughter had faded.

'Magic,' replied Hogshead and was instantly annoyed at the childishly wheedling tone that had crept into his voice. 'Gimme some magic!' he shouted in as angry a voice as he could muster.

'Ha!' So thou seekest magic, I surmise! What willst be thine calling? Really dangerous spells and charms to curdle the very life bloo— No! ha ha! Thou seekest wonders to poppeth the eyes of audiences. Am I correct?'

'Oooh, yes plea . . . Yeah! Get it!' Silently, through clenched teeth Hogshead cursed himself. They'd never say anything like 'Oooh yes please' in 80-millimetre Superthaumination. 'Bring it here! Show it to me!' he added in a tone which he hoped could be described as imposing. 'I want your best!'

'Hmmm, ye bestest, eh? Thee'd better have lotsa doshings, lots and lots of cash. Knowest thou, boys and girls, imports aren't of the cheapest! Especially if you wants an assistant, too. Anyone from the audience'll do . . . oops.'

'Assistant?' coughed Hogshead, scowling suspiciously and peering into the gloom as a cloud of confusion started to form. 'Familiar, surely?' His mind formed an image of Clint Machismo, the magic lantern star, as he caught the first glimpse of a sniff of a lie. Hopefully he tried to form his facial muscles into some passing similarity, attempting to impress Ye Great Entranco with his knowledge of magic and procedure. The gloom of the room made it less effective.

'Yea, verily, of course. They're all familiar with even the most complex workings of every item, essential knowledge to preventeth acciden . . . What wouldst thou have me perform . . . er, demonstrate first?'

Hogshead grinned with excitement in the gloom as he recalled the list on the parchment advert. Now what had sounded interesting?

'Show me the "Casket of Swords"!'

'Ha! Ye "Casket of Swords", is it? Death-defyinge perils brought to you in ye comfort of thine own home. Watch in awe as I plungeth these eight swords, these razor-sharp swords, please feeleth free to check them sire, as I plunge them through my beautiful assistant's nubile body without drawing the slightest drop of bloo—'

'Show me!'

'Can't. Being repaired, quick release lever's up the spout,' muttered Ye Great Entranco quickly, shaking his head as if to dislodge something painful. Then he continued more confidently, 'What else wouldst thou have me enact . . . er, display?'

Hogshead scratched his chin and only briefly wondered precisely what a high-level spell would be doing with a quick release lever. 'Reveal to me the secrets of the "Ottoman of 'Orrors"!'

A hollow tone wrapped itself around Ye Great Entranco's

voice as he answered. 'Ye "Ottoman of 'Orrors", is it? Well, ladies, gentlemen, boys and girls, here is a treat to stupefy and shock. Contained within ye walls of thys box are perylls and curses to make ye hardiest of Pandoras weep and faint. For thine delight and delectation, here for tonight and one night only, I, Ye Great Entranco, can reveal these misfyts of alchemistry to you . . .'

'Reveal it!' enthused Hogshead, his eyes popping and itching with the aroma of dogweed.

There was a muffled curse in the gloom. 'Choose again. I'm, er, fresh out of "Ottoman's of 'Orrors". What about card tricks? Or filling cones of newsparchment with milk, eh? Oh, I know, what about animism kits, eh? You know, making animals out of inflated pigs' bladders? That always goes down a treat at parties, especially if you get the kids to blow them up first. Sure-fire hit. Fetch the catalogue and demo box, Ygor.' There was a low grunt of assent and the shelf-door creaked open.

Hogshead snarled and muttered something very unsavoury under his breath, shifting uncomfortably and noisily on the whoopee-cushioned pouffe.

'Don't you fancy any of them?' asked Ye Great Entranco, beginning to wonder about this customer's lack of appreciation of his flatulent wares. 'They're some of my most popular lines, but if you're looking for something a bit more . . .'

'Where's the "Tomb of Termination", Entranco?' shouted Hogshead, losing his patience as another volley of unwarranted raspberries launched themselves from his nether regions.

'The "Tomb . . ." Aha, what of it?' spluttered the figure in the gloom, in a voice that sounded oddly panicky. Hogshead got the distinct impression that Ye Great Entranco desperately wanted to race around the room barring and bolting anything that could open.

'The "Tomb of Termination". I want to see it!' growled Hogshead, rapidly tiring of this farrago. At that point he would have sworn that the ravens of defeat were circling above, readying themselves for a carrion feast of gutted hopes.

'It's been too long . . . I . . . I . . .' began the wizard, panic highlighting the edges of his words.

Questions, like startled pigeons, exploded into the rarefied atmosphere of Hogshead's mind clucking and begging to be asked. He opened his mouth but, at that very moment, the door creaked open again and Ygor burst in with a blazing candle and large wooden trunk tucked under his vast armpit. He would have looked for all the world like some boy making off with an illicitly gained piglet had it not been for the fact that he was the better part of seven foot tall in his stockinged tootsies.

But it was the sight of the wizard that really snatched at Hogshead's attention. Cold eyes peering terrifyingly out of a stark, death-white face. Talon-like hands curling and uncurling rhythmically around a crimson glowing carved staff of power. Sigils and runes of evil power crackling and fizzing across the surface of his inchoate robes.

Hogshead would've been overjoyed if Ye Great Entranco had been blessed with just one of them. He stared in totally heartfelt disappointment at the cloth-capped man in matching cardigan and slippers.

'You're no wizard!' shouted Hogshead, leaping to his feet and pointing accusingly.

'Am so!'

'Then where's your robes, eh?'

'Er . . . I, at the cleaner's. Ygor?'

There was a low grumbling of affirmation.

'Well, then, show me the "Tomb of Termination"!' blurted Hogshead suddenly beginning to doubt the veracity of the advertisement torn bodily from the guide which supposedly promised 'Magicks and Mystreyes to Boggle the Mynd! Booke early to avoyde ye dysappoyntement!' He didn't get the answer he might have expected.

There was a yell, a wild rustling of clothes and the hands of the cloth-capped Entranco snatched Hogshead around the throat. The voice snapped hard into his ear as the stranglehold tightened. 'Who are you? Why d'you want the "Tomb of T . . . Termination"?'

'Ow, that hurts!' whimpered Hogshead.

'That's nothing to what the . . . the Tomb can do!'

'I just liked the name,' gasped Hogshead, writhing for the second time in far too few minutes.

'The name? Yes, they always liked the name,' whispered the voice, now edged with the madness of a grief-stricken past. 'It was always the favourite. Went down a storm every time. They lapped it up, screaming for more. Screaming. Screaming! But no, never again will I perform the "Tomb", not since . . .'

'Since what?' croaked Hogshead, his pulse throbbing in his neck. 'Not since what?'

Ye Great Entranco made a hideous gulping noise as if he was fighting a losing battle with a vicious gang of ruthless emotions. 'No, no. Not since . . . Benji!'

All it needed was a dramatic series of tumbling chords and the scene would've been B-movie perfection. They never came.

'Benji?' spluttered Hogshead, wrestling with bewildered disbelief in the now stark silence.

'That damn rabbit . . . I barely escaped with my life!' sobbed Entranco pathetically and then suddenly stopped. 'That's why you're here, isn't it? *He* sent you?' His grip tightened around Hogshead's throat.

'What? No! And who? In that order. Get off!' he croaked.

'You're from Strappado?'

'Who?' gulped Hogshead, his mind whirring.

'I knew I couldn't hide for ever,' spluttered the cloth-capped great one now quivering with terror as he released Hogshead's throat. 'Bound to catch me sooner or later. Well, make it quick. Is your sword sharp? Don't make me suffer any longer, please.'

Hogshead scratched his head in utter confusion.

'Don't you think I've suffered enough these last years?' continued the silhouette, falling to its knees and pleading. 'The fear that every customer would be my last, or that maybe that innocent-looking six-year-old's birthday party was a trap. Months I've lived in fear of this moment, the terror of revenge. And the nightmares. Every night I see it all over and over again. I'd done it a thousand times before. Laughing terribly as the birthday girl straps her pet into the Tomb of Termination, egged on by the party guests, nobody believing that you can

147

saw the wretched pet in half before their eyes and have it emerge moments later unscathed. The sadistic laughter . . . all part of the act, all in the cause of entertainment. Why didn't I check the release catch? It all might have been so different. Oh, why that night? Why did it have to be Strappado's niece's cutesy fluffy bunny under the axe?'

Hogshead shrugged: a gesture somewhat lost in the subdued lighting.

'It wasn't my fault,' begged Ye Great Entranco, rapidly approaching hysteria. 'The trapdoor release. That damned rabbit's tail caught in the trapdoor release! The axe wouldn't have hit if it hadn't caught . . . Oh the blood! The guts. The screaming!'

And with that Ye Great Entranco collapsed in a sobbing heap.

'I think it's time you left,' growled Ygor, looming ominously.

'What about my magic?' whined Hogshead.

'You won't find anything you want here,' insisted Ygor, snatching Hogshead's arm and propelling him towards the door.

A peal of sobbing poured from the lungs of the once Great Entranco. 'He could've been the best,' growled Ygor. 'He'll never perform the "Tomb of Termination" again. But for that one slip he'd have been a hovelhold name. Had it all planned out, next week it would've been. In seven days he would've made history. The only man to make Mahtelloh Tower disappear!'

'Yeah, yeah, very touching I'm sure. But where does that leave me, eh? Where am I goin' to get any real magic?' moaned Hogshead as he was ejected through the insect-eaten entrance.

'But you can catch him on stage tonight at Ye Silver Spittoone!' added Ygor cheerfully. 'Whole new show, some amazing transmogrification spells . . .'

Hogshead, his illusions shattered, trudged away barely seeing any of the other stalls.

Deep in the wriggling labyrinth of Losa Llamas a heavy oak

door creaked open, and Uhrnest the guard-cum-porter struggled through hauling a large cart laden with strange and interesting-looking parcels and packages.

'I'm back,' he grunted beneath a veritable torrent from his sweating brow.

Phlim leapt up from a heap of high-energy thaumatronics like a meerkat spotting a hyena. He tossed a strand of hair out of his eyes, squealed with delight and sprang over the desk, his lab-cloak flapping behind him.

'Did you get everything?' he squeaked.

Uhrnest nodded and solemnly wished he hadn't. It would have been a stack easier to haul back if some of the heavier items had been temporarily out of stock.

'Even the pattern recognition crystals?'

'Yeah,' grunted Uhrnest. 'They was on special offer, buy two and get a free runic alignment board.'

'You little angel. I could kiss you!'

'Eeurgh, I'd rather you didn't.'

'Have a beer, then,' enthused Phlim as he leapt on to the cart and burrowed eagerly through the boxes, his heart racing wildly. The weeks of work had been worth it. His pulse fizzed excitedly as he ran his hands over the stocks they said would never arrive. But here it was, the culmination of weeks of work. Without the manufacture of the scrying crystals, their sale, the purchase of lead piping and its subsequent conversion into far more valuable gold he would never have found the necessary cash to fund this project.

'Just help yourself,' added Phlim to Uhrnest as an after-thought, pointing to a large barrel at the far side of the junk-filled laboratory.

Uhrnest needed no second bidding. In seconds he had snatched a leather flagon off a shelf, shoved it under the tap and turned it enthusiastically. For a moment nothing happened, then suddenly there was a massive bubbling sound, the barrel trembled and violently frothing ale erupted from the tap at great velocity, splashing everywhere and drenching the hapless guard.

'Damn, damn, damn!' cried Phlim. 'Still too much incantium dioxide in that widget. One day I will achieve that authentic draught taste from a barrel. Still,' he mused as he stared at the froth-covered silhouette of Uhrnest, 'it's got a good head.'

Noting this fact somewhere in the capacious recesses of his mind Phlim snapped his attention back to the pile of boxes and within a few seconds had snatched up a vital package, leapt off the cart and scurried back to the mass of peculiar crystals, pentagrammatic circuit boards and runic oscillators upon which he was currently working.

Uhrnest licked cautiously at the rapidly clotting froth, smacked his lips appreciatively and tucked into the world's first man-size helping of real ale mousse.

The technical wizard's hands darted from wire loom to thaumistor, plugging here, connecting there, fusing the newly purchased pattern recognition crystals into the untidy mass and standing back to admire it all. He had to admit it, it didn't look much, but there before him was yet another stunning breakthrough in the field of thaumaturgy, the latest triumph of magic over nature, just one more stroke of sheer genius. He just hoped it would work.

So did the secretive observer ells away, watching the entire scene through the crystal-clear compound eyes of a MIN sneeke. He looked over his shoulder at a matching heap of wirelooms and pentagrammatic circuit boards and sighed. If the thaumaturgical physicists' version worked better than the version they already had then he might bother completing it. Otherwise they'd make do with the thirty-year-old model. He shook his head and chuckled, laughing at the pathetic filing system and short memories the thaumaturgical physicists had. Didn't any of them remember having invented an almost identical device three decades ago? Obviously not. 'Keeping watch,' he told himself. 'Eyes peeled in case this one comes up with a striking innovation.'

In Losa Llamas, Phlim leaned forward, grabbed two trailing wires, wrapped each firmly around the terminals of a square black box and flicked a switch. Immediately power surged out from the duraspell battery,* flooded through the thaumic circuits and lit an array of tiny red bulbs. Thrilling visibly Phlim reached out, snatched a large painting of a rune and held it in front of the pair of recognition crystals. The device rattled and whirred, clucked to itself thoughtfully and then lit a single green bulb. Phlim leapt for joy, snatched another card and held this in the same way. The device lit a red bulb in response and Phlim leapt even higher. There was no doubting it: the thing worked.

All he had to do now was connect the output to a steering circuit instead of two useless bulbs, mount the whole thing in that chassis over by the far wall, cover it with the pod-like body and it was ready.

In minutes he had done almost all this and more, for outside, strewn about the passages was a series of odd rune-bearing cards, arranged like the breadcrumbs of a lost child's forestry trail.

It was just as Phlim was tightening down the cover with his psychic screwdriver and Uhrnest was tucking into another pint of ale mousse that Practz burst into the lab.

'Might've known it would be something to do with you!' he sighed, waving one of the runic cards. 'What's the meaning of this, eh?'

'Ah, Practz, you're just in time. Would you like the honour?'

'What honour?'

---

*Rumours abounded as to the superior power values of duraspell batteries over the conventional hex-acid types. And so, in two widely publicised contests, between alternatively powered state-of-the-art virtual ecology creations, the truth was sought. In the first, two tap-dancing wallabies were set loose simultaneously on a wooden dance floor. Sadly, the incessant rattling of heels on polished mahogany chewed unbearably on the tester's nerves and resulted in the untimely destruction of said wallabies beneath the tester's size twelves.

In the second trial, two virtual penguins were set loose upon the waters of Lake Hellarwyl, the one to reach the far shore first being deemed the one supplied by the finer power source. All was going well for the duraspell penguin, its flippers thrashing energetically away from the hex-acid penguin, but two-thirds of the way across, disaster struck. It was sixty-three feet long and hadn't been seen in decades. 'Hetty' the Lake Hellarwyl Monster terminated the trials prematurely by erupting from the peat-soiled depths and devouring the pair of virtual penguins in a couple of minor chomps. Having spent all their advertising budgets on such sad escapades the battery companies gave up. Even to this day nobody is entirely certain which is the better thaumic power source.

'You can be the first passenger in this!' Phlim moved out of the way and swept his hands expansively over the low-slung three-wheeled contraption squatting on the floor. Practz stared at the torpedo-like body with a tiny raised windscreen and scratched his head. 'What is it?' he asked with trepidation. He'd known Phlim long enough to be sure that where his inventions were concerned appearances were normally deceptive.

'It's the greatest advance in transport that Losa Llamas has ever seen . . .' began Phlim.

The MIN observer chuckled to himself.

'Spare me the rhetoric,' grunted Practz. 'What's it do?'

'Takes you anywhere in Losa Llamas you want.'

'Oh, just like legs,' grunted Practz underwhelmed as ever.

'Faster, with far less effort and in stacks more comfort. Sit in, I'll show you.'

'Well, I, er . . .'

'Surely you aren't going to turn down the chance to be the first passenger?' oozed Phlim who knew seventeen out of the twenty-one sure-fire ways to get Practz doing anything he wanted. It was fortunate he didn't know the other four since they were either far too expensive or arrestable offences.

Faced with the double-edged prongs of being accused of cowardice *and* missing out on a groundbreaking thaumic event, Practz climbed into the snug cockpit as Phlim took the runic card and laid it on a table behind him.

'Er, shouldn't it have something to steer with? Reins or something?'

'Aha! No. That is the beauty of the runicycle!'

'The what?' Practz exclaimed. The MIN observer grinned to himself. Thought so, he mused and leant forward; it's even got the same name. 'Wonder if it's as good as the model we've been running around on.'

'That,' pointed Phlim. 'The runicycle guides itself, responding to these instructions scattered in a cunning pattern around the corridors. It sees this—' he held up a card – 'and it turns left. This and it turns right, that and it stops, see?' he added, pointing to the card he had just taken from Practz and placed on the table.

Practz nodded, feeling surprised that he was actually impressed.

'Never again,' continued Phlim, 'will Uhrnest there have to haul heavy loads through the miles of passageway. A runicycle could easily be made to haul a cart.'

Uhrnest raised an appreciative flagon of mousse and hiccupped noisily. It seemed the bubbles were going to his head.

'A brief circular demonstration run has been set up, so if you are ready?' asked Phlim. Practz nodded. Phlim flicked a switch and stood back. The runicycle hummed into life and leapt forward, its pattern recognition crystals scouring the floor two feet ahead of it, searching for instructions. In a second it was out of the door, Practz squealing with terror and shocked delight in the manner normally associated with teenage girls at the top of immense rollercoasters. The runicycle's crystals spied a rune, identified it correctly and commanded the steering for a sharp left. The torpedo-like tricycle screeched through the door, whistled around 90 degrees and zipped off down the passage with Practz still squealing madly and an unseen sneeke in hot pursuit. Time after unexpected time the runicycle snatched sideways as other instruction cards flashed into view, were processed and acted upon. Less than a minute after cannoning out of the laboratory Practz and the runicycle were screaming back towards it, having completed the mile-long circuit perfectly. It scanned the last rune, veered right and shot through the lab door. It was then that things began to go horribly wrong. Instead of re-entering the cavern, applying its brakes at the given signal and rolling to a relaxing halt, it thundered through the door at full tilt, raced under the table and hit the far wall with a sickening crash, a tinkling of shattering thaumatronics and a scream of rage from Practz.

As the dust settled Phlim heard the terrifying sound of Practz's teeth gnashing mercilessly as he hauled himself from the tangled wreckage.

A hand sprang out of the swirling cloud, snatched Phlim by

the throat and its owner bellowed, 'Stop, you said! You told me it would stop!'

'Yes, yes, when it sees that rune, over there,' choked Phlim pointing frantically behind him.

'That one on the table,' growled Practz.

'Yes, yes!'

'How's it supposed to see it up there?' snarled Practz as bits of runicycle fell from his hair.

'Ah. I see your point,' whimpered Phlim.

The thudding sound of his head repeatedly striking the table echoed beautifully down the passageway.

The MIN agent chuckled again and abandoned work on this model of the runicycle.


Panting in the deepest, darkest part of a tiny alley, just upwind of Ye Silver Spittoone, Arch Sergeant Strappado checked his false nose, beard and glasses and snarled. A heady mixture of anger and terror surged through his body. Images of that night two years ago bombarded his memory, fuelling the anger; the knowledge of what would happen to his major organs should he be recognised fuelling his terror. He shuddered at the thought of what would happen if any one of Ye Spit's clientele saw through his disguise. Arch Sergeant Strappado knew with alarming certainty that there wouldn't be anyone within that infamous low spot who hadn't either been arrested, or had a brother who had been arrested, or had heard of someone whose brother's dog had been arrested by his very own long lore-enforcing arms. It could get very messy if he was rumbled.

Fleetingly Strappado wished he had his usual complement of fifteen armed constables as back-up and cursed. He knew that couldn't be: this was private, this was for him, this was a chance he couldn't afford to miss. And besides, he couldn't afford to bribe them on their night off.

He took a deep breath and slunk out of the shadows, oozing down the alley towards the doorway, past the hastily scrawled blackboard message declaring that

And as he shoved open the door and was hit square in the face by the Atmosphere, his thoughts raced back two years to that fateful night.

Ye Spit had been exactly the same then as it was now, jammed with revelling cutthroats, assassins, murderers and tax inspectors fleecing each other in a thousand different ways, swigging vast flagons of Hexenhammer, snorting huge amounts of exceedingly illegal narcotics and all beneath the over-affectionate fug of dense fumes which inhabited that hostelry ever since the fans had packed up. Now the Atmosphere in Ye Spit was legendary, not least for its unnerving habit of grinning unexpectedly at the unwary from distant corners. It had once been just the type of air content to mess people's hair on balmy afternoons by the river, or rarely strip a dandelion clock for sheer devilry. But they were the days before the years of enforced company with the clientele of Ye Spit introduced it to the heady pleasures of alcohol and other more flavoursome narcotics. It learned fast. It knew the signs of a brewing argument, the delightful tension seconds before a fight and it was always there, Cheshire-cat grinning in darkened corners, no longer just air . . . now fully fledged Atmosphere.

But two years ago there had been a difference. Instead of being alone, as he was tonight, Strappado had entered with a companion similarly attired in long shapeless cloak of nondescript brown, floppy hat obscuring most of the face and matching false nose, beard and glasses, the best he could do at short notice. He had tried to talk her out of it, but she had insisted.

The hubbub in the bar had dropped a few decibels into the realms of merely painful as the regulars had cast wary eyes over the newcomers. Even the Atmosphere had raised a wisp of a curious gossamer eyebrow and swooped over for a closer look. Almost as one, the less ethereal occupants of the bar

155

clapped eyes on the obvious disguises, shrugged and turned back to the particular brand of swigging, fleecing, snorting or murdering in which they had previously been engaged. Anyone, they reasoned, that desperate for disguises must be in real trouble, and anyone in that much trouble must be a real criminal type and therefore eminently qualified to sup in Ye Spit. The Atmosphere wasn't so sure. There was something missing on one of them, now what was it? Ahhh yes . . . facial hair.

Strappado had led his wife Viv to a suitable table, removing two comatose revellers with a swift boot, and headed off to the bar. Moments later he had returned with two frothing flagons of Hexenhammer.

'Where's my Naildriver?' snapped Viv as Strappado had placed the ale before her.

'Ssssh!' he urged. 'Look, I told you, hardened criminals don't drink cocktails! Just shut up and wait for the m . . . mmm . . . the show!' The Atmosphere pulled up a plume of smoke and settled closer to the newcomers, sensing the oddly conflicting moods, one buzzing with thrilling anticipation, the other quivering with terror. If the Atmosphere had been able to peer inside Strappado's mind it would've seen constant replays of his last experience of a magic show splattered with the final few seconds of a piebald rabbit's existence.

'Humph. You could've got an umbrella in it,' snorted Viv, staring at her flagon. 'It looks sort of bare, don't you think?'

'Be quiet, dear,' growled Strappado.

*Dear?* pondered the Atmosphere. In all its years in Ye Spit it had never heard one customer call another dear. Well except for the pair of arch-criminals known as the Proscenium Twins, but they were thespians, they didn't count. Always calling each other luvvie, or darling, or some such sickening epithet.

'Just hush, dear,' continued Strappado. 'We don't want to attract attention to ourselves, do we? I only smuggled you in 'cos of the show tonight. You know the rules in here about women.'

'Damn sexists,' snarled Viv. 'I tell you, this place needs a woman's touch. Brighten it up a bit, few flowers here and there, scatter cushions, curtains . . .'

Fortunately, before she had the chance to get into the full swing of an interior make-over, the lights dimmed – an event greeted with a flurry of shady parcels being handed over in return for pouches of cash – and Skroht'm, the barman, banged on the bar for hush.

'Gentlemen!' he croaked in a voice unused to yelling anything but 'Time Gentlemen Please!', and then only very rarely, 'It's my great pleasure t'introduce f'your delight an' stuff, the one, the only, Ye Great Entranco!'

Ye Spit was filled with a tumultuous round of apathy and nose-wiping, a state which would have been shattered by Viv had not Strappado grabbed her wrists and prevented her jamming her fingers in her mouth and launching several large blasts of appreciative whistling. There was no doubt about it, she was excited. She loved magic shows and here she was right on the front row, keen for a dextrous display of prestidigitation. The Atmosphere lapped it up.

And then, swathed in a plume of smoke, Ye Great Entranco leapt on to the table top and four barrels supplied for him. A large black crow perched on his shoulder for a moment, glaring inchoately at the crowd pondering which pocket looked the ripest for a swift plunder.

And Strappado's heart clenched with fury as he recognised the vicious unconvicted rabbit murderer. His mind snarled at the pathetic attempt at disguise. If Entranco thought that a quick shave would throw Strappado off his trail, he was very much mistaken. It took all of the Arch Sergeant's willpower to prevent himself erupting from his seat and dragging the magician out of Ye Spit. That, and the sure knowledge that he wouldn't sing basso profundo again once he was spotted. He would bide his time; there was bound to be a perfect opportunity soon. If not, then it would have to be the 'Can I have your autograph?' ploy at the stage door later. The Atmosphere slunk around Strappado's ankles, purring as it thrilled with his anger.

A single candle guttered in the rafters above the magician's head, casting strange shadows floorwards. He swirled about in a long dark cloak for a few moments while he insisted on showing the already bored audience the inside of his vast sleeves, a task made impossible by the low light levels. He rolled up his right sleeve as far as his bony elbow, waved his bare forearm in the air flamboyantly, before thrusting it inexplicably up the left sleeve, fumbling about, and with a practised and nauseatingly exaggerated flourish, tugging a bunch of parchment carnations from his sleeve to a surge of rampant yawning. With Ye Spit's clientele's attention suitably disengaged the crow swooped silently off Entranco's shoulder and began dipping into a variety of pockets.

Had Viv's eyes been in possession of stalks they would have been on the tip of them, oscillating excitedly, transfixed by the waving carnations.

Entranco bowed automatically, putting a brave face on the audience reaction, then with a flourish he whisked off his long conical hat and using a series of poorly mimed gestures and grimaces attempted to make it clear that there was in fact nothing up there either. Strappado was convinced that the magician was trying to show that he had never in his life suffered from alopecia or dandruff. So it came as something of a shock when Entranco leapt off the barrels, swiftly removed the Arch Sergeant's hat and placed his own conical headgear in its stead. Strappado squeaked with alarm, trembling as he felt a pair of claws sink into the more tender parts of his scalp, followed swiftly by an unnatural warmness, as if a feather-lined flat cap had been landed there. He had to fight with his arms to prevent them snatching that grinning axe-murderer by the throat; neurons fought muscle desperately.

The magician grinned in wild oblivion to his danger as he tugged his hat away and revealed a terrified pigeon, trembling under the piercing glare of almost total general uninterest. Viv squealed her wild approval, startling the quivering bird into an unfortunately timed bowel movement and an eruption rafter-wards in a flurry of embarrassed feathers. Strappado leapt erect, knocking his chair flying, wheeled on his heel and fled out the back door snatching a bar towel to polish his freshly decorated head as he thundered past, blushing almost as much as he fumed.

Entranco barely batted an eyelid at this untimely departure and launched into the rest of his act. 'Gentlemen,' he declared, 'I need a volunteer!'

They were the four words Viv had waited her life to hear a stage magician utter. Without the cold glare of her husband to restrain her wrists, her hand shot skywards accompanied with a barrage of plaintive 'Me, me, me, me's. And then she amazed even herself. Before she realised it, she had leapt off her chair and sprung up on to the stage next to the magician. 'Me!' she said. 'I volunteer!' The Atmosphere wheeled and cavorted cheerfully above the rafters.

Entranco peered out into the gloom of Ye Spit, shrugged and nodded forlornly, intensely disappointed that there wasn't a gorgeous teenage girl upon whom he could work his spells (and hopefully his charms). He turned away, opened a large case and with a flick of a deft wrist erected a large screen which was covered in a clichéd array of silver moons and rabbits peering over the rims of inverted top hats. Privately he unscrewed a small dark jar and swallowed two pink pills (readily available from Mal Fease the Magickal Merchant) with a shudder.

Then he stood and went through a complex mime to show that what the audience was about to see, if they could be bothered to pay the slightest attention, was real and not done by mirrors or trapdoors or anything other than honest-to-goodness magic (also available from Mal Fease, the Magickal Merchant's for a very reasonable fee). He ravelled and unravelled the screen, spun it around to show the back, jumped up and down on the stage, jammed swords between the barrels underneath and then finally made Viv stand behind the backlit curtain and tried vainly to draw everyone's attention to the silhouette cast thereon.

And then he started. He really would have appreciated a drum roll instead of the drone of muttered conversation, but it was not to be. Viv stood stock still as he swirled his hands about mystically, muttering strange words and swaying back and forth. The candle spluttered behind the curtain making the silhouette twitch unnaturally as Entranco chanted louder and faster. The candle twitched again and some of the crowd looked up as the black shadow on the curtain seemed to grow horns. A guttering candle couldn't do that to a silhouette – could it? And then, as the magician changed the key of his chanting, the black shape appeared to shrink, its neck growing longer, the rim of the hat twisting and changing into what looked like ears, the tail of the coat writhing and turning into a real tail, the hands losing their fingers and the shape arched forward on all fours as its nose and mouth elongated into a snout – and it began bleating.

With yet another showy flourish, Entranco leapt on to the stage, tugged on a string and the curtain flashed upwards, spinning and flapping at the top of its travel, to reveal a fully horned goat chewing insistently at the inside of the magician's case.

'Get off!' he squealed, slapping the goat across its backside as Strappado stomped back in, having removed the last traces of guano from his head. Awestruck he stared from their empty table to the goat and back again. 'What have you done to my wife . . . ?' he screamed and instantly regretted it as the goat bleated in panic and all eyes turned on him.

'er . . . wife's friend. Wife's friend,' he blurted. 'She . . . he was sitting there and . . .'

'Volunteer,' grinned Entranco and slapped the masticating goat as it tore another strip off the velvety lining of his case.

'Turn her . . . him back!' shouted Strappado. 'Now!'

'So soon?' boomed the magician. 'The crowd are just starting to enjoy it. I've got the "sacrifice" trick to come! Based on the eternally popular "Tomb of Termination" . . .'

Strappado strode forward menacingly, withdrew a Lore Enforcement Agency standard issue fourteen-inch gutting knife from inside his cloak and held it directly in front of the wizard's liver. The Atmosphere grinned over his shoulder.

'Change her . . . him back or I get to do *my* sacrifice trick!' he growled with full Arch Sergeantial impact. The Atmosphere wriggled with anticipation of the coming punch-up.

'Oh, come on, I only got one volunteer,' wheedled Entranco. 'Just a few more minutes, just till I get to the finale and—'

'No! Change her back! Now!' growled Strappado, poking the magician in the liver significantly.

'Can't . . . it's d . . . dangerous to change back too quickly, and besides . . .' There was a brief flash of terror in his eyes. 'Her? You say "her"?'

'Yes, yes, keep quiet. I know she shouldn't be in here but she insisted and . . . why are you shaking your head like that?'

'Er . . . nothing. Nothing at all. No problem. Ha!' If he'd known she wasn't a man he would've handled that last mantra very differently, very differently indeed. Entranco knew only too well the problems of imposing a transmogrification spell on a person of the wrong sex . . . ohhh, the horror stories, the bearded ladies . . . He shuddered.

'What's wrong?' barked Strappado.

'Er, n . . . nothing, just a bit, er . . . cold. That's all.'

'What are you waiting for? Do it!' Strappado's knife bit into Entranco's navel.

'Yeah, yeah, sure I normally do this bit behind a screen . . .'

The look on Strappado's face seemed to make the idea of moving screens about just a little unnecessary right now.

And with that, Entranco's voice faded into a hurried resolution spell; gabbling the words, he hurled consonant after syllable at full speed. Strappado's jaw dropped in horror as the goat spasmed grotesquely, bleated and began doing very odd anatomical stunts. Its legs lengthened, the nostrils shrank and the horns shrivelled inwards with a slight sucking noise. It was only then that Skroht'm, the barman realised that for the first time in its entire history Ye Silver Spittoone was entirely silent. And worse, no one was drinking. All eyes were on the stage as the goat's fur squirmed backwards and disappeared under the surface of smooth female skin.

The lecherous cheering and rampant applause which exploded from the massed throats as they stared at a remarkably naked Viv could be heard half a mile away. Unanimously the crowd realised that all of a sudden this show had really taken a turn for the better.

161

Strappado snatched off his cloak and leapt to the aid of his shivering wife, covering her quickly to the obvious disappointment of the extremely interested audience. Then he turned, stood and stared at the spot which up until very recently had been occupied by Ye Great Entranco.

The Arch Sergeant shouted something suitably unprintable and made to rush off in hot pursuit until he noticed that all eyes were still on Viv. She sat there, bewildered and bleating oddly. He could almost smell the effect that the brief glimpse of flesh was having on them and knew what he had to do. He spun around, snatched her off the floor and battered his way to the door in the sure knowledge that he had saved not only his wife but also his eardrums. The battering they'd have got if he'd left her there just didn't bear thinking about.

All that had been two years ago, and his wife had been a living hell ever since. Whilst Viv undoubtedly looked as normal as could be expected after having been transmogrified into a goat, it soon became all too apparent that everything was not as it should be. In the ensuing years she had taken to wearing a bell around her neck, bleating during moments of extreme excitement and unaccountably spreading straw on the floor of their hovel. But worst of all was her appetite. Strappado had lost count of the number of mattresses she had devoured in the last twenty-four months and he seemed constantly to sport fresh teeth marks on his boots despite the fact that he had taken to getting her scraps of leather to chew on from the local cobbler.

Well tonight, two years on, Ye Great Entranco would pay for his tragic mistake. How dare he risk showing his face in Fort Knumm again.

Seething angrily, Strappado swaggered up to the bar of Ye Spit in his finest assassin-type impersonation, ordered a flagon of Hexenhammer with a shiver of *déjà vu* and took a table near the stage just as the candles dimmed and the magician leapt on to the barrels and table top that passed as a stage hereabouts. A large black crow perched on his shoulder. It seemed that little had changed in the last two years. Except that Ye Great Entranco was sporting a beard again.

Strappado's sense of reliving the past was overwhelming as Entranco produced a tattered bunch of parchment carnations from his sleeve, an event greeted with stunning apathy by all but one of the spectators, and the crow shot off on its tour of pocket duty.

In that instant Strappado knew he had his man in his sights; he almost couldn't believe that he was staring at his hated target. Muscles tensed in his lower intestines as adrenalin surged cheerfully through his body. And the Atmosphere pricked up its ears sensing an incident of coming interest.

Entranco swept his conical hat off his head with a flourish and proceeded to demonstrate the lack of anything hidden within, then jumped offstage and reached for the brim of Strappado's floppy fedora.

'Gotcha!' cried the Arch Sergeant and for the second time was present during one of those all too rare moments when everyone in Ye Spit had simultaneously stopped talking. All eyes turned at that instant, attention held by the sudden glint and rattle of professionally drawn handcuffs arcing towards the magician's wrist. And, much to the intense satisfaction of the Atmosphere, panic exploded as they recognised the disturbingly familiar tones of the dreaded Arch Sergeant Strappado. The crow went wild. Flapping madly it was first out of the window, having to escape bearing only a brass pocket sundial and a pouch containing five groats.

Tables somersaulted in all directions as guilty customers leapt from their stools and scrambled for any available exit, expecting the swift, sharp invasion of fifteen heavily armed and armoured constables. They shoved open windows long sealed by centuries of nicotinic tar, kicked open trapdoors buried 'neath decades of caked spit and sawdust or simply stampeded towards the front door.

Strappado turned too late to avoid the size twelves of Ikhnaton the Assassin in his chest as said Personnel Eradicator decided to make good a swift escape before he had his collar felt for failing to renew his AA membership.*

*Assassins Anonymous. Only assassins correctly accredited and able to deal death

As the Arch Sergeant was trampled into the floor of Ye Spit, Entranco saw his chance. Trailing handcuffs from his fortuitously freed wrist he bolted for the door, burst into the night and sprinted wildly away heading madly for the only safe-ish place he knew of in Fort Knumm, Mal Fease's warehouse at 21–21b Puce Street.

'Come back with my handcuffs!' screamed Strappado from the grime-caked floor. 'That's stealing, that is! I'll have you for that as well!' He struggled out from beneath a table, hauled himself upright and sprinted shakily off to issue himself another warrant and kick some troops together. Now it was more than personal. Now he could have the troops for free.

Cursing as he ran, Strappado was wild. How could he have let the swine get away so easily? Damn that conjurist! If only everyone in Ye Spit hadn't stampeded he would have that damned creature safely locked away behind . . .

'Wait a minute,' snarled Strappado, kicking an eighteen-inch rat out of his way. 'No stampede, no escape!' Damn! This was bigger than he thought. In a split second his expert infiltrator-spotting mind made the connection. A conjurists' enclave in Fort Knumm!

Everyone, absolutely *everyone* in Ye Spit was in on it. They were all Comrades-in-Charms. Well, that was it, all the evidence he needed. And if they'd helped Entranco escape then they'd probably hide him.

From now on there'd be no more Mr Nice Guy. From now on anyone seen doing anything even remotely magical in a public place would be arrested, cuffed and frog-marched into the Lore Enforcement Agency Interrogation Cells for a damn good seeing-to. He would get to the bottom of this conspiracy if it was the last thing he did.

up to the exacting standards of the Bureau of Sedition's BS 5750 were allowed to ply their trade in Fort Knumm, thus allowing petty acts of illegal murder to be identified and dealt with by the Lore Enforcement Agency. Unfortunately, the compulsory use of pseudonyms along with the strict confidentiality rules set up to maintain assassins' professional identities made all this almost impossible for the overworked Agency, who now only took to investigating killings if a relative complained. In triplicate. Twice.

164

Well, that and preventing Ye Great Entranco ever perform-
ing again.

Half an hour later a man and his alarm macaw peered out of the
shadows and sighed underwhelmedly.

'You absolutely sure this is the place?' asked Quintzi Cohatl
miserably as he stood in gloomy shadows in downtown Fort
Knumm.

'Absolutely,' slapped the nano-sprites in his ear. '21–21b
Puce Street, right over there.'

'It had better be,' growled Quintzi. Hiking for hours through
the forest after such an early start and sneaking around the back
streets of Fort Knumm on an empty stomach had done nothing
to improve his mood. 'My bones are killin' me. Just down the
hill, you said, just over the next rise, just round the next corner!
Pah! It's been miles and I'm knackered. I don't know why I
listened to you.'

'Because you want a new scrying crystal, that's why,'
reminded the nano-sprites petulantly. 'Because, apart from the
single groat that lurks in your left-hand pocket, you have
nothing of worth to rub together and because without it your
future is as rosy as your average glacier!'

'Don't talk to me about futures!' grumbled Quintzi. 'I didn't
say anything about hiking gods know how far to get a scrying
crystal. Give me a blast of that thaumy-stuff, will you? My
bones are killin' me!' begged Quintzi.

'No way,' came the paradiddled reply. 'We've barely
enough to keep us going, let alone any spare.'

'Oh please,' he wheedled. 'I'll buy you some when I'm rich.
My knees are so . . .'

'You can't buy it!' snapped the nano-sprites. 'It's naturally
occurring, morning after a full moon on the south-east side of
some weirdy tree.'

'Look, I'll just mash a few of them mushrooms up and . . .'

'Shut up!' snapped the nano-sprites, sensing odd vibrations
in Quintzi's eardrum, vibrations which their short experience
in the outside world had taught them meant one thing. Peril.

'What the . . . why?' spluttered Quintzi and then he heard the sprinting feet coming closer by the second.

He held his breath as a blackly menacing figure screeched around the corner, clattered down Puce Street, skittered to a halt and began pounding on the door.

'Come out!' screamed Arch Sergeant Strappado smashing his fists angrily on 21–21b's door-knob and waving a sheet of hastily prepared parchment. 'I know you're in there!'

'No, I'm not!' came the muffled answer from Ye Great Entranco. He was obviously flustered and a little confused by the recent events in Ye Spit.

'Ha! Gotcha!' squealed Strappado excitedly. 'You can't deny it now. Let me in!'

'Clear off, warehouse's closed!'

'I've got a warrant!'

'What for?'

'Your arrest!'

'What? I'm innocent!' Entranco crossed his fingers and attempted to prevent his knees trembling. He failed.

'Hah! What about stealing Lore Enforcement Agency property!' yelled Strappado through the keyhole.

'I never did . . .'

'Are they your handcuffs dangling from your wrist, eh?'

'Oh, er, I thought they were a gift. Want them back?'

'Yes! With you attached.' Strappado whirled away from the door, cupped his hands around his mouth and bellowed a series of sharp orders into the night.

Seconds later fifteen heavily armoured and yawning Lore Enforcement Agency troopers stomped around the corner tugging large heavy carts and shoulder-charged their way through the door of 21–21b Puce Street with a large amount of groaning.

'But this is more than just stealing handcuffs!' growled Strappado. 'This goes back a long way. The name Benji mean anything to you, eh? Piebald, five pounds, distinctly lop-eared?'

Entranco's eyes were pools of terror. He knew he'd been

arrested by a complete manic obsessive. He could tell, he could hear the deadly throb of axes just waiting to be ground.

'Er . . . can I have a lawyer . . . ?'

'Two years of hell it's been!' screamed Strappado, ignoring anything Entranco had to say and inventing a stack of verbal evidence to be taken down and used against him.

Quintzi Cohatl watched from the far side of the street as, a few minutes of crashing and banging later, Strappado cheerily frog-marched the magician out of Mal Fease's warehouse following a very unfortunate incident when Entranco had just *happened* to slip away for a moment and simply had to be pursued in an extremely noisy and destructive manner about the building.

'. . . and it's all your fault about my bleating wife! How dare you interfere with her, damned stage magician. Bloody irresponsible I'd call it, stomping into my local, transmogrifyin' people left, right and centre, then clearin' off without a care in the world leavin' the like of me with a mad mattress-chewin' wife! An' you call that entertainment?'

'What's mattresses got to do with it?' winced Entranco as he was bounced around the corner, his arm creaking in an expertly applied half-nelson.

'Don't play smart with me, sonny. Do you have a clue how much mattresses cost, eh? Do you? I ought to arrest all the likes of you for conjuring without due care and attention! Well that's the last time you get up on stage, matey. I'm closing you down! Permanently!'

At almost that very instant the first of the heavy agency carts erupted from the warehouse laden with shelf-loads of magical equipment of all kinds. Potions and packets of pills rattled beside wands and grimoires of spells as thirteen other carts followed. Quintzi's eyes bulged in horror as he glimpsed the final cart rattling away down Puce Street, its thaumic load crowned with the unmistakable glinting sphere of the last scrying crystal.

'Where's that going?' squeaked Quintzi desperately as he watched the whole of his future unravel.

'Behind a very large and very locked door, I'd guess,' tapped Nimlet.

'But . . . that's mine. I need it. How will I know who wins the Grand Kingdomnal before I can place my bets tomorrow?' he wailed pathetically. 'I'm ruined, ruined!'

It was suddenly too much for him. Leagues from home, all but groatless, exhausted, unemployed and suffering from voices in his head. Being sixty-five really wasn't turning out to be a great deal of fun.

As if in agreement Quintzi's knees gave up and he slithered pathetically to the ground, shaking his head. 'That's it,' he blubbed. 'I'm doomed to destitution. It can't possibly get any worse. Can it?'

Helpfully, in the soothing manner for which meteorology was so renowned, it started to rain.

'Oh, why me?' pleaded Quintzi rhetorically.

'Stop being so pathetic,' snapped the nano-sprites angrily against his eardrum. 'We're nice and warm!'

'I want to be pathetic. I'm good at it.'

'Hold your head straight,' snapped Nimlet. 'We don't want rain getting in here.'

Miserably Quintzi tipped the left side of his head skywards and grinned with his last ounce of humour as a cold drop wriggled into his ear.

The nano-sprites screamed, shivered and complained for hours after that.

# 'Big Boys don't scry . . .'

Quintzi Cohatl would have been the first to admit that it wasn't the finest night's sleep he'd ever had. The rain had continued unbroken all night, running in rivulets down the small of his back, fusing his aching arthritic bones into a solid osseous lump. If it had carried on sleeting down much beyond five in the morning, it's doubtful he ever would have moved from that secretive corner opposite Mal Fease's stripped warehouse. As it was, he nearly didn't make it. He was only saved by a mushroom and a ton of willpower.

In the barely perceptible way it has, dawn crept shyly into the sky. Quintzi shivered again, cursed and moaned miserably as his stomach writhed in excruciating emptiness. Almost without thinking about it his left hand snaked into the blue punnet he had been carrying, scrabbled about for a few seconds and withdrew a greying chunk of what had once been a shimmeringly blue-veined mushroom. It was in his mouth and being chewed at before he realised.

In seconds his stomach acids had ruptured the cells releasing the massive stores of vitamin hex, for which *Agaricus thaumagensis* was justifiably famous, his gut had snapped it up and latent enzymes were busily accessing the bound thaumic energy.

'Woooooooaaaaah!' he yelped, in precisely the way muesli doesn't make you. In moments he was stretching his ageing knees, waggling his finger in his ear and, for the first time in his life, squawking down Tiemecx's feathery ear.

'C'mon, c'mon! Wakey, wakey! We've got work to do,' he enthused like a holiday camp commandant. And just as forcefully he was on his feet and shuffling determinedly towards the Fort Knumm Lore Enforcement Agency building.

A lot of things had become clear to him last night as he had sat awake in a growing puddle of rain and despondency. And the main thing was that he desperately needed that scrying crystal. Without i      was totally lost; up a creek without a paddle, or canoe; no chance of ever earning any sort of honest living around here.

Incredibly he had also worked out the whereabouts of said crystal. It was very kind of the Lore Enforcement Agency to surround the entrance of 21–21b Puce Street with nice blue and black tape saying DO NOT CROSS OR THE LORE'LL GET YOU!

Quintzi Cohatl hobbled furtively out of a deep shadow and flattened himself against the back wall of the Agency building. Eyes peeled for movement, he rummaged about once again inside his left ear and whispered conspiratorially, 'C'mon, c'mon. Get a move on! I've told you what to do.'

The nano-sprites mustered their energies, swooped from his lobe and disappeared between the bars in the high security window grumbling and cursing the fact that they had agreed to locate this crystal. If only they hadn't been so desperate to get the Hextirpator they could've bargained.

In seconds they were zipping wearily down the corridors of law enforcement, flitting under doors, dodging through keyholes and sneaking their inquisitive selves into room after room, searching for the stash of magical equipment recently confiscated from Mal Fease's warehouse. Their thaumic antennae wriggled, sniffing the air for any hint of a high-density flux field, or a sign that there was anything even remotely magical nearby. Suddenly Nimlet twitched animatedly, zipped on ahead and hovered excitedly in the air.

'Can you smell it?' he buzzed as the other two caught up. 'Can you? Just behind that door . . . found it. I'm sure!'

'Well, what are we waiting for? C'mon!' And with that Udio vanished through the keyhole.

Screams of fury and the release of frustration rattled around the square stone room, punctuated by the creaking of heavy torture apparatus and renewed squeals of victimised anguish.

'. . . and that's for the time she chewed up all the tea-towels in the house!' shrieked Strappado madly as he swung from the vast wheel of the rack and increased the tension on a ragged-

170

looking body strapped to the machine. It seemed that Quintzi wasn't the only early riser that day.

'Aaaargh! Look, I'm sorry I ran off with your handcuffs, okay,' pleaded the victim. 'Thought you were the editor of *Thaum and Garden Magazine* wanting payment for those dodgy Hex Line adverts we ran last month,' screamed the magician, his joints creaking horribly. Nimlet noted with some concern that either the victim had an extremely poor choice in tailor, or he had suddenly grown by a good three inches.

Strappado sneered, spun away from the rack and glared at the array of instruments of torture, maiming and pain infliction on casual show. He tapped his chin thoughtfully as he perused the grotesque skeletons hanging from the far wall; skeletons made up of iron masks, metal collars, handcuffs, thumbscrews, manacles and a host of excruciating ironwork for inflicting pain on hundreds of other parts of the anatomy. He flicked through the jungle of chains hanging from every available inch of stone ceiling, some ending in cuffs, others in leg braces and others in a variety of screw-closable fastenings designed for every protuberance from the ear down. Then he grinned wickedly, unhooked a device that looked like a cast-iron codpiece and hurled it into a furnace.

'Just warm it up a little,' he growled. 'Wouldn't want it to be too uncomfortable for our little Entranco now, would we?' he added, leaping on to the rack wheel once more and yelling about the suffering of two years living with a woman who thought she was a bleating goat.

'I can smell magic!' insisted Udio, buzzing agitatedly around the interior of Inquisition Suite Thirteen. 'Where is it?'

'It's no good,' tutted Nimlet miserably. 'It's in him.' He buzzed dejectedly about, indicating the gradually lengthening form of Ye Great Entranco. 'We can't get at it.'

'What d'you mean?' snarled Udio. 'Course we can! I'm starving!'

Suddenly he zipped out of the air, plunged at Entranco's wrist and muscled his way between the skin cells, ignoring the cries of concern from Nimlet. Seconds later he was in the magician's bloodstream, bouncing and rattling uncontrollably

171

amongst torrents of blood cells, frothing plasma and, crucially, floods of thaumaglobin. Everywhere he looked Udio could see it, spinning in shimmering vortices around him, bobbing provocatively. He darted forward, latched on to a single molecule and tugged desperately, failing to see a net of microscopic chains binding the thaumaglobin molecules together. He struggled, writhed and spun wildly, like a miniature great white shark in a trawl net, and totally failed to succeed in anything other than wearing himself out almost completely. Dejectedly, he emerged from Entranco's ankle a few moments later and buzzed embarrassedly up to join the other two nano-sprites.

'Told you,' snapped Nimlet. 'Got to wait until he's actually doing a spell, that's the only time it's free.'

'What?'

'Ever thought of the mess that having unbound thaumaglobin zipping about inside a body could do, urghh,' shuddered Nimlet. 'You know, spontaneous combustion, sudden mysterious disappearance, major organs dissolving, anything! C'mon, let's get out of here!'

As Nimlet zipped through the keyhole and back into the corridor, Strappado bent over a set of bellows, blew the furnace to full inferno and then, with the flamboyant enthusiasm of the professional sadist, withdrew a glowing metal codpiece, decided it wasn't quite hot enough yet and hurled it back in. He whirled back to Entranco and stared into his sweating face. 'Sixteen times I've redecorated the windowledges in the last two years,' he sneered through clenched incisors. 'Sanded the teethmarks out and started again from scratch every time. That's worth at least three more turns, don't you think?'

'Look, I hate DIY as well as the next man but, I ... aaaaargh!' Entranco's elbows popped worryingly. He felt like a top E guitar string rapidly passing F sharp.

'And that's for my niece's rabbit, Benji!'

Cringing and praising their good fortunes at not possessing tender anatomies, the nano-sprites veered left and resumed flitting in and out of high security cells. Nimlet checked out two before erupting back into the corridor in a state of extreme oscillation. 'Found it! Found it!' he buzzed and vanished through the locked door again.

'Found what ... ooooh,' cooed Udio as he and Skarg'l flashed into the room. The three nano-sprites stared at the entire contents of Mal Fease's Puce Street warehouse jammed unceremoniously into a tiny cell. Boxes of ready-mix spells were piled randomly in heaps next to stacks of dumped multi-pack convenience charms and yet more crates of Instant Rabbits. Vast piles of off-the-peg wands were slung against unrecognisable devices of obscure origin and even more obscure thaumic use. And there, perched on a mound of ensequinned top hats, the crowning grail-like glory: a single palely glowing sphere.

Quintzi did a little jump of joy a few moments later and then snarled, 'About time too! What took you so long?'

'There were a lot of rooms ...' put in Udio. 'Had to check them all.'

'So where is it, eh?' growled Quintzi as images of a prosperous future swam just out of his mind's reach. 'Tell me where the crystal is!'

'Tell you?' tapped Nimlet coyly. 'You never said anything about telling you where it was. Find it, you said ...'

'Don't be awkward! Tell me!' pleaded Quintzi.

'Well, I could ... on one condition.'

'What? What? Name it!'

'You get the crystal – we get some breakfast!' bargained Nimlet.

'Is that all?'

'Oh, yes!' bashed Nimlet. 'C'mon then, it's around the other side.'

It didn't take long for Udio to chew away at the ageing mortar around the bars in the ground floor window and loosen them enough for the arthritic Axolotian to tug them out. Then, creaking and complaining habitually about several degrees of personal discomfort, Quintzi hauled himself on to the window-ledge, teetered for a moment, grabbed out in the dark for the curtains to steady himself and tumbled inside with a crash. Rubbing his head and cursing to himself he realised, far too

173

late, that cells rarely have curtains fortuitously placed to allow the steadying of criminal entrants.

Three doors down, the ears of Arch Sergeant Strappado leapt erect. He stopped in his tracks and froze, listening intently, crimson codpiece smouldering in fiery anger. Alarm bells rang in his head as he ticked off all the officers he knew damn well weren't in at this time of morning. Then he eliminated all the cleaners he'd personally thrown out of the building earlier, just so they wouldn't hear the screams, and came to the startling conclusion that there were officially only two people in this building at the moment, and, since one of them was strapped to a rack and the other had strapped him there, it was highly probable that a third someone was currently engaging in actions which Strappado had most definitely not sanctioned.

It sounded like it was about three doors away on this side . . . three doors? Strappado's alarm bells switched to klaxons of terror. Someone was breaking into a roomful of magical equipment. His heart pounded with panic. Gods, but they had moved quick! he thought. Too quick. His eyes flicked suspiciously around the room, warily scanning the walls for any apparent auditory device.

They must have agents in this very building! In his very force! Damn those conjurist infiltrators! How dare they blatantly break into his . . . Then his heart missed a beat. What did they want? Had he stumbled across a high-level conspiracy, or a deadly spell-smuggling ring? Or could it be something far worse?

'You, stay there,' he growled at Entranco, snatched a red-hot poker out of the furnace and dashed into the corridor.

'Hey! Oi! Come back!' screamed the arrested magician after the fleeing figure. 'What about me? Hey! You can't leave me here!' The door slammed shut. 'Typical. Bloody typical that is! Lore Enforcement Agency? Can't trust 'em. Start an investigation, never finish it!'

Quintzi Cohatl's jaw was somewhere around his collarbone as he stood staring at the vast magical stash and the single scrying crystal perched atop one of the heaps. His heart pounded with anticipation. There, tantalisingly close to him,

174

lay his perfect future. Unlimited resources gained from gambling on an undying list of dead cert. All he had to do was scramble up the heap of magical oddments, tuck it into his pocket and . . .

'Hold it right there! Hands high! Don't move!' snapped Arch Sergeant Strappado, bursting in through the stealthily unlocked door and yelling as many aggressive-sounding commands as sprang to his panicking mind. 'You've got some explaining to do, sonny!'

Quintzi whirled around and stood staring cross-eyed at the tip of the red-hot poker. 'Er . . . explaining . . . er, yes.' The highly honed lies section of his brain leapt into action, looking for an opportunity to chip in with its infamous capability for stretching the truth to unforeseen elastic limits.

'What the hell d'you think you're doing in here, eh!' bellowed Strappado, suddenly horribly aware that he was totally without backup. Thoughts whirled in his seething mind, not least the fact that this intruder, bedecked with bald head, scruffy beard, golden toga and filthy socks, well . . . he didn't really have the appearance of a magical mafia-type conspiracy's deadly leader. But, he warned himself, that could be a disguise. Who knew what appearance-altering spells were within easy grasp of conjurist infiltrators? Who could say that they weren't messing with his mind right now?

'I . . . I was looking around,' blurted Quintzi, realising that he was horribly out of practice at the gentle art of fabrication. The nano-sprites cringed.

'Anything in particular sir had in mind?' cackled Strappado sarcastically. 'Or do you normally just stroll into a high security area unannounced?' He brandished the poker once more with prime inquisitorial elegance.

'I didn't stroll . . . I . . . I . . . er, the window. Just came out in my hands.'

'What?'

'Not really very high security, is it?'

'Who are you to say what's high security and what's n—' Suddenly, in mid-rant, Arch Sergeant Strappado bit his lip and turned crimson. Could it be that this was exactly the right person to pass hypercritical judgement on his security? Look at how easily he had removed the window bars from three-foot-thick walls. How come he knew where the most valuable stash of magical contraband was being stored? There could be only one conclusion. This had to be the work of MIN.

Strappado had only heard the vaguest of rumours about the shady goings on in Mystical Intelligence.* Could he have inadvertently run across one of their investigations? Swiftly he swung the red-hot poker out of sight and grinned sheepishly.

'Sorry, I, er, didn't mean to criticise,' he blubbed apologetically and looked at his toes. 'Please, er, do look around and I'll be glad to help with anything that you may require. Anyone from Mystical Intelligence is always welcome to fly in and investigate our security.'

Quintzi stared blankly for a moment, baffled by the sudden change of tone. Then, never one to duck the chance of a lifetime when it presented itself, he grinned and pointed to the glowing sphere on the top of the heap of thaumic detritus.

'Stop grovelling and pass that to me,' commanded Quintzi, hoping he had gauged the situation correctly. In an instant, much to his immense relief, Strappado had dropped his poker, scrambled up the pile and was offering the scrying crystal to the Axolotian, admiring his style. He knew precisely what it was he wanted; this had to be big, he had to have been monitoring every move to know what he was after.

'This vital evidence, eh?' oozed Strappado in a conspiratorial whisper, desperate to sniff something of the MIN agent's mission. 'Contain clues, does it? Essential pointers to catchin' all them nasty, horrid wizards, hmmmm?' Strappado had long known of the rumoured fulminating rivalry between the non-wizards of MIN and the showy magic users they policed.

Quintzi's mind whirled. 'Wizards?' he mouthed.

Strappado's eyes flashed left and right, searching once again

*It was unsurprising that he had only heard whispers, since one of the requirements of becoming a Mystical Intelligence operative was that the candidate's voice couldn't be heard over a range of more than three inches, even while screaming at the top of his or her voice. This made for an almost bomb-proof ability to keep vital secrets, but didn't really help in times of acute personal crisis.

for hidden ears. 'Sorry, "hush, hush", is it? Delicate operation?'

'Er, very delicate,' shuddered Quintzi recalling the effect of dropping a crystal on to solid floors and not understanding a word of the ranting Arch Sergeant.

'I can help,' yammered Strappado. 'Undercover, like. I can sniff 'em out. Brimming with local knowledge me, you know. Just say the word. In fact I'm already rounding the suckers up, filthy blighters. I'll help, and I won't even charge overtime. Be a privilege to help stamp out them bloody magic users once and for all . . .'

And suddenly a tapping in the back of Quintzi's mind obscured the wittering Arch Sergeant's flow. 'Say "yes"!' chirped his fabricampus in a flurry of squirted lies. 'Say it!'

'Yes,' grunted Quintzi, shaking his head.

Strappado's face lit up. 'I can? You will? You'll let me help with MIN work? Yes, yes, yes! Right, I can hand one over right now or I can get the names of other wizards and then carry out a stack of dawn raids and . . .'

'That won't be necessary,' said Quintzi under instruction from his fabricampus. 'This is fine. All I need for the moment.'

'Sure?' asked Strappado, diving into the pile of gadgetry, tugging eagerly at boxes of astrolabes and athanor burners with overwhelming gusto.

In seconds he was back, offering a host of devices to Quintzi with a gaze of expectancy and awe. Resisting the overwhelming temptation to pat the Arch Sergeant on the head, the Axolotian made for the window.

'Anything else you need?' spluttered Strappado hard on Quintzi's sandalled heels.

'N . . . no, no, that's splendid! I'll be in touch if there's anything more,' he added over his shoulder as he vanished into the dawn, his treasures tucked Fagin-like under his criminal toga, his mind not daring to believe what had just happened.

Strappado whirled cheerfully around in the swiftly vacated room, his heart pounding like a teenager with her first valentine, overjoyed that someone, whoever it was, at MIN wanted him to help with his investigation. 'They'll be in touch!' He felt like springing out into the night and screaming his involvement at the top of his voice . . . but he knew he couldn't. It was hush, hush – top secret – need to know basis. It was his secret mission!

Already he was alert to the chance of a second contact, his eyes peeled and ready for the call.

He wheeled on his heel and sprinted back to the Inquisition Cell, ready to get as much vital subversive information out of that damned magician as he possibly could, armed only with the vast array of tools to hand. He chuckled evilly at the thought.

Then changed his mind and headed off towards the briefing rooms. He had very important new orders for his men. Yes! It was time to introduce 'Operation De-Mage'.

The crowd went wild as War spurred his horse hard, raised his mallet and galloped wildly towards the spinning ball. It bounced once off the verdant grass and a Knight Templar was on it, his gaze piercing through the visor, calculating the sphere's trajectory with stunning speed. With a whinny his horse pirouetted and was in mid-charge.

'Behind you!' squealed Merlot excitedly brandishing his Apocalypse Four supporter's scarf. 'C'mon War, get your finger out! Strike.'

As if in response to the heckling from the box, War spurred his steed on, his mallet helicoptering above his head, eye squarely on the ball, lining up . . . His apocalyptic arm swept long and low and suddenly the Knight Templar was in his way, cutting through and scooping up the ball. War roared, followed through illegally and almost decapitated his opponent.

Merlot punched the air wildly and Arbutus performed a swift backflip. They both knew the final would be tough, but *this* . . . classic gamesmanship. War was always a tough opponent.

Abruptly a whistle rang out across the field and a white parchment was thrust high into the air for all to see – another foul point against War.

'Oi, ref . . . you blind?' ranted Merlot. 'He deserved to get hit. Nobody tackles War from behind. Send him off!'

For a moment the game was halted as War's latest casualty was dragged off the pitch.

Merlot reached triumphantly for another glass of wine and gave his scarf a joyous wave. This was turning out to be one real blistering match. For a brief second his thoughts strayed momentarily away from the sporting spectacular as he wondered who it was that had been so kind to treat him to all this. He really ought to find out and express his appreciation. He stood, turned, reached out for the handle and . . .

Behind him there was a flurry of excitement on the pitch as the substitute was waved, cheered and booed on. Curiosity sprang cheerfully into his heart as he turned back to the match with a shrug. He really should find out who was the substitute . . . After all, there was still plenty of time to discover who had given him the ticket later. Especially when all the injury time was tacked on to the end.

No sooner had the bolts been unshot from the door of Tedd Sert's Wagering Emporium than an over-eager figure in a gold toga burst in waving a single groat and obliviously trampling the owner.

'Everything on the nose of Armadillo Flash in the eight-thirty!' declared Quintzi Cohatl to an empty desk.

'You what?' growled Tedd Sert picking himself off the floor and dusting footprints off his tunic. His nose quivered. Someone was actually wanting to place a bet – without him bribing them. Already the day was looking up.

Quintzi wheeled around. 'Armadillo Flash. In the eight-thirty. C'mon, c'mon, take the money. It'll start soon.'

'You serious?' growled Sert, sauntering over to the desk. 'Everyone knows that camel isn't worth spit!'

'D'you want to take my cash or not?' pressed Quintzi.

'If you want to give it away, sure. But, I wouldn't bother filling out a slip if I were you.' Tedd Sert sniggered. It was always the same at opening time. Desperate gamblers pressing their money on him and insisting that today their luck had changed, flinging their final groats on complete no-hopers. He loved it, of course. In the first three hours he normally made just enough profit to cover the afternoon crowd – the smart-arses who spent months studying 'form' and knowing what the 'going' was like. Worst of all they knew whether winning a nine to four odds on favourite was better than a ten-to-one either-way. Or not.* Sert looked at Quintzi's mad glinting eyes and knew for certain that there was another hundred per cent profit coming his way.

Quintzi thrust the hastily filled in parchment slip under Sert's nose and pressed a coin eagerly into his fleshy hand.

'One groat on Armadillo Flash and . . . what's this?' A smirk leapt on to Tedd Sert's face. 'You *can't* be serious? All the winnings placed on Black Scabbard in the nine-thirty. To win? Studied the form have you? Har har!' Without thinking, Sert dropped the groat into his tunic pocket and stuffed the slip on to a six-inch nail hammered through a block of wood on his desk.

'No. I just know that my luck has changed,' grinned Quintzi, nervously caressing the crystal sphere hidden in his deep toga pocket, then he snatched the quill once more and began scrubbling a list of other names and times on another betting slip.

'Dream on!' mocked Sert as he stared derisively at the list. 'Hobbling Horatio hasn't won anything in the last five years. Well, not unless you count that raffle two years back!'

'I feel lucky,' glared Quintzi and shuffled off to await the results of his first wager.

Half an hour later there was the weary fluttering of wings, the scrabbling of claws and a pigeon's head appeared at the 'results' window. A murmur of excitement rippled around the now populated Wagering Emporium.

Tedd Sert grabbed the bird, tore the sheet of parchment out of the tube strapped to its leg and unfurled it.

'Results of the eight-thirty from J'helt Numm. First across the line . . . I don't believe it!' An expectant hush fell. 'Strewth! Armadillo Flash, well I never did.'

---

*Tedd Sert hated to admit it but, he wasn't sure either.

A wave of grumbling, shaking of heads and ripping of slips filled the room as all except one of the punters stared financial defeat, once more, in the face.

'I'd take the money and run,' advised Sert as Quintzi insisted on the placing of his winnings on Black Scabbard in the nine-thirty. 'Used up all your luck today, just you see.'

Half an hour later Tedd Sert scratched his head in wonder as he read another pigeon-delivered slip declaring that Black Scabbard had romped home easily, finishing ten lengths ahead of the favourite.

Reluctantly he placed one hundred and fifty-three groats on a twenty-five to one outsider and scowled. Today had not started as well as he had initially hoped.

A few hundred yards away from the Wagering Emporium a crowd of uniformly shrouded folk had gathered on a tiny patch of litter-strewn wasteground. Alternately peering over their shoulders warily and scrutinising the ground ahead upon which they were to tread, the Divers Tribe of the Cautious Newt crept towards the hastily constructed bonfire and the cauldron shackled above it with three lengths of over-strength chain link. Three times a year they came from all over Fort Knumm to gather in a state of delicate paranoia and celebrate the triurnal festival of Ghramm Maslar the Eternally Concealed.

It was the rigid belief of all Devotees of the Cautious Newt that their state of well-being could be likened to the delicate gossamer skin of their immortal amphibian deity – easily punctured and immensely difficult to mend without major surgery. Only by avoiding everyday dangers like the proverbial plague could a nirvanic state of existence be achieved and through this, the ultimate goal of immortality. It was consid-ered the height of blasphemy to expose oneself to unnecessary risk and, five years ago, following the realisation that most muggings occurred at night, the traditionally nocturnal festival was shifted to mid-morning, just before elevenses. The bonfire and safety candles didn't look quite as pretty but what the hell, it was worth it for the added impunity.

Unfortunately, other dangers presented themselves. Not

least the exposure to harmful stellar rays which beat down from above, causing freckles and increasing the risk of being laughed at. But these dangers came as little surprise. They all knew that life could be likened to a ferocious female of the canine variety. And besides, the Great Ghramm Maslar, before becoming Eternally Concealed had warned of the perils of hanging about in the sun too long, amongst a catalogue of many other dangers, claiming that the Only True Way to avoid all risks and thus achieve Immortality was to be nailed inside a reinforced wooden box and stored in the cupboard under the stairs. One hundred or so years ago when Ghramm Maslar had been sealed in, he had made a vow that he would never speak, as this might wear out his vocal cords over the Ages of Immortality which he was destined to enjoy. It was unfortunate that as a result of this vow none of his devotees ever found out he'd died of boredom one wet Sunday afternoon eighty-six years ago.

But that didn't stop him being guest of honour at his very own festival. Applauding gently so as not to risk repetitive strain injury, the gathered Divers Tribe of the Cautious Newt welcomed the sacred wooden box as it was pulled in on an ageing trolley by four strapping devotees.

A flurry of charms and protective spells were clutched and murmured amongst the crowd as the Great Crated One was parked, bricks chocked against the wheels, just in case, and the reclining bulk of High Priest Furt was tugged on, waving from his sedan chair. It was Furt's firm belief that since the life-force flowed through the souls of one's feet it was immensely damaging to one's Immortal future to be constantly stamping about all over it. He highlighted this point with devastating effect using a cockroach to represent his life-force and showing what happened to it after ten minutes' furious clog dancing. Even before the sticky patch of ex-cockroach had been cleared up he had leapt on to a convenient sedan chair and had never risen since. It was amazing how influential that box of fortune cookies had been.

'Devotees!' proclaimed Furt in his traditional welcoming whisper. 'It is good to see you all here on this day of cautious festivity in honour of Maslar.' He pointed to the box. 'However, before the traditional non-lighting of the symbolic bonfire and the reaffirming of our Creed of Prudent Circumspection, may I ask your sympathy for our more unfortunate brethren who cannot be with us today. Three devotees have been severely reprimanded for heeding not the Code of the Green Cross by causing injury to themselves and shame on our sect by getting themselves run over . . .'

The crowd tutted and wagged their fingers pointedly, shaking their heads in risk-free remorse as the High Priest continued down the list.

'. . . and finally,' he whispered. 'It is my sad duty to inform you of the demise of Brother Gest, who has been lost to our cause after accidentally strolling into a magic lantern palace during a showing of *Pirates on Parade* starring Clint Machismo. So overcome by the wild images of derring-do and the wanton swashing of buckles was he that, after recovering from a dead faint, he flung off his knee-pads-of-faith, discarded the crash-helmet-of-caution and is now to be seen on the set of *A Pirate Function* as Machismo's stunt double. We shall remember him in our charms of warding.'

The crowd shook their heads and cast spells of protection over themselves.

'But, on a happier note, it is now almost time for me to ceremonially open this festival.' Furt pulled a large parcel out of his pocket and began to peel off the protective layers. After he had removed almost a dozen tea-towels and been positioned closer to a length of muted yellow ribbon he raised his hand and brandished an ancient knife which positively hummed with throbbing bluntness. Cheerfully, he donned a pair of gauntlets and began happily sawing away at the ribbon.

'Not so fast!' yelled a man in the crowd, flinging off his black covering robe to reveal the hated uniform of the Fort Knumm Lore Enforcement Agency. Terror flashed through the ranks of devotees, who whirled on their heels and picked their way across the wasteland carefully so as not to twist their ankles.

'Get them!' yelled Arch Sergeant Strappado to his crack

team of troopers as they followed his example and flung off their sunproof robes. 'Round up the damned magic users in the name of Operation De-mage. Slam them in jail!'

'Don't leave me!' whimpered Furt, wriggling his toes as his carriers fled carefully.

Shrieking with laughter, Strappado hurled the tribesfolk of the Cautious Newt into waiting cage carts and gleefully anticipated the expression on the man from MIN when he saw how efficient he had been.

And as High Priest Furt was literally dragged away (his sedan chair had been hitched to the back of a cart) he cursed this grossly unforeseen risk and vowed, if he survived, to instigate identity cards during festivals. Couldn't be too careful, he thought as he rattled through the backstreets of Fort Knumm. Give a free festival and you never know who'll turn up.

An unsuspecting pigeon squawked frantically as it was wrenched impatiently off its perch and roughly separated from the vital message it was carrying. With a grunt Tedd Sert hurled the bird into a basket in a cloud of feathers. His fingers clawed at the slip as the sweat of apprehension trickled down his brow. Good news, it *had* to be good news.

The massed throng in his Wagering Emporium held their charged breath. In truth, there was little room to do anything else. All day they had been flooding in as news of the stranger's gambling phenomenon had spread. Of the twenty-five races run today in various parts of the Talpa Mountains one man had correctly predicted the victor in twenty-four. It was unheard of. With unprecedented accuracy he had plucked from his hat the names of half a dozen ageing goats, a trio of moth-eaten camels and a whole host of other extreme outsiders. His one groat bet was now worth three thousand and twenty-four . . . and he had placed it all on the last race of the day.

Speculation was running at fever pitch as the roomful of gamblers watched his every move, turned his reasoning over in their minds and vainly attempted to fathom his system. Fortunately for Sert this took up so much time that no one had possessed the foresight to follow Quintzi's 'fortuitous' winning streak. It was either that or the superstitious crowd believed that after twenty-four perfect wagers his luck was bound to run out.

As Tedd Sert unravelled the recently delivered slip and looked at the result, his face fell.

'I take it the news is in my favour?' asked Quintzi with a certain nonchalance.

'Yes and no!' barked Sert angrily. 'If you are wondering whether Spoonfed Slob romped home to unfaltering victory in the five-thirty, then the answer is "yes". But, if you want to know whether you're walking out of here clutching upwards of sixteen and a half thousand groats in winnings, the answer is "*no*!" Nobody can predict twenty-five wins on twenty-five races. Unless they've got a system!'

'Guess it was just my lucky day. Told you it had changed. I won. Hand it over,' countered Quintzi.

'Luck? Pah! That had nothing to do with it. You've got a system! Look, I'll pay out five grand if you tell me your system.'

'No way,' answered Quintzi. 'I tell you, it's my lucky day.'

'It's a fix, a set-up. You cheated! Shop's closed, get out all of you!' yelled Sert pounding his fists angrily on the desk.

The crowd jeered and stood their ground. For years they had faithfully lined Tedd Sert's pockets (albeit thinly), following his 'daily suggestions' and now, when it looked like he was finally going to shell out . . . well, they weren't going to miss it, even if it was to a complete stranger with funny clothes and a jeering parrot on his shoulder.

A few side bets started up on whether he would get away with keeping the cash.

'I won!' insisted Quintzi forcefully.

'Cheated!'

'Won!'

'Cheat . . .'

'Won . . . Wait a minute,' shouted Quintzi, holding up his hands dramatically as an idea suddenly struck him, propelled by the tidal wave of euphoria from a day's faultless victory.

'You're a gambling man,' he leered, staring at the emporium owner.

'Er, yeah,' grunted Sert with the confidence of a newt on coals.

'What say we settle this matter with . . . a wager?'

The crowd cheered enthusiastically.

'Wager? What did you have in mind?' choked Sert warily. 'There's no more races today.'

'Doesn't have to be a race, does it?' Casually he wriggled his left pinkie in his ear, rattling the nano-sprites to attention. 'How about something a little closer to home? A gnat more immediate? Something that there can be absolutely no doubt about?' Quintzi looked up at the ceiling and the ageing oak beams, recalling the fun he had had with a recently destroyed barn.

'I'm listening,' struggled Sert under the weight of eager gazes.

'Hmmm,' grunted Quintzi as he stroked his beard thought-fully. 'I bet . . . I bet that beam up there won't continue to support this ceiling for more than, ooooh, the next three minutes.'

'What?' gaped Sert, disbelieving his ears as much as he did secondhand cart dealers. The crowd deflated. What insanity was this?

'That beam there?' pointed Sert, shaking his head.

'Yup. Three minutes from now and that'll come crashing down. How about double or quits?'

'You mad? This some kind of publicity stunt? That's been there for three hundred years!'

'And it won't last another three minutes, you'll see.'

'Double . . . or quits?'

Quintzi nodded.

'You're on. Ha!' exploded Sert, shaking hands quickly through the grille.

Quintzi whirled around, shouted a few numbers enthusiasti-cally and the crowd started to count, baffled and somewhat disappointed by this turn of events.

If, they mused, he'd won that much money in one day, why

was he blowing it on such a stupid whim? But then, all his other outside follies had come good. What's to stop this one? Nervously they edged back. Just in case.

Unseen, three tiny spots of light flitted out from Quintzi's ear and zipped ceilingwards, plunging into the very flesh of the beam and searching for any weak points within.

'. . . thirty-five . . . thirty-six . . .'

'Better get the cash out of the safe,' jeered Quintzi.

'Fat chance,' snapped Sert, folding his arms and settling smugly back in his chair.

The two stared at each other across the desk, locked in non-physical competition like grand chess masters.

'. . . ninety-nine . . . one hundred . . .'

'Hear that creak?' jibed Quintzi. 'Definite creaking noise, that was. Definite.'

The nano-sprites worked away at the molecular level, snipping through countless millions of lignin fibres and weakening the structure terminally, Quinzti knew very well that this wasn't strictly gambling, but what the hell, why change the habit of a daytime?

'. . . one hundred and fifty-one . . . one hundred and fifty-two . . .'

'Less than thirty seconds,' grinned Sert. 'Face it, you've lost!'

'It's not over yet,' returned Quintzi as the beam creaked and a wisp of plaster dust fell on to the desk.

Alarmed, the crowd stopped counting and took another nervous step backwards.

'Gimme the cash!' growled Quintzi as yet more ancient oak cross-fibres were ripped asunder and left flapping with all the structural integrity of your average lemon sorbet.

Quintzi started the counting off again, and on the count of one hundred and seventy-six, Tedd Sert screamed and looked up as the beam jerked, creaked wildly and fell out of the ceiling in a shower of plaster, spiders' webs and dead beetles. It arced past his nose with a scant inch to spare, crashing into the desk and scattering hundreds of betting slips high into the air. In a second the crowd had scarpered through the front door and were huddling in the street to see what other damage would occur.

Miraculously Tedd Sert's Wagering Emporium remained standing. At least, it did until moments after Quintzi Cohatl emerged carrying two huge sacks of cash, sporting a grubby sheen of plaster dust and an immense grin. He swaggered smugly in front of an awestruck crowd and kicked the door shut.

He and his parrot didn't stay around long enough to find out if the structural creaking and splintering noises were in fact as architecturally terminal as they sounded.

Across Fort Knumm, Hogshead was trying to figure a way of getting his hands on one of the delicious-looking pies that were arrayed upon a large stall in a square. Unfortunately the mountain of a baker was in absolutely no mood to even consider for a millisecond the possibility of giving one away. Hogshead had tried that, as well as feigning acute malnutrition, setting up decoys and attempting to steal one and simply sprinting past in a desperate snatch and grab.

None of his ploys had worked and now he was starving. The simple truth was, and this also applied to every single spell in the Thaum and Garden Show, if you ain't broke you can have it.

Miserably he rummaged about in his pockets for the fifteenth time in the vain hope that he'd missed a little cluster of several dozen groats. He hadn't. It was hopeless. He should just get up and struggle back to Cranachan, forget all about that mysterious device and all the spells for sale and bury himself in the single book that Merlot hadn't confiscated.

And he would've been on his feet and begging for a lift if it hadn't been for a bearded mandolinist who wandered into the square, hurled his cap on the ground and struck up with a jaunty reel.

Hogshead was amazed. It was out of tune, out of time and he was out of his head on some dodgy-looking cider, but nobody seemed to care. In minutes, the gap-toothed busker's cap was filling with flung groats.

Hogshead fumed at the unfairness of it all. If only he had a mandolin then *he* could siphon off some of this sudden fountain of cash. If only he could play a jig or a reel but . . . Hang on! He could do something *far* better than that.

He never thought it would come to this. Never had he expected his big break to be so, well, publicly shabby, or so blatant. A small group of friends in a back room, he had imagined, but this? . . . He cringed as he thought it through. It would be okay as long as there was nobody out there he knew. He stood nervously, coughed in a very pathetic manner and launched four flaming spheres into the air.

It had the desired effect. Much to the annoyance of the stall holders and the mandolin player the people spun around and proceeded to 'ooh' and 'ahh' at Hogshead's magical display as the spheres were joined by a fifth and gradually metamorphosed into a quintet of tumbling armadillos.

And as the plated mammals bobbed above the heads of the awestricken audience the attention of a pair of polo-neck-and-dungaree-clad ruffians was snatched and transfixed. They glanced quickly at each other, nodded and plunged into the crowd, gauntlets flexing excitedly, orders of 'Operation De-mage', ringing clear.

The crowd scattered, the ruffians grabbed Hogshead and, snarling only that 'The Boss wants a word!', dragged him away kicking and screaming.

Unseen, five armadillos hit the ground, shook their heads, blinked and scarpered in five different directions.

It was almost dawn before Quintzi managed to clear his extortionately priced and rapidly rented room of eager punters frantic to hear how his 'system' worked.

It was a task achieved only by vast amounts of lying and the donation of the better part of a thousand groats to the hastily created Wagerers' Benevolent Drinking Fund. A sturdy body of men and women whose task it was to alleviate the tension of overwhelming gambling success by drinking to the victor's undying health – all fluids subsequently imbibed being paid for, naturally, out of a healthy slice of said victor's winnings.

189

Quinzti was toasted and cheered down Ye Spit well into the wee small hours.

Alone at last, he leapt on to the creaking bed, uncorked a bottle of vastly overpriced wine and raised a glass to his lips.

'Not so fast!' came a voice in his left ear.

'What is it now?' groaned Quintzi.

'You got yours. Now it's our turn! You promised this morning, remember?' tapped the nano-sprites.

'Come back in the morning. I'm knackered,' mumbled Quintzi, downing a vast swallow of wine.

'Okay, if that's the way you want to treat us. It's no more Mister Nice Sprites!'

Suddenly it felt as if someone had maliciously jammed a searing red-hot poker into his ear and wiggled it. 'Aaargghh! What the . . . Stop. Stop!'

'We'll keep that up all night if necessary,' growled the nano-sprites.

'What d'you want from me?' moaned Quintzi clutching the side of his head and nervously sniffing the air for any sign of charred earlobe.

'Our souvenir of the Auric Triangle. Get it out!' commanded the nano-sprites in the certain knowledge that he would obey.

Miserably Quintzi tugged the hextirpator out of his cloak pocket and set it down on a bedside table. 'There, happy now? Can I get some sleep?'

'Uh-huh. Mushrooms. Get 'em out!'

'What?'

'Take two. Now shove them in . . . Hold on just a . . .' The confidence of the nano-sprites suddenly took a nosedive. A bucket of reality's ice water drowned their enthusiasm. There was in fact nowhere to insert the mushrooms. Silently they screamed. There must have been another part to it, a crusher. Without that vital device it was utterly impossible for them to get their thaumic tendrils on the vast dam of magic locked up in the punnet of fungus. Unless . . .

It was Nimlet's idea. His problem-solving mind whirled the mallet of logic hard on its nut of insolubility with a satisfying crack. He leapt at Quintzi's eardrum as the Axolotian waved the punnet around and asked, 'What do I do with these now, eh?'

'Eat them!' bashed Nimlet. 'All of them. Now!'

'What the . . . Owww, all right, all right!' he cried as his ear ignited once more.

He shovelled the greying fungi into his mouth, thrilling with anticipation of the coming rush. He kind of liked favours like this.

Quintzi threw the final fungal offering down his throat, washing it quickly away with the remains of the glass of wine, lying back and readying himself for the exquisite feelings he knew were only seconds away, rolling in as unstoppable as a tidal wave with a mission.

'Now! Remove that tube from the device,' commanded Nimlet, somehow making it sound as if it was coming from a set of desperately clenched teeth, 'and insert the needle into your arm just above the . . .'

'Whoa!' squealed Quintzi. 'Now hold on. Nobody said anything about n . . . n . . . needles!'

'Would you prefer a little more earache?' battered the nano-sprite ominously.

Quintzi stared at the needle, glinting in the pre-dawn moonlight. 'I . . . I . . .'

A pneumatic drill revved up next to his eardrum.

'Okay . . . okay . . . okay!' Trembling, he picked the needle up, looked away and jammed it painfully into a convenient artery, almost fainting at the thought of it.

'Light that burner!' battered Nimlet as the other two trembled in confusion.

'Burner! What are you on ab . . . Whooooooaaaaaaahhhhhh!'

Inside Quintzi's stomach the mushrooms were releasing their thaumic cargo into his bloodstream, flooding his ageing body with free vitamin hex.

'The burner!' hammered Nimlet, and buzzed out of his ear. In a second he had zipped into the wick of the athanor and was vibrating furiously. Friction heated a tiny spot, raising the temperature and in a flash igniting the fuel.

Quintzi's eyes rolled into the top of his head as pumps began to move within the hextirpator, sucking, pulling vitamin-hex-rich blood up through the needle, along tubes and into the complex purification mechanisms. It ran down columns packed with thaumophilic extractants, was pushed up heating columns and finally, after being recombined and activated, three drops of shimmering one hundred proof thaumaglobin appeared at the end of the tiny tube. With a shriek of unbridled ecstasy the nano-sprites zipped into liquid magical heaven.

Of this Quintzi was completely unaware, his body was gripped in the rush of thaumaglobin overdose. His major organs were mamba-ing in sheer delight, his veins pulsing frenzied tangos of rapture, his spirits soaring on euphoric wings of gossamer bliss. And for only the third time in fifty-odd years, the follicles on his shining dome began to extrude hair, his arthritic joints slithered smoothly over perfect cartilaginous surfaces. Years seemed to slip off him, lines on his face filled out, muscles swelled, hair sprouted dark brown not grey and his midriff grew to the well-fed proportion he had sported in his teenage days. For a glorious five minutes he felt utterly tremendous.

But then, abruptly, it stopped. As the final milligrams of thaumaglobin were slurped from his system by the magically starved nano-sprites, Quintzi's body returned to its original aged, osseous state of near-decrepitude.

Actually, that's not strictly true. There was one fundamental difference, one completely new addition to the list of aches and pains that infested his body. Quintzi had a craving – a totally overwhelming desire to feel like that again. And again. And . . .

Now if only it could be done without recourse to needles.

'Every night!' shrieked Quintzi an hour later. 'I've got to jam a n . . . n . . . that into my arm every night just so you can . . . can feed?'

'Yup!' tapped the nano-sprites on the inside of his ear in the chirpiest manner he had yet heard.

'But that's disgusting!' spluttered Quintzi in confusion, his head awash with terifying armies of needles stretching away into a pincushioned future.

'Tough. That's the way it is. You're not up to much. Full of impurities and a ton of non-thaumic drivel. Now if you'd been a real prophet . . .'

'What's that got to do with anything! Okay, so I lied my way through college at the Prophetic Institute and bluffed my way into a job at the Fruit Protection Agency, but so what? I was good at it!'

'Lucky.'

'I won the Augury Academy Awards. I would have been in the *Good Seer Guide* next year . . .'

'If it hadn't been for a few fires, yeah, sure.'

'I didn't see it coming . . .'

'You didn't see anything coming. That's the problem. If only you were capable of producing your own thaumaglobin like any honest prophet or wizard. But no, we happen to be stuck with you so it's needles at midnight for . . .'

'Wait a minute,' cried Quintzi suddenly as mention of the 'n' word crystalised a thought in his seething stylophobic mind. 'You saying prophets produce their own thaumywatsit?'

'Very good,' tapped the nano-sprites sarcastically. 'It's so nice to have an attentive audience.'

'And the same goes for wizards?' he pressed, rubbing his punctured forearm and staring out of the window thoughtfully. Something was hatching. He hadn't been an expert practitioner in the arts of scheming and fabrication for the past fifty-odd years to know a chance to shirk when he sniffed it.

Early on in life Quintzi had realised there were two ways to get things done: solitarily, or by the ancient and noble art of coercion. And, if at all physically possible, he'd always plump for the latter. So what if the art of coercion called upon a little illegality along the way? That just added to the fun.

'Wizard, witches anything that uses magic. Doesn't matter, they all need thaumaglobin to carry all them precious little thaumic particles to their spell-flexing fingertips,' confirmed the nano-sprites.

'Excellent!' grinned Quintzi, leaping off the bed and trying to ignore the faint dizziness he felt. 'No more damned needles for me!' In a moment he was in his stockinged feet, padding towards the front door of the guest-house and disappearing off down the street. The nano-sprites blinked at each other inside the darkness of his ear, totally confused.

Ten minutes later, after sending the nano-sprites ahead to scout, he screeched to a halt outside the back window of a small hut, the garden of which was devoid of vegetation and any semblance of grass. He raised a curious eyebrow at the string of chewed washing that dangled on a line, shrugged, pinned himself to the wall and began fiddling with the catch on one of the windows. Easing it stealthily up he stepped inside, padded his way up the creaking stairs and into a small bedroom, barely managing to contain a startled shriek of amusement as he peered at the scene within.

It was not, he had to admit, the type of bedroom one would have expected Arch Sergeant Strappado of the Fort Knumm Enforcement Agency to kip in. Not expected, that is, unless you knew his wife.

Fragments of half-chewed boots and strips of leather littered the floor, almost, but not entirely, obscuring the thin layer of straw spread patchily around. The bare skeletons of long-dead mattresses lay like the sun-bleached remnants of beached leviathans, bent, twisted and thoroughly useless. Teeth marks were scattered randomly amongst the edges of cupboards, the windowsill and three of the bed's four legs, grinning white against the age-darkened wood. And within all this disorder, two figures slumbered gently, one breathing heavily and occasionally twitching as he dreamt of part two of the inquisition he would enjoy later that morning, the other snoring as she breathed in, bleating as she breathed out.

Thus had it been for two years, the peaceful harmony of a snoozing couple. But things were about to change.

Quintzi crept around the end of the bed, barely containing his amusement as Viv bleated gently in her sleep. But suddenly, leaping faster than a frog on a barbecue, he lunged, snatched Strappado across the mouth and whispered in his startled ear. 'Your Kingdom needs you!'

The Arch Sergeant's eyes slapped open and stared unbelievingly at Quintzi for a moment, blinking as he recognised the face of the man from MIN.

'A mission!' whispered Quintzi. 'Up for it? Top secret, hush hush, undercover eradication.'

Strappado's eyes glowed in the dark as excitement snatched at his innards. His head nodded wildly, burning with questions. Eradication of what?

Quintzi glanced over his shoulder as if he had heard something, the whites of his eyes flashing left and right melodramatically. A surge of adrenalin flooded Strappado's thaumaphobic, mage-hating body.

'Need this kept quiet. Suspect in a murder investigation broken out, given us the slip. Hiding here in Fort Knumm among the low-life magic user community.'

Strappado trembled as he heard this. Could this be true? Was he actually going to be able to legitimately beat up a few damned itinerant, stinking mages? As if to answer, Viv bleated and rolled over, dreaming of pastures and cheese-making.

'Suspect in disguise. Your mission, should you choose to accept it: round up and arrest any known, stinking magical scum for interrogation immediately. Bring 'em in and your kingdom will be eternally grateful!'

And suddenly, before Strappado could answer with anything more than a nod, Quintzi swooped around the end of the bed and out of the Arch Sergeant's hut, eager to get the most of his nano-sprites in another day's 'gambling'.

Three streets away, he collapsed in a fit of wild laughter, clutching his ribs and reeling with the memory of the expression of eager devotion on Strappado's face. So easy. And now it was time to find larger, more private accommodation.

Strappado lay in bed and positively buzzed with pride-filled excitement. His help had been sought out and selected. He had been chosen by MIN! And amazingly, he had been ahead of them. Oh, how efficient he'd look tomorrow.

Seconds after this surge of joy, his heart raced at the prospect of beating up a few mages who even so much as looked like they might think about resisting arrest. What a day he had to look forward to. What a day!

Ellis Dee was furious. He had never believed it could take so long to collate all the eyewitness reports of his 'subjects'. Why he had let Praquat head it up, he'd never know:

After questioning absolutely everybody about whether they remembered anything unusual that night and then spending the best part of six hours dismissing alleged sightings of choruses of tap-dancing badgers and hang-gliding armadillos, Praquat had recalled everyone for a hour and a half session of hypnoregression each, followed by a spell of intensive aromatherapy to rebuild their karma.

His two days of in-depth investigation had turned up the incontravertible fact that the hextirpator might or might not have been stolen by a teenage black female Caucasian in his mid-sixties.

And the strangely anonymous en-dreadlocked Zhaminah wasn't much less frustrated by it all. But that could have had more to do with his constant irritation at how much he had forgotten about interrogation. Two years spent in deep cover locked certain skills far out of reach. His mood could also have been attributed to the stream of violently threatening communications with a certain Commander Furlansk back at the headquarters of the Mystical Intelligence Network. Right now his entire financial future and three-quarters of his favourite organs depended on the safe recapture of the hextirpator.

'Damn you,' he cursed in the privacy of his own tree house. 'Answer me!' Angrily he stabbed his index finger at the dark grey shell of his mollusc and awaited a reply. Now that he had a lead he *had* to report it.

Years ago technicians working for the Mystical Intelligence Network had been investigating the odd phenomenon of underwater communication between individuals of the horn-shaped Tuleph Whelk. It had long been known that the male of the species was capable of issuing a shrill siren-like sound which could be carried for miles through the shallows of the Eastern Tepid Seas. In fact it was a surprise that one of the tacky tour operators working in the area hadn't exploited the chance to offer Whelk Male Voice Choirs to gullible punters.

But one factor had always remained a mystery. How do the females communicate? It was obvious that they did, for whole klatsches of them could be regularly witnessed wriggling aimlessly through the shallows. After decades of painstaking research (which spawned a complete set of delicious whelk-based recipes) technicians discovered that the whelks forced jets of water through tiny orifices burrowed in their shells, thus emitting a high-pitched shriek. Similarly tuned receptacles in other shells were capable of vibrating in sympathy and thus receiving the message.

It wasn't long before octave dividers were inserted and MIN operatives were issued with the first of these Tuleph Horn Communicators. Within the first year an array of booster shells were secreted in grids throughout the known world and, lo, the first shell-net Tuleph Horn system was born.

Zhaminah snarled as he listened to the normally soothing sound of the sea issuing from the horn, then he blocked up specific orifices and shouted again down his specific frequency.

And amazingly he received a reply.

'Yes?' snapped the thin voice.

'Agent Zhaminah here, reporting latest development regarding that device beginning with "H"!' he stated, encoding his words in case anyone was eavesdropping.

'You again,' tutted the reply. 'Found it yet?'

'Er not as such, but I've uncovered a description of the suspect!' he enthused hopefully.

'Well. Spill it!' crackled the thin reply.

'The culprit is a female black Caucasian in his mid-sixties believed to be in possession of an alarm macaw, or not.'

There was a strangled scream, a click and the sussuration of the sea returned.

Zhaminah scowled. Something told him that perhaps that last report wouldn't improve his promotional chances much.

Excited pupils dilated eagerly, watching as a vast armoured

claw arced out of the sky and smashed into the expanse of blue-grey carapace. Staggering beneath the onslaught of the blow the decapod waved frantic antennae, shuffled backwards and launched a scything retaliation with its own deadly claw, catching its attacker firmly by the front two legs and flipping it on to its knobbled back. In a second it lunged, dealing death in an armour-piercing instant. Cheering echoed hollowly in the background as the crowd of onlookers yelled enthusiastic encouragement to the armoured victor. And another wave of betting slips were torn asunder or exchanged for paltry sums of cash.

Quintzi Cohatl grinned to himself as he scribbled the name 'Pulveriser' on a scrap of parchment and casually closed down the near future round-up of the Fort Knumm Boxer Shrimp League on Scry Sports. Swiftly he took a swig of the remains of a skin of red wine, tugged on his boots and lurched out of the room followed by a zipping trio of nano-sprites.

He stomped on through two more rooms and exited from the back door, wincing as the light hit the back of his eyes. Scrying, he found, was easier with the curtains closed. Blinking he lurched across a small courtyard and staggered arthritically into the vast outhouse, grinning as he surveyed the straw-strewn interior. It hadn't taken much to persuade the owners to go on an all expenses paid trip to Shirm for a few weeks. It was amazing what ten thousand groats could do to alleviate the reluctance of hovel owners. They'd even put themselves out and brought a sack of sunflower seeds for Tiemecx, although he had been surprised that it cost a hundred groats a pound . . .

'Yes,' he muttered to himself as he patted the tubes, columns and single glinting needle of the hextirpator. 'Perfect, just perfect!' He chuckled under his breath. 'But now, it's time for some fun!'

Backing out of the door he slammed it shut, turned a key in a vast padlock and spun on his heel. Striding purposefully down the hill away from the extortionately priced hovel he followed his nose through the dark backstreets and headed towards the lower Slove district of Fort Knumm.

Taking its name from the almost terminally sluggish River

Slove, this area of dilapidation and mouldering aquatic algae was avoided like the plague by all but the most nasally challenged of citizens. There was only one exception.

Those with any interest in the Fort Knumm Boxer Shrimp League flocked there eagerly in nose-bound droves. And today was no exception. Following a particularly lethal season, which offered spectacular viewing pleasure but presented vast substitution problems for the breeders, the final ten six-inch shrimps were to be pitted together in one, no-holds-barred, mashing match. It would decide the ultimate winner of the Golden Pincer Award. Today was a day whereupon vast amounts of cash were destined to change pockets.

And Quintzi knew whose pockets most of it would end up in. With the list of the order of destruction clutched firmly in his fist he couldn't possibly fail.

Swooping around the tattered remains of an ageing barn, he thrilled as he heard the hubbub of expectant punters betting money rashly on the fortunes of doomed crustaceans.

'Ten groats says Aggravator falls in the first five minutes!' declared Quintzi, striding up to a small balding man waving his hands in a strangely unfathomable manner. Automatically the wagering clerk held out a slip and reached for Quintzi's proffered coin. Just as the transaction was about to be completed a hand flew out of the sticky air, slapping Quintzi's coin out of his grip, and the hand's owner stepped in the way.

Quintzi's face dropped as he recognised the dust-covered figure of one Tedd Sert, owner of the now structurally condemned Wagering Emporium.

'So, come to ruin the Fort Knumm Gold Pincer have you?' accused Sert. 'What system you using today, eh?'

Quintzi took a step backwards as a dozen angry faces turned his way and growled. Every one of them had been present at the strange and frightening events which had transpired in the Wagering Emporium, and every one of them knew that it hadn't been entirely honest wagering that had occurred.

'I'm here for a spot of honest wager—' began Quintzi. Tiemecx cringed and debated fluttering away to a safe distance.

'Honest?' barked Sert. 'I'll bet you have no intention of using honesty!'

'Fifty thousand to one on!' declared the balding wagering clerk and began waving his hands furiously as he took bets. Forests of densely whispered conversation sprang up all around as baffled punters were fed extrapolated rumours regarding Quintzi's recent dishonourable behaviour. And as the number of rumours grew, so did the inaccuracy of the whispers, and with it, a sense of steadily mounting unease. Even some of the boxer shrimps began to get skittish in their paddock pools.

'I've come here to place a few bets on . . .' began Quintzi again.

'No you haven't!' interrupted Sert. 'You've come here with only one thing in mind. Destruction!'

'No. I . . . here, take my bet will you,' offered Quintzi, looking to the balding wagering clerk.

'Your money's no good here!' said Sert. 'I know your sort. Profess to love gambling but secretly you're trying to destroy all the wagering emporia in Fort Knumm!'

Quintzi shook his head, feeling a wave of anger rise inside him. This buffoon had crossed him yesterday, questioning his every bet in that same irritating manner, sneering as the first three came good, snarling with the next two and screaming with the last twenty. How dare this creature get in the way of his fortune? Feelings of superiority seethed within Quintzi's chest as Sert poked him in the shoulder to emphasise each point.

'You're from the Anti-Wagering League, aren't you? C'mon, admit it! You want to destroy the last haven of pleasure the likes of us can have, don't you?'

Quintzi's mind whirled in confusion for a few moments. What was it with the citizens of Fort Knumm? Why did they insist on accusing him of being something he wasn't? If he wasn't a MIN agent, then he was a member of the Anti-Wagering League, whoever they were.

'No! I just want a bit of a flutter,' protested Quintzi, becoming horribly aware that the contest was about to begin. If he didn't get his bet on soon, he'd miss it completely. Several thousand groats waved sorrowful farewells and wiped tears from their streaming eyes.

'Bit of a flutter?' crowed Sert sarcastically. 'What d'you think this is? A butterfly farm? Clear off, we don't want your cash!'

And then, with the final volley of finger-jabbing something clicked inside Quintzi. His temper surged. If he wasn't going to get his way then no one else was. Years of frustration swelled to the forefront of his psyche, boiling in crimson conflict. Tiemecx swallowed nervously.

'Okay!' bellowed Quintzi, his face purpling, his body seeming to grow with fury. 'You're right I don't want to place bets. I detest shrimps, I loathe boxing and I spit on every one of your pathetic creatures!'

The crowd swelled in the exact manner normally ascribed to angry seas. Tiemecx fluttered surreptitiously out of the war zone.

'Just give me the cash!' bawled Quintzi. 'You know damn well I'm going to win it!'

'Well, you can't have it until then,' countered Sert sounding far more stroppy and girly than he had intended.

'Oh no?' whispered Quintzi, his eyebrow arching in rhetorical query.

'No.'

'Ha! Wanna bet?' grinned Quintzi. Cold shudders of all-too-recent memory wriggled seditiously down the spines of the punters who had witnessed yesterday's events. 'You see,' he continued in a dark tone, 'I bet that if you don't hand over all your cash, right now, then something very, very nasty will happen to a particular ten boxer shrimps currently nestling in their paddock pools, just over there.' He pointed dismissively to his left.

The crowd, as one, took a deep breath, rumours and vivid memories of splitting beams filling their minds.

'Is that a threat?' scowled Sert.

'Threat? Oooh, no, not at all. Merely a feeling I have in my fingertips. An "odd" feeling you might say, ha ha! It's funny but every moment you hesitate in handing over lots of dosh I can feel those odds changing, getting more and more likely that an accident will occur. Can you sense it too? Do you feel, ahem . . . lucky?' grinned Quintzi sharkishly and waggled a finger in his ear. The nano-sprites needed little bidding; they knew what Quintzi had in mind and began buzzing eagerly.

'As long as *you're* here in our sight,' growled Sert attempting to hide the uncomfortable feeling in the pit of his intestines, 'then those boxer shrimps are perfectly . . .'

'Safe?' interrupted Quintzi, raising a greying eyebrow and shaking his head ominously. 'Have you checked the solidity of that small jetty over there? The one with all those barrels on, see?' he pointed to his left. 'It would be *so* unfortunate if that were to, ahem, collapse unexpectedly, spilling barrels into the paddock pools in a hail of crushed crustaceans and smashed shrimps.'

'Never happen!' whined Sert. 'That jetty's been there three hundred years and is a solid as . . . ah.' *Déjà-vu* clamped hard around his throat. Recollections of a certain scene not too dissimilar to this one flashed across Tedd Sert's mind. Nervously he slapped plaster dust from his shoulder.

Quintzi grinned. 'I ask again, do you feel lucky?'

Sert's mouth dithered in gasping indecision. Something very odd was going on here. This wasn't gambling, it couldn't be. It wasn't stacked his way.

'I feel so lucky, lucky!' whispered Cohatl harshly, rubbing his palms together in anticipation.

'Well, *I* bloody well don't!' shouted a frantically cigar-smoking man suddenly bursting through the crowd, jingling under a wealth of necklaces and ostentatious rings. Harvee Goldfysshe, promoter of fayres, fêtes and boxer shrimp tournaments, squinted at Quintzi through a growing fug of bluish smoke. 'Twenty thousand groats says that jetty stays intact, okay?' barked the promoter, shaking a sack of cash. He had seen Quintzi's obvious signal – nobody wiggles their finger in their ear unless it's a signal – and he knew, right there and then, that the jetty had been sabotaged, joints sawn through, slowly smouldering fires, ton and a half of dynamite –

could be anything. All that mattered to him was that the damned tournament happened. He'd have to pay back the hundred thousand to Scry Sports if it didn't.

'Twenty thousand?' gagged Quintzi trying desperately to keep a straight face. 'That'll do nicely!' And in a flash of gold toga he snatched the sack, turned and strode purposefully away, a sharp lick of victory curling on his upper lip.

Up to his midriff in black mud, one of Harvee Goldfysshe's personal assistants scoured the underside of the jetty for any apparent sabotage.

'Nothing!' he shouted.

'There must be!' yelled the promoter angrily a few minutes later. 'I don't pay out twenty grand for nothing!' Surely he hadn't just lost his 20 per cent in front of all those punters, had he? Been had? For nothing?

'No sign,' confirmed the assistant, beginning to sink. 'Er, can someone give me a hand. I . . . I'm going under!'

'So will I be if this gets out,' growled Goldfysshe. 'Never promote anything else. Never! Pull that jetty apart I want evidence!'

Even as he rounded the corner of the barn Quintzi knew that something momentous had just happened. He hadn't had to win it. They had just given it to him! Okay, he'd had to put a bit of pressure on, but still . . . twenty thousand groats for just turning up and having a bit of a strop. Wow! That's better than some of the stars of the magic lantern get.

Baffled, and buzzing with not just a teensy bit of elation, Quintzi pondered three major fundamental questions. Was that a one-off? A strange combination of fates and fortune? If not, then how could he do it again?

'Now then, young man. How many times have I told you about it, hmm?' rasped a bonneted woman from behind a pair of almost opaque pince-nez. 'How many?'

'Far too many,' grumbled the Lore Enforcement Agency reception guard wearily to himself, his cheek slouching further down the palm of his hand.

'What was that?' snapped Mrs Arangue in her cracked

falsetto as she peered up at the guard behind the imposing range of the mountainous front desk, like some feral mole before the mass that is Mount Annatack. 'Don't mumble into your beard, now. It's not polite!'

'Yeah, yeah,' grunted the guard. It was like this every day. Mrs Arangue was always here, complaining about the parlous state of this, moaning about the shocking increase in that, or simply wittering on endlessly about the disgusting dropping of standards of some other trivial something or other. And today was no exception.

'Done it again, they have,' she yelled and would have pounded her octogenarian fist on the desktop if she had been capable of reaching that altitude. 'Littering the river. I tell you, there's barrels everywhere and somebody, though heavens know who, somebody has destroyed the little jetty in the middle of the river. I blame those shrimp gamblers myself. The river's never been the same since they came and started their wicked activities. Criminals they are, nothing but criminals! There's footprints all the way out to the jetty. That's evidence, that is! Evidence! Just match them to their shoe sizes and you've caught them red-handed!' Mrs Arangue paused for breath in her tirade, pursed her lips and gave the guard a hard stare. 'Well, what are you going to do about it?'

'Well . . .'

'Aren't you going to take fingerprints or anything?' rasped Mrs Arangue before the guard had a chance to attempt any fobbing off. 'You know, before the tide comes in and washes it all away, hmmm?'

'Yeah, yeah, sure. I'll send someone round,' he grunted, dripping enthusiasm from every bored pore. He knew there was no urgency, even if someone was going to take a look. The tide wasn't due in until next week.

'Used to be a nice river,' complained Mrs Arangue. 'When I was a little girl it was full of fish and teeming with birds . . .'

'Oh, I remember reading about that,' grunted the guard. 'Wasn't that the time of the fishmongers' revolt when they hurled rotting cod at each other from each side and you couldn't move for bleeding gulls squawking and carrying on . . .'

'That isn't the point,' countered Mrs Arangue, reaching for the handle of her umbrella in a manner likely to cause imminent offence.

'Cod Wars, they called it, didn't they?' smirked the guard and received a swift crack from a certain brolly.

'I didn't come here to be insulted!' rasped Mrs Arangue. 'I demand to see your superior officer.'

'He's not in. Call back next year.'

'Next year? But that's months away. I demand immediate action and shall remain here until something constructive is deemed to be being . . .' At least Mrs Arangue would have ranted something similar had she not been shoved roughly sideways by an expensively dressed figure with a cigar, stamping up to the desk and slamming his fist on the desk. The squat, balding man with him sniggered.

'Matter of grave importance,' snapped Harvee Goldfysshe at the reception guard and tapped his cigar ash on the desktop. 'Get Strappado here!'

'I demand to see him also . . .' began Mrs Arangue from the floor, before Tedd Sert whirled on his heel and glared forcefully at her.

Grumbling angrily, as was the normal conclusion of such daily fracas, Mrs Arangue bustled out into the streets and headed home for a nice afternoon's cross-stitch with a bottle of gin at her side. It wasn't *that* important that she see the Arch Sergeant today. There was always tomorrow. Or the next day.

If she'd known then that she wasn't going to have to wait that long before her next reason for complaining, and what it was that she would be up in arms about, she would have been skipping river-wards as fast as her ageing legs could possibly carry her.

'Strappado is busy,' reiterated the receptionist.

'Doing what?' snarled Goldfysshe.

'Parchmentwork. In his office!' answered the guard. 'Hey, come back you can't . . .'

'We know the way,' growled the promoter, stamping off down the corridor under a furious cloud of cigar smoke.

Moments later he had kicked Strappado's door open and was

205

marching unstoppably towards him. 'Okay, okay. What's the game?' he insisted.

Strappado looked up from the pile of cash he was counting from this morning's 'donations'. 'Ahhh, Mr Goldfysssss . . .'

'This some sort of new plan, eh?' snarled Harvee. 'It nearly had me. Nearly. Now gimme my twenty grand back!'

Strappado was clearly at a loss. 'What twenty . . . ?'

'Look,' Goldfysshe leaned ominously over the desk. 'I don't detest making my "donations" to the upkeep of the Lore Enforcement Agency any more than anyone else. But when you start such underhand techniques to screw us for more, well, that's just not on!'

'What are you shouting about?'

'Hear that, Sert? Touching, isn't it? Such devotion to duty.' He wheeled back to glare at Strappado. 'What am I shouting about? I'll tell you! "Twenty grand or the shrimps get it!" *That's* what I'm talking about. And I wouldn't mind if there *was* a real threat!'

'It was real enough yesterday,' shuddered Sert thinking of his beloved Wagering Emporium.

Harvee Goldfysshe stared at Arch Sergeant Strappado's jaw, took in the way it was flopping limply from side to side and realised that something was indeed wrong. Strappado wasn't a convincing enough actor to keep up this feigned ignorance for so long.

'You telling me someone's muscling in on my patch?' Strappado gasped after Sert had given him the full story. 'And they're using b . . . blackmail? Yeurrgh!'

Goldfysshe nodded. 'So what you going to do about it, huh? Seems to me you'd best find who's responsible or I'll start demanding my money back!'

'You can't do that!'

'Oh no? And what if the rest of Fort Knumm just happens to hear a whisper that you can't, er, "protect" them properly, eh? How d'you think that'll affect your "donations", hmmm?'

Goldfysshe didn't wait for the answer. He whirled on his heel and stomped out of the Lore Enforcement Agency building, his heart seething with acute fury. Nobody took him for a ride. *Nobody!*

Back in a certain grossly overpriced hovel high on a hill above Fort Knumm, Quintzi Cohatl tugged the cork out of another bottle of wine and filled a waiting flagon. Grinning lopsidedly, he raised his hand in a toast, and stared at the sack containing the larger part of thirty-two thousand groats, his mind whirring excitedly as he considered how far he had come. Two days ago he had one groat to his name and now ... Well, who knows where he could be in another two days? Who knows, if only he could foresee ...

'Idiot!' he thrilled excitedly. 'You *can* see the future. Those days of bluffing are ancient history!' With a grin he snatched his newly acquired scrying crystal out of his pocket and scrabbled with the controls. In seconds a picture filled the sphere.

'... lcome to the Fifty-Third Interkingdomnal rabbit-breeding championships brought to you by Scry Sports. Yes, watch those bunnies at it ...'

Quintzi grumbled and twisted at another knob. The crystal shimmered with static interference and suddenly crackled into a different picture.

'... but my darling. How shallst I prove my undying love is true? Wouldst thou have me face him on the duelling arena ... ?'

'Gah! Soaps,' he grumbled again spinning the knob and breathing a sigh of relief as *Thaum and Away* vanished into a swirling snowstorm. The crystal crackled, flashed and tuned into the broadcast he sought. There, in full-colour futurescope, was Channel Forth – *The Scry's the Limit!*

Eagerly he selected the character menu, rubbing his hands cheerfully as the crystal filled with lists of names. Quickly he rifled through to the 'C's and there, looking very insignificant amongst all the thousands of others was the name COHATL, QUINTZI. With the briefest wriggling of the cursor he highlighted his name and clicked. The screen flashed, turned black momentarily, fizzed and leapt once more into life showing a new and hauntingly familiar scene. Quintzi stared at the image of a balding man in his mid-sixties who was staring at a crystalline image of a balding man in his mid-sixties who was staring . . .

Tutting he reached out to adjust the scrying crystal's temporal lock and scratched his head as an infinity of balding images reached out and scratched their heads. Baffled, he turned to look over his shoulder. A chain of Quintzis followed. Snarling, he grabbed the temporal lock and spun it backwards, watching as the crystalline Quintzi scratched his head in precisely the manner he had a few seconds previously. With a grumble he spun the lock forward to snatch a glimpse of the future. The image in the crystal ran at double speed, catching up with his current actions, accelerating towards the immediate present . . . and stopped.

Quintzi shouted something unprintable as an infinity of other Quintzis shouted the same thing.

'Oi!' he cried, waggling his finger in his left ear. 'What's wrong with this thing? Is it broken or what?' he demanded of the nano-sprites, his voice dripping with angry frustration.

'Oh no. It's working perfectly,' came the tapped reply.

'Perfectly? Don't talk rot, the temporal lock's gone! I can't see my future!'

'Exactly,' answered the nano-sprites as if it was completely obvious.

'Exactly what?'

'You can't see your future. Not allowed.'

'What? Why can't I?'

'Too dangerous,' tapped the nano-sprites. 'Single biggest cause of terminal depression amongst seers and prophets is seeing what little surprises life has in store. If it's bad news, you feel wrecked and start looking for a convenient cliff to hurl yourself off. Good news, you know, money beyond your wildest dreams, unimaginable fame and a devoted posse of maidens – well, that's worse. What'll you do with your cashless, unknown, lonely self until then, eh? It's bad enough waiting for your Christmas pressies. And that's once a year. But ten years, fifteen? More than most folks can stand.'

'So how do I figure out what to do next?' whined Quintzi miserably.

'Like everyone else, stupid,' bashed the nano-sprites. 'You guess!'

Quintzi snarled as he muttered a string of blasphemies. 'Guess?' he growled under his breath. 'Guessing's for losers and no-hopers, for idiots in gambling emporia who can't see beyond the next race! Guess! Pah! I might just as well trust to the fickle hand of fate and hold my breath till it's my turn to dip into the sweet trolley of delight.'

'Yeah. Same as everyone else,' tapped the nano-sprites.

'What? The same as those morons I fleeced in the gambling emporium?' cried Quintzi riding on a surge of arrogance, recalling their amazed faces as he picked victor after victor. 'How can you compare me to those creatures? I must've looked like some sort of prophet to them. Especially with the final bet on the beam, ha! All or nothing if it collapsed. They'd have never seen anything like that if it hadn't been for me! That wouldn't have happened without . . .'

And then, as Quintzi poured another glass of wine down his throat, something hit him. The light bulb of an idea lit in the void of his mind, shining inspiration into a galaxy of shadowy doubt.

'Of course!' he chuckled evilly. '*I* made it happen. I'm a *prophet* that makes things happen!' In that instant he could see his future stretching away from him clearer than he would ever have seen it in any scrying crystal. And he knew it was secured. *He* had been in total control yesterday and earlier that morning when he had walked away with twenty thousand groats after simply threatening ten boxer shrimps. In a flash of wine-fuelled extrapolation he realised why they had taken his threat seriously – there was no doubting the fact that everyone had believed that his prophecy could have destroyed the boxer shrimps if he hadn't got his selfish way. Simply by saying it was going to happen, it would.

Yes! They knew that they were looking at the self-fulfilling prophet.

'*Self*-fulfilling?' mocked the nano-sprites. 'Chewed through

209

that beam yourself, did you? Ignited the melon barn by magic, eh?'

'Ah, well, *they* don't know that, do they? To them I'm dripping with danger; what I say happens!'

'Only if we want it to,' clarified the nano-sprites. 'Or have you forgotten that?'

Quintzi shifted gear, fixing this gilded opportunity firmly in his greed-driven sights, determined to nail it down securely. 'Hey! Hey, guys!' he began in a hugely reasonable tone of voice. 'We're a team. A partnership. I've given you shelter and . . . and food,' he added, rubbing nervously at his wrist.

'Whoopee! Our very own walking bed and breakfast,' jeered the nano-sprites.

'Yeah, well, you do treat my body like a hotel . . .'

'So when's lunch?' they snapped. 'If you want to make absolutely sure that we are healthy enough to carry out any fulfilments you wish, then we're going to need at least, ooh, three feeds a day.'

'Three?'

'Yup.'

'Three. You sure that's enough?' grinned Quintzi. 'You can have more if you really want it.'

'Hold on, you've changed your tune a bit,' tapped the nano-sprites suspiciously. 'Last night you practically fainted at the sight of that needle. What's the catch?'

'Catch? Oh, please, guys, whatever happened to trust amongst team-mates?'

'We've seen how you work, remember?'

'So you should know that I never lose anything that's even remotely handy. I want to keep you happy, guys. So, if you little darlings want a bit of a slurp, that's fine by me.'

'Now?'

'Soon.'

'How soon?'

'Well, I reckon that between here and . . .'

He didn't get far before a heavy boot kicked open the front door and two extremely angry-looking men burst in.

'Okay, so what's the scam?' barked Harvee Goldfysshe,

snatching Quintzi by the throat. 'How were you going to do it, eh?'

'What? D . . . do what?' spluttered Quintzi.

'The accident?'

'Accident? Er, you're going to have to help me out with this,' he squeaked, hoping that the nano-sprites would get the message.

Goldfysshe snarled. 'The jetty collapsing, sending a rain of barrels crashing through the paddock pools. Remember? The complete destruction of the entire Golden Pincer Contest!' reminded Goldfysshe with a wild shaking of the ageing Axolotian. Behind him Tedd Sert growled angrily.

'Oh, that,' answered Quintzi, sweating.

'Yes. Twenty thousand groats' worth of that! My men have been over every inch of that jetty and there's no sign of sabotage. How were you going to do it, eh?'

'Do it? I . . . Shame on you,' choked Quintzi, stalling for time and attempting, once again, to spin some safety net of lies to save his neck. 'You know I can't answer that. I . . . I . . . it's not professional!' he blurted.

'And what's professional about that, eh?' snarled Goldfysshe, showing a set of teeth that should have been for a check-up long since.

'Twenty thousand groats for a few minutes' public appearance is very profess—'

'Don't get cute!' growled Goldfysshe, squeezing Quintzi's throat tighter and forcing him backwards into a position not too dissimilar to one beloved by dramatically tango-ing couples.

Quintzi looked up into Goldfysshe's eyes. 'Ethics,' he choked. 'Taken a vow of silence. Cannot divulge . . .'

'You'll be divulging your lower intestine in a minute if you don't tell me!' snarled Goldfysshe brandishing a large knife significantly at Quintzi's midriff.

'Okay, okay, let me up!' begged Quintzi. 'I'll tell!'

Goldfysshe made a deep growling noise and tugged Quintzi into a rough approximation of a standing position. Tedd Sert advanced across the room menacingly, feeling a little safer

211

now that Goldfysshe had taken some of his fury out on something other than his anatomy.

'You want to know how I was going to destroy your little sideshow if you didn't pay up,' choked Quintzi in a voice of almost terminal gruffness. Secretly he thrilled at how tough it made him sound. 'I'll tell you how . . .' he growled, hoping that he could think of a plausible answer.

Goldfysshe snarled angrily and took a step forward.

'I . . . I was going to destroy it by . . .' struggled Quintzi. And then he had it. He stood proudly and threw back his shoulders. 'Yes that's it! *I* was going to destroy it! By myself! Simply by focusing my mind I can make things happen. What I predict comes to pass! The seeds of my wishes blossom into trees of destruction! For *I* am the Self-Fulfilling Prophet and what I say goes!'

Goldfysshe's head flipped back as he started to roar with terrifying amusement. 'Is *that* the best you can do? You sad man!' Tedd Sert shifted uncomfortably, unsure whether or not to laugh. The thought of another building dropping on his head didn't really appeal.

Quintzi stared at Goldfysshe's molars and cringed at the state of decay. Silent dental witnesses to a life of rich food and enamel-rotting wine.

'How long is it since you last went to the dentist?' asked Quintzi in as nonchalant a manner as he could muster. The change of tack took Goldfysshe by surprise.

'Dentist?' he spluttered, suddenly feeling uneasy.

'Far be it from me to pry into your schedule of oral care, but I really do think that you need to go. Now!' observed Quintzi threateningly and waggled his finger in his ear to stir up the nano-sprites. 'It's entirely up to you, but I do feel absolutely sure that if you continue in your present manner, then a really bad toothache is, well, inevitable.'

'That a prophecy?' mocked Goldfysshe. 'Or a threat?'

'Both!' declared Quintzi, hoping the nano-sprites were paying attention. 'In less than a minute your mouth will be a mass of screaming agony! I predict it. It's a prophecy!'

'And your face will need extensive remodelling,' threatened

Goldfysshe clenching his fists as, unseen by him, three microscopic motes of light made up their minds and zipped towards a random selection of cuspids and molars. It was worth protecting Quintzi just this once more. He had promised them another feed, after all.

Tedd Sert took an uneasy step backwards as he witnessed the unnerving grin of confidence that flashed across Quintzi's face. The three nano-sprites vanished into Goldfysshe's teeth, homed in on a bundle of nerves each and attacked.

'. . . know a good butcher who could fix you up, just right,' snarled Goldfysshe. 'You'll be good as new in . . .' His hand clapped to the side of his face as deadly magical jaws locked around the raw ends of nerve bundles and began to gnaw. In seconds, dull hammer blows of agony were pounding from his molars, searing stabs of suffering were lancing from his incisors and cataclysms of chronic affliction erupted from impacted wisdom teeth he never knew he had. His root canal was aflame with the napalm of pre-emptive retaliation.

Tedd Sert watched in horror as Goldfysshe collapsed to the floor in writhing buccal torment, legs thrashing as he clutched at his cheeks.

'Ever had any trouble with ingrowing toenails?' asked Quintzi, staring pointedly at Tedd Sert's right foot.

'N . . . no!' whimpered the erstwhile Wagering Emporium owner, his mind filling with images of throbbing tootsies raw with screaming inflammation.

'Good,' grunted Quintzi. 'And I foresee a continued absence of sock-bound distress for a very long time. As long as you keep away from here and make sure you tell everyone about the awesome power of the Self-Fulfilling Prophet!' He grinned as he stepped over the screaming form of Harvee Goldfysshe. 'And I'll know if you've done it. I'll know if you haven't 'cause I know where you are going to be before you do. I can arrange for all sorts of discomfort and misfortune to float your way. Just don't ever forget – prophecy is a threat waiting to happen!'

Cackling madly with the fizzing thrill of victory, Quintzi

strode out of the door, down the stairs and away towards the centre of Fort Knumm.

Right then, if he had had the choice, Hogshead would've changed places with Harvee Goldfysshe in a second. If only his problems were as simple as excruciating toothache . . .

At that very instant, he found himself swinging from a pair of manacles in the sweltering atmosphere of Interrogation Room Five between two members of the Divers Tribes of the Cautious Newt.

'Told you!' moaned the one on his left. 'Didn't I tell you it was too risky?'

'What is?' challenged the one on the right. 'You trying to tell me you've just figured out that hanging around inside interrogations rooms might just be putting ourselves in the tiniest bit of danger?'

'Shut up,' growled a guard wearing studded leather armour, which seemed to have more studs than leather, as he bent over a bellows and blew the furnace into a raging frenzy. Another guard cheerfully sharpened an array of unrecognisable, but highly dangerous-looking, devices in the manner normally reserved for expert chefs about to carve a joint.

'Yeah, shut up, Tymorus,' repeated the devotee on the left of Hogshead. 'You don't know what you're talking about. And besides, I'm not talking about physical pain. I'm talking . . .'

'Let me guess,' interrupted the one on the right. 'Spiritual risk, perhaps?'

'Exactly,' agreed Tymid with a brief grimace of joy. 'I always said that magic was a danger to our faith. It's turned me into a blasphemer now.'

'Eh? How d'you figure that?'

'Look at us!' wailed Tymid peering pointedly down at his feet. 'I have failed to follow the example of Ghramm Maslar's teachings "No Gain Through Pain". My wrists are smarting something blasphemously, I can tell you. How's that going to improve my chance to reach the nirvanic heights of immortality, hmmmm? I'm tellin' you, Magic made me a blasphemer!'

'*Au contraire*, dear Brother in the Newt,' countered

214

Tymorus from Hogshead's right, above a whoosh of flames from the furnace. 'This situation offers us a chance to increase our faith simply by facing the risks assaulting us head on and avoiding them with the quiet dignity of not screaming.'

'What? Have you lost your marbles? Has it failed to register that we are in no position to dodge fate's missiles whilst shackled to this wall, especially since there are two lunatic guards preparing to gut us in the name of what they laughably call "justice"? Oh ... er, ha, no offence,' grinned Tymid sheepishly as the guard at the furnace growled aggressively.

'Again I feel compelled to disagree,' offered Tymorus. 'Look not upon our immediate surroundings as strewn with perils beyond our control. Consider it as a haven.'

Hogshead shook his head in horrified bewilderment. How had he ended up here with these lunatics spouting pseudo-religious babble? Had his life gone *so* far off the rails? And just because he was caught red-handed partaking in a bit of thaumic juggling?

'Look on the bright side,' insisted Tymorus, waggling his manacles evangelically. 'There are some risks from which we are currently totally protected.'

'Are you mad?' gagged Tymid.

'Be fair. There is absolutely no risk of us being run over by a forty-ton wagon train while we're down here ...'

'True,' conceded Tymid.

'... or of getting sunstroke ...'

'Agreed, but ...'

'There's one you forgot!' blurted the guard with the sharp implements, leering professionally. 'You ain't got no risk of gettin' a pension! Har har. An' I tell you what, jus' t'stop you gettin' infection from any o' me weapons, I'll sterilise 'em first. Just leave 'em in that furnace for 'alf hour an' they be right bug free. Course they might be a little bit hot later, but can't 'ave everythin', eh?'

Hogshead whimpered pathetically and began to wish he was back in Cranachan. Though he would never admit it, it was beginning to occur to him, as his arms ached, his toes throbbed and a pair of guards readied a painful reception, that maybe this magic stuff wasn't really as safe as it could possibly be. Perhaps Merlot had been right: plants were safer.

Suddenly the door was kicked open and Arch Sergeant Strappado burst in, strutting cheerily towards the dangling prisoners, rubbing his hands together excitedly as he awaited the arrival of the man from MIN. He would be so pleased when he saw how thorough his round-up had been. There were fifteen interrogation suites brimming with yet-to-be-convicted magic users. Soon the eradication would be complete!

The guards quivered to attention and snarled threateningly at the prisoners.

'And what are these filthy low-life scum-sucking wastes of space up for?' demanded Strappado.

'A very long stretch,' chuckled one of the guards, thinking about the rack in the next room.

Strappado winced at the ancient joke and dealt the guard a swift elbow in the ribs. 'What charges?'

'Oooh, no charge,' giggled the guard as he doubled over. 'All torture's on the 'ouse!'

As the guard's fingers made horrid scrunching noises beneath Strappado's boots the other guard filled the Arch Sergeant in.

'Three counts of grievous bodily charms, one count of conjuring without due care and attention and a pair of giving and receiving stolen hoods, not to mention unlicensed use of flameballs in a public . . .'

'Sounds fine to me!' declared Quintzi Cohatl as he burst in through the door and stomped up to Strappado. 'I'll take charge of these now,' he whispered confidentially. Awestruck, the guards watched as the Arch Sergeant nodded subserviently and saluted the balding stranger with a flourish normally reserved for parades.

'Are these the conspirators you have been searching for?' fawned Strappado attempting to maximise any slim chance of future recognition from MIN . . . Oh, what joy it would be to have them call him up!

'Can't tell yet,' squinted Quintzi impressively. 'These damn conjurists are devious. Appearances can be deceptive, especially with a bit of transmogrification in action. But I'll make 'em crack, they won't stand up under my "special investigation".' Quintzi winked at Strappado during these last two words, somehow adding a whole atmosphere of mystery and excitement to the phrase.

Hogshead swallowed what he felt would be one of a very finite number of swallows remaining to him.

Strappado cleared his throat and smoothed the front of his studs nervously. 'Will you be requiring any assistance in your "special investigations"?' he quivered, almost salivating with eagerness. Years he had waited for any excuse to inflict oceans of unjustified agony on the entire thaumic population. And now, he was so close he could almost taste . . .

'I was hoping you would offer,' grinned Quintzi briefly before scowling even harder at the trio of dangling prisoners.

Fireworks of delight erupted in Strappado's roiling heart, blossoming into anticipatory lupins of joy. 'Anything, anything!' he begged, his mind whirling at the free-range possibilities of unlimited torture in the name of justice.

'Take them down and load them into one of the prison carts waiting out front,' Quintzi ordered and clicked his fingers imperiously.

The Arch Sergeant leapt forward eagerly, snatched keys off the baffled guards and set about the manacles with glee. They were being taken to a secret location. Could it be MIN Headquarters?

Working faster and more efficiently than he had ever done in his life Strappado yelled orders at the guards and whisked the captives out into the open, hurling them into a waiting cart. In one bound he was up in the driving seat, panting desperately.

Quintzi, his arthritic knees creaking painfully from the mad dash through the bowels of the Lore Enforcement Agency, looked up at Strappado and shook his head.

'I'll drive,' he ordered.

Instantly Strappado kicked the driver into the street and offered Quintzi the reins.

'Alone,' insisted Quintzi as he creaked up the steps and snatched the leather straps.

'But ... I ... I ...' spluttered Strappado, pulling a face which demonstrated the word 'crestfallen' perfectly. 'Where are you taking them?'

'Believe me, it's safer that you don't know,' murmured Quintzi, enigmatically tapping the side of his nose. A second later he had pushed the Arch Sergeant off the cart and cracked the reins across the flanks of the rhinos with a shriek of 'Ha! Ha! Mush!'

In moments all that remained was a cloud of rapidly settling dust and Arch Sergeant Strappado picking himself out of the gutter and heading towards the sniggering guards.

'Me and MIN,' he sneered through a hastily put-on brave face. 'We're like that! Okay?' he added menacingly as he crossed one finger over the back of another in the age-old symbol of assumed kinship. 'And anyone who says we're not'll have me to answer to. Clear?'

The guards nodded and, when Strappado was safely out of earshot, collapsed in a fit of giggling.

In the humming gloom of the Sneeke Room, deep within the headquarters of the Mystical Intelligence Network, an operative stared into the compound image of a small room. He'd been staring at this screen for hours and so far nothing had happened. Well, nothing, that is, if you were to ignore the occasional outbursts of either extreme jubilation or spitting anger from the cloaked resident of the box under surveillance. And, since there weren't any orders for the operative to inform anyone of bursts of extreme jubilation or spitting anger, he didn't. This was quite a source of relief. Right now, approaching Commander Furlansk with any news was a very risky thing to do.

Suddenly the image in the screen changed, the operative squeaked and sat bolt upright, his attention snapping to full alert. The cloaked figure on the screen stood, jammed his fists into the small of his back and attempted to rub away some of the stiffness of watching a polo tournament. With a weary flick of his wrist he tugged a small rodent out from beneath his conical hat and flung it to the expectantly waiting owl.

'You're all right,' muttered Merlot, hoarse from a particularly enthusiastic cheering session a few minutes ago. 'Any time you want a snack you just tug at my hat. Me, I've got to do a bit of hunter-gathering. Hmmm, should I wait for the interval, or nip out now while they're faffing about changing substitutes again?' His stomach rumbled, cast its vote and the matter was settled. 'Back in a few minutes, Arbutus . . .'

Alarm bells rang in MIN headquarters as the operative pounded on a red button.

'What is it?' choked Commander Furlansk.

'Target on move, sir,' barked the operative tensely.

'Stop him!' growled Furlansk. 'Pizza movement.'

The operative's head whirled around and stared up at the Commander. 'Shouldn't that be pincer, sir? Pincer movement?' He was very lucky to escape with only a black eye.

'Pizza movement!' he repeated. 'That button, there!'

And as Merlot strolled towards the door of the box, Commander Furlansk's fist pounded on an unsuspecting button.

In the corridor outside Merlot's box a dozing figure was jerked to complete wakefulness by a sudden, unignorable electric shock to the back of her head. She leapt to her feet, slammed a red and white cap on to her head, slung the heated tray over her shoulder and sprinted off around the corner.

She only just made it in time.

'Refreshments, sir?' she blurted as she shoved Merlot back into the box and thrust a steaming slice of pizza under his nose.

'Why, yes,' flushed Merlot. 'That's just what I had in mind. How did you know . . . ?'

'Just a guess,' answered the usherette. 'Folks tend to get a little peckish at the interval. One slice or four?' she asked with a flash of teeth.

The wizard grabbed a handful eagerly, then began rummaging in his pockets.

'That's all right,' beamed the usherette. 'It's all-inclusive.'

There was a sudden cheer from beyond the door as the new

Knight Templar substitute was wheeled on. Merlot's head twitched, inquisitive. He flashed a grin at the pizza carrier and vanished into his box, dripping strings of melting dragonzola cheese.

In seconds he was thoroughly engrossed once more.

'Close,' grumbled Commander Furlansk. 'Too close. Be ready for the interval, hear?'

The operative nodded pathetically and returned to watching his target. Irritatingly, his stomach began to rumble.

Quintzi spurred the rhinos up the final few feet of the hill above Fort Knumm, zipped around the back of the gloomy hovel and galloped into the outhouse. Tiemecx the alarm macaw hopped off the windowsill where he had been waiting and settled on the top of the wagon. His beak dribbled, desperate for a sunflower seed to nibble.

'Okay, who's first?' oozed Quintzi at his first crop of prisoners.

'First? For what?' gulped Tymid, staring at the large kitchen table which had been hastily dragged into the outhouse and surrounded by four chairs.

'Lunch,' grinned Quintzi in as disarming a manner as possible.

'Lunch?' spluttered Hogshead disbelievingly.

*Lunch!* pined Tiemecx.

'Yes. Everything's ready,' smiled Quintzi, patting the table. 'There's just one thing missing. Guests. Er, allow me to introduce myself. I am Professor Cohatl of the Interrogation Efficiency Policy Studies Advisory Committee,' he lied consummately. Tiemecx shook his head in confusion.

'I don't understand,' spluttered Tymid looking shiftily around the outhouse. 'A few minutes ago we were dangling in a cell watching the guards getting ready for a good interrogation, and now, this?'

'I can see from that question that you are a criminal of above-average intellect, showing classic inquisitorial responses to situations beyond what you, yourself consider to be normality,' reassured Quintzi smoothly, drawing fully on his years of spontaneous bluffery to get precisely what he wanted. He knew the odds of him wrestling with these three criminals and winning was thousands to one against, so he had to try another, less physical way of getting them in those chairs.

Tymid shook his head. 'You saying I ask a lot of questions?' he asked.

'That is correct. It is a classic trait of the type of criminal who responds less well to traditional, more brutal, modes of extracting factually correct responses,' lied Quintzi barefacedly. 'My studies have shown that you will provide less information when interrogated over hot coals rather than, say, over a nice cup of tea. It is my firm belief that by removing the "terror" from "interrogation" a mutual bond of trust is established between inquisitor and "client", thus leading far more efficiently to an information stream of enhanced purity and clear factual accuracy. Now, gentlemen, would you kindly join me for a spot of lunch?' And with this last phrase still ringing in their ears Quintzi opened the door of the security cart and stepped away to take his place at the head of the table. Tiemecx fluttered to a nearby rafter and awaited the sunflower seed course.

Quintzi grinned wickedly to himself as the three prisoners followed and joined him at the table, failing totally to notice the hastily added leather restraints which were nailed to the armrests and legs of the chairs. They also missed the lengths of rope passing under the table to a central lever nailed inconspicuously near to Quintzi's chair.

As soon as all three were seated, he chuckled wildly and tugged on the ropes. Leather cuffs snatched tight around twelve major limbs and in an instant the three prisoners were totally immobilised. Hogshead screamed. Tiemecx fluffed his wings in confusion.

'What's going on? What are you . . .'

'Save your breath!' barked Quintzi, dropping all pretence of professorship with an unceremonial crash. 'I'm in charge now! I don't have to tell you anything!'

Hogshead gasped as Quintzi produced a strange magical-looking device from behind a barrel and set it up squarely in the middle of the table. He recognised it instantly and right now wasn't entirely sure that he was in the mood for a demonstration.

'So, I ask again, who's first?' scowled Quintzi menacingly.

'No thanks,' whimpered Hogshead. 'I don't smoke,' he confessed, pretending to confuse the device for one of the odd steaming flasks beloved by exotic traders in shady bars.

'Suit yourself,' countered Quintzi his eyes flashing madly in the gloomily Gothic interior of the outhouse. 'But your time will come!' With a flourish he swept the input tube out of the rear of the hextirpator and stood framed against a window clutching the needle. Any self respecting director of 'B'-movie horror with any sense of timing would have ordered a lightning crash for that very moment. Sadly, none came.

Not even when Quintzi leapt towards the writhing form of Tymid, rolled up his sleeve and skewered his wrist like some maniacal kebab chef. Screams echoed around the outhouse, barely masking the slurping and bubbling noises that issued from the hextirpator as Quintzi lit the wick of the athanor burner.

Hogshead's stomach churned with barely suppressed nausea as he watched red fluid, more normally located within the forearm of Tymid, advance up the input tube and disappear into the magically extractive intestines of the device.

If Hogshead could have raised his hand and asked to be excused, he would have.

He shook his head helplessly. He was hallucinating, that was it. This was all a bad dream and he would wake up in a moment. It couldn't possibly be true that he had just seen three tiny, almost microscopic spots of light zip out of their captorial madman's ear, could it? I mean, things like that just don't happen in everyday life. Do they?

He tugged against the leather straps around his ankles and wrists, concluding with sad panic that they were far, far too real for any dream.

'Lunchtime!' cried their balding captor suddenly, grabbing Hogshead's attention with the fascinated horror of a road accident spectator. Shaking in a cold sweat he focused on the magical device slurping crimson life out of the already drained-looking form of Tymid. And then, Hogshead's heart missed a quivering beat as, without fanfare or thundercrash to underline the dread, almost suburban, horror of it all, a tiny drip of transparent liquid oozed its way out of the end of the tube. And was leapt on by three sparkling lights.

'Eat, eat my little darlings,' urged Quintzi. 'Suck up those thaums! Drink and grow strong. There's plenty to go around! Plenty! Just as I promised!' Tiemecx tutted and tapped an irritated claw. Well, there's gratitude . . .

Quintzi glared across the table at Hogshead and Tymorus. 'And there's more where they came from!' he growled, and chuckled an evil laugh as he congratulated himself on setting up a perfect endless supply of 'donors' courtesy of Arch Sergeant Strappado. Bless his cotton socks!

'You'll never get away with this,' challenged Hogshead, not knowing precisely what it was that he wouldn't get away with but somehow failing to find anything more appropriate to say in the circumstances. He was certain that something of a decidedly fishy nature was going on: nobody strapped anyone down to a chair unless something dubious was about to happen. Well, except for some of the less strait-laced practices that go on amongst consenting adults in the privacy of their own hovels, but that was different. And besides, Hogshead was far from consenting. Or adult . . .

'Won't get away with it, eh?' gloated Quintzi. 'And who's going to stop me? It's already too late for you three, and nobody else knows where we are!' With a smugly melodramatic flourish he uncurled his index finger and touched it to the drip on the end of the tube. Irritated, the nano-sprites zipped aside as the surface tension broke in the gleaming droplet, flooding precious millilitres of 103-proof thaumaglobin on to Quintzi's criminal digit. Licking his lips like a cheap backstreet harlot eyeing a bottle of chilled champagne, he ran his finger across the inside of his teeth, closed his eyes and swallowed.

It took only a few seconds for the rush to start. Trembling like a stilt-walker in the throes of an 8.6 Richter scale earthquake and whooping madly, Quintzi leapt around the outhouse as a wild thaumic frenzy clawed at his lower intestine.

And in that instant, staring in witless terror, Hogshead realised what deadly scheme was unfurling before his all-too-innocent eyes. Precisely what it was about the expression of thaumic rapture writ large across Quintzi's face that he recognised first he could never be sure. Perhaps the euphorically quivering lip; maybe the delighted spinning of his pupils as they tossed like tadpoles in a whirlpool; possibly even the fervid frenzy of his cavorting major organs – whatever it was, Hogshead recognised a man in the velvet-iron grip of a fully-fledge thaumaglobin rush. He'd read about it in one of the more adult magical books he'd found in Cranachan Library before Merlot had snaffled them.

'Whoooooaaaaa . . . What a vintage!' cried Quintzi rising a good inch above the straw-strewn floor. 'Gimme some more!' His finger snaked out towards the hextirpator's tube. And the outhouse filled with the echo of a slurping gurgle as another concentrated droplet of thaumaglobin was wrenched from Tymid's pallid body. The nano-sprites gargled ecstatically in the crystal-clear fluid, the intensity of their glowing increasing with each newly absorbed millithaum.

Quintzi smeared another moist fingertip across his teeth, slurped and shrieked once more with wild abandon as the rush deepened rapidly towards stampede.

Behind him, Tymid grew paler and began to pant painfully like some ghostly cod hauled writhing from the depths of the oceans.

'Stop this!' cried Hogshead, biting desperately at the leather strap across his wrists.

'Lighten up, pal!' giggled Quintzi as he tango-ed around the table to some frenetic rhythm unheard by anyone but him. 'You'll damage your teeth!'

'What about him?' pleaded Hogshead.

'Ahhhh, somehow he doesn't look too interested in testing the tensile strength of his bonds,' sneered Quintzi, squinting at

Tymid's pallid features. 'In fact he looks quite content to just sit there, all quiet like.'

'Content? He's got no choice!' yelled Hogshead.

'Hmmmm, guess not,' grinned Quintzi, leaping on to the table and pirouetting around the hextirpator. Was it Hogshead's imagination or was their maniac captor looking somehow younger? Somewhat more lithe of limb? Tiemecx had spotted it too.

'Serves him right!' chuckled Quintzi, as he leapt off the far end of the table and landed in a full scissor-split that would have charmed the tutu off the most reticent of ballerinas. Then, clicking his fingers, he sprang back on his feet and whirled around to face Hogshead, pointedly ignoring the choking gurgles behind him as his cloak flew out like some mad vampire on acid. 'If there's one thing I really detest,' grinned Quintzi, his pupils gyrating dizzily, 'one thing that really gets up my nose, it's waste!'

'What? Who's wasting what?' spluttered Hogshead staring at Quintzi's face as years seemed to roll away from the furrows in his brow. Bewildered he watched as a dozen crow's feet wriggled their toes and fled from around his eyes.

Tymid gasped and turned the colour of wet newsparchment, his skin starting to look as worryingly translucent as an anaemic jellyfish.

'You guys, you're all the same,' giggled Quintzi. 'So sad. *So* serious. I don't know how you do it. All this wonderful . . . ooooh stuff rattling around inside and you always look so . . . miserable! Ha ha ha!' He flick-flacked backwards across the floor, shrieking as he leapt on to a barrel, spinning fast enough to make even the most devoted of whirling dervishes hang up his fez in shame.

Five more drops of thaumaglobin dripped out of the hextirpator and were snapped up by the ravening nano-sprites in a frantic feeding frenzy. And then, ignored only by the cavorting Quintzi as he cartwheeled along a rafter shrieking about how wonderful he felt, Tymid coughed feebly, lifted his head, stared imploringly about him through eyes drained of

225

colour, tried to mouth a final desperate, plea and sank forward flaccidly.

'Typical!' yelled Quintzi as he somersaulted off the rafter to land on the table and glower at the lifeless body of Tymid. 'Well, that'll teach him for not enjoying his magic as much as I have, HA!'

'You ... you've ... Look what you've done!' squeaked Hogshead in disbelief, straining frantically against the wrist straps.

'Hmmm, bugger, isn't it? And just when I was really getting to enjoy myself, too! How thoroughly selfish can you get?' moaned Quintzi, tutting as he stared at the terminated supply of thaumaglobin. Then, with a shriek, he sprang off the table and bounded behind a stack of hay bales only to emerge a moment later clutching a long black sack. In a matter of moments he had disconnected the hextirpator, unfastened Tymid's limp body and wrestled it into the sack, tugging the drawstring shut with a wild flourish.

'There's always one who can't stand the pace of the party, isn't there?' cackled Quintzi, hauling the sack towards the door. 'Just taking out the empties,' he called with his hand on the latch. 'You stay there and carry on enjoying yourselves, won't you. I'll hurry back. Byeeeeeee!'

And with a slithering of sack on gravel and a final slamming of the outhouse door Quintzi was gone. Close behind him was Hogshead's hope, a trio of nano-sprites and a very baffled alarm macaw.

Tiemecx, over the years, had become used to Quintzi's bald head. It was extremely odd to see him looking so, well, young and hirsute.

A few minutes later, down on the banks of the River Slove a certain Mrs Arangue was trudging along muttering about the state of society today when she stopped in her track and stared at a shady figure dragging a large sack towards the edge of the bank.

Her heart thrilled as she clapped eyes on the culprit and

226

focused hard in the twilight, sucking petty details of description through her pince-nez. With glee she filed away the fact that the offender was undoubtedly in his teens, dark haired and decidedly on the rotund side. And one other detail she surmised from her underbonnet observations. He was either incredibly stupid or definitely not a local. Or perhaps both.

Anyone worth the minimum of salt could tell you in a flash that disposing of anything on the slime-ridden expanse of Dregs Bank was almost a physical impossibility.

Only once a week did the tide ever reach up far enough to cover the glistening black mud with anything more than an inch or two of slovenly water, and then only for about ten minutes or so. Mrs Arangue cared not a jot about that. In fact it was better for her this way, strengthening her case a hundred-fold at least. Here was evidence: real, genuine, dyed in the wool, incontrovertible evidence!

With a skip in her step higher than it had been for a long while she spun on her heel and, handbag clutched tightly to her prying bosom, she strutted off towards the front desk of a certain Lore Enforcement Agency.

# Fireballs – Extra Large

'Psssst!' hissed a harsh female voice irritably.

Drub, the Fort Knumm Lore Enforcement Agency Officer, shook his head and trudged on past a vast ageing barn. He hated night shift on the banks of the River Slove; there were always far too many very odd flying insects zipping about down there. Things with buzzing wings, legs and no sense of direction, things with needle-sharp proboscies that could smell blood half a mile away, and things that seemed to have been designed to cause the most pain and suffering possible . . . and then there were the pale things that lived in the sludge laughingly referred to as a river. He shuddered and swatted an insect away, cursing his luck that he was always bitten on this shift. Pre-emptively he slapped at the exposed flank of the back of his neck, hopefully flattening any would-be mosquito's hopes for a swift slurp of a snack in seconds.

'Pssssssst!'

Nervously Drub looked around at the sudden sound, outstretched palm ready to eradicate anything with insectile wings he spotted within a hundred feet of his body. A drip of sweat trickled down his neck.

'Pssssssssssssst!'

The officer spun around, tugging his truncheon out of its holster and clenching his fists. Anything that made a noise that big was something not to have sinking its mandibles into your jugular unannounced. No way!

'You deaf?' whispered a tiny woman from the darkness of an ancient barn doorway as she peered around an almost opaque pair of pince-nez. 'Or just ignorant? I've been ''Pssssst''-ing you, in case you haven't noticed.'

'I thought you were a . . . the insects . . . oh never mind,' blurted Drub by way of explanation, slouching in insect-free relief. Unseen, a pair of mosquitoes bored their hungry way into the back of his neck and began to slurp happily.

'You callin' me an insect?' snapped the unmistakable figure of Mrs Arangue.

'No, no, I . . . How can I help you?' growled the officer in his most polite manner, glaring at the woman.

'It's more like how I can help you, young man,' she huffed importantly. 'I've got some real evidence.'

'Regarding what?' asked Drub, sifting through his memory as he attempted to recall what crimes they were supposedly investigating around here. There was that kidnapping last week, or the theft of fifty-three feet of lead flashing off a roof two weeks back and . . . ah, of course, the boxer shrimp doping conspiracy. He tried to stifle a yawn. He never got anything interesting to poke into. Nothing ever happened on the banks of the Slove.

'Just bring the evidence down to the station in the morning and I'll take . . .' he began boredly.

'Don't talk rot!' hissed Mrs Arangue. 'How can I bring it in? It's impossible!'

'Eh? What is? I don't understand. If you've got evidence, you can bring it in!' mused Drub. 'Hire a cart, or thumb a lift or something.'

'Normally that would be fine. But not when it's the whole bloody river! Look!' She pointed to a string of footprints in the mud of Dregs Bank. 'How can I bring that in? And don't say a bucket and spade!'

'I . . . er, ahem.' Drub barely stifled the urge to slap his forehead with frustration. Mrs Arangue had caught him again. As if he couldn't guess the answer, he asked, 'So what is it evidence of?' Part of his mind was trying to work out if it was worth calling upon the services of one of their crack forensic artists just to keep her from complaining of Enforcement Agency apathy.

'Littering!' declared Mrs Arangue. 'It's always the same around here, people have no respect for the appearance of their environment. Can't you see that big black sack out there. Look!'

Drub could barely disguise his amusement. He could've put hundreds of groats on that answer, she never spotted anything else. In all the years he had been pounding this forsaken beat she had never reported anything new. There could be a massacre going on about her and all she'd see was the little red dots on the floor and the messy disorder of a few stray limbs.

'Well? What are you going to do about it, eh?' pestered Mrs Arangue, prodding him in the abdomen with a finger case-hardened by years of just such activity.

'I'll make a note of . . .'

'Note?' she squeaked. 'And what will you do with that once my back is turned? Will that end up in the river too?'

'Now look here, I am an officer of the . . .'

'And so you should behave like one!' railroaded Mrs Arangue, tapping her foot with acute irritation. 'When a crime is reported you should act, hmmm? If you don't you're a disgrace to that uniform.'

Mrs Arangue stared up at him over her pince-nez, her lips working with annoyance. It was a sight to strike terror in the heart of any grown man. And he was no exception. With each passing moment under the red-hot lamp of Mrs Arangue's fulminating gaze the foundations of Drub's resolve crumbled, slipping away into the dust of inevitability.

'Wh . . . wh . . .' he spluttered as she tapped her foot to the pounding rhythm of insistence, her eyes burning unblinkingly into the back of his head.

'Come on. It's time for action!' she pestered from behind an expertly wagged finger.

'What . . . what d'you want me to do?' blurted Drub and instantly regretted it. One of the first rules of the Lore Enforcement Agency was, never let the public take control. Especially Mrs Arangue.

'Good boy, that's the spirit,' she grinned with a tone of voice that, inexplicably, made him want to roll over and have his tummy scratched. 'Now, go fetch that sack!' she declared.

He was three feet nearer the bank when he suddenly stopped, whirled on his heel and thrust his hands on to his hips in the universally recognised stance of defiance. 'Now hold on a 'minute,' he began convincingly. 'I'm not a binman! I know the uniforms are pretty similar but I'm an officer . . .'

'So behave like one and fetch that sack!' she interrupted, tutting like a matron.

'No. I don't collect litter on duty, you should know that. Now, if you don't mind, I'll just be about my business . . .'

'Littering is still a criminal offence hereabouts, isn't it?' asked Mrs Arangue in the tone of voice used by one who didn't know the meaning of the phrase 'fobbed off'.

'Of course. A dumping like that'll be worth at least three months in solitary if I have anything to do with it . . .'

'And we still require at least a soupçon of evidence to make a conviction stick?'

'Yes,' Drub replied warily, sensing that these questions were definitely, as always, heading towards a conclusion of her choosing. Cunningly structured collies of questions herding the bleating sheep of his resolve into a corner.

'Well, there's your evidence,' she declared, pointing at the offending black sack still perched on the glistening mud of Dregs Bank. The beak of an over-eager Noleff Tern tugged hopefully at the corner of the sack, sensing something inside. And in that instant Drub knew that something was up. In all his years patrolling this stretch of the Slove he had never seen a Noleff Tern wheel out of the sky and partake of a little spontaneous foraging. Those particular birds were far too fussy to take an interest in anything normally found floating on the Slove. They'd turn their beaks up at anything less than julienned carrots. Well, unless it was meat of course. Drub had heard tales of entire swarms of Noleff Terns scrapping for hours over the most meagre of snips of bacon rind. And looking at the frenzied glint in that bird's eye, there was more than bacon in that sack.

Drub swallowed nervously. If someone was hurling joints on to Dregs Bank then something was horribly, dreadfully wrong.

'Go fetch it!' insisted Mrs Arangue commandingly as a large pallid creature slithered past a foot from the bank.

In a second Drub's resolve was shattered. 'Hold on, hold on, you don't get me fooled that easily. This is just some cheap way of getting me to clean up the river . . .'

'I don't suppose Arch Sergeant Strappado would be hugely impressed if he heard that one of his men was deliberately ignoring evidence . . .'

'You wouldn't!' coughed the officer nervously. He knew what Strappado would do to some of his favourite parts of his anatomy if he was to hear of such dereliction of duty. Red-hot pokers loomed far too close to his kidneys.

Mrs Arangue grinned as if to say, 'It's up to you. I mean, if you really enjoy the things that Strappado can do then go ahead, ignore the sack and live in constant fear of freshly griddled kidneys!' Instead she said, 'I only want what's best for you. Isn't it about time you earned a promotion?'

Before he knew it, he was up to his shins in sticky black mud, heaving as he powered his way towards the offending sack. Nervously he glanced down as another pallid creature slithered under the surface and disappeared. He swallowed, blotted it from his thoughts and forged on ahead. Worms, he shuddered, he'd temporarily tried to ignore the eighteen-inch monsters that lived out here. Despite the cloying sludge his pace actually picked up. It was the closest anyone had ever come to having a bow wave on Dregs Bank for years.

Sweating with a wicked mixture of exertion and terror, he slowed down, reached out for the sack and stopped. He could feel the piercing gaze of Mrs Arangue on the back of his neck, drilling into his bull-like muscles. The pair of mosquitoes sucked harder. The Noleff Tern squawked and looked accusingly at him.

What was he doing out here? A sudden wave of burning anger-fuelled curiosity welled up inside him. This had better be worth it! This had better be a sack of something more than just litter, otherwise that Mrs Arangue would be . . .

Cursing under his breath now, and fending off the flapping tern, he unfastened the string at the top, loosened the neck and peered inside.

Unseen and undetected, a tiny insect-like creation whirred out of the sky and, diverted from its normal routine by the unusual sight below, settled on Drub's shoulder and peered down with unblinking compound interest.

It was at that very instant that Drub screamed.

Pale eyes glared forlornly from within a face of anaemic horror. Lifeless features yearned limply for release from the confines of the sack. And Officer Drub shrieked with joy.

It was incredible, the chances of it happening were, ooooh, hundreds to one against, but here it was, a body in a bag. An *unauthorised* body in a bag. He could tell in an instant that this wasn't the work of an AA-registered assassin. All members of Assassins Anonymous utilised the correct procedures of attaching all necessary receipts to the right earlobe and countersigning the backs with their membership number. But this had nothing.

Drub's heart pounded with excitement as he recalled Mrs Arangue's strident words. '. . . saw who did it! . . . show you where he is now . . .'

Much to the extreme irritation of the Noleff Tern he sealed the sack again, swirled around and swung the top of it over his shoulder. The move was too quick for the sneeke perched there and a second later it was crushed with a cracking splat. Oblivious, Drub ploughed his way back to the shore through the waist-deep furrow, his mind surging with questions like, 'Whodunnit!' and 'Why?', his arm fending off a wild beak.

In seconds he had created thirty-five distinct and separate motives featuring sordid love triangles involving the essential scantily clad heroine, disputes with drug rings, streetwise gangsters rubbing out unwanted competition . . . And not one of them was even close to the truth.

Wading out of the river he stood before Mrs Arangue, a glint of a tear of joy at the corner of his eye. 'Before I go any further,' he declared officiously, 'there's just one thing I want to ask.'

'Well, get on with it,' she snapped.

'Apart from seeing what transpired here, did you have anything at all to do with this?'

'Ohhh, what a thing to ask!' she barked. 'I ought to take you across my knee and . . .'

'All right mum, sorry. I had to ask. I mean, you've done a

few odd things in the past just to get me a promotion, haven't you?'

'I only want what's best . . .'

'Yeah, but fitting yourself up for shoplifting three months ago. That was embarrassing! Especially since I wasn't on duty that night!' Wild wings powered out of the sky. Drub ducked.

'Pah!' flustered Mrs Arangue, dodging the irate bird and trying to forget about her criminal record. 'You going to let me lead you to the wicked culprit so you can arrest him, eh?'

'After you,' grinned Drub and, punching the air occasionally and avoiding the bird's squawking, he snatched at a dangling apron string and followed his mother away from the river leaving a slithering trail from the muddy sack of evidence.

In the secret safety of MIN headquarters a grey-clad operative scratched his head at the sudden loss of transmission from the remote-controlled sneeke, rewound the memory crystal and stared with awe at the pallid face of, judging by his clothes, some sort of magic user.

This was something his superior officer should know about. A dead wizard. He would be pleased.

'Three,' grunted a tuxedoed man holding up the requisite number of fingers to the dealer. His cards fluttered perfectly into range, spinning gently to a halt on the green baize cloth of the table. The gambler flipped the cards over, scanned their surface with a wary eye, snarled and slammed the entire hand on to the table with a curse.

'Fold,' he growled after dropping a five-groat coin into the irritably shaken swear box. There were a great many things the dealer would put up with at his table. But he really detested cursing.

'Two,' snapped Punt, the next player, with an eager grin. He knew there was over three hundred and fifty groats in the pot. And that pot was going to be his, he could feel it. His fortune was really in the bag now. Across the table he could swear he could see the shimmering voluptuousness of Lady Luck blowing him a plethora of serendipitous kisses.

Greed spreading across his face, Punt snatched up his two

cards and barely contained a shriek of delight. He turned the cards over, his lucky leather gaming gloves creaking as he blinked and stared into the faces of Mr Bun the Baker and Miss Fit the Undesirable, his heart fluttering with exquisite excitement.

'Raise you twenty,' he declared, hurling away two unwanted cards with a flourish and clutching two completed nuclear families, each smiling with the overwhelming happiness which gave the game its unimaginative epithet.

The other players snarled under their breaths as they tossed in the requisite coinage and the next player took his additional cards.

Punt watched as, with almost painful slowness, the next three players took their turns, selecting cards, rearranging their hands, or simply folding with a disgusted curse and a five-groat fine. Soon there were only three players left.

Punt's heart quivered. He had never been in such a good position. 'Raise you thirty,' he drawled in a poorly accented whisper as he attempted to keep a poker face. A shower of coins swelled the pot's total to way over the four-hundred-groat mark.

And then, just as he had hoped, one of the opposing pair grunted flatulently, hurled his cards on the table and sat back in his chair glaring and folding his arms.

Lady Luck hitched up her stockings and pouted lasers of encouragement.

Punt locked his gaze on to his last opponent and attempted to telegraph waves of hatred through the ether, trying, as had been done to him on numerous occasions, to put him off. He assumed an expression of what he hoped was swaggering malevolence and awaited the first twinges of the undermining of his opponent's confidence.

Rapt in such taut concentration it was not really surprising that he didn't see a man who looked at least two days over sixty-five push open the door and hobble into the Gambling Parlour, gasping for a well-earned drink. Of course, Punt failed to see him for a host of other reasons, not least the fact that he was sitting with his back to the door.

But in a few minutes even folks in the most private of seating positions would be horribly aware of what had just walked in.

Quintzi Cohatl shuffled up to the bar, his arms aching from hauling a large black sack down towards the River Slove and hurling it in. Smacking his lips expectantly he scrambled up on to a tall stool and casually ordered a large flagon of Hexenhammer.

It was something of a disappointment, he mused as he slurped at the frothing ale, that the effects of the thaumaglobin had worn off quite so quickly, returning him with unceremonious abruptness to his normal appearance and, worse, his horribly familiar aching joints. Still, there was a glimmer of fizzing optimism lurking on the horizon. He'd only taken two drops . . . who's to say what would happen with a few dozen more buzzing around his system?

As this thought rattled around inside his head and opened up a grand vista of arthritis-free possibilities, he chuckled evilly and took another thirsty swallow of ale.

'Will, sir, be partaking of our facilities tonight?' asked the barman with an ingratiating flash of his teeth.

'Eh?' croaked Quintzi as he was shaken from his thoughts. 'What? What facilities?'

The barman pointed to the clusters of green baize tables, nestling under low lights, dotted in smoke-filled corners, and swept a hand towards a bevy of waiting beauties ready to remove any winnings for a flash of thigh, or more. 'Our gaming tables and post-table hospitality are legendary throughout Fort Knumm. Nowhere can offer such a menu of possibilities – five-pack snap, thirteen-card pontoon, and, of course, our house specialty Happy Fam—'

Quintzi's eyes bulged as he focused on the heaps of cash crowning each of the hundreds of tables. And an idea hatched.

'Yes,' he grinned almost to himself as a host of dangerous thoughts coalesced into what passed as a plan. Exuding an air of casual malice he waggled a finger in his left ear, looked at the barman and declared, 'I shall take full advantage of the, er, facilities. Bring the boss out here.' He ended with a grin, the like of which the average great white shark would be proud of.

236

'Er, Señor Harloh is busy . . .' smiled the barman again, adjusting his serving tunic with a hint of discomfiture.

'Fetch him here,' insisted Quintzi, staring at the barman's gleaming row of dental enamel. 'Fetch him now or you might find yourself getting sudden excruciating toothache,' he threatened and just for a moment three sparkling motes could be seen zipping out of his ear.

'Toothache? My teeth are fine,' grinned the barman. 'In fact it was my ability to show vast expanses of toothy whiteness that enabled me to secure this fine position.'

'Right now, at this precise moment of time, those little pearlies are just perfect,' noted Quintzi with an air of casual malice. 'But have you ever stopped to consider their ongoing future?'

'Oh yes, I floss regularly. I've got years left.'

'Years? Ha! I was actually thinking in terms of a shorter time scale. What about, say, in thirty seconds from now, hmmm? Are you absolutely certain that if you continue to stand there *not* fetching your Señor Harloh away from whatever it is he is supposed to be busy at, are you convinced that you won't feel as if your root nerves are being gnawed at by ravening monsters?'

'How many have you had?' smirked the barman, missing Quintzi's point and adding a false giggle as if he had got the punchline to an obscure joke. 'If I didn't know better, I'd think that sounded a bit like a threat.'

Quintzi's face broke into a crocodile smile. 'Didn't know better, eh?' he mused with icy condescension. 'And I suppose that you know better than the laws of chance, hmmm? You are completely certain that there isn't even the remotest possibility of you suddenly, and irrevocably, developing a screaming toothache which will remain as long as you don't go and bring the boss here, now?'

'Absolutely certain,' smirked the barman with a sparkle of flawless whiteness. He knew that one of his jobs was to engage in strange philosophical conversations with some of the more inebriated of customers. 'That is the most far-fetched concept I have ever heard. The chances of me suddenly developing

237

toothache are about one in a . . . aaaaarggghh!' His hands clutched at the side of his cheeks as he collapsed behind the bar.

'Normally I would agree. However, odds have a habit of altering very drastically when you are addressed by the Self-Fulfilling Prophet,' snapped Quintzi peering over the glass-ringed expanse along with a dozen others at the bar. Gasps of alarm blossomed around him as people stared from the writhing barman to the ancient figure grinning at him sadistically.

'The Self-Fulf . . . Aargh! My molars! Sure, I'll fetch the boss . . .' He scrambled to his feet and, miraculously, the incessant gnawing attacking his raw nerves stopped abruptly. Panic regarding his welfare and an overwhelming sense of acute dental preservation added wings to his heels and in seconds he was gabbling an explanation to the fat cat owner of the infamous gambling joint, bar and grill.

'Slow down!' ordered Monty Harloh irritably from beneath a bevy of overly attentive maids draped decorously across him and his king size chaise-longue. 'You tellin' me this . . . this old git just *gave* you toothache, zap, just like that?'

The barman nodded frantically, wincing as he felt a large molar rattle ominously in its socket.

'And then it vanished again just as . . . Florence? Is that your hand? . . . ahem, just as quick?'

The barman continued to nod, blushing slightly as he saw where Florence's hand was positioned. He felt certain that no towel maid would ever do that to him.

'And this makes you think that something . . . Florence! . . . something strange is happening?'

The barman's neck was beginning to ache with the constant flurry of nodded agreement.

'Listen pal, you are gettin' way too sensitive about those teeth of yours. Gods! If I thought somethin' odd was goin' on every time my teeth tingled well, I'd give up eatin' iced Lemming Mousse right now . . . Florence, that is *very* distracting! . . . It'll take an awful lot more than that to persuade me this . . . oh, what's his name . . . ?'

'The Self-F . . .' began the barman.

'The Self-Fulfilling Prophet!' screamed a voice from the door as a panic-stricken man sprinted through it. 'He's here! You're doomed, doomed!'

Monty Harloh sat bolt upright, scattering salaried affectionate maids in all directions, and turned to face the crimson visage of the owner of the pile of rubble which had once been known as Tedd Sert's Wagering Emporium. 'If this is a cheap publicity stunt to help rebuild your . . .' began Harloh.

'No, no. It's a warning!'

'What? You on his side?'

'No. I'm being altruistic,' answered Tedd Sert defensively.

'Yeuch! If you're going all religious on me, stop it!'

'I'm simply trying to stop him breaking your bank the way he destroyed me.'

'What? Never! Nobody breaks the bank of Monty Harloh. I'll deal with him now before things get way out of hand.' He stomped towards the door, spun around and addressed the towel maid. 'And Florence, I'll be back in a few minutes,' he winked lecherously. 'Keep your fingers warm!' Then he whirled on his heel and was gone.

Seconds later he was hit square in the face by a scene of utter chaos. It hadn't taken long for a few of the ex-regulars at Tedd Sert's Wagering Emporium to clap eyes on Quintzi Cohatl as he propped up the bar and hassled a certain barman. And as soon as he had been spotted, tongues began to wag. In moments, the wild truth was embroidered upon, vast tales of exaggeration pinned hastily to its improbable backside and hoisted aloft for everyone to hear. And for the first time in the history of Monty Harloh's Gambling Joint, Bar and Grill, not a card was turned, ale poured or steak torched.

Harloh reeled as he took in the scene, realising in seconds that not one groat of profit was currently being wrenched from his customers' grubby pockets. Something had to be done.

'What is the meaning of this . . . ?' he bellowed above the relative silence of stilled roulette wheels and static dice.

'Nice place you've got here,' grinned Quintzi sadistically. 'Lots of people. Big. Profitable.'

'Is this all your doing?' snarled Harloh.

'*Moi?* I simply came in for a quiet drink and . . . well, something happened,' oozed Quintzi playing innocent. 'Seems that some of your more vocal clients have been spreading vicious rumours about my, er, abilities.'

'And what might those abilities be?' growled Harloh with a sickening feeling he already knew the answer.

'Oh, nothing much,' mused Quintzi taking a casual sip of ale. 'Just an overwhelming desire and knack for, ahem, self-fulfilment.'

A wave of gasps rippled around the now still room and blasted at the concentration of one Punt the gambler, currently still staring intently at his opponent.

'You know the sort of thing that would make me feel ever so fulfilled,' continued Quintzi, nonchalently tugging a pickled morello cherry off a thin stick. 'Just the usual thing – more cash than you can shake a stick at amassed almost instantly and *without* the need for dreadfully inconvenient side issues such as working for it.'

'Ho ho, is *that* all?' guffawed Monty Harloh to a shocked audience. They had heard what this Self-Fulfilling Prophet could do if he didn't get his way. It didn't seem like such a good idea to irritate him. Some of the more wary punters edged towards the door.

A flash of anger crossed Quintzi's face. 'Yes, that is all. Not a lot to ask for since that is, more or less, the position in which you, conveniently, find yourself.'

'I worked for this!' challenged Harloh, spreading his arms wide as if to encompass his empire. 'Built this with my own hands . . .'

'Ahem . . .' coughed Quintzi with an expression that telegraphed a modicum of disbelief. 'Your very own paws?'

'Well, metaphorically speaking, of course,' admitted Harloh. 'I mean you wouldn't expect me to actually get *my* mitts dirty with bricks and mortar, would you?'

'Tut, tut, course not,' pouted Quintzi in mock sympathy for a second before turning sharply and fixing Harloh with a gaze of ice-cold threat. 'Just as you wouldn't honestly expect me to have to prophesy that this place will come tumbling down around your ears if you don't give me, say, 25 per cent of all the profits made here.'

'What?' chuckled Harloh, amused at the effrontery of this ageing man. 'Twenty-five per cent is a little steep,' he began as if he was considering a genuine offer. 'I was thinking a little lower. A nice round figure. Nought.' He burst out laughing at his feeble joke. He was the only one.

Just behind him Tedd Sert was trembling, recalling with vivid clarity the events that had occurred in his Wagering Emporium.

'Say yes,' he muttered under his breath. 'Just agree to whatever he wants!'

'Are you mad?' snapped Harloh at Sert. 'What can this pathetic arthritic creature actually do, eh? Attack the foundations with his walking stick? Lot of harm *that'll* do, I don't think!'

'I . . . I know what he did!' yelped Sert, tugging at Harloh's sleeve, eyes wide with impending doom. 'I've seen it! I don't know how, but my Wagering Emporium. He . . .'

'Gods! Listen to yourself, Sert. You're raving! Who's to say it wasn't just simple subsidence? I mean, you were pretty close to the river and the mud is notoriously . . .'

'Having trouble making your mind up?' interrupted Quintzi with a grin. 'It's a fascinating dialogue, but don't take too long, will you? It would be so sad if you were too late to prevent a, ahem, disaster.' Casually he took another sip of ale, his little finger hooked pompously.

'Say yes!' pressured Sert, looking warily at the ceiling for any newly forming cracks.

'But 25 per cent?' sputtered Harloh, feeling somehow very uneasy.

'It's worth it, believe me. I know!'

'It's an awful lot of . . .'

Suddenly there was a scream of alarm and a clear patch of floor appeared where there had been a massed throng. Some erstwhite gamblers shook frantically, brushing a fine white powder off themselves as if it was boiling pitch, while others looked at the bare patch on the ceiling.

241

A jolt of panic lanced through Harloh's heart, for in that instant he realised that a thin stream of plaster dust was dropping down from one of the beams.

'Ooops,' giggled Quintzi, dipping a cherry into his flagon of Hexenhammer with an air of apparent uninterest.

Harloh reddened angrily and whirled into action, adrenalin surging as he drew his sword and snatched Quintzi by the throat. 'I'll kill you! Hack your head off and mount it on a spike as a lesson to . . .'

'Won't do any good,' answered Quintzi, rapidly turning cross-eyed as he stared at the gleaming blade under his chin. 'I'm only telling you what'll happen if you don't fulfil your destiny and give me 25 per cent . . .'

'How's that supposed to affect anything, eh? Money's never changed the course of things before!' snarled Harloh, a hint of bewildered panic edging his every word.

'So, questioning the Laws of Inevitability now, are you?' croaked Quintzi as a perfectly orchestrated creak echoed around the hall. It was all he could do to not grin with admiration for the nano-sprites. They were really getting the hang of this.

'Say yes before it's too late!' begged Tedd Sert as tables began to be ransacked by the panicking crowds.

Another shower of plaster dust tumbled ominously from the ceiling.

'Succumb to your destiny! Smooth the paths of inevitability!' insisted Quintzi. 'Gimme the cash!'

There was a vast rumbling creak of shattering timber and an ancient oak beam scythed through the ceiling and crashed into the bar. Barrels and bottles went spinning in all directions.

Harloh screamed wildly, writhing in the final agonies of indecision. Then sense prevailed. 'Take it, damn you! Take it.' He dropped his sword and began hurling coins at Quintzi desperately leaping around the hall and snatching groats from several dozen tables. 'Just stop it all. Now!'

Quintzi shoved a pair of gnarled fingers in his mouth and whistled once. Abruptly the sounds of disaster abated and, known only to himself, the nano-sprites swooped back into his ear, chuckling excitedly.

'I'll see you,' grunted Punt's opponent in a distant dark corner, tossing twenty groats on to the heap of well over five hundred on the table between them. Punching the air joyously Punt turned his cards over to reveal two perfectly formed families. 'Full house!' he declared, spreading his arms wide to scoop his winnings into his lap.

Scant milliseconds before Punt's fingers contacted the glittering pile of cash a pair of arthritic hands scooped the winnings into a waiting sack and Quintzi legged it exitwards, staggering out of the plaster dust and card-strewn chaos and giggling under the combined load of well over thirty thousand groats.

Oh yes, he thought, he could definitely get used to this way of life!

Punt swore profusely as he suddenly saw the error of his ways. In a flash of evangelical fervour he realised there were other, far easier ways to win vast untold amounts of cash. He was on his feet and out the door before his cards hit the floor.

It had to be said, he'd really lost track of time.

Normally, Merlot found that keeping track of that most ephemeral of elements was, on the whole, less than easy, but here, in his private box with wine on tap and a real humdinger of a polo match unfolding ... well, even Arbutus wasn't entirely positive how long the game had lasted.

It was only as the last Knight Templar was being hauled off the pitch and the interval was announced that Merlot happened to glance at the stack of empties in a heap in the corner of the box and realised that perhaps tempus had fugited a little further than he had thought.

Suddenly there was a curt knock and the door was pushed open by a young satyr carrying a large heated tray of pizzas. 'Want anything for the interval?' he asked cheerily and geared himself up to launch into his full spiel of readily available toppings.

Merlot stared at the crusty spread and licked his lips as the aroma of freshly toasted herbs leapt up his nostrils. He stood, swayed slightly and lurched towards the feast, completely unaware of the sudden panic that had erupted in a certain observation room in the secretive depths of MIN headquarters.

'What's that doing there?' barked Commander Furlansk pointing at the pizza-selling satyr. 'I left strict instructions that no one, repeat *no one*, was to be allowed access to that box!'

Merlot, under the unblinking gaze of the sneeke, pointed at a spicy Ammorettan Death Lizard and pineapple twelve-incher and grinned hungrily at the satyr.

'Don't know where you put it,' hooted Arbutus, fluffing his flight feathers huffily. 'You can't have digested the last one yet.'

'Eight and a half groats, mate,' said the satyr.

'Do put it on the bill, there's a good chap,' grinned Merlot, reaching out.

'What bill's that then?' asked the satyr, snatching the steaming pizza away.

'This box is all-inclusive, refreshments and stuff, you know?' dribbled Merlot.

'Not what I've heard, mate. Eight and a half groats.' He held out a palm and waved the pizza in his other hand.

Merlot drew himself up to his full height and glared at the youth. 'Now look here, the charming young lady who came in before you supplied me with some rather tasty victuals for free.'

'I bet she did,' grinned the satyr somewhat lecherously.

'No, no. Pizza, you oaf. Two slices, gratis.'

'Sounds like you got a bargain there. But this is still eight and a half groats.'

'Extortionate,' grumbled Merlot, salivating irritably.

'Look, I don't have to stand here listening to your fantasies, mate. I've got stacks more boxes to visit before the end of the interval. Nobody's interested once the play's on. Now, d'you want this, or not?'

'Well, yes, of course I do . . .'

'Eight and a half groats and it's yours.'

Muttering under his breath about rip-offs and the state of

take-aways today Merlot thrust his hands in his pockets and began to rummage for change. Sixteen balls of string, twelve dozen spiders, a nest of strangely coloured wires a pile of unidentifiable fluff and a goldfish later, he managed to cobble together the correct amount.

The satyr winced as he accepted the coins, wiping scales off his palm, and threw the pizza at Merlot. 'Enjoy,' he spat and whirled on his hooves, muttering under his breath.

Merlot felt certain that it sounded unnervingly like 'Hope it chokes you', but he couldn't be absolutely certain. Anyhow he had his pizza, that was all that mattered right now. He tugged open the flat parchboard box, snatched a scalding slice out and, balancing it carefully on his fingers, he sank his teeth in.

'Happy now?' tutted Arbutus from the back of the chair.

'Huh?' grunted Merlot, turning to look over his shoulder. Elastic strings of unbreakable dragonzola cheese stretched from the pizza like sticky hawsers unwilling to let go, snagging around his beard with tepid inevitability.

'Happy now you've got your second pizza in a few hours?'

'Mmmm,' nodded Merlot in enthusiastic agreement.

'Doesn't something strike you as a bit odd about it, though?' asked Arbutus, staring accusingly at the savoury snack.

'Mmm mmm,' replied Merlot shaking his head in denial.

'You sure?'

And then it hit him like a bolt from the blue. He chewed the spicy mouthful and swallowed quickly. 'Dreadfully sorry, old chap. How could I have missed it. Do forgive me.' He reached up and, with the briefest of fumbling, tugged a mouse out from beneath his hat and held it out.

Arbutus stared at the offering, fluffing his wings haughtily as strings of unwarranted cheese laced themselves irremovably from the rodent. 'Not for me,' he hooted.

'What's up? Lost your appetite?' muttered Merlot, dropping the mouse and snatching another mouthful of pizza.

'I'm still full.'

'Then what's the fuss about?' mumbled Merlot around a particularly spicy patch of Ammorettan Death Lizard.

Arbutus tutted disgustedly and frowned. It was quite

remarkable how a forehead of feathers could really emphasise a good furrow of irritation. 'Have you no memory?'

Merlot shrugged and wrestled with another stringy bite.

'Honestly. How you ever got to be a wizard I'll never know. Does it not strike you as odd that you had to pay for that . . . that snack,' spat Arbutus, 'when there was no charge for the previous offering? Do you not find it a little suspicious?'

Merlot swallowed and stared intently at the owl. 'Do you know, I do. Something about all this has been nagging at the back of my mind and I think it's disgusting.' He put the box of pizza down and began rummaging once more in his pockets. 'Now I don't mind a little entrepreneurial spirit once in a while, just so long as it doesn't mean I have to pay for my pizza.'

Arbutus slapped his wing to his forehead in despair.

Merlot muttered and grumbled to himself until he grunted with satisfaction and tugged the ticket to his box out of an inside pouch. 'Now we'll see,' he announced and began to read the small print on the back. 'Nope,' he declared finally and threw it away. 'Doesn't say anything about being charged eight and a half groats for refreshments. I knew something didn't add up. Just wait till I get my hands on that satyr.' He leapt to his feet.

'No, no, no!' hooted Arbutus. 'Think about the girl.'

'Yes, such honesty. She could have got away with at least four groats and I wouldn't have noticed . . .'

'I sometimes wonder why I bother,' grumbled Arbutus before turning and fixing Merlot with a severely hard stare. It seemed he needed it. 'The girl is the dodgy one . . .'

'No, no. How can you say that about a dear sweet . . .'

In the depths of MIN, Commander Furlansk was furious about two things as he watched this conversation unfold. One: he hadn't a clue what it was they were saying since no one had been able to figure out precisely how to get sound from a sneeke, and two: no one had ever offered him the chance to go on a course in lip-reading. Mind you, he mused in a brief, and extremely rare, millisecond of whimsicality, lip-reading wouldn't help much with talking owls.

'What was she doing hanging about outside the door before

246

the interval, hmmm?' insisted Arbutus, adopting a pose not dissimilar to the great detectives. Incisive, strident, thoughtful. It was undermined completely only by the fact that he was without a pipe to puff on between thoughts, was only nine inches high and completely feathery.

'Just happened to be passing I expect . . .' flustered Merlot.

'Going where? Nobody's interested in food while the match is on.'

'Well, *I* was . . .'

'And why didn't she charge?' hooted Arbutus insistently.

'All-inclusive in the box . . .'

'Ahhh yes. Who *did* supply you with the box, hmmm?'

'Well, I . . .'

A tiny stab of doubt finally wriggled at the itchy edge of Merlot's mind. Something definitely didn't add up to four. What had he done for someone that they'd be so grateful to give him all this? Anonymously?

'And why d'you suppose there is a little bug-eyed creature up on that shelf watching every move you've been making?'

If Commander Furlansk hadn't realised yet that perhaps something was a little amiss in the box, he did at the instant when Arbutus swept a self-satisfied wingtip towards the sneeke and Merlot stared straight out of the compound image of the screen.

Merlot's stab of doubt turned to an itch, felt a bit more confident and decided it was time to nag.

'Security?' whimpered Merlot desperately, hoping that there was a *very* simple and rational explanation to the bug-eyed insect and that he hadn't been surreptitiously kept out of the way while persons unknown set about some mysterious and despicable deeds.

'No chance,' hooted Arbutus. 'You've been surreptitiously kept out of the way while persons unknown set about some mysterious and despicable deeds.'

'I was afraid you'd say that,' gagged Merlot sheepishly. 'The third chukka's about to start.'

Even if there had been glorious audio capability on the sneeke monitors of MIN, nobody would have heard a thing.

Any sound of Merlot's sudden shimmering exit from the box, the racket of Arbutus's squawk of irritated alarm and the frantic fluttering of his mad last-minute plunge through the rapidly disappearing halo of tinsel, all of this would have been drowned by Commander Furlansk's squeals of furious alarm.

Had Hogshead's wrists not been strapped firmly to the arms of a certain heavily built chair, then he would almost definitely have been rubbing his eyes frantically and pinching himself to make sure he wasn't in the midst of a vast and horribly realistic nightmare. Or perhaps he would simply have been quite content to chew at his fingernails as the terror of recent events sank in. He would however have been far better off legging it out the back door quick sharp.

As it was, fate dictated that he was in fact strapped disturbingly tightly to said chair and therefore all he could in fact do was sit staring unbelievingly at the strange magical device squatting on the table before him, now immobile and worryingly silent after its wild period of gurgling thaumic extraction. Hogshead shook as he recalled the horrific events which were already trying furiously to fade into the realms of unreality. Could it really have happened the way he recalled it? And, worse still, could it be true that either he, or Tymorus, was going to be . . . gulp . . . next?

A wave of panic surged through Hogshead's body, its frothy peak curling unstoppably, crashing in on top of him, carrying him way up the rocky beach of terror to leave him gasping, soaked in a cold sweat of fear. And in that instant Hogshead decided that, whatever it was their captor had planned inside that scheming mind, he wasn't going to wait around to find out about it. He was certain that life-enhancement, fun and a hugely enjoyable romp through the guilded empire of the senses, it wouldn't be.

Straining madly, Hogshead's teeth clamped hard on the leather strap around his right wrist and started to chew frantically, squirming wildly as the leather squeaked noisily against his dry incisors.

'What are you doing?' asked Tymorus from the other chair. 'Be careful, you'll risk your teeth.'

Unheeding, Hogshead tossed and struggled for ten full minutes, like a jester in a strait-jacket, before collapsing back into the chair in exhaustion, with nothing more to show for his escape attempt than a lather of sweat, a nagging toothache and a dreadful taste of dead animal in his mouth.

'See?' offered Tymorus. 'A risk for nothing. Relax and face the world calmly. Don't you know that stress is a real killer?'

'Shut up!' barked Hogshead, panting angrily and scowling at the straps. Briefly he wondered precisely what wicked alchemy had been employed in the tanning of that leather. And just as swiftly he realised he didn't want to know. What if the rumours regarding the extensive usage of pickled dogs' intestines were true? It certainly tasted bad enough to be possible. His stomach did a strange flip of extreme nausea.

'By facing the perils of life calmly we can rise above them. Learn from the teachings of Ghramm Maslar: in avoidance is preservation,' offered Tymorus with not a hint of evangelism. It was the first time he had found himself with a captive audience to be converted. 'Take the air that we breathe and compare it to yourself. Both are facing a runaway forty-ton wagon train, the air flows around, avoids injury and remains a step closer to immortality – have you ever seen a bruised cloud? – whilst you would struggle against it, ending up with a stack of compound fractures and a massive hospital bill at the very least. What does that say to you?'

'Always check the handbrake is firmly applied before leaving a wagon train unattended,' snarled Hogshead pedantically.

'No, no,' wheedled Tymorus. 'That's not the point. See, the air avoids danger . . .'

'Look pal, it may have escaped your notice but it's become a little difficult to avoid anything right now.' Hogshead writhed against his wrist straps to illustrate the point. 'Or are you capable of sprinting off down the hill to get help with that chair strapped to your back, eh? Your toes that strong?'

'Sarcasm is the barbed tongue of wit, it damages . . .'

249

'Shut up and get real! Have *you* ever seen an air molecule strapped to a chair, eh?'

'Well, there are bound to be some trapped under your wrist,' answered Tymorus after a moment's reflection, feeling not a little unsure about which way this discussion was going.

'Exactly. So . . .'

'They are there to remind us that in any situation only the believers will be saved,' proclaimed Tymorus. 'Only the truly faithful avoid all dangers.'

'What? You suggesting that air has faith?'

'Well, I . . .' flapped Tymorus. 'Look, that was a metaphor, all right? You're just being picky now.'

'Yeah, well I'm not in the mood for deep theological discussions, all right? I just want to get out of here before that nutter comes back for one of us.'

'That won't happen,' stated Tymorus in a surprisingly matter-of-fact tone. 'Never does in a hostage situation.'

'What?' bleated Hogshead.

'It's obvious. He's had his show of strength to keep us quiet and add a very effective threat scenario. Now he'll start to bargain with . . . er . . . with, er . . .'

'Exactly. With whom? Who'd pay for our release? We're not hostages. Besides, what have we got in common?'

Tymorus would have shrugged his hands if he could have moved. 'Well, I've got an itchy backside,' he admitted.

'Snap,' growled Hogshead.

'. . . and I could really do with going to the loo . . .'

'Shut up! I was trying to ignore that.' Hogshead shuffled in embarrassment and strained once again at his wrist straps. 'It's no good, I can't break them!' he grunted in frustration. 'Ohh. If only I was stronger . . . or an expert escapologist . . .' moaned Hogshead thinking of the Great Abscontini who could free himself from strait-jackets and sacks and chains while dangling upside down from a flaming rope over a vat of piranhas. It made four leather straps seem easy.

'. . . or a magician,' grunted Tymorus thinking of what would be next on the bill if Hogshead were an escapologist. Magicians *always* followed escapologists like clowns always followed lion tamers . . . just in case anything went wrong. It was amazing what a well aimed flash bomb or bucket of tinsel could cover up.

'Of course!' shrieked Hogshead.

Tymorus stared at him blankly.

'Look, you won't tell anyone, will you,' whispered Hogshead almost shyly. 'Only I'm not really supposed to know how to do this, but, well, needs must . . .'

'Do what?' asked Tymorus.

'This!' declared Hogshead closing his eyes, mumbling and wriggling his fingers against the arms of the chair.

'Oi! This is no time to sleep!' cried Tymorus.

Hogshead ignored him, relaxed and sent out two anger-enhanced tendrils of his mind.

And then Tymorus shrieked with alarm. Well, you would if four eighteen-inch-diameter fireballs suddenly erupted into being scant inches from you while you were strapped immobile in a chair. It was all well and good avoiding danger, but this was a little too close for comforting immortality. The strain it was placing on Tymorus's adrenal medulla was just too much.

The fireballs whooshed into formation above Hogshead, split into a regular rectangle and, as one, slowly lowered themselves towards his wrists and ankles. There was a brief scorching sound, a smell of burning leather and whiskers and Hogshead was free, the straps scorched to a crisp.

Victoriously he rolled off the upturned chair, staggered to his feet, his knees objecting with seemingly unwarranted pettiness, and made his way towards Tymorus.

He never got there.

Just at that very instant, the door to the outhouse burst open and a vast figure clad in the uniform of the Fort Knumm Enforcement Agency stormed in followed very closely by a tiny woman peering around a pair of almost opaque pince-nez.

Unseen behind them a gaudily coloured alarm macaw flitted through the door and perched on a handy rafter. It tutted to itself as it saw the rotund youth. Looks like Quintzi's been at that thaumy-stuff, it thought, and hoped he'd managed to find some sunflower seeds.

251

'There he is, Drub!' cried Mrs Aranque. 'Just like I said – teenager, fat, dark brown hair. Get him. Grab him! Clap him in irons! Hang him high!'

*Oh no*, shrieked a part of Hogshead's brain as the vast bulk of the officer swarmed eagerly towards him.

No, no, no, not again!

'He did what?' spluttered Arch Sergeant Strappado as a red-faced collection of incredibly irate civilians burst into his office.

'Ran off with four sackfuls of groats!' bawled Monty Harloh, spitting angrily.

'Oh, not again,' Strappado muttered to himself. 'And you let him?'

'No choice!' barked Harloh furiously.

'What? Just 'cause someone had toothache and a bit of plaster happened to fall off the ceiling coincidentally?' asked Strappado with a nervous tremor in his voice.

'Coincidence? You telling me that was coincidence? You've got no idea. You had to be there,' interrupted Tedd Sert. 'It was terrifying. Like . . . like he was using magic, or something . . .'

Suddenly Strappado's attention snapped to full alertness. 'Magic?' he squeaked, gripping his desk. 'Did you say magic?'

'Couldn't be anything else,' offered Harloh. 'It had nothing to do with chance. Believe me, my whole fortune depends on chance. I am something of an expert!'

Strappado's mind was whirling as he glued one and one together and came up with a soggy mess of a conspiracy. It couldn't possibly be a coincidence that this weird supernatural protection racket started at the same time that someone high up in MIN was sniffing around. Nah, they had to be linked. It had to be some kind of a hush-hush operation. Why else would he have been ordered to round up every magic user in Fort Knumm for interrogation? Why else indeed?

'Leave this to me!' he declared proudly, and only barely resisted the temptation to strike a pose pointing evangelically skywards. 'I can handle it.'

'Glad to hear it,' said Harloh, feeling a little confused at Strappado's sudden increase in interest. 'Want a description of him?'

'No, no, that won't be necessary,' grinned the Arch Sergeant hoping that one of them, just one, would be curious enough to ask him why.

'No description?' began Tedd Sert looking baffled.

Strappado grinned wider, readying himself to answer the inevitable question which was bound to follow. 'Why not?' He would stare nonchalantly skywards and declare enigmatically that he wouldn't require their services any longer. He had sources in very, very high places. Oh, the increase in his coolness quotient would be unparalleled. Now come on, one of you – ask!

He stared at Sert, guessing at the thought processes rattling away behind that forehead. 'You don't want us to give you a description of the culprit?' he murmured then pursed his lips in question 'W . . .'

Ask! grinned Strappado, edging forward. Ask, why not?

'W . . . w . . . why, that's up to you,' finished Sert. 'We'll leave you to it.' And with that, as if it had been rehearsed, the mob spun on their feet and left as Strappado deflated.

'Report!' demanded Commander Furlansk of the Mystical Intelligence Network as he swept into the Monitoring Room in his anonymous grey cloak and tunic and stood before the trembling junior who had mentioned an interesting find that might be of immediate use.

Nervously the junior pulled a few knobs and a pool of light flashed into life before him. A picture shimmered into view mysteriously and began showing images of a man trudging through the black sludge of a river. The viewpoint arced down and settled on the pool-filling expanse of a vast shoulder and polo-neck sweater. Two hands reached down, swatted a hungry-looking bird away and unfastened the throat of a black sack, peeling it back slowly. The shoulder shuddered as the pallid shrivelled features of a face appeared. The neck was retied, the image flipped around and a black shadow crossed the pool before shaking violently and ending in a flare of static.

Commander Furlansk snarled an ancient MIN oath and thrust a clenched fist into an open palm melodramatically. 'What does this have to do with anything of interest to me? Explain!' he commanded, as was his wont.

'W . . . well, sir, that is pretty much what I thought when I first saw this and it kind of got me thinking . . .'

'Get on with it.'

'Ahh, yes. Well, I was reviewing some of our earlier sneeke-derived footage of the use of the hextirpator, you know, looking for clues as to its current whereabouts . . .'

'Yes? The point, the point?'

'Er . . . sludge, sir.'

Furlansk made a noise deep in his throat. The type of noise that normally presaged imminent personal discomfort for the person or persons in the immediate vicinity.

The operative swallowed in terror. This wasn't going as impressively as he had hoped it would. 'S . . . sludge, sir, left in the hextirpator boiling flask after extraction was complete.'

'So?'

'Well I, er, estimated the volume of purified thaumaglobin extracted and compared that to the volume of remaining residue, sir.'

'Jolly, jolly good,' growled Furlansk. 'I am still awaiting the point to all this.'

'Yes. Well, then I looked at this face here, see?' He flicked back to the image of the body in the bag and with a flurry of careful hand movements pulled hard focus on the shrivelled pallid face.

Furlansk winced nauseously and looked away.

The operative continued his commentary, '. . . and I decided to estimate how much liquid it would take to bring him back to normal, see? Well, in this hand I've got the estimated percentage of fluid extracted from the mushrooms,' he waved an envelope cheerily. 'And in this hand I've got the same thing for the body in the bag. Would you care to have a look at them?'

Furlansk snatched the envelopes and tore them violently

254

apart. In a flurry of uninterest he stared at the two figures. 'Five per cent and five per cent,' he grunted. 'Well, whoopee-doo.'

'But . . . but don't you see?' urged the operative desperately, almost wishing that he hadn't started this conversation.

'No,' stated Commander Furlansk flatly.

'Er . . . the percentage volume of fluid extracted from each subject was the same.'

'I *can* see that.'

'So what if it's the same stuff that's been extracted? Using the same device?'

Furlansk stared again at the shrivelled look on that face and knew instantly that this was, in fact, the work of the hextirpator.

'Get me Zhaminah on the Tuleph Horn now!' was all he barked as he stormed out of the Monitoring Room and stomped back towards his office.

The operative trembled as he tutted and shook. 'G . . . gratitude,' he muttered. 'Just a little thanks would've been nice.'

Commander Furlansk's heart thrilled as he knew they were back on the trail of the hextirpator. Soon all the decades of inequality would be evened out. Soon MIN would rise and grab their share of the theurgic pie hogged so long by the magicians!

No longer would damned wizards resist arrest by simply vanishing in a puff of tinsel. Gone would be the days when mages could skip parking fines by metamorphosing their carts into canaries.

Soon the thaumic potential would be equalled. And then MIN would show who was *really* boss.

The combined jingling of a little over thirty thousand groats cheered the mood of Quintzi Cohatl marvellously as he creaked his way up towards the extortionaly rented hovel on the hill. As a gross act of prophetic blackmail the, soon-to-be-legendary, Monty Harloh job was a dream. No capital outlay, no real damage and a stack of ill-gotten gains to show for it. Not to mention the few free drinks kindly supplied by the terrified barman.

'Oh, my little beauties!' cooed Quintzi to the nano-sprites

nestling cheerily in the darkness of his left ear. 'What a team we make. My brains and your thaums, brilliant! Tonight you are going to have a feast, a slurp-up meal, you might say. Ha, ha! See, I've got some plans. *Real* schemes hatching up here,' he tapped the side of his shining head. 'I want you chaps all fit and energetic!'

The nano-sprites fizzed and buzzed excitedly inside his ear, thrilling with the joy of an appreciative audience. A ten-thousand-spell service on a thaumatron just wouldn't seem the same after this.

'See, I've been thinking,' snarled Quintzi evilly. 'It's time to expand the business, get some efficiency going. I think it's time I had a word in the Mayor's shell-like. I should do more than just harvest the riches of Fort Knumm, I think. Expand and conquer, as they say in despotic circles. Then I wouldn't have to carry my own sacks of cash.'

Struggling to the top of the hill Quintzi skirted around the back of the hovel and staggered towards the outhouse. Raising his voice cockily he called ahead to his captives, 'Okay. Decided who's next for the hextirpator, eh, lads?'

It was only when he received a complete lack of reply that the seeds of suspicion germinated in his mind. His pace quickened as he scrambled towards the outhouse door. Flinging it open he stomped inside. Unseen behind him a dozen feet scurried covertly after him in the shadows of evening.

A look of horror flashed across Quintzi's face as he took in the scene within – the upturned chair, the rucked-up straw on the floor and, worst of all, the single prisoner where there should have been two.

'What's been going on here, then? He up and leave you, eh?' barked Quintzi, swinging his sacks of cash on to the table. 'How the hell did he undo the straps?'

Tymorus had his eyes screwed shut, trying desperately to obey the Irrefutable Recommendations of the Emergency Psalm of Ghramm Maslar – If All Else Hath Failed and Danger Loometh Large; Ignoreth It and It Might Just Goeth Away.

Sadly for Tymorus, it wasn't going to be that easy.

The Self-Fulfilling Prophet growled as anger flooded his

256

body and an alarmingly familiar hollow craving returned. He knew what he needed to make him feel better – thaumaglobin, and now! 'Well, I guess I'll just have to upgrade the straps and declare that you're next!' he gloated, sparks of madness flashing in his eyes as he snatched the needle of the hextirpator firmly in his hands. Advancing on Tymorus's exposed wrist accompanied by the kazoo-like humming of the nano-sprites, he high-kicked his way across the outhouse, grinning manically, whirling the needle between his fingers like some deranged drum majorette.

'Any last requests?' he whispered in Tymorus's ear as a metallic flash of light glinted off the needle tip.

Tymorus stared, trembling, his jaw dropping on to his chest, unable even to gurgle for help.

'Dinner!' buzzed the nano-sprites, wishing they had tongues to dribble. In a few moments they would be diving into their life-giving thaumaglobin. 'Quick! Do it now. Fire up the hextirpator!'

Glints of crimson sunset flashed off Quintzi's teeth as he fingered the needle, chuckled evilly and plunged it deep into Tymorus's terrified wrist.

The devotee of the Cautious Newt whimpered, bit his lip and cursed at the blasphemy of having pain inflicted upon the temple that was his body.

With a flourish of expectation Quintzi lit the burner, thrilling as he watched the remnants of last time fizz and bubble in the reflux flask. Soon those roiling millilitres would be joined by more, purified and deposited at the end. More essential thaumaglobin. His liver flipped in anticipation.

And just as his spleen readied itself for a swift mamba of joy there was a sudden knock at the outhouse door. Quintzi froze guiltily, then spun on his heel and listened, glowering over his shoulder at the door like some Gothic horror star from a magic lantern show. Had he locked the door behind him? Angrily he squinted at the outlet tube of the hextirpator, a knot of craving welling inside him. Tymorus gurgled and began to look pale around the gills. The door was pounded again and a voice shouted. 'Hello? We know you're in there!'

'Friends of yours?' growled Quintzi at Tymorus as the nano-sprites hummed impatiently inside his ear, eager for food.

Tymorus shook his head in denial and stared horrified at the tube sucking at his wrist.

'Hello?' called the voice at the door again. 'Er, Mr Prophet, sir? Are you there?'

Quintzi gritted his teeth, annoyed at the disturbance, but a small and powerful seed of pride was germinating inside him, propagated by the words 'Mr Prophet, sir?' Nobody had ever addressed him like that. Well, except in his dreams but that didn't really count. A stack of things happened in his dreams which bore no resemblance to reality.

A plethora of nervous reactions struggled through his body. What did they want? Who were they? He found his heart beating faster. He stared longingly at the hextirpator, craving the euphoric feel of a pure thaumaglobin rush in his veins.

'Hello?' called the voice once more.

Quintzi trembled as the valves and columns sucked at Tymorus's wrist, desperately needing a bit of magical courage before he found out who was calling.

And then, with a gurgle, the first drop of pure magic trickled out of the hextirpator. In a flash Quintzi's tongue was on it, lashing the quivering droplet from the end of the tube faster than a starving toad on a mosquito. He thrilled as the magical essence flashed into his organs in a wave of euphoria. The nano-sprites didn't get a look in on the next half-dozen droplets either as Quintzi slurped up the liquid wildly, feeling his nervousness ease as fast as his aching joints.

'Hello? Mr Prophet . . .'

The years tumbled off Quintzi, his body metamorphosing into the portly rotundity of his distant youth. With a squeal of ecstasy, and a crackle of shorting magic fizzing from his fingertips, he cartwheeled to the door, wrenched it open and exploded into the air to stand in mock nonchalance before his visitors.

'How can I be of service?' oozed Quintzi, scraping the ground in a low bow as he rapidly approached his early twenties.

The crowd shrieked and vanished into the shadows as they caught a glimpse of Quintzi's face – madness incarnate, eyes reeling around the inside of his skull in a rapture of theurgic rush. One immensely exposed-feeling spokesman stood for a moment, grinned sheepishly and fell to his knees in what he hoped was a suitably devout position.

'Lost your voice?' mocked Quintzi to a terrified silence. 'C'mon, spit it out, I haven't got all day,' he snapped after a few seconds of prone inactivity from the uninvited callers.

The sound of gurgling horror issued from the inside of the outhouse as the hextirpator sucked harder.

'Er, I . . .' began Punt nervously, embarrassed at the quivering note of awestruck subservience that had crept into his voice. 'Well, I . . . me and the lads here, well, they were there, we saw what you did back in Monty Harloh's an' . . . er. Want any disciples, like?'

'What?' smirked Quintzi in arrogant amazement, his knuckles cracking with fizzing free magic. 'Disciples?' He tapped his cheek with a melodramatic index finger.

Punt knelt and wondered if this had in fact been as good an idea as it had seemed at the time. And then his mind flashed with the envious recollection of his pot of winnings being snatched away by . . . well, it sort of looked like him, but he'd seemed quite a bit older in Monty Harloh's.

'We could help. Er, carry your bags, put posters up advertising forthcoming public events, act as bouncers and . . .'

Quintzi laughed frantically as he was regaled by a growing catalogue of duties to which a faithful band of disciples could apply their collective shoulder. But as the laughter continued, oiled smoothly by the ecstasy of thaumaglobin and the relief of a non-arthritic body, it changed from the shrieking amusement of utterly surprised disbelief to the harsh demonism of evil realisation; as Punt laid on thick swathes of the sweet butter of smarm, so Quintzi began to believe that perhaps, if he was a prophet, then what he really needed was a devoted following to lap up the pearls of theurgic wisdom that would undoubtedly fall from his mouth.

'. . . and even a bit of worship and devotion when it was required,' finished Punt looking up at the strangely youthful man. Was it his imagination or had something happened in the last few moments? Was this the secret the Self-Fulfilling Prophet could offer – an answer to the ageless horny chestnut of eternal youth?

Another bout of gurgling could be heard from inside.

'So what's in it for you, eh?' sneered Quintzi imperiously, trying to cover up the guilty noises off. 'Besides the opportunity to serve with a prophet of my stature, of course.' He polished mocking fingertips on his cloak.

'W . . . well,' answered Punt nervously, backed by a host of baffled, but hopefully nodding, putative disciples dragged from the gambling arenas of Fort Knumm. He took a deep breath and swallowed. He knew this was going to be the hard bit. 'Seeing as you are so good at making such vast amounts of cash so easily and effectively, er, all we'd require is just a bit of a share of the . . . er . . . profits,' grinned Punt, imagining the sacks full of gleaming groats which could so easily be his. But a nag of extra-curricular interest in fountains of youth frolicked shyly at the back of his mind.

Tymorus coughed and wheezed desperately in the background.

'Nice idea, guys,' cackled Quintzi, tugging the door shut. 'I'll give it some thought . . .'

'Wait, wait!' begged Punt, jamming his foot unceremoniously into the doorway.

Quintzi stared at the pallid face of Tymorus and the hextirpator tugging at his wrist.

'Just think,' continued Punt. 'We've got lots of local knowledge between us. We could show you all the best places to offer prophecies and . . . and you'd never have to carry all those heavy sacks of money around ever again,' wheedled Punt in a determined impersonation of acute fervour. 'We could do it. We'd do anything.'

'Anything?' grinned Quintzi, his mind whirring. A spark of pure magic crackled painfully off the tip of his nose and shorted itself on the door-lock.

'Er . . . y . . . yes,' whimpered Punt, feeling unsure.

The nodding faces backed him up, grinning eagerly at Quintzi exactly the way the crowd of turncoats in the Grand Municipal Temple at Axolotl hadn't when they'd heard about a certain unfortunate mishap with a few barns.

'So, it's a perfect match, you see?' concluded Punt. 'We all benefit! What d'you say? Fancy a quick worship now, eh?'

And in that instant, any resistance was trampled beneath the eager spaniel of blind optimism and crushed into the carpet of a gleaming future.

Things were looking good for Quintzi. Especially the future.

'Very well,' he pronounced. 'You first task is to dispose of this,' he added after a few moments' scuffling in the barn. 'Carry this to the river!' And he hauled a laden black sack from the outhouse.

In a woody clearing high in the Auric Triangle there was a shimmering of tinsel, a shrill whine and suddenly a man clad in a gaudy cloak and polo supporter's scarf appeared, seemingly from nowhere. He blinked, readjusted his pointy hat and stared around him for any signs of a particular rotund youth. Questions would have to be asked of him as to whether he had come across any hints of any strange and mysterious deeds afoot. It was a long shot but he knew how interested Hogshead was in such dubious things. His eyes strafed the clearing, scanning all points of the compass for clues that anything was amiss. But before he had scoured more than 90 degrees of arc a tree exploded in a wild flurry of feathers and a livid tawny owl swooped at him.

'Arbutus, my dear, nice of you to drop in . . .'

'Don't give me that! It was *my* idea, okay. Don't forget that,' hooted Arbutus. 'Now, I know you had to have a hasty getaway but there's hasty and there's *hasty*! Now that was . . .'

Merlot only managed to prevent Arbutus chewing his ear off by the very narrowest of margins, maintaining the integrity of his lobe by hurling a furry snack into Arbutus's chattering beak. It was then that he spotted the erect form of a small tent hidden in the trees. Muttering to himself about the ignorance of youth he stomped towards the tent, attempting to hide the fact that he was not a little relieved that Hogshead hadn't actually got round to upping sticks and heading back to Cranachan.

He stopped outside it, grasped the flysheet and tugged it backwards, preparing his index finger for a good wagging to tell Hogshead off thoroughly for not having packed up. He needed to make sure they both knew who was boss.

'Now then, my boy, what is the meaning of you still being here when I specifically said – oh.' It didn't take long for Merlot to discover that the tent was totally empty.

Tutting, he scowled around the clearing and suddenly caught sight of a solitary figure dashing between trees and bushes in a manner that looked as if it was meant to be furtive.

'Hogshead! Come back here you . . .' He stopped in mid-sentence, a rare thing for Merlot. Confused, he watched the furtive figure grasp at the base of a suitable bush, tug hard and reveal a three-wheeled, low-slung contraption with a pod-shaped body and a tiny windscreen. Merlot's mouth hung open in bafflement; somehow he didn't think he'd taught Hogshead quite that much magic. He squinted hard and peered across the distance between them trying to pull the fuzzy figure into focus. *Was* it Hogshead?

Then there was an odd crackling sound and to Merlot's amazement the figure raised what looked like a whelk to his ear. Incredibly it began to talk, in a thin and very angry-sounding voice.

'He's gone? But where to?' gasped the figure in the runicycle.

A series of fizzing syllables rattled out of the shell.

'I only asked.'

Another fizz of commands.

'Sir. On my way!' The en-runicycled one put the shell back in his pocket and began rummaging about in a pouch in the cockpit, muttering. 'I knew he'd never keep that wizard out of the way for very long. Ridiculous idea giving him tickets to the bloody polo tournament . . .'

Suddenly a tirade of thin crackling insults blasted out of

Agent Zhaminah's pocket, abruptly reminding him that he hadn't quite disconnected the call properly.

From behind a convenient tree Merlot watched the MIN agent hurl a large card to the ground before the runicycle. A second later he fired the device into life and was zipping away through the trees.

Muttering to himself Merlot strode up to the card and squinted at the motley array of runes carved into its surface. In a flash he had translated it and realised that something very odd must be going on. Well, he felt certain that it wasn't every day that the instructions, 'Fort Knumm. As fast as possible. Now!' were fed into any old runicycle that happened to be lying around under a convenient bush.

Almost before the rune board had hit the ground Merlot had started to dissolve in a shimmering of tinsel, attempting to remember the way to Fort Knumm.

There was a jangling of vast keys, a creak of an ageing door and with a beam of self-satisfaction Drub the Lore Enforcement Agency Officer kicked Hogshead into a cell and slammed the door shut.

'Well done, son,' smiled Mrs Arangue, wiping a tear of pride from her eye and resettling her pince-nez. Nobody was sure how long it had been since anyone had been arrested for murder in Fort Knumm. Ever since the introduction of the Assassins Anonymous Agreement nobody had ever been disposed of without someone knowing about it in triplicate at least three weeks in advance of the event.

But this, an unauthorised dispatch, well, the culprit would hang for certain.

Hogshead picked himself up off the far side of the stinking cell and pinched himself. Could this really be true? In prison. Again! Something was definitely drastically wrong with his lifestyle.

Ignoring the leering grin from Drub as he stared through the hatch in the door, Hogshead trudged towards a heap of rags in the corner and flopped into them miserably, preparing for a really good, no-holds-barred sulk.

But before he could get started a gaudily coloured alarm macaw flitted on to the windowsill and peered in at him expectantly. In a second it had squeezed between the bars and had hopped on to the cell floor, staring up at Hogshead with an expression that somehow crossed the barriers of species communication.

Hogshead knew that bird wanted something to nibble, and it wanted it now. He started rummaging around in his tunic pockets.

Quintzi Cohatl cackled wildly as he cartwheeled down the street, flicked himself off his forearms and bounced to a perfect halt in front of a vast and hastily painted poster. Seven drops of pure thaumaglobin raced around his body, spurring his hyperactivity to ever-growing heights of madness.

'Excellent!' he declared, patting a grinning Punt on the head. 'He can't possibly miss this! Ha, ha! Come on, my dear devotees!' He pirouetted on the spot and strode out along the banks of the Slove, a snake of disciples in tow.

What a joy it was to be at the head of this column of people, leading them onward towards a brighter, better future. A future with him as their spiritual as well as civic leader! This was what his whole life had been leading towards, he was certain. He was a born leader. Okay, so it might have taken a while to get here, but better late than never. He'd just have to do a lot of catching up, making up for lost time. His mind flicked back just a day to when he had first approached this river tugging a large black sack, alone, facing a future which only he saw. And now look at him, his footsteps filled by a host of followers, all sharing his images of the glories of self-fulfilment to come. They carried his second martyr aloft, his second theurgic casualty. Shame the nano-sprites had been so hungry and he'd been distracted . . . Still, it was all in a good cause.

'. . . and so we are gathered here to fling this worthless sack into the river, turn on our heels and march on towards our brilliantly publicised meeting with the Mayor!' concluded Quintzi to a stirring, if confused, reception of cheers. Most of the throng had to admit privately that they'd expected another spree of prophetic profiteering rather than a cosy chat with Mayor Khulpa.

But they didn't know about the plans Quintzi had for a lucrative takeover bid.

'Come on!' he shrieked, punching the air and cartwheeling along the edge of the River Slove towards the middle of Fort Knumm, his heart skipping excitedly.

In his wake he left droves of eager followers nailing posters to any available vertical space, covering everything and spreading the words:

IS THE FUTURE ALL IT'S CRACKED UP TO BE?
OR A CONSTANT STRUGGLE UPHILL?
HOW'D YOU LIKE TO BE SELF-FULFILLED?
HEAR WHAT YOUR MAYOR THINKS!
TONIGHT, OUTSIDE THE TOWN HALL

And just as the last of Quintzi's devotees hightailed it along the riverbank, a small woman bustled into view, cast a wary eye over the rolling back of Dregs Bank and stopped in her shocked tracks. Unbelievingly she blinked, rubbed her eyes, polished her pince-nez and stared again. Anger fumed inside her as she saw another black sack littering the shining expanse of damp mud.

'Drub!' she shouted as she turned on her heel and raced back towards the Enforcement Agency, her arms wheeling.

'A murder, you say?' gasped Arch Sergeant Strappado.

'Yes, sir. An *unauthorised* murder!' answered Officer Drub smugly and polished his fingernails on the front of his black dungarees. 'No parchmentwork to be found anywhere. It's the first one in years and I have the culprit locked up, sir!'

'Already?'

'Yes, sir, here he is!' Drub stood and pointed through the bars in the cell.

'Well done! There'll be a promotion in this for you!' declared Strappado.

'And a massive pay rise, sir?'

'And a massive pay rise!' repeated Strappado, extending his hand in a rare gesture of warm approval . . .

At least, that's how it went in his dream anyway. After the excitement and the effort of dragging a black sack of evidence all the way back to the Lore Enforcement Agency Building Drub had felt worn out. And in the cool darkness of the cells, it hadn't taken him long to drift away into the restful shallows of sleep.

But while Drub breathed heavily, Hogshead was busy. It hadn't taken him very long to discover that the brightly plumaged alarm macaw, who seemed to have adopted him, was actually far more intelligent than it looked.

Only a few minutes after he had discovered a souvenir from one of his botanical lessons lurking in his tunic pocket and begun to share the beech nuts with the bird, he had half-jokingly muttered 'fetch' and pointed to a stick on the cell floor.

Amazed, he had accepted the stick from the eager macaw, dropped a beech nut into its beak and hurled the stick again. And then the idea had hit him.

He emptied his pocket, pointed to the stash of nuts and pointed out of the cell door at the snoozing guard, waving his arms in a series of complex gestures.

Tiemecx's eyes had bulged at the extent of the reward for such a simple task. He'd squawked assent and hopped through the bars in the door. Hogshead could barely believe it. Someone had really trained this bird well.

If only Hogshead knew the truth he wouldn't have been quite so impressed. Tiemecx would do absolutely anything for a nibble. Claws scratched on the stone floor as the bird waddled forward, assessed the situation and hatched a plan of action.

Barely daring to breathe, Hogshead watched as Tiemecx hopped on to the arm of the chair, stood on one leg and, using his curling beak and devastatingly nimble claws, nonchalantly unhooked the vast bundle of keys from the snoozing guard's midriff. In a matter of seconds the bird had squeezed back into the cell and was gleefully tucking into the stash of nuts. Hogshead stared at the keys, scarcely able to believe his eyes.

Should he go through with this? I mean, it *was* against the law to escape from a jail. But then, he was probably going to hang if he stayed here . . . for what, he hadn't a clue.

With his heart in his mouth he reached through the grille in the door and nervously tried the keys in the lock, barely stifling a scream of joy as the fifth one turned and withdrew the vast iron bar. Hogshead pushed open the door and sprinted away along the passage.

'A murder, you say?' growled Arch Sergeant Strappado a few moments later.

'Yes, sir. An *unauthorised* murder!' answered Officer Drub smugly and polished his fingernails on the front of his black dungarees. 'No parchmentwork to be found anywhere. It's the first one in years and I have the culprit locked up, sir!'

'Already?' growled Strappado sceptically.

'Yes, sir, here he is!' Drub stood and pointed through the bars in the gently swinging cell door.

Somehow Drub correctly predicted that he wouldn't be getting a massive pay rise in the foreseeable future.

'Guards!' shrieked Strappado as Tiemecx downed the last beech nut, looked around, squawked and took to the air on the trail of Hogshead, his new source of nibbles.

'Guards! Follow that bird!' yelled Strappado sarcastically. 'Drub wants it for murder!'

All eyes turned on Drub as he reddened with a mixture of confusion and acute embarrassment. He *hadn't* arrested a macaw. He was certain.

'Get back out on duty you pathetic idiot,' grumbled Strappado. ' "Murder," he says. I ask you. We don't get murders in Fort Knumm anymore. We've got a system!'

'Tonight?' asked Mayor Khulpa irritably as he stared at a hastily painted poster held aloft by Greebly the clerk. 'Why wasn't I informed? Public meeting, indeed! Pah! Not very public if I don't know about it, is it?'

'I'm informing you now, Your Worship,' winced Greebly pathetically.

'I might have been otherwise engaged,' observed Mayor

Khulpa. 'Could've had any number of civic functions to attend. Any number of free dinners laid on for me . . .'

'Er, tonight was unbooked,' groaned Greebly.

'What?' Khulpa clutched forlornly at his midriff of suitably civic proportions. 'No free dinner? What do you expect me to do? Fend for myself? What about the Guild of Fort Knumm Hand Masons? It's been weeks since they honoured me with a slap-up meal.'

'You were round there four days ago,' grunted Greebly, shaking his prematurely balding pate.

'Nonsense. It was close to a month. Has to be!'

'You were presenting the Lifetime Award for Long Service to Macramé and Cross-Stitch . . .'

'What? That ball of pottery string?'

Greebly nodded. 'Yeah. Thursday last week.'

'Hmmm. Well it's still time they invited me back. I'll go there tonight instead of this public meeting here . . .'

'I don't think you will!' declared what looked like a rotund teenage boy as he kicked down the door and swept flamboyantly into view. He was followed by a wave of confused-looking disciples. They were all asking themselves the same question. How could a visit to the Mayor make them all filthy rich?

'How dare you burst in like that!' began Greebly. 'Got an appointment?'

'Not as such, no. But I somehow suspect that the Mayor *will* see me anyway. It was his destiny.'

'Nonsense. I require an application in triplicate signed by three professionals who have known you for at least five years, and then . . .'

'By then it will be *far* too late! The Wheels of Destiny will have rumbled inexorably over your pathetic bodies.' Quintzi Cohatl strode imperiously across the municipal carpet and helped himself to a crystal glassful of brandy.

'Too late?' asked Mayor Khulpa with a sudden twinge of acute nervousness. 'Too late for what?'

'Oh, to save yourself the millions of groats that the future is certainly going to cost!' observed Quintzi in a coldly dismissive manner.

'The future?' blurted Khulpa incredulously. 'Who d'you think you are coming barging in here trying to tell me the future? We don't deal with that here!'

Greebly tugged at the mayoral cloak and coughed under his breath, horribly aware of the fact that he hadn't informed Khulpa of a few recently whispered rumours that had been flitting around the lower corridors. Well, they just hadn't seemed very important then. Just wild chit-chat . . .

'Oh, maybe I do deal in the future,' grinned the Mayor sarcastically. 'Oh yes, I have a vision.' He raised his eyes skywards and spread his arms evangelically. 'It's vision of . . . of *you* being hurled out of this room by several of my larger guards if you don't put that glass down and get out. And take *that* lot with you!' He wagged a flabbily dismissive finger at Quintzi's newly fledged devotees.

Greebly cringed and took refuge behind his master's bulk.

Surprisingly Quintzi just sipped his drink and smiled that now distinctively reptilian smile. 'I don't think so.'

'Oh no? And why's that then?' challenged Mayor Khulpa, stepping forward in a childishly threatening manner.

'Because it is the future. I know it well. In fact, you might say that I wrote a book, as it were.'

'Don't talk rot. Nobody can do that!' spluttered Khulpa, having obviously forgotten everything there is to remember about the subtle art of diplomacy.

Quintzi's eyebrows shot up his forehead as he fixed the Mayor with a tungsten carbide stare. '*I* am not a nobody!' he breathed, nostrils flaring. Everybody took a step backwards and was covered in a dense axminster of silence.

Cohatl took another sip, rolled the ancient Koh Gnyack around his mouth and sucked air noisily through his teeth. Then his face relaxed into a broad smile and he strode towards the Mayor.

'Dear, oh dear,' he tutted, slipping an overly friendly arm about the mayoral shoulders. 'We really shouldn't be arguing, you know. You see, you have no choice. Like it or not, the future is coming. And unless you listen *very* carefully to what I say it will be excruciatingly messy and expensive for you.'

'Says who?'

Cohatl's face creased into a feral grin. 'Says me. I invented it.' He tapped a palm twice on Khulpa's cheek and strolled arrogantly away.

'Nonsense!' flustered Khulpa. 'Nobody *invents* the future. It simply happens. Cause and effect . . .'

'Ha! You're so right, Mayor! You see, *I* cause the problems and *you* suffer their effects!'

Greebly coughed nervously and tugged at the Mayor's expensive sleeve. Khulpa turned and stared at the ashen-faced clerk pointing with terror at the madman strutting along the Official Civic Desk and scattering parchment messily. 'It's him! Him!' he mouthed desperately and pointed to the poster.

'And there are more than just financial considerations,' growled Cohatl ominously. 'Employment casualties, for example!' Casually he stepped on to the pristine green cushion of the Mayoral State Carver and then to the floor, leaving a large dollop of the River Slove where Khulpa's backside normally dwelt.

'Employment?' flustered the Mayor as fear seeped through his politically thickened skin. He knew that jobs meant votes and votes kept him in office.

Cohatl smiled icily and snatched the Chain of Office from around Khulpa's overfed neck. 'Who'll be wearing this in the future?' he asked.

Khulpa's hands flashed to his neck as he squealed and clawed at the absent chain looking for all the world like a man in the final throes of poisoning. 'You can't do that! Who do you think you are bursting into my office unannounced, drinking my brandy and snatching my . . .'

Quintzi's disciples cheered cautiously.

'I *know* who I am,' snarled Quintzi, spinning the chain around a portly index finger. 'And the future knows who I am! Now it's time to introduce myself to everyone else!' His disciples cheered. And with that, he whirled on his heel, tossed the now empty crystal glass high into the air and strode towards the door by which he had entered.

Khulpa watched sparks of light glint prismatically off the tumbling tumbler and squealed. Before he knew it he was dashing forward, palms outstretched, eyes locked on and targeting. With a grunt he launched himself rugby style and just slid his hands between the glass and the office carpet.

'Nice catch,' grinned Cohatl and disappeared into the corridor twirling the Chain of Office.

'Great to see you haven't lost track of priorities,' observed Greebly, slapping his forehead in despair.

'Eh?' grunted the prone and panting Mayor.

Greebly raised his palms heavenward for a moment than ran them around his neck as if stroking a large and incredibly valuable official ornament of gold and diamond.

'Arghhh! Oi! Come back with my chain!' screamed Khulpa, suddenly feeling worryingly naked. That chain meant a lot to him. It was his passport to almost four hundred dinners a year; without it he would certainly go hungry. 'There's no escape. My guards will stop you!'

'I don't foresee any problems there,' echoed Quintzi's voice as he dashed off down the corridor followed by a totally baffled herd of devotees trying frantically to work out what that chain would be worth divided by . . .

Sprinting faster than he had in years (except for the time when there was that catering cock-up at the Fort Knumm Hand Maidens Ball three years ago and only the first five people at the serving hatch managed to get a portion of Lemming Mousse) Mayor Khulpa whistled through the door and plunged down the corridor hot on the thief's trail. What a nerve! If he'd wanted the Mayoral Chain so badly he should have bought an election, as Khulpa had himself. But he wouldn't get far, there were guards everywhere.

Drub, the Lore Enforcement Officer, trudged along the banks of the River Slove on automatic as his mind whirled in confusion. So far he was totally at a loss even to begin

271

explaining the events back at headquarters. Nothing seemed in the least plausible about it all.

Could it be that he had, as Strappado suspected, flipped his lid and arrested a macaw on murder charges? No, that was impossible . . . wasn't it? There was the body. He shuddered as he recalled that shrivelled face. A macaw couldn't possibly have done that, could it? A vampire macaw? No, no! How would it have put the body in the sack and dragged it on to Dregs Bank?

No. There had to be a simple explanation. Drub went back to first principles, recalling precisely what he had done. Right, first he arrested the suspect as indicated by Mrs Arangue, then he'd dragged said suspect into the cells, fetched Strappado and when he came back . . . there was a macaw in the cell and the suspect had gone. Uh-huh. Conclusion? Easy: the boy had turned into a bird.

The vast majority of Drub's confused brain squealed with despair and, had it been a democracy of neurones then that particular train of thought would have terminated there, all musings, wishes and contemplations being unceremoniously turfed off on to another line of speculation.

However, in a disused corner of his mind a clump of conclusions leapt upright and made it entirely obvious that they weren't going to quieten down until they'd had their say.

He was right. The boy *had* turned into a bird. Simple. He was the wizard that Strappado was after. A criminal shape-shifting murderer turned macaw in order to make good his getaway. Just wait till Strappado heard that one. Oh yes!

He whirled on his heel, lurched into a sprint and trampled an eagerly scuttling woman sporting a pair of dark pince-nez.

'Drub! Come back here!' she cried from the bank, flat on her back. 'Now!'

Reluctantly he obeyed, snatching her up off the muddy footpath with a sickening slurping sound.

Before he could put her down and race back to Strappado with his burning news she grabbed him around the collar and declared. 'Another one. I've found another one. They're at it again!'

272

'At what again?' he asked unthinking.

'Littering the river. There's another one of those sacks on Dregs Bank.'

'Another!'

This was worse than he thought. How would Strappado react when he gave him the news that he had a *serial* murdering shape-shifting wizard loose in Fort Knumm?

Somehow he didn't think it would go down too well.

Sweating profusely now, Mayor Khulpa spun wildly down a spiral staircase in the Town Hall, his feet barely touching the steps. Ahead he could see the grinning figure of the thief and the wave of disciples. Behind he ignored the desperate gesturing of Greebly. What did that buffoon know about mayoral decorum? I can chase my chain if I so choose.

The corridor widened at the base of the staircase, sweeping majestically towards the front entrance and the pair of vast guards standing either side.

'Stop them!' croaked Mayor Khulpa. 'Hold them! That's an order!'

The guards flicked into life, strode forward in front of the doors.

'See?' shrieked the Mayor triumphantly. 'No escape! Give me back my chain.'

Quintzi stood totally still for a moment, scowling at the guards, and rummaged deep inside his cloak. In a second he was holding a crystal sphere on his palm in the stance beloved by actors when presented with a skull called Yorick.

'A vision!' declared Quintzi, staring at the blank sphere. 'I see two guards revelling in the joys of riches. I see two doors, not too dissimilar to those before me, and miraculously they are swinging open, their handles tugged by guards clutching small sacks of groats. Small sacks like these!' he announced. And miraculously two sacks of coins arced out of his pockets and were caught easily by the suddenly grinning doormen. If Khulpa hadn't been panting so frantically he would've spat and cursed something very nasty indeed. Not very incredibly, the doors creaked open.

Quintzi entered the square before the ornate Town Hall, stepped sideways, raised his hands for silence and addressed the throng that had gathered in response to the rash of posters littering Fort Knumm like the pox.

'Ladies, Gentlemen, and most especially the Children. May I welcome you all to this evening's debate on the future of Fort Knumm. And I'd like to welcome your Mayor . . .'

The main entrance of the Town Hall exploded in a flurry of curses and the sweating bulk of Khulpa erupted into view, snarling. His clothes of office hung in disarray about his shoulders, his neck flabby and naked without a certain official lavatory pull.

'What are you lot staring at, eh?' he snapped to the fifteen-thousand-strong crowd of criminals, cutthroats and a few hundred assassins. 'Where's that bloody thief, eh?'

Twelve hundred thieves took a swift, sharp intake of breath and instantly closed ranks. How dare he insult thieves so publicly! It was an honourable profession, there were rules. Not just anybody could be a thief, oh no. Took skill, years of practice. How dare he . . .

Before Mayor Khulpa could lurch towards Quintzi Cohatl, Punt and several of Quintzi's devotees sprang forward, snatched at the Mayor and hauled him off to a specially prepared chair facing the gathered crowd.

'Gimme back my chain!' squealed Khulpa, struggling. Greebly stood at the door and tutted. He'd tried to warn him.

'So!' declared Quintzi, addressing the crowd dramatically. 'You're all here to find out about the future, eh?'

The crowd shuffled nervously. If they were entirely honest with themselves they would probably have to admit that they'd turned up simply to see what all the fuss was about. Rumours, wildly enhanced gossip and the tallest of tales regarding this so-called Self-Fulfilling Prophet had transpired to raise the curiosity levels of the average Fort Knumm resident to far above that which was normally expected. It couldn't all be true, could it? He looked so young.

'Well, it's all here, the future is in the palm of my hand!' He strode up on to the head of one of the pair of stone Ammorettan

Death Lizards that curled their way either side of the granite staircase. A gasp of wonder rippled around the crowd as he pointed to a shimmering glass sphere in his hand.

Expertly his thumb depressed the tiny power toggle and the sphere hummed into life, images swirling into coherence within.

'. . . lcome back to Scry Sports and our coverage of One Man and His Hog . . .' declared a voice within. Quintzi coughed noisily, waggled his thumb frantically on a small knurled dial and the sound diminished. He continued to stare at the silent broadcast of next year's Lammarch Warthog Trials and expertly adopted an expression of acute concern. In the sphere a pair of warthogs swooped around under expertly whistled guidance, gathering a flock of sheep together and driving them towards a pen. Cohatl's lip twitched as he spotted the fitting irony.

'I can see the future!' he decreed. 'Your future under that Mayor!' Lying was undoubtedly getting easier and easier for him.

Another wave of shock spread around the crowd as they heard his words. The future? Could it be true? Those who had witnessed his earlier exploits leaned forward, craning their ears to listen to the pearls of far-sighted wisdom that would undoubtedly come tumbling down soon.

'And I'm sorry to say . . . ooooh! no . . . it doesn't look good!' added Quintzi just as, coincidentally, a stubborn-looking ram wheeled around and began to challenge a carefully advancing warthog. The sphere filled momentarily with a full-screen view of a worried-looking shepherd. 'Shocking!' he continued, somehow managing to make his face turn pale. He raised his arm in a dramatic sweep of forward-looking desperation and winced. His shoulder creaked with worryingly familiar arthriticness.

'What can you see?' called Punt, looking up from in front of the stone Death Lizard. 'Tell us!'

'I . . . I . . .' Quintzi's head reeled for a moment as he stared at his reflection in the sphere. Was it his imagination or was he starting to look a little more wrinkly? No, surely not, just a trick

275

of the light. He pulled himself together with an effort, took a breath and resumed his prophetic vision.

'I see ... I see windows smashed in the streets. Lore Enforcement Agency officers sprinting wildly through an assembled mob, waving truncheons. I see a crushed toy bear pounded beneath fleeing feet ...'

Ten children wailed simultaneously and tugged at their parents' sleeves.

'I see chaos and ruin, destruction and irreparable damage. And I ... no. It cannot be true!' A pained expression flashed on to Quintzi's face as if he had witnessed a sight of ultimate betrayal, the nadir of back-stabbing perfidy. 'Surely not!' Expertly he milked the crowd of all their emotions, steering their gullible hearts, already mistrustful of Mayor Khulpa, towards a stunning (if invented) revelation. Quintzi glanced towards the sweating bulk of Khulpa and winced in a manner that a stage actor would have given all his curtain calls for. A creaking pelvis just happened to make this a little easier.

'Tell us!' yelled Punt. 'What do you see?'

'I ... I ... no. It's too horrible ...'

The crowd roared in disapproval. They wanted to know. They hadn't hung about out here wasting valuable drinking time to find out that the future just wasn't very nice. They wanted reasons. Ye gods! just talk to any marginally inebriated pessimist and he'd tell you the future was a mess for free. They wanted facts.

'As duly elected representative of this town,' declared Mayor Khulpa, shouting around the wall of Quintzi's self-appointed devotees, 'I demand that you inform us of the information to which you have so recently become privy!' He grinned to himself as he heard the masterful use of language. True, he wasn't entirely certain he knew what it all meant but, well, neither did anyone else.

'You don't want to know,' warned Quintzi, wiping an imaginary tear from his face as if the knowledge he now possessed was tearing him apart from inside.

'Oh, but I do!' insisted Khulpa, feeling that at last he was regaining some control.

'Believe me, you don't!'

'Oh yes I do!'

Quintzi shook his head and a shock of grating bones struck a chord of terror within him. 'No!' he shouted involuntarily, as he realised that the effects of the thaumaglobin were wearing off.

'YES!' bellowed the crowd. 'Tell us!'

'Er . . . very well.' He rallied well and would have launched into his final push had not his chin suddenly erupted in excruciating itchiness. Alarmed, he realised that his chin was sprouting plumes of whiskers like there was no tomorrow. Fighting down rising panic he flipped up the hood of his cloak and spun around, back to the mob, holding the crystal high like a priest at some vast altar.

The crowd edged forward straining to ensure that they heard every one of Quintzi's words. It was an unnecessary move. There was no way that Quintzi was going to let them miss any of this. Not now it was all so close.

'Above the shattered chaos of destruction . . .' he yelled in apparent anguish, choking as his larynx aged. 'Beyond the turmoil of misery and suffering, I see . . . I see him laughing!' Quintzi pointed stiffly at Mayor Khulpa's heart.

The crowd took a menacing step forward.

'I see increased costs for repairs, spiralling expenses for . . . a word . . . a strange word . . . protection!'

A flurry of shop owners and other traders shouted in disapproval. They already paid extortionate amounts to the Lore Enforcement Agency as a so-called 'Immunity Charge' – a strangely calculated monthly payment which, if coughed up in full, substantially decreased the chances of any unfortunate incidents occurring to the property or persons paying it. Interestingly, the higher the monthly costs, the safer one was. Well, at least until you fell behind . . .

'And he is behind it all!' croaked Quintzi smacking his lips and beginning to crave another magical fix. 'Leave Fort Knumm under his control and the entire future is utter doom and gloom. You'll languish in anguish, be in a ferment of torment, you'll wallow in the throes of sorrow and woe!'

The crowd, like an angry sea in a Force Ten gale, swept towards the steps of the Town Hall, their hands punching the air like the peaks of white water, their voices deafening in a rising tumult.

And then into this seething aquatic analogy strode Quintzi, hood tugged far down over his ageing face like some ancient prophet who knew about roses and noses and whose name rhymed with toses. He held up his palms, halted the tide and declared in a voice that somehow everyone managed to hear, 'Of course, there is an alternative to that dreadful future, if you're at all interested.'

Arch Sergeant Strappado would cheerfully have continued smashing Drub's forehead against the Lore Enforcement Agency cell walls well into the night after he had heard his theories of serial murdering shape-shifting wizards on the loose. But he was disturbed by a sudden incoming report carried by a suddenly incoming officer.

'Disturbance in the Town Hall Square,' spluttered the officer, panting wildly and wincing as he caught sight of Drub's forehead which was already turning a nasty shade of bruise. 'Close to a riot situation, sir!'

'Let them fight! I'm busy!' Strappado punctuated his words with the repeated pounding of Drub's forehead. 'I don't care.'

'But, sir, they're about to lynch the Mayor.'

'Good. About time that good-for-nothing scrounger got what he deserved. Now gimme the bad news!'

'Er,' the officer scratched his head. 'The Mayor's all right, sir.'

'What?'

'Well, he's all right for the moment, sir. The crowd was stopped from ripping him apart by . . . by a sort of fat kid with brown hair and . . .'

'Sir!' whimpered Drub desperately. 'That's him. That's the one who turned into a macaw!'

'Macaw? He feeling all right?' asked the other officer.

'It's him, I tell you!' insisted Drub. 'And . . . and the Mayor's next!'

278

'You sure?' snarled Strappado, spinning him around.

'Yes. The description matches . . .'

'No. I mean about the Mayor. You sure he's next?'

Drub nodded wildly.

Strappado's face brightened considerably. 'Ooooh goody. I don't want to miss this. Assemble *all* the guards!' he ordered. 'Full riot gear. I want a front seat!' He blasted from the room in a whirlwind of giggling enthusiasm.

Hogshead could barely keep upright as he hurtled through the deserted streets of Fort Knumm. He'd lost count completely of the number of times he'd caught his toe in a crack in the cobbles and gone flying across some street or other, only to end up bouncing off a wall or coming to rest in a puddle of a decidedly unsavoury origin. He hadn't any kind of clue which way he was running. And frankly he didn't have a chance to care. Just as long as it was away from the guards who had to be chasing him it didn't matter. He knew he must be doing well: ever since his jail-break he hadn't seen any guards.

Suddenly, he heard a screech of tyres, a yelling of voices, and a host of spat curses issued from an odd torpedo-shaped vehicle as it leapt out of a sidestreet and almost flattened him.

'Watch it, alley hog!' he cried at the finger-waving man in the anonymous grey clothing.

He sprinted on, whirled around a sharp corner and slammed into the back of a knot of people which seemed to stretch as far as his eyes could see, which was to the Fort Knumm Town Hall.

'Of course,' declared the hooded figure on the steps who was clutching a small crystal in an oddly evangelical pose, 'there is an alternative to that dreadful future, if you're at all interested.'

The angry wave of the crowd halted in mid-surge and turned their ears once again to the Self-Fulfilling Prophet. But now their blood was surging with the anger of the riot. Right now, placid listening to a speechifying prophet was not high on their collective agenda. Right now they wanted to make somebody pay for all the years of misery they'd suffered under the rulership of Mayor Khulpa. And there was only one man with the correct currency. The Mayor himself.

Quintzi raised his aching shoulders above the crowd and winced as he felt a wrinkle reappear across his forehead. His stomach rumbled hollowly, craving the life-enhancing elixir of thaumaglobin. He could really do with a few drops right now.

'Those images of destruction,' he croaked desperately, keeping his head down. 'That chaos and ruination which I have been privileged to witness, as a result of my specialist foreseeing powers . . . It *can* be avoided!'

Unknown by anyone else, three spots of light lurked miserably in his left ear. 'How d'you like that, brothers,' snarled Skarg'l the nano-sprite. 'His specialist powers? Pah! Any mug with a few spare groats can get one of those damned crystals. That's our brothers' specialist foreseeing powers being abused, that is!'

'So what?' grumbled Udio. 'It's nothing to do with us. We're just here to fix things, patch 'em up when they go a bit squiffy. Gods, you know I really miss ruptured destiny valves,' he added as wistfully as a tiny mote of light can get.

'Me too,' grumbled Nimlet. 'There just isn't the same satisfaction in pulling bits of wood apart just 'cause he says so. It was fun at first but now . . .'

Having sprinted at double time through a series of very short short-cuts, Arch Sergeant Strappado burst out from a tiny side alley and arrived panting at the back of the mob in the Town Hall Square. With a flurry of swift hand gestures and martial arts kicks he commanded his band of accompanying guards to open a path for him, quick sharp. He didn't want to miss any of the Mayor's imminent demise. Well, it wouldn't be right for such a high-ranking member of the Lore Enforcement Agency to miss such an event. And besides, he couldn't stand the way Khulpa insisted on inviting himself around for dinner and then proceeded to polish off all his favourite brandy.

As the guards began to clear a path towards the Town Hall steps, the mob started to chant wildly, blood heat rising in a tide of anger and hidden unrest. They weren't interested in the future any more. That could wait. Right now they wanted Mayor Khulpa!

The crowd surged forward uncontrollably, the front line rising up the bottom steps like a boiling tide of fury, their collective mind seething with the will to sweep up the steps and smother the Mayor in a frenzy of clawing savagery.

This was better than Strappado had expected. He might even be able to join in if no one was watching too closely. And he would have done too.

It was only the unexpected shimmering of tinsel which suddenly appeared on the steps and began to coalesce that stopped the mob on the steps. Never had the fifteen thousand cutthroats, assassins and common sneak thieves seen anything quite so, well, distracting. Their jaws dropped in awe, they stared in wonder as the buzzing of silver bees grew in intensity, spun around each other and formed a column of pure magic. A shimmering cascade of spinning stars began to coalesce on the top of the Ammorettan Death Lizard. It pulsed mysteriously, swelling swiftly as it solidified into a tall, vaguely cylindrical form. Hogshead bounced up and down frantically at the back of the mob, trying desperately to see what was happening. His heart leapt as he recognised Merlot's distinctive arrival. Relief began to grow within him.

Quintzi Cohatl snarled angrily as he watched the wizard form, spitting fury that his grand plan had been disturbed so publicly, detesting this intrusion and cursing his body for aching so viciously. If only he could just call a halt to the whole thing and sit down with a nice few drops of thaumaglobin. If only he could regain the control which was slipping away . . .

And then suddenly, almost as if reality had hiccuped, there was a blinding flash and a tall man was standing there, clad in a long robe the colour of E major and trimmed with a C-minor collar and cuffs. Strangely he was also wearing a long black, red and purple scarf and a matching shirt, unrecognisable to all but anyone with a knowledge of polo as those of the Apocalypse Four Supporters' Club. 'Greetings,' he declared.

It was as far as he got. For in that same flash Quintzi knew exactly where his next pick-me-up was coming from. 'Grab him!' he screamed, flinging his hood back and beckoning wildly at his devotees from atop the other Ammorettan Death Lizard. 'Jump on him. Now!'

Suddenly shocked at the odd transformation that had occurred beneath the hood, the mob halted in their tracks.

Strappado stood perfectly still, his jaw sagging limply on his chest, stunned by the tinsely entrance. Blinking, his gaze turned from the newly coalesced wizard to the unmistakable form of his MIN contact and from there to the statuesque figures which he was calling upon to help. Thoughts of promotion uppermost in his mind he yelled at Quintzi's disciples: 'Well go on, then. What are you waiting for? Grab the bloody conjurist infiltrator! Grab him! Now!'

When his MIN contact found out that it was he who had given the order he would be a member of that elite group faster than you could whistle the Cranachanian Kingdomnal Anthem. And since that only consisted of four bars, it was very quick indeed.

Before he could correctly work out that certain folks weren't running towards him to shake him warmly by the hand, Merlot was flattened to the deck by a mob of Quintzi's seething devotees, his hat tugged down over his eyes. Within the second he was pinned down by a dozen of the more portly disciples and the Self-Fulfilling Prophet himself had leapt off the stone lizard and landed in an arthritic heap next to him. Barely pausing for breath he swept the hextirpator out of his cloak pocket and waved it threateningly at Merlot.

'That's it. Arrest him! Clap him in irons,' enthused Strappado from the middle of the crowd.

Hogshead jumped up and down behind the crowd in an attempt to see a way through and find out where Merlot had suddenly vanished to. Had he imagined his arrival? Could he be hallucinating? His heels clattering on the cobbles, his ankles screaming, he sprang once again, at the very same instant that Quintzi Cohatl leapt off the stone head of the Ammorettan Death Lizard on the Town Hall steps, spread his arms wide and tugged the hextirpator out of his cloak with a wild shriek.

Hogshead hit the ground with a splat and shook his head in

282

horror-stricken denial. His heart skipped a terrified beat as the all-too-recent memories of an ageing madman jamming needles into a captive's forearm flashed across his mind.

But it couldn't possibly be – could it? Here? In front of everybody? Hogshead leapt above the crowd once more and stared for as long as he could at the figure swatting an owl away.

'We can do this easy or hard, take your pick,' snarled Quintzi at the pinned and mounted wizard.

'I say, this is all rather impolite,' mumbled Merlot and tugged his hat away from his eyes. One of Quintzi's devotees grabbed the top of the conical headgear and snatched it off, slapping it on his head like some sort of war trophy. It was only as a dozen rodents sank their claws into the top of his scalp that he realised something was horribly wrong. Screaming, he snatched it off and hurled it away. Merlot's hat arced over the far side of one of the stone lizards on a vapour trail of mice.

'Yes,' grunted Merlot in disgust. 'Very uncivil I must say, er . . . is that . . . a needle?'

Quintzi nodded and angled the said device before Merlot's nose. 'Wonderfully sharp. It won't hurt a bit.' He grinned.

'Hurt? What do you mean?'

'This!' declared Quintzi, plunging the needle deep into Merlot's wrist and lighting the athanor burner with a flourish.

Merlot's eyes rolled into the top of his head. 'I don't wish to be rude but are you a qualified physician? Have you correctly sterilised that n-n . . .' spluttered the wizard, feeling his head swim. Needles always seemed to send him a bit funny. Even the ones that fell off pine trees made him a little woozy. He didn't really understand it, but . . . As his pupils migrated into the safety of his head he collapsed in a dead faint.

And in that instant, in the moment Hogshead recognised the man's distinctive gestures and stance, stacked them high on the back of the recent memory and overturned the lot in a multi-fact pile-up on his personal information highway, he knew who it was up there, up before the whole population of Fort Knumm, readying himself for who knew what ruinous activities, there, swatting owls away from ... Owls? Hogshead's heart was in his mouth. He hadn't been hallucinating. Merlot was here. He scanned the scene and whimpered as he recognised the beard of the figure buried in an avalanche of disciples. And somehow, through the screaming of the restless crowd, Hogshead heard the hideous gurgling of the hextirpator.

He had to be stopped, and now! Snarling wildly he tore blindly at the backs of the people before him, elbowing his way forward frantically, elbows and knees gyrating in all directions.

After a minute and half of this, the brute whose leather tunic he had been attempting to burrow through picked him up and hurled him away out of the square, grunting something along the lines of, 'Now then, sonny, no need to push. We'll all get a chance to show the Mayor what we really think of him!'

The exact phrasing was, however, somewhat more colourful and descended into the sub-shades of the really unprintably insulting.

Witnessed only by Punt and a few other close devotees, the hextirpator continued to bubble and fizz. Abruptly it gurgled obscenely and oozed a gleaming droplet of purified thaumaglobin from its tube. Quintzi Cohatl cackled delight and snatched the invigorating droplet on to his fingertip, slurping excitedly, trembling in anticipation.

With a shriek, the rush hit. He leapt to his feet and bellowed with the confidence of rapidly approaching youth. Now he was ready to regain the mob's attention and twist it to his will, bend it to his ultimate benefit.

'Ladies and Gentlemen, my plan is stunning in its elegant and unfailing simplicity!' he yelled, buttering up his audience as he approached his mid-forties. 'I have the power to see the future, to witness any and all of destiny's forthcoming snags. And for a modest fee, payable in advance of course, I can make this information available to all whom it affects. Yes, you scratch my back and I'll make sure that you don't break yours! Now, I can't say fairer than that, can I? What d'you say?'

A roar filled the Town Hall square, drowning Strappado's

incomprehensible gagging as he pointed at the rapidly unageing figure. MIN agents shouldn't be able to do that, should they? Wasn't it just a smidgin too . . . magical?

Quintzi leered out at the crowd, trying to gauge their mood. 'Personal prophecies, *and* I throw in the Mayor!' he declared. The crowd went wild. After all, it did seem fair enough, especially with a ritual mugging thrown in. They all paid 'Immunity Charge' now, and for what? If this madman was prepared to give them something other than just enforced poverty in return, well, who were they to argue? Almost as one, the crowd's gaze settled on Mayor Khulpa's midriff.

There were only three pairs of eyes that looked directly at Quintzi Cohatl and didn't see a rosy future, and they belonged to Strappado as he watched his supposed future with MIN retreat as fast as Cohatl's years, Hogshead who knew for certain that this madman had to be stopped, and a grey-cloaked figure who had parked his runicycle round the back of the Town Hall.

Leaping about at the back of the crowd like a dwarf on springs, Hogshead knew that somehow he had to get through the crowd. There was no telling what that madman Cohatl would do if he wasn't confronted face to face.

But with mounting frustration he had to admit he hadn't a clue how to reach him. Nothing, saving fire or flood, would shift that crowd more than a couple of worthless inches. And then, in a flash of sheer inspiration it hit him. Suddenly he knew what to do. Stepping back from the crowd he chanted a few desperate words and almost singed his mop of hair as three fireballs – extra large sprang into unsupported existence.

'Fire!' yelled Hogshead dramatically. 'Help, help! Fire!' And with that he plunged into the crowd, the trio of torches spinning just over six feet above the ground.

Never had a crowd parted so swiftly. It came as a very satisfying spectacle to see the effect the imminent prospect of singed earlobes had on the fluid dynamics of a random mob. In moments Hogshead was surfing towards Quintzi on the afterwave of a spreading current of panic, his arrow-straight course converging on the hated Self-Fulfilling Prophet.

'. . . and with *my* help your future can be assured!' insisted Cohatl staring skywards in a paroxysm of fervent ranting as he reached for a perfect youthful retirement. In a matter of minutes he could feel it: with just the right push he would be well on the way to finding himself lapping lustily at the heady liquour of luxury.

'Yes, people of Fort Knumm. Pay me and I can offer you the perfect future. Disagree and the very stones of the Town Hall will fall on top of all of you . . .' The nano-sprites wriggled and buzzed in anticipation of another destructive mission.

'Not so fast!' screamed a grey-cloaked figure from the top of the Town Hall. All eyes flashed roofwards as a rope cascaded down and the figure abseiled perfectly on to the top of the Ammorettan Death Lizard. In a fluid continuation of the movement he drew a very large and hummingly sharp sword and leapt down to land near the gurgling hextirpator.

'Years I have awaited this!' shrieked Agent Zhaminah of the Mystical Intelligence Network. 'Thousands of groats I've invested in that! It's mine! I want it back. But first . . .' He shook off his gloves, reached out a trembling fingertip and scooped four drops of purified thaumaglobin from a small receptacle. His eyes widening with barely suppressed excitement he dropped them on to his tongue. He had to be the first to try it, to prove that MIN would never be beaten by magicians again. Commander Furlansk would be so proud . . . if only there was a sneeke in the audience.

'No magician can ever dominate MIN again!' declared Zhaminah, his dreadlocks and goatee beard waving. 'The days of their magical supremacy are numbered . . . WHHHHAAAAAAAAOOOOOAAAAHH!' He rose a full three inches off the steps as his first thaumaglobin rush hit. 'Once MIN have the power, we can rule!' Sparks of blue lightning fizzed around his hair as his body tried to absorb the thaumaglobin. He snatched another drop, flexed his fingers and began to concentrate his whirring thoughts. How long he had practised this, his first spell, he would never know. It had been years of dry runs in the privacy of his tree house in the Auric Triangle, rehearsing the words over and over again, without an audience and, crucially, without any of the power necessary for its ultimate thaumic completion. His liver vibrated frantically as it discovered the thrill of the mamba, his spleen began to tango and his pancreas learned to jig.

Zhaminah held everyone's attention riveted as his fingers curled and uncurled, his lips moved and he began chanting. Fizzing crackles of cerulean energy bounced along the length of his arms as if he was standing on a fifty-thousand-volt supply. The crowd edged nervously away as he reached the climax of the spell, then with a shrug of practised shoulders and a gritting of teeth he finished its casting. There was a crack of lightning and a shimmering black cylinder flashed into existence. It turned hollow, one end opened into a rim and, with a coincident flash of unnecessary pyrotechnics something moved inside.

Agent Zhaminah shrieked with theurgic excitement as he pulled the tiny bunny out of the shimmering topper and held it up for the crowd's applause.

Nervously Mayor Khulpa edged out of his seat and crept away.

'See!' shrieked the MIN agent. 'It's so easy. Ha! And now, for my next trick I shall . . .' He whirled on his heel, snatched the tiny tube of purified thaumaglobin from beneath the hextirpator and threw it down his neck.

Despite their confusion the crowd applauded.

It was as if the orchestra which Zhaminah's organs were dancing to suddenly tripled the tempo. He squealed as several hundred millithaums coursed wildly through his body. Deep within, his liver vibrated madly and his spleen ached for a tango partner to whirl around in a frenzy of passionate terpsichory. Fireworks of thaumic energy zapped out from his eyebrows and fingertips.

'Ha! For my next . . . trick . . . I shall . . . uh-oh!' His intestines rumbaed uncontrollably. He hiccuped and sent a sheet of purple flame blasting twenty feet into the air. And at the very instant that his spleen succumbed to temptation and snatched his pancreas in a passionate embrace, a whistle rang out long and loud from a Lore Enforcement Agency Officer's Standard Issue Whistle.

Drub's finger pointed hard and unwavering at the mop-haired rotundly youthful figure of Quintzi Cohatl and shouted, 'That's him! Murderer! Get him!'

In a flash he was batoning his way through the crowd.

The Self-Fulfilling Prophet swore profusely. This was definitely *not* going right. Other people were stealing his show, bellowing in an unruly manner, pulling rabbits from hats without his express permission ... Well, he'd show them. 'That threat about the Town Hall crumbling isn't an idle one, you know!' He waggled his finger in his ear and barked angrily at the fizzing nano-sprites inside.

And then something strange began to happen to the nano-sprites. As Quintzi attempted to regain control of the crowd by showing them the evil future that was, according to him, completely inevitable, and to scare the proverbial willies out of them all, the nano-sprites' fairy-godmother genes somehow began to tune in to the crowd's wishes. As the crowd surged forward and was offered the alternative to a dreadful future, 'if they were at all interested', a tidal wave of bombarding and conflicting images of wish-fulfilment rattled into the nano-sprites' minds.

Assassins and undertakers dreamed of a future pile of recently dispatched bodies, whilst aromatherapists and acupuncturists urged the fates to deliver droves of living patients, albeit not entirely healthily. Bank clerks wished for stacks of cash secured safely behind impenetrable vault doors, whilst burglars hoped for a few crates of all-purpose vault-piercing dynamite. And for the first time in their tiny lives the nano-sprites were privy to a new and alarming sensation – utter confusion. Never before had they experienced the concept of mutual exclusivity. Things before had either been broken or fixed, faulty or perfect. They buzzed in bewildered bafflement, trapped between Cohatl's visions of a gloriously wealthy future as ruler of Fort Knumm and Officer Drub's overwhelming urge to slam him in jail and hurl away the key.

MIN Agent Zhaminah on the other hand was buzzing in far

more than bewilderment. His spleen hurled his pancreas about in gay abandon as he hiccuped another thirty-foot sheet of flame skywards. His intestines knotted and writhed as if they were suddenly possessed of intelligence, his pupils whirred in his skull and his entire body began to vibrate wildly.

An area of clear ground began to grow as people panicked and edged backwards, keeping clear of the dangerously oscillating stranger.

The first sign that it was too late for Zhaminah was the brief spurt of steam which shot from his ears. Then he simply put his hand over his mouth and said, 'Wooops!'

A second later all that remained was a smouldering heap of very ex-MIN agent. The crowd, as one, screamed in horror as the windows in the Town Hall shattered. Everyone wheeled around and fled.

Quintzi's jaw was ageing rapidly as he stared at the events around him. His eyes drank in the scene – windows shattered in the streets, the Lore Enforcement Agents sprinting through a massed mob and there, crushed in the wreckage, a child's dropped teddy bear.

It wasn't fair. If only he'd realised he'd seen it all coming.

Suddenly two huge hands shot from the crowd, snatched him by the shoulders and two voices snarled in each ear, ''Ere. I wanna word with you!'

Quintzi dangled helplessly between the arms of the Lore Enforcement Agency. 'I am arresting you for the murder of two . . .' began Drub before Arch Sergeant Strappado opened his autocratic mouth.

'Oh no, matey,' he seethed. 'He's mine. All mine!'

'But I got him first,' whined Drub. 'Well, before he turned into a macaw, of course!'

'He's mine!' insisted Strappado with a glare of red-hot-pokerian intensity. 'I'm having him for breaking and entering the Lore Enforcement headquarters . . .'

'. . . and breaking *out* of the Lore Enforcement Headquarters's cells . . .' added Drub.

'. . . plus impersonating an officer of the Mystical Intelligence Network . . .' countered Strappado.

'. . . er . . . and impersonating a member of a gaudily feathered bird species?' offered Drub.

'Stealing my chain of office!' shouted Mayor Khulpa from behind one of the stone Death Lizards.

'Shut up, you lot!' bellowed Arch Sergeant Strappado, glaring redly. 'I'm in charge here and he's mine, all right? Any objectors? Anybody have anything to say about that, eh?'

Quintzi shrugged his shoulders and sighed. 'Bugger,' was all he said before he was dragged away across the litter-strewn expanse of the Town Hall Square, his heart heavy with the feeling that if he'd tried just a little bit harder then maybe, just maybe, he could have foreseen a suitable escape route.

It was highly fortunate that Officer Drub didn't look over his shoulder at the exact moment when Hogshead struggled out from beneath a large hoarding that had been flattened by the crowd's hasty exit; fortunate for Hogshead since Drub probably would have squealed with delight and slammed him behind bars for the two murders, and fortunate for Drub's sanity since it would have curled up its toes and gibbered as it tried to figure out precisely how he had changed places so cleverly with the old man currently under his partial arrest. It was also quite handy for a certain gaudily clad wizard currently lying forgotten on the top step, a tiny device sucking unstoppably at his wrist.

Hogshead blinked as he stared around him, then gasped and sprinted up the Town Hall steps.

'Merlot! No!' he cried, hearing that dreadful slurping. His heart seethed with terrified anger, gripping his body, driving him on. 'No, no!' he screamed. Without thinking, he snatched at the hextirpator's needle and tugged it free of the wizard's frail-looking wrist, flinging the hated device against the wall. It struck the edge of a windowsill, cracking the glass flask, spraying heating oil in a wide arc. The fire caught, grabbed the flammable wave and ignited it in a Molotov flare of blue and yellow flame. A wave of searing heat blasted back, seeming to devour every molecule of oxygen, snatching Hogshead's breath for an infinite stifling instant.

'Feel better for that, eh?' croaked Merlot weakly.

'I hate it, it's so . . .'

'Dangerous?'

'No, worse. I've seen what it can do, it's . . .'

'Magic!' coughed Merlot, fixing Hogshead with a sharp scolding gaze. His beard seemed to turn unnaturally dull. 'Told you magic's dangerous, didn't I?' he whispered feebly. 'But you wouldn't listen. No, wouldn't lisss . . . Pah, teenagers, always know best.'

Hogshead stared in silent horror as Merlot shimmered translucently. The cracks in the stone steps winked momentarily through the ancient wizard's body, grinning like some cubist carrion bird, waiting, ready for the inevitable.

'Merlot! No!' squealed Hogshead, shaking him by the shoulders.

'And you still think Micturan Fire Lizards would be good fun, hmmm?' Merlot's lip curled fractionally at the corner.

'No. I don't ever want to . . . Merlot!'

The wizard's gaze unfocused, seeming to stare into an approaching infinity, eyelids closing . . .

'No don't! Please . . . Merlot!'

Hogshead's eyes burned desperately into Merlot's face, yearning, seeking some final spark of vitality.

Unseen behind him, three spots of light fizzed and buzzed.

'I say we should,' insisted Nimlet.

'I must refuse, brothers,' argued Skarg'l. 'The proposal has not been correctly submitted.'

'You what? Just 'cause he hasn't said "I wish"?' snarled Nimlet.

'I was really looking forward to a good "fixing",' mused Udio. 'Got myself real worked up. Feel a bit, well, cheated right now.'

'Exactly!' insisted Nimlet. 'C'mon, what are you waiting for!'

And suddenly he was gone, powering swiftly towards the prone wizard, squeezing between the cells of skin and plunging along sluggishly pulsing vessels. In seconds he had zipped through the swirling complexes of anatomical design and finally forced his way into the tiny gland at the back of the wizard's brain.

Alarmed he stared about the inside of the pineal glance, shocked at the dullness of the cells, worried by their apparent inactivity, panicking at the dread lack of thaumoglobin production. If he didn't know any different he would quite categorically have concluded that there was no way anything other than the barest minimum of thaumic activity was currently going on, as if the magical spirit had deserted the corporeal shell. He wasn't far wrong.

'Wakey, wakey!' he squealed ineffectually. 'C'mon, get your pseudopods out! This is no time to be slacking!' Nimlet spun agitatedly, kicking cell walls here and there like some mad sergeant-major at a platoon of sleeping-bagged privates. 'Move, move! Get pumping!'

A thaumocyte twitched and waved a tendril almost dismissively, apparently exhausted by the hextirpator's toll, helpless.

'Merlot! Look, just say something. Do something,' pleaded Hogshead, shaking his inert and worryingly translucent shoulders. 'Don't just lie there. C'mon, twitch, cough . . . It's not hard.'

Arbutus wadled forward, picked up a finger in his beak and let it drop, tutting and shaking his head forlornly.

Then, with the slightest of tinsely whooshes which went unseen by Hogshead, as if by magic, the wizard's eyelid fluttered and he coughed feebly.

'Merlot?' yelled Hogshead.

The wizard's eyes flicked open suddenly and he looked around in confusion. 'Ah yes. I'm *so* glad you asked me that young . . . young . . . Ahh Hogshead. Yes, you must be Hogshead. Sorry, must've dropped off!' He rummaged about in his cloak pocket and produced a small round piece of fruit, 'Do you like peaches?'

'Merlot! You're back!' squealed Hogshead.

'Er . . . er . . . back? What's wrong with my back?' he floundered for a moment.

Arbutus flicked his head to one side and cooed thoughtfully, tapping a flight feather against his beak.

'No,' spluttered Hogshead. 'You. *You're* back. Here . . .'

'Yes. And where else would I be, hmmm?'

Arbutus tutted and rolled his eyes, questions mounting inside his avian head.

'Oh, never mind,' grinned Hogshead. 'I just thought . . .'

'Tsk, tsk. Dangerous, that,' grinned the wizard and slapped a hand on to the top of his head. 'My hat!' he proclaimed. 'Where's my . . .'

'Don't worry. I know where it is, I think.' And with that Hogshead was off.

Chuckling gently to himself Merlot rummaged once again in his capacious pockets.

'Okay,' hooted Arbutus with a hard stare. 'What's the score?'

'Aha! There it is,' smiled Merlot, producing a bundle of wires and pentagrammatic circuit boards from his pocket. 'My favourite toaster,' he declared melodramatically.

'Toaster?' spluttered Arbutus. 'That's nothing like a . . .'

His beak was suddenly trapped between Merlot's fingers and he watched baffled as the wizard stared around him with an expression remarkably similar to that adopted by folk who know that there is a bluebottle in the room but haven't a clue precisely where it is.

'My poor toaster,' he continued. 'I really, really wish it was working as well as it once used to.'

Almost before he had finished, three tiny fizzes of light swooped down on the bundle of junk at lightning speed. Merlot could have sworn he heard a flurry of zipping giggling as he tugged a level ten containment box out of another pocket and dropped the nano-sprites inside.

'Found it!' declared Hogshead, waving a gaudy hat from behind one of the stone lizards a moment later as Merlot slammed the lid shut and hid the box.

'C'mon,' whispered Arbutus secretly. 'What's the score?'

'Damnation. How did you know?'

'What – all that shimmery, showy, fading in and out dramatic nonsense . . . Pah, never fooled me for a minute. I knew damn well you'd just slipped off for a quick peek at the game. What's the score?'

'You won't tell him about my little, er . . . lesson?'

'Spill it, the score?'

'Apocalypse Four are way ahead. If they don't win now, then . . . Ahh, thank you my boy. I do feel somewhat naked without that.' Merlot took his hat off Hogshead and slapped it conically on the top of his head. 'Could catch my death without that,' he added and winked at Arbutus.

'That's not funny,' winced Hogshead and looked miserably at the ground between his toes. 'Not funny at all.'


Trembling nervously beneath the fiery gaze of his new overseer, Quintzi Cohatl shook the bones.

'Well?' snarled Arch Sergeant Strappado, nonchalantly heating up his favourite red-hot codpiece. 'C'mon. Give me an answer. I haven't got all day.'

Gripped in terror, Quintzi's hands shook as he sweltered under the scorching gaze of fury.

'You said you could predict where and when and by whom the next crimes were going to be committed! Well do it!' barked Strappado, casually tossing a roast chestnut to the multicoloured macaw perched on an iron maiden.

Quintzi's hand flashed open involuntarily and dropped a dozen or so shrew bones. He stared at the arrangement of thighs, crossed his fingers under the table of Interrogation Room 6 and said, 'There's a really high probability of the removal of property from an abode in . . .'

'No. *No*! Speak properly!'

'Er . . . I . . . I can't see . . .'

'Oh, would you rather we play poker?' grinned Strappado waving a red-hot iron casually around.

Shaking, Quintzi gathered up the bones and hurled them on to the table once more, desperately wishing that he had been able to see the future.

If he'd known all this was going to happen then . . . ah, avocado storage seemed so attractive right now. Certainly far less personal risk involved.

The bones formed an equally incomprehensible picture.

'Er . . . robbery on Puce Street in half an hour,' lied Quintzi.

'Good, good!' grinned Strappado, edging closer. 'Now, about the three-fifteen J'helt Numm Gold Goblet? Yataghan Boy, he a good bet?'

Quintzi whimpered and swallowed very nervously. If only he could remember precisely who had finished where.

The gentle chirping of harfinches filled the air and barely masked the bubbling of a small pot. The rotund youth held his nose and sat upwind of the stinking contents, cringing with immense gratitude that he wasn't the one who'd be forced to down it in one.

'It's ready!' he declared with a final stir.

'Wonderful,' croaked the white-haired wizard. 'I simply can't wait, what?'

'Now, now. That's not the attitude!' snapped Hogshead. 'You need this to get your strength back. It's just like you said: sprouts, spinach and these funny blue-veined mushroom things. C'mon, down in one!'

'Must I?'

Arbutus scowled at Merlot through piercing orange eyes from a low branch. 'See?' he whispered. 'I didn't tell him. Now if you really want to explain that all this isn't necessary, feel free. I won't stop you.'

'Eat it all up!' insisted Hogshead, loving every minute of putting that fortnight's botany class to good use and feeling rather pleased with himself at the almost miraculous recovery the wizard had made.

Merlot cringed, held his nose and swallowed the thaumically rich brew, coughing irritably.

'There, now isn't that better?'

'Could've done with more garlic,' he grumbled. 'And some honey. Medicine always needs honey.' Then, with a flourish, he hurled a card down in front of the shining new runicycle and trundled forwards into the back games cavern of Losa Llamas.

'No, no, no!' he shouted suddenly, slamming his wand on the wooden floor. 'C'mon, you can do better than that!' he yelled at the Thaumaturgical Physicists gathered together. 'Up, down, up, down! Flex those thaumiceps! Practz, stop flagging. You can do fifteen more float-ups for that. Gods, anyone'd think you've never had to levitate before. Spells are for life, not just Hallowe'en!'

Hogshead looked at Arbutus and grinned. They both knew it wouldn't be too long before he got all his unique strengths back.